PROWLERS

ff

PROWLERS

Maurice Gee

faber and faber

LONDON · BOSTON

First published in 1987
by Faber and Faber Limited
3 Queen Square London WC1N 3AU
This paperback edition first published 1989

Photoset by Parker Typesetting Service Leicester
Printed in Great Britain by
Richard Clay Ltd Bungay Suffolk
All rights reserved

© Maurice Gee, 1987

British Library Cataloguing in Publication Data

Gee, Maurice
Prowlers.
I. Title
823[F]   PR9639.3.G4

ISBN 0-571-15297-X

ACKNOWLEDGEMENTS

I have made several borrowings from Glenn Busch's *Working Men* and David Gee's *Our Mabel* and am pleased to acknowledge the debt. I would like to thank Dr Royd Thornton of the Cawthron Institute, Nelson, for permission to use the Institute's library and consult its archives. The Lomax Institute in my novel resembles the Cawthron in size, constitution and one or two parts of its history but no close likeness is intended. The Lomax scientists are imaginary, although some of their work was first done in the Cawthron by its staff.

I am grateful to the New Zealand Literary Fund for its generous encouragement and support.

M.G.

THANKS M

I do not like her. She's beautiful without any contrivance and I don't trust nature to that degree. Nasty things lie under surfaces. That's the sum of my wisdom learned through lenses – my lifetime of squinting through bits of glass. Tup said magnification banished fear. So it seemed to me for many years. Now I know it shows empty places, endless recession, and how can we hope to travel there? We're trapped at the intersection of two planes (is and ought, there's two good names), we're buried at a crossroads with the stake of our limitations through our heart. An evolutionary dead-end, my opinion. Said as much to that girl, but she was kind, gave me a verbal pat and a smile like a sticky sweet. She's blue of eye, a Lotte Ogier eye, and pink of cheek, and honey-tongued, and oh so patient with this smelly dodderer, myself; but whispers, 'Shit!' under her breath when her tape plays up.

I don't like that. Don't like her. I wish she'd leave me alone and stop this infernal scrape scrape with her questions. It gets her nowhere with me that she's grand-daughter of my sister Kitty, and this job, all she can get with her fine degree! keeps her from drawing unemployment benefit. I don't care if she starves. I don't care if she goes on the streets. That won't bother a girl so free with faecal expletives.

Calm down. Read your pulse. Is it still there? Do I still have a pint or two of blood? See the yellow dent the biro leaves in the ball of my thumb. It's beyond my resources now to plump that bit of flesh out.

Beauty lies under surfaces. There's a contradiction. So soon? It does not matter. Contradictions are beautiful. Tensions are beautiful. And beauty is inadmissible! So, all my life, to the very end, I kick the feet from under myself, and pick myself up. What fun it is knocking these bits of skin off. The blood flows, see?

Start again. I do not like her; like you not, Kate Adams, your plumped-out lip and bright kind eye and snake-hissed lavatory word. The skin peeling on your arms – don't you know the dangers? Your moving breasts. That's too much cheek. Put on a brassière, you slut, before you come questing here again.

Questing is a good word. It's inadmissible. Confusion is a good word. Extraordinary to be confused after a life so full of magnifications and clarity. And mysteries penetrated. And governing principles understood. Kitty used to infuriate me by saying of Lotte Ogier, piano teacher – a Meissen shepherdess, pink, befrilled, a weeping German monster, greedy, cruel – that her eyes were so blue and clean she must take them out at night and wash them in a basin of cold water. Bile rose in my throat to hear her say it, a bitter taste came on my tongue, and pulses made a flutter in my temples. I cried, 'You can't take out eyes, you're being mad,' and I got my new anatomy chart and showed Kitty the human eye in horizontal section, a structure I had *understood*, and made my property, and showed her how it was continuous, from sclerotic and cornea and crystalline lens to the optic nerve which carried the impressions to the brain, and it was mad, *mad*, to talk of washing it in basins of water. The thing would be dead then, you could never put it back. Kitty defended herself. She had not been talking of optic nerves but Lotte Ogier, a different matter. You couldn't cut her down the middle and make a chart of her ('Oh yes you can' – and I flipped pages), and eyes, after all, were things you looked at, not just with, and they could have meanings of all sorts. And she quoted some line about 'speaking eyes', which made me screech, 'Eyes can't speak'; and then we grinned, for we had moved into self-caricature, a saving place; and Kitty looked at my chart then, for she had wide interests, and understood the eye in a trice, though she let me explain, and marvelled at the good sense of it all. That pleased me immensely, for it was my good sense. Yet Lotte Ogier's clean blue eyes always made me tremble after that.

Kate Adams has that eye. Washed and bright. She's a thing of lovely surfaces. How complete the young are, you never think of bits when faced with them. Organs, blood, bowel – that Burma road – murky secretions by the kidney-bowl; none of that. They seem all joints and surfaces and their parts are teeth and hair, no parts at all, but continuous. Yet this one peels. Is she starting to come apart, as I come apart? The last thing I want is to pity her. Admiration, dislike, interest, lust, fear, as I watch from my multiple eyes. Pity with all this? I'm glad she's gone, reduced to neuronic shifts in my brain.

I take my handkerchief (it crackles like paper, and how that made her twist her nose) and wipe the sore grooves that run from my clown's mouth down to my jawbone – which I consider now turning into the jawbone of an ass and hacking at friends and enemies with. She did not kiss me there but on the forehead. My mother used to kiss me on the lips, full on the lips, and Kitty too, and even Dad. We were a kissing family and must have put armies of germs about. But Kate has taken my germs, no doubt at all, from the chair she sat in, from my fingers' touch, and touch of my mind. Minds, the boy Noel screeches, cannot touch, but I tell him to shut his gob, he's had his say. Kate stowed her tape-recorder in her ethnic bag – embroidered sugar-sack it looked to me – pecked me at the hairline, ran prophylactic finger on her mouth, and off she swayed. She'll edit this weekend and bring her transcript round to me next week. It's all lies. I gave her a batch of sterile slides, but touched her with my mind, its many parts, and will see if we can get a culture there.

I've flown apart. There are bits of me floating off as I spin and spin. Can I persuade them back by being still?

Here they come, the asteroids, the basalt moons.

2

I don't want them. Start again. The girl upset me. I'm not like this, not a mad old man. I'm Noel Papps. I'm dux of Jessop College. I'm Pettigrew Scholar. Here I come, I'm Dr Papps, I'm head of Soil Science. I, alone, discover what is wrong with the Plowden Hills, why they won't grow, and I, Noel Papps, repair that error (Whose? I ask the bishop). I put in what they haven't got; and look at me now, I'm Director of the Lomax Institute, I'm Sir Noel.

Have I reached the end? Is that all? One paragraph and a joke? My God, is this my entry? Where are the days? They were brimful. They burst like crates of apples. They ran off down the lawn like apples spilled, I have not the hands to grab them all. Where are they gone, lying in the long grass, lying in the hydrangeas. Slaters crawl in brown caves pecked by birds. I crush cider-flesh with my feet, walking by.

Piffle! Rot! I'm not Kitty. This is her stuff. Get yourself out of my head now, Kit. Go on. Minds can't touch. I know my days, they're marked on calendars, eighty years. Not one is lost, not one lasts a moment longer than I allow it to. I'm in control and all those forces outside law – fear, grief, desire, comedy, ambition, hatred, love – are cellular in me and know their place and wait until I stain them to their lawful show; and that's no boast. Amazement and clear sight go hand in hand.

So what shall I choose, where am I now? Shall I be with Tup Ogier in the playground, leading him to where a praying mantis eats a fly? It's a blue one, iridescent, oil-sheeny, and its buzz half-hearted and its legs giving life away as hooked arms hold it dinner-wise and jaws chomp its head. 'A beauty,' Tup breathes. 'God-horse in some places, Papps. Lovely creature, eh?' The mantis eats the fly's head like an apple, stopping only to munch a leg like a celery stick. 'See how its jaws work. Mandibles. They're lateral, not horizontal like ours.' He has his little glass out from its hinged leather case and lets me look. I see yellow jaws that work unhurriedly in time with the crunch of fly tissue. 'The strength there, Papps. If he was as big as us he could chew iron bars.' 'She,' I say, looking at her abdomen; and he pats me and says, 'Good boy. Look, here's pudding.' The mantis eats unborn maggots from the fly's abdomen. They wriggle, tiny grubs, but there's nowhere to go. Untimely ripped, my father would say; born into the monster's iron jaws.

If mantises could burp this mantis would. Her lovely arms wipe her lovely mouth. There's not a fly-scrap left, and she's cross-eyed, she's blotto, and will fall off her twig if she doesn't watch out.

'A bird should come along and eat her now.'

'Ha! Good boy.'

That was the first lens I looked through, Tup Ogier's magnifying glass, which he called 'my truth-teller'. 'No more superstition, Papps, when you look through this.' 'No, sir,' I said, not understanding. Years later, he gave the glass to me, and I joked, 'She tells the truth but she can't prophesy.' He stroked her with the ball of his thumb. 'She does enough. The end of fear, Noel. Look after her.' I took her – let's say *it* – home and dropped it in a drawer; and it lies there now, with a litter of specimens I'll never classify – marble from the valleys and granite from the hills I play the game of name and number with; or would if I had the interest; and gold, a tiny nugget, and a splinter of black basalt speckled with olivine.

Tup's glass and all her kind tell me nothing now.

4

When he gave you his attention you couldn't tell which eye it was that saw. Which eye must you fix yours on, like a man? One was always out of line and though it wasn't that you chose it always came to fix on you and make you blink, and the other was the one over your shoulder. Tup, the least shifty of men, shifted them. Yet I believe that's impossible. Impossible, too, that it was the outward sign of an inner flaw, his maculation, for moral health made a running fire on his skin. He wore a ragged ear, but that was no flaw, that was a prop – mauled by a wildcat in Peru, bitten by a Burmese pirate in the China Seas. His teeth were under pressure from each other, they jutted or lay back like head-stones in an old cemetery. With all this, an energetic springing of coarse hair, pads of it on cheeks and wrists and fingerbacks; horse-lips, ape-man jaw, yeti-feet; and you had a man of ugliness so majestic that children new at his school had been known to hide their faces at the sight of him. 'Imagine having to kiss him,' little Irene Lomax breathed. Tup was a walking contradiction, and a lesson for me in deeps and surfaces.

He took the four of us – a Blyton four, said clever Kate, not an hour ago, and was miffed at having to explain – into the little lab he'd made in a storeroom at school and gave us a lesson in blowpipe analysis. The occasion comes spinning back to my centre. Beauties of shape and significance make me a little breathless as I set it down to study it; and speculations threaten me about chance and fate. None of that. I will not fall down that hole.

We were Kitty and Noel Papps, Irene Lomax, Phil Dockery, and Phil and I had helped capture Edgar Le Grice, the Jessop fire-raiser. Our story appeared in the *Daily Times* alongside news of the landings in the Dardanelles. I'd better get us down in our right balance. Algebraic symbols would help, Kitty as x, Phil as y, and so on, and then I could compare and bind together, and display us in our proper magnitudes; and Tup and Le Grice could come in; others too, Lotte Ogier (a subtraction from Lotte Reinbold), and the Gasman, Les Dockery, a negative number, and a dozen others, and I might end up with an axiom. Instead I have these powers that won't obey, and a sense that individual being rests on lawlessness. So I'll enter the maze without that help, and the only cotton thread I'll hold is me.

Noel Papps was a boy just turned thirteen. An ugly fellow – like this sick baboon, old Sir Noel. He gave an impression of sootiness, sooty eyebrows, sooty hair, and dark blood in his cheeks; and a rubber face, lips you could stretch and let fly back, an ill-formed nose, a squashed potato, and eyes very dark, smart-alec eyes that signalled the boy's anxieties too well. He asked himself how he would get on, having, so to speak, no exterior. He declared what was inside without moderation, desperately. He was clever. Like fat boys he must be a character, and he was part way to it when things happened in Jessop that made him something else.

That's Noel Papps, a bit of him. Or is it marks on paper? One begins with an axiom, one doesn't end. Begins with a truth self-evident. Say *Noel Papps* and leave it there. What's the place of all this attribution? Sooty. Ill-formed. That stands already, doesn't it, in *Papps*? Smart alec though. That is better. That somehow changes the rules. It prods the thing into a jerky step. We advance some way into the dark with that. I could have some interest in this game. There's a buzzing in my ears. I could become a devotee. There are things I'll never see again, not now; shadowy forms I'll never reach. But *smart alec* – yes. And *desperation*. Progress like that makes one ambitious.

Let's get on.

If I hadn't been a scientist I would have been an actor. I made up my mind that's what I'd be. I practised stretching my face, I practised snarling. I laughed, heh! heh! heh! and I did murders. Sometimes at the bathroom mirror I'd try Robin Hood, but I was a clever boy, as I've said, and I wasted only a moment before inflating into Friar Tuck. I was very good as the Sheriff of Nottingham too. My eyebrows came down to hide my eyes and my teeth grew points. When I played the Kaiser in our school's patriotic pageant I had a face all ready to use.

Kitty was Britannia. She sat on a throne and held a trident, just like the lady on the penny. Irene was Gallant Little Belgium. 'Britannia, Britannia, oh pity our distress . . .' And Phil Dockery, the Port Rat, barefoot boy, flea-bag Phil in his ragged pants, was New Zealand. That came about from my cleverness. I was chosen for New Zealand, and being hero tempted me, and the rifle and uniform, but not as much as the spiked Hun helmet and the moustache. 'I tear this poppy Belgium from her stem!' I knew my part. There was something else though, and sometimes it increases me and sometimes diminishes. Although it's a fact I can't focus on it, which is upsetting. I'll put down this: I was sorry for Phil. We were not friends, but Mrs Beattie had marked him down as Hun, and I saw what he would lose. So I pointed out how tall he was. She stood us back to back and even without shoes he had an inch on me.

'New Zealand should be tallest, Mrs Beattie. I can do the Hun. You watch.' I stretched my rubber face and lunged so fierce at Irene that she screeched, and I made as if to twist her head from her neck. Mrs Beattie, fat and silly – silly in behaviour, fat in her mind, but clever in a number of pin-pricking ways – recognized me; saw the centre of strength that would hold up the shaky structure she assembled, and was left with Phil Dockery as New Zealand. Turning this grubby Port Rat into our soldier boy brought her cruelty out. She tweaked his ear and tugged his greasy hair, and wiped his germs from her fingertips with a folded handkerchief. 'Whait cliffs, Dockery, whait, not whoit. You sound like a navvy from Liverpool.' How all the goody-good girls, in their pinafores and pink ears, laughed. Irene laughed, though she would have to stand by him and have his arm around her in the end. The bolder girls pretended they had seen fleas jumping over.

I fought with Phil Dockery in a corner of the school grounds. Crazy with insult, he tried to twist my head from my shoulders. But I was rubber, I changed shape, he could not hold me. I stayed alive until Tup Ogier came and broke us in half as though breaking an apple, and marched us by our necks off to his room to tan our hides. But there he only let his strap roll out like an ant-eater's tongue and rolled it up again and put it away and spread a chart of the human brain on his table and showed us where the evil passions lived. He told us the brain was a flower, see how it opened like a rose – the cerebellum – but down here in the stem a worm was eating, here in the medulla oblongata, the reptile brain. That's where Phil and I had been, splashing with the crocodiles in the swamp. I thought that was unfair. Phil had been trying to kill me but I had only been trying to stay alive. I didn't protest though, because

7

the chart had taken my breath away and I had no time for unimportant things. Tup strikes again. Every time he aimed at me he scored a bull's-eye.

'Sir,' I said, 'sir' – and I could smell a strong sweet scent – it penetrated me. Life was a series of shocks and recognitions. I had perhaps a dozen steps to make, and this was one; and when Tup rolled the chart up and sent me away, keeping Phil back to swab iodine on his knee, where my loose toe-cap had razored him, I felt as if I had been given a taste of some new food and its flavour lingered in my mouth and penetrated my cerebellum. In lunchhours I sneaked inside and opened Tup's drawer and studied the chart; played games with it, sailed down this river and that, explored the hemispheres like continents and found scaly birds and man-eating fish; but came always back to names and outlines, for the real adventure started there – in control. That was the thing I smelled like a rose.

And I sneaked up to the belfry and spent my time with Miss Montez, stroking her, poking my fingers in her apertures. She had lovely fingers, she had lovely toes, and a pelvis like a gravy-boat. Beautiful joints – Tup rubbed them with mutton fat – and a curve in thigh and forearm no woman with flesh on her has ever equalled, not for me. The measured knitting on her skull could not have been done better with a machine. Her eyeholes had a symmetry and balance that made me want to weigh and measure them. She was yellow. Tup told me later she was probably a man.

Phil and I carried her down for a lesson. She was wired to a wooden frame and Tup moved her arms and legs with a set of levers at the back. 'Children, say hello to Miss Montez. She's my good friend of many years. I met her first on a river steamer in Brazil. A Portuguese lady, a soprano at the Manaos opera. She threw herself into the river for hopeless love of an Italian tenor – ' and so on, aimed at the girls. The piranhas ate her – 'look, you can see the marks of their teeth on her bones' – and the tenor sang an aria that made everyone cry. Then Tup bought her from the captain for seven shillings.

'That's all lies, sir,' Kitty said.

'When we don't know the facts we're entitled to invent,' Tup replied.

There were facts enough for me, her bones were facts. He raised her arms like mantis arms – but likenesses were nothing beside names. Tup told me them: occipital and parietal, clavicle and scapula, humerus, ulna, femur, fibula, and lovely toes and fingers, phalanges. Mouthing these, I possessed Miss Montez. I entered a world shining with order, bright with controls, where two follows one and three follows two. To know the name of things is my desire; our only proper knowing is through names. Circles are completed in the noun, margins and boundaries are clear, and we are free from vagueness, free from fear, with every object known from every other. The name, the name, is the single proper epithet.

And having said that, what about the verb? Isn't breaking down and building up the thing that chemistry is all about? For I'm a chemist. Nouns create a landscape without movement or sound. Nothing happens. Verbs bring activity and change. Yes, I agree with that argument. But I see predication as closer naming. Noun and verb unite in my craft or science.

I say this as though it remains true all my life. It started long ago when I was young, uncertain of what was real and what was not, afraid, and glimpsing powers (seeming to glimpse) – ready for religion, that is. The answer did not come from there, and never can for me, not now, even though the answer that I found doesn't hold. The name's a lovely shell, lovely container, but outside and in, chaos, harmony, unknowable. I remember now, better than occipital, parietal, the hollows in her skull, the aching void.

I go on too long about Miss Montez. Miss Montez was not my bride, the oxidizing flame was my true bride. Let me come to her by even steps. And in all these words find one big name? I don't hope for it. Nor is my question theological. Anything considered, but no theology, never that. By big name I simply mean my life. I'll be selective – direct, evasive – and perhaps come close to it, a shadow shape. I'll go along by predication. That's the method. But acting shall be my vehicle. I've placed that talent second long enough.

How I shall howl! How I shall laugh!

4

But I shall also say things quietly and try to put them in their proper place. Howls and laughs will be imperatives, chronology will be my discipline. So – the patriotic pageant, that comes next.

I can say my speeches to this day: 'No scrap of paper binds me. Might is right. The weak I feed into my iron jaws. What care I for truth and peace and justice? I tear this poppy Belgium from her stem. I trample her red petals in the mud –'

Mrs Beattie wrote it with the vicar of St Bede's. The Kaiser had the best lines. Kitty, on her throne, might cry, 'Fight we must and fight we will. Who will follow? Speak!' and Egypt, India, Canada step forward – 'I', 'And I' – and poor Phil, rifle shouldered, at attention, 'Mother of Empire, furthest are we from Home of all your sons, far far we lie from those dear *whait* cliffs – ' but that was all just wind and I had words. My moustache went crooked and I tore it off and held it like a blade in my hand, killing laughter. And in the end, though I squatted shrinking at Kitty's feet, though she held me snarling till I died, with her trident digging in my back, while everyone sang 'Land of Hope and Glory' and the hall joined in, I knew there had been one peak in the night and I, Noel Papps, had stood on it alone.

Before we could take our bows, Jacklin, our MP, came bounding on stage. 'Friends, people of Jessop, children of Jessop school . . .' He was a doggy fellow, oh how he wanted to be patted, to be loved. And how ready he was to snarl and bite and prove this way his devotion and worth. He pumped with his little fat arms. We smelled him – tobacco and ripe meat – and heard, the nearest, Phil and I, a bubbling in his guts, and heard him fart, poot, poot, poot, three little woofs. 'What a glorious night! And what a lesson we've learned! Out of the mouths of babes, eh? True patriotic feeling.'

Tup Ogier, in the front row, shook his head. He'd had words with Mrs Beattie about the jingoistic huff and puff in her pageant. Lomax, the mayor, who had filled Jacklin with the food that caused his borborygmus, began to pull his lower lip. And perhaps Jacklin had not meant to speak real words but lost his judgement. Real words came out in the end. 'Which of us wouldn't like to shoot a Hun right now? A Hun or Turk? For Empire. For Mother England. Remember those lads in Gisborne, how they wrecked that German pork butcher's shop? He'll never show his face again. And that one in Wellington, with the name no civilized person can pronounce. Von this! Von that! We'll show 'em, eh? We'll show 'em, with these young soldier lads and lasses at our backs. Von, two, three, out!'

When the laughter had died down he put his hands on his knees, he almost squatted, and leaned his face into the audience. 'What a pity it is we haven't got any pork butchers in our town.'

A man at the back said in a loud voice, 'We've got that piano teacher down the road.' It was Edgar Le Grice.

Now there's a name. I feel when I've put it down I've said enough. Jacklin I need a lot of words for and at the end he's barely there. Edgar Le Grice though – that's enough. He comes spinning back like a moon. And he's black. He's red and black. And he has fire in his head. You see it burning there behind his eyes. He's on his feet below neat-lettered Sunday School texts and the paragraphs make his head start out of a page. A hulking fellow, silent. I've seen him once before, squatting beside his hydraulic ram and watching over his shoulder as Tup marches us up the river bank for swimming in Bucks Hole. We're on his property but have right-of-way and Tup keeps us strictly to the path. The thump thump of the ram is the beat of Le Grice's rage. He never moves, he's like stone there.

Now here he is, with 'love' and 'Lamb of God' about his head, but different words coming from his mouth. 'Why should she grow fat here when we've got soldiers dying over there?'

Others took it up, young fellows mostly. Cries, thick and brutal, filled the air.

Lomax mounted halfway up the steps. 'Now, wait a minute, boys, wait a minute.' He tried to say we didn't want any trouble in Jessop, not tonight; but Le Grice said, 'Shut up, Lomax. Your daughter goes there for piano lessons.'

'Not any more,' Lomax cried.

Le Grice took no more notice; ignored Jacklin too, flapping on the stage. He said in his passionless way, while rage leaked from his eyes, 'We're not having her, so follow me,' and I seemed to hear again the ram's thick beating.

Although I did not know it, my father had gone, which was brave of him. With a name like ours it would have been more sensible to go home quietly and lock the door. But he ran down the road with Tup Ogier and found Frau Reinbold at her piano. He threw his coat on her and took her along the alley by the park and hid her in the bakehouse, with Kitty and Irene to look after her.

Tup faced Le Grice's mob from the middle of Frau Reinbold's garden path. Phil and I arrived in time to hear the end of his speech and had not heard his voice so lost before. He was a man of too many words. On the other side of the white picket fence was Edgar Le Grice.

'She's your fancy lady, teacher, so shut up.' He kicked the toy gate and sent it spinning off its hinges. They knocked Tup Ogier down and ran over him. Sunday-suited for our pageant, black and dense, they wedged through the door, one stopping to wrench Frau Reinbold's plate from the wall and spin it like a discus into the street.

We helped Tup Ogier up. His tattered ear was bleeding. I felt the bottom fall out of one of my certainties. We sat him on the garden seat and he panted, 'Stay away, boys, they've gone mad.' My father came back. 'It's all right, Tom. She's in the bakehouse. She's all right.' A smashing of glass came from the house. The noise seemed to fracture my teeth, I felt them throbbing. Tup tried to stand up but my father held him. 'They'll tear you to bits. Get the police, boys.'

'Mr Lomax went for them.'

The French doors bulged and burst. Le Grice appeared, with curtains draping his torso. He tore them in handfuls from their rings and balled them and flung them into the garden, where they opened out and floated like scarves and settled on the round-headed shrubs. He leaned back inside and gave a heave and seemed to lift the Bechstein over the step. Men with white mad faces came beetling round its sides. They beat it across the flower beds, kicked it like a donkey and tipped it three feet into the sunken garden. One jumped on it and struck it with an axe. The letters of the name sprang out and looped to my feet. (And my father lifted the spiked Prussian helmet from my head and put it down behind a daphne bush.)

The axe made kindling of the ebony wood. The keys came out and made a waterfall. Wires sighed, and hammers did a caterpillar walk. Edgar Le Grice had gone back into the house. Now he appeared in the doorway, with a bottle held stiff-armed above his head, and throat lined up as though he meant to swig. He jumped on the piano, shouldered the axeman away, stood wide-legged in the broken keys. Liquid spun like glycerine and fractured into glass at his feet. He held the bottle until it was empty, then flung it back-handed at the house, where it burst on the wall and rained his mob with splinters. Le Grice had sucked motion, speech, intention, even fear, from us all. We were like the sleepers in the castle and could not move as he passed among us, but could see. The rattle of his matches brought us awake.

'No!' shouted Tup Ogier.

'Ha!' cried the mob – a breath in time with the fire's explosion. Le Grice seemed lifted by it and thrown back. He landed on his feet on the garden wall, and stood wide-legged, lit-up, facets of him flashing red and yellow. I think of him now as pleochromatic, but that's a defence, that's a retreat, it leaves out black. And as the piano crackles and the flames turn crystalline, it's black I see: Le Grice spinning at me, basalt moon.

5

'A tragic family,' Tup Ogier said; and that was with their story only half told. Everybody knew it but my mother told it best, especially stirring pots at the stove or beating dough on the kitchen table, when her busy-ness became a kind of counterpoint to the story. The Le Grices had been lazy and proud, treating their farm out there in the river bend as a country estate, and he, Edgar's father, not doing a hand's turn but strolling with a walking stick – called it his ash-plant – and pointing out this and that wanted doing. He owned property in town and ran for mayor but failed because he was too snooty to ask for people's votes. He thought the highest place should be his by right.

Mrs Le Grice, the old lady? Well, my mother said, fixing us, then slapping dough, she wasn't always old, remember that. A beautiful woman, in her day – if you go for the sort without any flesh on their bones. And of course she could spend as much as she liked on clothes. A fashion-plate, and very social too. They had garden parties there, and English lords and ladies to stay. But all that changed, my mother said; and could not be satisfied, for it came about from the death of a child. Lucy was her name, Lucy Le Grice. To hear my mother tell it, she was a kind of fairy or woodsprite, flitting about the farm, among the lords and ladies, picking flowers. She drowned when she was nine, in a river pool, called Girlies Hole later, where classes from our school had swimming lessons. Her brother, Edgar, was meant to be watching her, but he had gone off

13

fishing with his mates. They found her in the deep part, down past the rapids, floating under the water like a fish, with her eyes wide open.

'Oh, the poor thing,' Kitty said, her own eyes brimming.

'I've seen her photograph. It's all over the house,' Irene Lomax said.

My mother gave her a puzzled look. She disapproved of Irene, that confidence and knowingness, yet was pleased Kitty should have the mayor's daughter as a friend. A part of her story, too, was robbed from her – that no one ever saw Mrs Le Grice after Lucy drowned. I waited to see if she would work it in. Cecil Le Grice, she went on, became a shadow. He wasted away and died from grief. As thin as a matchstick, she said, and his skull nearly breaking through his skin. And, she said doggedly, not looking at Irene, no one saw Mrs Le Grice after Lucy drowned, not close up. They saw her on the porch sometimes, but she went inside if people called. She wore sandshoes and a garden party hat. The tennis court grew weeds and the fences rusted. All the workmen left and Edgar Le Grice tried to run the farm. Gorse came down the hills. He grew into a hulking silent fellow.

And at forty-five (it's not my mother now) he started burning buildings round the town. He burned a grocer shop and a quarry shed and the band rotunda in the park and Dargie's Livery Stables. He tried to burn Lomax's seed and grain warehouse, but Phil and I stopped him. It happened on the night after the pageant. The day too had its terrible event.

I find it hard to go on. Not because of terror, I can face that. Because of shifts, because of dizziness. Nothing will be still. Poverty and abundance transmute. And this is that and that is this. And *it* was so, but yet not *so*. What other option but silence do I have? Imperfections strike at me like hail. And there, you see, this double focus, which is a kind of seeing round corners, a view through mirrors cunningly placed, when all I want is to look *straight* at the *single* thing. Obliquity makes me dizzy, multiplicity smothers me. Yet I'll go on. I think that if I'm silent I'll soon die.

Frau Reinbold then. She sat at our breakfast table, and, 'Oh, you are spoiling me,' and, 'I shall grow fat,' she cried as my mother ladled porridge into her plate. Plump and pink and sugar-spun Frau Reinbold, with eyes so sparkling blue they looked as if she took them out at night etc. etc. 'Outside it was Walpurgisnacht. But Kitty and Irene – two angels.'

'She was more like a devil with that fork,' I said.

'Ha!' The Frau seized her spoon and poked my ribs. My mother frowned.

'If you've finished, Noel, go and get ready for school.'

I was reluctant. I'd worked out what a fancy lady was and I was a little drunk with Frau Reinbold. My father came in and said Tup Ogier was in the sitting room and wanted to talk to her. 'Ah, dear Thomas,' she cried, dabbing her lips with a hanky and tweaking her cheeks to colour them up, though already they were pink as cherry icing. Dad showed her out, winking at Mum; and according to Kitty, who peeped through the door, Tup Ogier held Frau Reinbold in his arm – like this, she demonstrated – and wiped tears from her cheeks with his own hanky. Mum looked into the hall then and made a charge at Kitty with the flyswat, so she saw no more. But, 'Fancy having to kiss him,' Irene Lomax breathed.

We sat in our desks with fingers folded and looked at Tup with interest and respect. His ragged ear was yellow with iodine. Lady-powder smudged his black waistcoat. 'Tup tup, tup tup,' he sang as he moved about.

'Sir,' Phil said, 'my father reckons Mr Le Grice must be the fire-raiser.'

'Well, Dockery,' Tup replied, 'we mustn't start rumours. We must leave the fire-raiser to the police.'

'Sir,' Kitty said, 'those bumps you told us about, on people's heads – '

'Phrenology,' I said.

'It's not a science remember, it's like astrology, a pseudo-science.'

'Yes, sir. Would a fire-raiser have a special bump?'

'If we believed in it, Kitty, he certainly would. Just here, above the ear. Destructiveness. Quite close to music, strangely enough. I wonder what harmonies he hears.'

'Sir, can we see Miss Montez?'

'Ah no, not today. Arithmetic.'

'Do Germans have a special bump?' I asked, meaning fancy ladies.

'No, Papps, certainly not.'

'Germans have got square heads,' said a boy called Ray Stack.
(Hay stack.)

'Who told you that?' Tup said.

'My father. He says it's square with a hole where the brains
should be.'

'Ha, ha,' we laughed uneasily.

Tup breathed through his nose. 'Arithmetic.'

'Was Frau Reinbold's piano worth a lot of money?' I asked. I
could not stop rubbing myself against her.

'Enough. Enough. Books out.'

'It was a Bechstein,' Irene said. Her own Bechstein was sold and
replaced with a Broadwood. And her music teacher was Mrs Wil-
son now. Irene had been Frau Reinbold's Wunderkind. 'Bechsteins
are the best in the world.'

'They can't be if they're German,' Ray Stack said.

'Sir,' Phil said, 'what about the war? Are the Turks still floating
mines down the Bosporus?'

Tup Ogier held his finger up. 'Another word and out comes Dr
Brown. Arithmetic.'

In the afternoon we went swimming in the river. Mrs Beattie led
the way and Tup came in the rear, watching to see no boys sneaked
into the tomato gardens. The girls turned down the path to Girlies
Hole and we crossed a wooden one-way bridge – for English lords'
and ladies' carriages – and went up the river bank to Bucks Hole.
Over the paddocks the Le Grice house sat brown-sided, rusty-
roofed, with yellow gorse behind it on the hills. The rocking-chair
on the veranda was the one Mrs Le Grice was sitting in when they
carried Lucy home. She rose and put her hands on her throat and
squeezed a peacock scream out of herself. (That's my embellish-
ment. I've no idea if it's true, but now it's down I'll leave it, for it
seems to include judgement as well as decoration – though why
should I judge?)

Mrs Le Grice, Irene Lomax said, never cut her nails. They curled
over her fingertips and clicked like knitting needles when she
touched anything. Her hair came down to her knees and sometimes
she plaited it and used it like a club to hit her son. I don't need to
say that's a lie. Irene must have enjoyed herself telling Kitty. It's
true her mother took her there several times and made her play the
piano for the old lady. And it's likely the music room was full of

16

photographs of Lucy Le Grice, and five-finger exercises were on the piano still, and the piano had dead notes and played like a wire mattress (she was oddly mature in some of her language, Irene), and dust rained from the curtains if you tried to pull them back, and came from the sofa in little puffs when the old lady patted it for Irene to sit down. Irene claimed Mrs Le Grice mistook her for Lucy, and that's likely too. 'You must practise harder, Lucy,' she said, which made Irene cross, for her mistakes were the piano's fault.

We watched the house and kept to the path and passed the hydraulic ram going thump thump thump. At Bucks Hole Tup took the temperature of the water while we stripped on the shingle fan. 'Sixty-eight, nice and warm,' he called. Chicken-scrawny, most of us, white-bummed, with patterns printed by singlets on our backs. But one or two, like Phil, were already men, and stood hands on hips, showing it. A bit of a midget there, I ran for the water, with hand neatly cupped. Later on none of us cared, the water shrank us all to tiddler size.

Tup took Phil and me and several others along the bank to the deep part of the pool and tested us for our diving certificates. He flipped a tobacco tin, hammered flat, into the water. It fluttered like a leaf going down and vanished in the translucent green; and in I went, second, after Phil, and the bottom of the pool was magnified as though I looked at it through Tup's glass. I went along the gravel like a crab, with puffs of sand springing from my hands. The element enclosing me was death. Meniscus silvery, it bulged and bent. No guarantee of my world still in place. It might have been snuffed out while I was gone. Other things, not people, waited there. I had the tin, and kicked, clawed up fast; and broke into my natural element, and must have looked, with open, haunted eyes and hollow cheeks, like some traveller from the underworld. That, anyway, is my fancy, for I'm not looking straight ahead.

Tup reached for the tin, but never took it. Two girls came running on the path. They stopped at the shingle fan and stood side on, not to see us naked boys, and cried their messsage at the trees: 'Sir, come quick. Mrs Le Grice has fallen in the pool.'

The scramble for clothes then! Tup, with a shout, had gone. 'Get dressed, all of you. Meet me on the bridge.' We ran along the path but did not stop. The bridge drummed under our happy feet. We ran through the head-high scrub to Girlies Hole. Tup had Mrs Le

Grice lying face down on the grass and was giving her artificial respiration. Water trickled from her mouth and liquid flecked with blood from her English nose. A tiny wax white ear bloomed on her head. Her false teeth lay on the stones as though she had coughed them out.

'Is she still alive, sir?'

'I'm not sure. I told you boys to wait on the bridge.'

Kitty was kneeling by Mrs Le Grice's head. She had patted the old lady's hair into a bun and placed it on the base of her neck. Now she tried to squash a balloon of air caught in her dress but it moved somewhere else. So she took the old lady's sandshoes off and tipped the water out.

Tup stopped his counting. 'Get an ambulance, some of you boys.'

'I sent for one,' Mrs Beattie said.

'Well, Dockery and Papps, you'd better go up to the house and fetch Le Grice.'

We went up the path and over the bridge and ran side by side along the road to the gate. A drive curved to the house, a perfect arc, with dust as white as flour in the wheel-ruts. We passed a square of blackberry enclosed in rusty wire, where bits of a tennis net were wrapped about a post. Ripe berries hung in clusters over the walls of a fallen pavilion. The rocking chair was on the house veranda. It was woven seagrass, ravelled like knitting. A doorway opened into a hall where glass tear-drops gleamed on a chandelier. We climbed up and knocked on the jamb.

'Maybe he's not home.'

'What's that noise?'

We jumped from the veranda and walked round the house to the back yard. Edgar Le Grice was sharpening a sickle. He held the blade two-handed, working a treadle with his foot, and sparks streamed from the wheel and ran up his arms. White sparks, black-haired arms. Red tartan shirt. Belt of heavy leather, buckled with brass, and a spike like a dog's tooth through the hole. His belly and chest were barrel-hard.

We moved to let him see us. The wheel stopped. He set the sickle down by his feet. We heard him breathing through his nose.

'Your mother fell in Girlies Hole, Mr Le Grice.'

'Mr Ogier's doing first aid.'

18

Le Grice took a step, somehow drunken. He was stunned by the arrival of a moment – but I'm guessing. I must say what he did, which was to run. We followed him like dogs at heel, and he ran with a long limping stride, his feet beating dust from the ground, past the house and tennis court, along the road. We saw an ambulance beyond the bridge, with its doors wide open, and children standing in a group, and Mrs Beattie pushing them away. Ambulance men brought Mrs Le Grice from the path, lying on a stretcher.

Le Grice shouted, 'Ma!'

They slid her in the way my father slid trays into the oven, and waited at the doors as he galloped up. 'Ma!' He went up clumsily and banged his head, but did not notice. I could not see Mrs Le Grice but saw his hands reach out and hold her face.

Tup Ogier came up the path. He held the old lady's teeth, and offered them. I had been refined and drawn by a kind of osmosis into Edgar Le Grice's grief. I was outraged, and drew myself away from Tup. One of the ambulance men hooked the teeth on his finger and dropped them in his·pocket. They closed the doors and drove away.

'Will she die, sir?' Kitty asked.

'I don't know. She's very ill. But you did very well. You were very brave. Irene too.'

'Everyone into lines now,' Mrs Beattie said.

'Oh, I think they can make their own way back.'

We went in a cluster round Kitty and Irene. They had pulled Mrs Le Grice from the pool.

'She just walked into the rapids,' Kitty said.

'She thought I was Lucy. She called out,' Irene said.

The old lady tumbled through the chute and floated into Girlies Hole. She kept raising her head, and giving little bleats like a lamb. Then her face stayed under water. The girls swam up and tried to turn her on her back but a bubble like a pudding in her dress got in the way. So they floated her along, trying to hold her head on one side. Kitty nearly drowned, she said, when the old lady's hair wrapped round her throat.

Mrs Beattie tucked up her dress and waded in – 'up to her bloomers,' Melva Dyer said – and helped pull Mrs Le Grice to the bank.

'She sicked up.'

'She had dribbles coming out her nose.'

So the others. Irene and Kitty, knowing their value, kept out of it. If I understand the word right, they'd had a Blyton time.

Phil's and mine came in the night. Chronology holds, images fatten up. Here we are, standing on a street corner under a gaslamp, eating pies. We've come from helping in the bakehouse, where Dad has made Phil soap his arms up to the shoulder, and put him in an apron and tucked his forelock under a cap, then washed his own hands a second time; and Phil has been neat and small in the presence of food and has worked with his arms at his sides, minimized, not to put the mysteries in danger. Wolfing his pie, he becomes himself, and grabs and gulps the crust I offer him. (He brings no lunch to school but scrounges sandwiches from other boys.) 'Your old man makes good pies,' I hear him say. I'm sickened by his open-mouthed chewing, the glue of mince and pastry on his tongue. I don't really want him as a friend, but the intimacy of our fight won't go away.

Wind rumbles in the swollen night. Palms clash their branches in the park and the lamp at the entrance lights up the polished wood of a children's slide. Beyond the river the dome on Settlers Hill gleams like a head. Tup Ogier is working there tonight, but clouds swelling up from the east will cover Mars and spoil his view.

'Old Tup gave me a look through the telescope. We looked at the moon.'

'When?'

'Monday night. We saw the craters. We looked at Mars too. Tup reckons there's no real canals.'

Jealousy and rage make me dizzy. Tup is mine. I'm betrayed. Phil is stink-bag Dockery from the Port, with horse shit on his ankles and snot wiped on his arm. I put my hand on the lamp-post to keep from falling, but the sky dislocates and turns on its side. There's an external agent in this: the breaking of glass. I reach out now and tap my tumbler with the paper-knife. A sound, clear as bells; but it's no good. I want that sharp fracture, icy silence, and I'd like to throw the tumbler at the fire grate.

Phil says, 'Glass!'

'In Lomax's.'

We're threaded on the sound and can't get off. 'Come on,' he says.

We run down an alley between brick walls. A pile of dirt lies half in the light, with shapeless footprints climbing into the dark. Phil puts his foot in one but I don't dare. 'He's a giant.' He climbs to the top and puts his head over the wall. 'Long way down.'

'It might have been a cat.' I remember the cat, a ginger Tom with yellow eyes and a torn ear. He's my invention. He burns like a flame, which Phil snuffs out.

'With feet that big? Hey, a broken window.'

I climb the pile of dirt and look at it. A black hole, a nostril, shows in the pane. 'Get your cissy shoes off,' Phil says. I sit on the dirt and take them off and stuff my socks inside.

Phil straddles the wall and lets himself over. He drops and his feet slap on paving stones. 'Come on, Papps.'

I howl silently, dropping down. It's come into my head I'm on my way to being killed. We cross the cobbles, slinky as cats, and rub along the warehouse wall. Phil puts his head through the broken pane and I squint along the side of his cheek. Blades are poised to slice our throats. Our arteries are delicate and bare.

The warehouse is a brick shed half as long as a football field, with skylights in the roof, from which starlight and gaslight diffuse through the room. Huge bins, head-high, stand along one wall and sacks of grain are stacked along the other, plump as loaves. At the far end is a loft where empty sacks are stored. No light penetrates, but we see a movement there, and hear the tinny boom of an empty can. We hiss with fear. I see Phil's tongue come out and wet his lips.

Edgar Le Grice strikes a match. His red balaclava blooms like a rose. He pulls a piece of rag from his pocket and sets it alight and his hand is on fire; but he doesn't feel, he looks as if he means to eat the flame. Then he leans down and touches sacks and they spring alive, he's printed on the ground of his fire. His red round head and black coat make him bird, and down he jumps, or flies, with coat-wings spread and one hand flaming, and lands on sacks by the ladder's foot. He touches bags of seed and makes them flower. Flame runs along and he lopes with it, keeping pace and yodelling delight. He looms at us in the window. He has no ambulatory motion I can see, and I screech and jump away. Glass has sliced my fingers (not the only time in my life looking through windows makes me bleed), but I don't feel. I run and Phil runs with me, along the cobbles to the double gates, where we can climb.

A door opens in a larger door. Le Grice comes into the bay where drays load up. The burning rag is gone from his hand. He jumps from the lip into our path and sends Phil tumbling with a whack of his arm. I scream like a swamp hen as he faces me. I don't know whether he's going to wrap me round or break me in pieces. There's a tearing noise and a stink and my pants fill up.

Le Grice looms over me. I puzzle him; and perhaps he knows what I've done and sees a child and is sorry for me. Just for a moment our eyes meet. A grunt comes from his throat; a twisting – is that grinning? – on his mouth. He puts out his arm and moves me aside. Then he's running, and back from his detour into normality, for he looks over his shoulder at Lomax's and raises his arm and yells at the flames. He jumps and catches the top of the wall and hauls himself up. Phil, limping past me as I squat, grabs his leg, but Le Grice scrapes his fingers off with his other boot, and straddles the wall, and looks a last time at the fire gargling in the warehouse. He jumps down and smacks away up the street.

'Come on,' Phil yells, but I crouch holding my belly and my rubber face signals agony. He climbs the gates and runs to give the alarm.

What do I do? That warm filthy weight is in my pants, and stink about me; and horror in my brain. I mustn't be found. I see a hose looped over a tap and I run bandy-legged and stick the nozzle in my pants and turn it on full-blast and hose the shit out, front and back. The force of the water nearly tears my penis off – but I'm clean, I'm clean, and nobody knows. I know, of course.

Men arrive. By that time I'm at the door in the big door, holding my arm against the blast and hosing water on the nearest sacks.

Tons of grain and seed are lost, but the firemen save the building. Phil and I are heroes. We tell them who it was and police drive out to the farm and arrest Le Grice.

I'm full of self-importance. But also I have secrets on my mind.

You see, Kate Adams, why I dislike your language?

6

Covered in prickles today, full of temper, all that sticky sweetness washed away – an improvement, I think. This is closer to the real girl. She wore the same blouse and skirt and I asked if they were all the clothes she had. They look as if she found them on a flea-market stall. Her shirt hangs out, giddy-gout, and the sleeve is partly torn from the shoulder, leaving a slit two inches long through which I had the desire to insert my tongue and touch her skin. It looked as if it would taste of salt.

That's a strange desire in an old man. I don't know whether to be proud or ashamed, and I'm pleased there's scientific curiosity mixed in it.

She said, with envy and contempt, 'I see why they call it the dress circle.' The envy's natural, the contempt, I suppose, results from lessons. Possessions corrupt and success can never be honest; yet, poor things, they want them all the same.

She leaned over the rail to watch a man casting for trout in the river. I told her it was Archie Penfold, my doctor. He did the stretch between the bridges every Wednesday, his day off, and hadn't managed to catch anything yet. 'It looks all wrong,' she said; fisherman in river, with houses on wooden piles up the hill and suburb spread out on the other side. And city beyond, with parks and cathedral, and an advertising balloon dipping and bouncing in the wind; and ships in the port, trucks on the reclamation, scallop boats dredging in the bay; and pale blue mountains on the other side, streaked with snow. 'You can see too much.'

'I've got Jessop under a microscope.'

She wrinkled her nose, questioned the morality of that. 'The people living here,' she said, giving a minimal thumb-stab at the 'circle', 'have got too much money. And too much time on their hands.'

'I'm poor,' I said, and wiped my eye, 'and I've got very little time.'

She grinned, admiring my act. 'There's plenty of life in you.'

Kate Adams, it's there, in ample measure, but the difference is, you see, there's a big hole in the fence and it can bolt away any time it wants. That gives every moment a sharp edge. That makes me want to taste the salt on your skin in a spirit of *interest*, not desire.

It's something I need to know, or needed to. I don't now. That's the old part of being old. The moments have no continuity.

'Come away from that rail or you'll fall into the river and scare his fish. Show me your transcripts.'

She sat in the wicker chair and took some typewritten sheets from her sugar sack. A tea ring decorated the title:

Lomax Institute Archival Project
Sir Noel Papps, Director (1955–68), talking with Kate Adams at his home
in Jessop, 7 December, 1984.

'I'm not much of a typist.'

'I can see that.'

'The girl at the Institute's going to make good copies.'

'Quiet,' I said. 'Let me read. You can make some tea.'

Adams: Can we start with biography?

Papps: Me? I was born in 1902 in Jessop. My father was a baker. My mother was the sixth daughter of a mill-hand at White's Landing.

Adams: Yes?

Papps: Yes what?

Adams: That's rather bare. I'd like more detail. What about Papps? It's German, isn't it?

Papps: Originally. But we're British for a long while now. My great great great-grandfather it must have been, came over from Hanover in the time of the Georges. Paap was his name. P-a-a-p. Somewhere along the line it changed to Papps. My grandfather – he was a furniture maker – emigrated to New Zealand in the 70s. Came to Jessop. Ran a joinery business. My father didn't follow him. He baked cakes. Started up on his own at twenty-five. He'd bake all night, then drive his cart over the hill with a contract load of loaves for the shop at White's Landing. That's where he met my mother.

Adams: Interesting.

Cold ashes. The fires are someone else's and they're dead. I started skipping – jumped my mother and father. They're not mine to fool with; yes, fool, for if I gave more than names and dates I'd be fitting them out in funny hats and paper noses and putting grins on their faces and tears in their eyes. Anyone else I'll do that to, even if

24

I love them, but George Papps and Dora Papps are pre-existent, and free from the sort of imperialism I'm embarked on now.

Kate came back and put my tea down. She poured spillage from the saucer into the cup. It seems she can't move without slopping things.

'Where are you up to?'

'Here.'

'Alfred Lomax?'

Adams: You must have been, what? twenty-three when the Lomax Institute started.

Papps: Yes. I was away at university. I heard about it.

Adams: Did you know Alfred Lomax? I mean, he was mayor all those years. You must have been aware of him.

Papps: I was. He had what you'd call a high profile. And his daughter Irene was my sister's best friend.

Adams: Kitty?

Papps: Yes, Kitty.

Adams: Irene Lomax. She was a sort of pianist, wasn't she?

Papps: More than sort. She was superb. She was magical. She should have been world famous. Could have been.

Adams: What happened?

Papps: None of your business. And it's got nothing to do with the Institute. Stick to Lomax.

Adams: All right. Tell me about him.

Papps: He was self-important. There's nothing wrong with that, most of us are. He was chasing a knighthood and never got one. All he ever got was an OBE.

Adams: Poor thing.

Papps: He did a lot for Jessop, in the footpath and drainage way. And of course, he started the Institute. But he was . . . switch that thing off.

'I'm not in the gossip business.'

'I remember what you said, though. I made some notes when I got home.'

'You did not. What did I say?'

'Lomax was a randy little stoat.' She grinned. 'So what? All men are randy little stoats.'

'That sounds like chapter and verse.'

'What if it is? It's still true.'

I told her to tear up her notes or she'd get no more interviews from me. I even threatened to tear the transcript up, and I put it on the sun-deck rail and held my finger ready to flick it into the river – where Archie Penfold had at last hooked a trout.

'Go ahead,' she said, 'it's only a carbon.'

'Why is it always gossip and scandal you people want instead of facts.'

'Aren't they facts? That Alfred Lomax was screwing his office girl?'

'Don't speak like that. It's got nothing to do with the history of the Institute.'

'How do you know? It might have been because of that he set up the trust. So people would remember him as more than a randy stoat. What did you say his wife died of?'

'Mortification.'

'And then he got a housekeeper and started screwing her.'

'That's enough! Go away!'

Instead she leaned over the rail and shouted at Archie, 'Throw it back. Go and torture your patients.' She was burning with anger and he was suitable object. I saw the black O of his mouth. I'll have to tell him when he calls that this Harpy has nothing to do with me.

She sat down. 'You men aren't happy unless you're killing something.'

'Chapter and verse.'

'Alfred Lomax killed his wife.'

'She died of complications following childbirth. She was too old. You're not to take any of this down.'

'I can remember.'

'What's the point?'

'You're not the only one I've been talking to. And whenever you come to anything real you all say, "Switch that off." Then you dish out the dirt.'

'What dirt?'

'Who wasn't up to his job. Who pinched his research from someone else. Or stuck his name on someone else's paper.'

'Did they say that about me?'

She wouldn't answer.

'We were really pretty tame at the Institute.'

26

'The only decent one was Pearl Winwood.'

'Have you talked to her? She was a very pretty girl.'

Kate made a sound like tearing paper. 'That's all you ever say, you old men. Not, she was good at her job. Just, she was pretty. Well-developed frontally, one of you said.'

'Percy Trigg.'

'You sit in your chairs sniggering, playing your little sex games in your head . . .'

'Did Percy try something? Give your bum a pat, eh? He drove Pearl Winwood out.'

'Did he? I'll remember. I'll ask her.'

'She won't talk. Pearl's a lady.'

I was well aware of what I was saying. I wanted to punish her for a number of things: Archie, the stories she'd heard about me, my slopped tea, her ugly language. But what a marvellous pragmatist she is. She looked at me a moment, with lip turned back, and the points of her eye-teeth grating together. (Cave-woman eye-teeth, beetle-crackers.) Then she took my tea and poured it in my lap. It was only lukewarm. She doesn't make a good cup, which I must tell her. She shouldered her bag and stamped out of my house. The sundeck trembled.

I begin to like Kate Adams very much.

7

I've read through the transcript and it's accurate as far as it goes. How far is that? An infant step, except that infancy is a natural time and these are unnatural exchanges.

Adams: When did you first get interested in science?

Papps: As a schoolboy.

Adams: Primary? Secondary?

Papps: Oh, primary first. Then secondary.

Adams: Was the teaching good?

Papps: Yes, very. At primary, at Jessop Main School, we had a man called Thomas Ogier. He was very gifted as a teacher.

Adams: Didn't you just have nature study then?

Papps: Tup Ogier went a lot further than that.

Adams: Yes, I see. How is Ogier spelled?

Their spelling is atrocious. *O*, I said, and *g* and *i* and *e* and *r*. And Tup had made his brief appearance in my life. I can't let it go at that.

One Saturday afternoon he took the four of us across to the school and gave us a lesson in blowpipe analysis. He was trying to get Phil interested in science in the hope that he'd go to College and make some use of 'that good brain up there'. 'Sir, sir,' I cried, 'can I come?' Irene and Kitty said, 'Me too?' But only I had really heard the words. Blowpipe analysis. It meant equipment and techniques and procedures, it meant taking apart, finding out, putting names. I trembled as I walked along behind. Remember too: I had seen a black moon rising. Remember I had pooped my pants.

We went into the lab and Tup sat on a stool behind the bench while we lined up on the other side. But the pedagogical arrangement did not suit him. 'No, no, come here. Round here. Now, when we analyse minerals there are two ways. There's a wet way and a dry way. With wet we use reagents in solution – things like hydrochloric acid. I'll show you that another day. Right now I want to demonstrate the dry way. It's more fun.' I remember that little speech word for word. It had terms I understood instinctively, that never needed any explanation – analyse, reagent – and a name, hydrochloric acid, strange to me, that fell into my mind with a splash and rattled like an egg boiling in a pot. I remember too that I was offended. Did Tup think I was here for *fun*?

'Here's our equipment. Bunsen's burner. Although there are portable lamps for use in the field. And our little friend the blow-pipe. You blow in here, the air comes out here, bends the flame, carries it over the assay. What do you think this bulge in the centre is for?' He expected no answer, but Kitty said, 'To make you blow harder?'

'No, Kitty, you don't blow hard, you blow steadily. Anyone else?'

I knew. First it was intuitive, then it was logical. There was a humming in my mind, part power, part joy. 'Sir, it traps the moisture in your breath. So it won't spoil the experiment.'

Tup was startled; by the answer, by my dogmatic tone. 'Have you been reading in my Rutley, Papps?'

'No, sir. But moisture would change things. Wouldn't it?'

'Yes, it would.' He blew through the pipe. 'That's dry air coming out. It's not easy. You needn't think it's easy, young Papps.'

I knew it would be easy for me. Tup explained that the blast of air must be continuous. You kept your cheeks puffed out and used them like a bagpipes and breathed in through your nose at the same time. He lit the burner and put his watch on the desk. 'Time me. Two minutes is enough. I'll do the oxidizing flame. You don't know what that is, Papps, by any chance?'

'No, sir.'

'You put the nozzle in the flame. All the air gets burned. Watch.'

I watched. The others timed him. I saw the flame bend over, make a curtsey. Inside the transparent cone a cone of blue, which kept itself abased though its colour was proud and pure. It never trembled. I shot a look of admiration at Tup, who brought this about. Red-faced, ugly, he winked at me.

'Two minutes, sir,' Kitty sang.

Tup stopped blowing. The flame stood up, stood apart. She and I had a dialogue.

'You see, I'm not even panting. That's because I breathed normally. I could have gone on for five minutes if I'd wanted.' He ran the mouthpiece under the tap and dried it on his handkerchief – unclean. Irene made a face at Kitty. 'Now, Phil. See what you can do.'

The flame did a ragged dance. It lay down, sprang up, lay down. Phil watched it, cross-eyed. A gluey sound came from his nose as he tried to breathe. 'I could do it, sir, if I practised.'

'Try again.' Tup was anxious for him. Love, of a paternal kind, had got in. He was, I think, confused by a desire to do Phil's part, he willed him excellence, his cheeks inflated as Phil's inflated, his eyes too went cross-eyed, and orders came for the flame to lie steady. She knew none of it. She waited for me.

'Well, well, that was better. Rome wasn't built in a day, Phil.'

'It's just, I've got a cold sir.'

'Yes, of course. Here, blow your nose. Give it a minute or two. Kitty, you try.'

Kitty washed the mouthpiece and dried it on her sleeve. She did better than Phil. The flame made little trembles, dips and bows, but she controlled it. And having done that, wasn't interested any more. Kitty was a magpie, collected shiny things; bits of information, mental and physical skills; but was always moving off in some new direction. She was scatty, she was sharp, she was everywhere

– and comes together later, points in one direction, a creature of great mass, Cyclopean. Now, in the lab, she sees that she can make the blowpipe work if she wants, and knowing that, stops wanting and is ready to go away.

Irene, scarcely touching the mouthpiece with her lips, has a turn. She's no good. The flame hops about, it evades her. Irene had a narrow nose, and narrow passages no doubt, and suffered all her life from allergies and sinus infections. She could not breathe in and blow out at the same time. She made another face and put the blowpipe down.

It was my turn. But Tup said, 'Just a minute, Papps. Have another go, Phil.'

I didn't mind. I could wait. I even smiled as Phil made his attempt and did it better. He gave me the blowpipe and I stuck it in my armpit, made it clean. Tup knew what was coming. He would have liked to stop me; but in another way had seen my measure and was in a state of expectation.

I put the mouthpiece to my lips and put the nozzle in the flame and swelled my rubber cheeks, and looked, I suppose, like one of Aristophanes' comic slaves, but my ugliness was beside the point. The flame surrendered. She surrendered. She gave herself to me. Pale blue, and clothed in her transparency, she lay down. She lay as still as stone, as hot as suns, as cold as ice, and breathing through my nose I possessed her. You think it's funny? I overstate the case? You think that, Kate? An ugly boy blowing through a pipe into a Bunsen burner flame – and speaking, in his old age, of surrender, possession. I don't care. I have special knowledge. My beginnings were my high point in science. I've been through troughs and I've stood on peaks, and earned a comic handle to my name, but in Tup Ogier's lab, on that Saturday afternoon, I knew the consummating moment.

'That's enough, Papps.'

Yes, that's enough. I'll say no more, as the funny man advises on TV. I gave Tup the blowpipe and stepped back and stood in a corner. Phil had another turn, and carried on his wrestling match with me, and I watched him with indifference. It had nothing to do with winning. I began to pity him at last. The flame would not recognize him, danced away.

'No, Phil, you breathe in, you blow out. Two actions going on

30

side by side.' But he could not break himself apart and put himself together. That would mean turning aside, that would mean delays, and he was headlong, and interested only in things that lay in his path. I saw the moment he gave me Tup in his lab, flames and pipes, as not worth having. I saw the change of colour in his eyes, saw him shrug, saw him turn aside. He turned surrender into victory, and went away and got on with his proper business. The girls had gone already. Tup and I were left alone.

'Well, well, Papps. Had enough?'

'No sir.'

He ran his finger along the ragged top of his ear. He only did that when he had lost. He went to the window and watched Phil cross the playground, and he sighed; but I showed no mercy.

'You said there was another sort of flame, sir.'

'Yes, yes. You're a greedy sort of fellow, aren't you, Papps?'

He showed me how to make the reducing flame. I did not like her as much as the oxidizing. I liked, if you'll excuse me, penetration. I was happiest when the nozzle was in. But I made the flame perfectly. The prolonged steady blast was no trouble; and no laboratory skill has ever troubled me.

'Sir, can we do some minerals?'

'Why not? Why not?'

I had begun to interest him. When he had forgotten Phil on that afternoon he set himself to see how far he could stretch me. He began to be excited. I stayed calm. My only fear was that he would stop. But he began to be like a man stacking boxes – another one, another, and still the tower held.

We reduced metallic oxides on charcoal blocks. We made a borax bead. And when Tup turned to the blackboard behind him and wrote $Na_2B_4O_7.10H_2O$, I closed my eyes, I nearly fainted. *This* was taking apart. *This* was naming. We took up iron and copper on the bead and tested them and the flame went green and red and blue. He told me why. The why was as beautiful as the colour. The why and the colour became one.

'Good heavens, five o'clock. Your parents will be wondering where you are.'

We stood side by side in the boys' lavatory and peed together on the slimy wall. 'Urine is mainly urea. That's a crystalline body,' Tup said. 'There's also sodium chloride and uric acid. And other things.

Hippuric acid. Various pigments. Chemistry, you see, is everywhere.'

We walked across the cricket pitch to the gate. 'Would you like to do some more, Noel?'

'Yes, sir.'

'Phil might like to come along too.'

'I don't think so, sir.'

'No? Well, perhaps not. Remind me on Monday after school. We'll make some microcosmic salt.'

I dreamed in bed of microcosmic salt. The words rattled like dice in a box and wouldn't come out. I've no doubt I was tossing and groaning, but I slept easily when the oxidizing flame came into my dream. Edgar Le Grice also came, and held his black coat out to smother me, and behind him squat red flames gulped and sucked. He turned into the black moon, gleamed like coal. My blue reclining flame licked at him. It made him spit and crackle and leak grease. It turned him white and crumbled him to ashes. With cheeks swelled out, and breathing through my nose, I blew him away.

8

Dear Mr Papps,

Excuse me for not calling you Sir Noel but I couldn't do that and keep a straight face. I'd like to call you Noel and think I should as you're my great uncle or whatever, but you still haven't invited me to, have you?

I suppose I've put your back up now – as if I hadn't done that already! – but actually I'm writing to say I'm sorry for that business with the tea. Sorry! Sorry! But I did enjoy it, especially the look on your face. You looked as if you were going to throw a mental, as the kids say. Anyhow, I hope it doesn't mean I can't come again because I haven't finished with you yet. I've finished with the Lomax, just about. One interview to go, with Royce Lomax, and it's all wrapped up. Then it can sit in a butterbox until someone comes along in forty years and does a centennial history of the place – and tells the world how marvellous you all are. In my opinion you were a scungy lot, with a few exceptions.

I've got a new project, not PEP, all my own, and that's what I want to see you about. I need your help. I suppose I can call? Yes? OK. I'll come on Friday. I hope you didn't get scalded down there.

Luv,
Kate.

Help meaning money, no doubt. She's not getting anything from me. And she's not getting any more information. I know what her project is, I've been waiting for someone to dream it up – my biography. The answer's no. Why should I give myself away to some Tom Dick or Kate who thinks my life is simply a career? If there's something to say about me I'll say it myself. I'll tell my own lies and my own truth. Who for? That stops me short. There has to be one other besides myself. She – ah yes, she – burns it for me, page by page, in the fireplace in the livingroom, while I sip milk and whisky, new-born.

Is it my biography, Kate? The answer's no. If you mind your manners I'll let you do the burning.

You'll get nothing useful from Royce Lomax. The man's a wimp, to use one of your terms. You'll get a lot of palaver, that's all. Sweaty little fellow, he sweats words, and none of them stand up to be looked at, they slide away like jelly on a plate. The last time we spoke, three or four years ago – I was stupid enough to go to his exhibition and saw hills like worms, lakes like livers and kidneys, trees like penises, caves like eyes – he told me his work owed a lot to primitive animism, and geomorphology, and some Chinese system or superstition (I forget the name), some hierarchy of powers in the earth that were either benevolent or malign, according to the angle, physical and mental, of one's approach. There were red stickers going up all around us, but he sweated because he was afraid people were buying for the wrong reasons – for the penises I suppose – and he told me he'd like to give me a painting because I'd been Irene's best man-friend. No, I said, I didn't have room in my house for pictures, too many books; but I should have taken one. They sell for two or three thousand dollars today.

Irene's mother died when Royce was born. I see what a curious sentence that is. But Irene's the Lomax I'm concerned with. There she stands with Kitty, with Rhona, with Ruth: a quartet of women conversing at the centre of my life. The men circle round – Phil Dockery, Tup Ogier, and the rest – and sometimes *I* don't have a central place. Irene settled there with as much authority as a new particle joining an atom.

Kitty brought her in one afternoon and Irene sat at our piano without invitation and started to play. I looked up from my homework, then stood up, and Mum came from the kitchen and listened in the doorway, with a potato half peeled in her hand. Irene played – without music, that impressed me! – 'The Harmonious Blacksmith'; a very hard piece, my mother said later. I moved so that I could see her hands. I would have done better to turn my back and be impressed by Handel, not Irene. I could not connect her skill with ribboned curls, narrow nose, stuck-up voice, skinny Reen. She was changed. When she played another piece with crossovers in it I made a little squeak of ecstasy.

She sat a moment with her hands in her lap. Then she looked at my mother.

'Your piano needs tuning, Mrs Papps.'

'Oh?'

Irene pressed a key and made a face. 'It's really not a very good piano.'

'We'll have to get a new one just for you.'

'Could we, Mum?' Kitty cried. It was rare for her to misread Mum.

'Be thankful for what you've got.' Mum went back to the kitchen and would not come out, even though Irene played some more. She was showing off most of the time. But now and then she seemed to forget about that, and I saw the equal skill of going slow, I heard the music. She created it, and ruined it for me, did Irene. Ever after, I've thought of music as from her. Music seemed to hum about her like a swarm of bees. Don't laugh at that. She was harmonious, like her blacksmith (hers, you see, not Handel's), and even when she was being 'bloody', to use Kitty's term, or when she was depressed or sour or self-pitying, and when she was sick, and sick and dying, nothing was ever out of tune, sounds answered each other and compensated and everything found a proper place. In one thing only, in one thing, I heard the clash of discords, and

34

even about that I'm not certain any more. And I can't hear anything, even the Sallies playing for dollars on the tray of a truck, even the Saturday night heavy rock beating up to the circle from parties on the flat, without hearing it through Irene.

She was back with Frau Reinbold – Mrs Ogier now, acceptable though only just. Kitty had lessons from her too, but Kitty, as I've said, was not to be pointed. In any case, Irene was way ahead and out of sight, so what was the use of going on there? I don't mean Kitty was a quitter. She had taken what she needed from the piano, but still had many other things to learn; and at the end of it, who she was and where to go. For Irene piano was a passion and a way. She loved what she hadn't learned about it more than what she had. She gathered in new skills greedily. I think of the mantis eating the fly. Insatiable but fantastically neat.

Mrs Lomax died. Mortification was the cause, the hard birth of Royce opportunity. Lomax didn't have the appearance of a lecher, he had pained eyes and pinched face and slanting-sideways jaw and an elongated nose that some invisible goblin seemed to be stretching. He had a hollow chest and one of those pot-bellies of a sharply-defined sort, like a football pumped up hard in his trouser-front, and down at ground level turned in toes. I never really believed in his mistresses because I could not picture him 'doing it', as we said. Even now I can't. I try to see his cold nose nuzzling in the valley of his secretary's bosom and the picture's ludicrous. But he had her all right, and several others. It was never a scandal, it was a whisper, and it grew so loud it made a kind of sub-ethereal roar in our town. He resigned from the mayoralty 'for business reasons', and his poor wife, poor, high-flying, nose-in-air Mrs Lomax, English-vowelled, county-bred, shamed already by a pregnancy in her forties, went into labour early and did not survive.

Royce survived. Irene survived. Lomax survived, triumphantly. He hired a nurse for the baby and a housekeeper for himself. His business – many businesses – prospered in the war years. He grew very rich and in today's money would have been a millionaire several times over. This made him respectable again. His benefactions included a new roof for his church.

As Irene's friend, Kitty saw more of Lomax than I did. She never said much about him, apart from the fact that he lived upstairs and put his hands behind his back when he talked to her. I was in the

35

house only once when he was alive. Phil and I came down Montrose Street on our way home from college. (Have I mentioned that Phil's father, Les Dockery, had gone to the war and Phil lived with the Ogiers now? And here he was in a uniform as well pressed as mine, and the flea-bites gone from his wrists and ankles, walking on Nob Hill as though he belonged there.) Lomax, with a handkerchief round his hand, was trying to crank his car and barely managing to turn the handle.

'If that was a sheila he'd get 'er started,' Phil said. 'Need any help, Mr Lomax,' he sang out.

'Ah boys,' Lomax said, 'I've hurt my hand.'

'Let's have a go,' Phil said. He turned the crank-handle two or three times. 'She's not firing.' He had less idea of what went on in engines than I did but had heard some mechanic use the phrase. 'Hop in Mr Lomax and give her some choke.'

Lomax did as he was told but still the engine would not start. 'I'll have to call a tow-wagon, unless you boys . . .?'

We pushed the car home with Lomax sitting up at the wheel.

'Aren't you the ones who caught Edgar Le Grice?'

'Yes,' we said.

'I hope I gave you something.'

'Half a crown.'

'That's all right then. I think you've earned a piece of cake today.'

We followed him up a path spread with scoria. I put a piece in my pocket and Tup identified it later on: volcanic slag, all the way from Auckland, and shipping it down must have cost a mint. The sound of Irene playing exercises came over the lawns. We saw flashes of white inside a dark room and I knew that must be her hands.

'Tiddily-pomp,' Lomax said, not jocular so much as defensive. Then looked at me sharp. 'You're Papps, of course. You've got that pretty sister.'

'Yes,' I said.

'She'll grow up to be a beauty. But you boys mark my words, good looks are not that important. Good looks often get in the way.'

'What of, Mr Lomax?' Phil asked.

Lomax saw his phoney innocence. 'Now now,' he said, 'now now,' and looked severe. 'You're young chaps yet. You concentrate on getting ahead.'

He opened the front door and took us down the hall into the

kitchen. There we found the housekeeper, Mrs Clark, a woman with a small head on a large body and arms as quilted with fat as a baby's. Shiny flattened curls covered her head like silver beetles. Her fatness was the fatness of indulgence and her air of pained bewilderment came, I guess, from her having to work in the kitchen although a fancy lady.

'Ah, Mrs Clark,' Lomax said, 'give these lads a slice of cake, will you? And a glass of fizz-pop.' He sat down at the table and took a small notebook and a gold propelling pencil from his pocket. He wrote and tore the page out and folded it and gave it to Phil. 'Be a good lad and drop that off to Mr Drayton at the garage on your way home.'

'Good as gold, Mr Lomax,' Phil said. He expected another half crown. But Lomax only said, 'Go easy with that cake, Mrs Clark. I'll want a piece with my cup of tea.'

She put two mingy slices on a plate: seed-cake, which I loathed, and not baked by my father. The fizz came from a bottle already opened and was flat.

'There boys, tuck in,' Lomax said, while Mrs Clark dabbed up crumbs half-heartedly and put them on her tongue.

Lomax went to the door. 'Oh Mrs Clark, blisters on my hand. I wonder if you'd come upstairs and put some ointment on?'

'Now?' Mrs Clark said. Her eyes went ointmenty.

'It's rather sore. Immediate relief, that's what I need. You boys can let yourself out, eh?' He gave us a tiny wink from his slanting face.

'Yes, sir.'

'And rinse them glasses,' Mrs Clark said. Going up the stairs, she made a glottal cry. Phil, at the door, said, 'Pinched her bum.' I ran to see but they were gone. He came back to the table, looked at his cake, and pushed it aside. 'They must have better stuff than this.' He found a tin of biscuits in a cupboard and a new bottle of fizz in the safe. 'We can tell them Teeny-Reen said we could.'

We feasted, and left our glasses unrinsed on our plates, and stood in the hall to see if the chandelier was moving. Irene was doing chords in some difficult sequence and I was sure it was her sound that made the lustres tremble. Phil wouldn't have it. The rhythm was all different, he said. 'I wish she'd shut up so we could hear.' He crept up the stairs and peered through the railings. I went the other way and looked in the open door at Irene practising. It seemed impossible to me her skinny hands could make such thunderous sounds. She sat upright, in her Girls' College uniform, with her hair pulled back and tied with a ribbon. Her profile was severe, the line cut sharp, as though with scissors. Odours and vapours filled the house, stirrings in a moral atmosphere, and Irene seemed to me breakable. I wanted to break her. I wanted to save her as well. The two upstairs, her father and Mrs Clark, had me excited; and Irene had me hot and had me cold. The vapours and the odours coiled in me.

Royce sat on the floor, chewing a rusk. Coloured wooden blocks lay all about him. He looked at me and seemed uncertain whether to laugh or cry. I made faces at him and brought him down on the side of tears. Irene stopped playing.

'Quiet, Royce.' She looked at me and seemed to go cross-eyed. I saw her father in her long-nosed face. 'What do you want?'

'Nothing. We helped with the car.'

'Well I'm practising, so go away.'

Phil came along the hall and pushed by me into the room. 'Gidday, Teeny-Reen. Play us a tune.'

'I will not.'

'Something with trills in it, eh?' He stepped his fingers along the keys. Irene brought her knuckles down on his wrist.

'Ow! That hurt.'

'Don't touch my piano.' She closed the lid.

'You're a bitch, Irene.'

Royce wailed and crawled across to her. She picked him up and he buried his face in her shoulder, leaving mucky rusk-smears on her dress.

'Your old man's upstairs with Mrs Clark.' Phil put up his forearm, waggled it. 'Rumpity-bump.'

'I know what my father does. And you stink, Phil Dockery. So get out.'

'Come on, Phil.' I pulled him to the door. 'Sorry, Irene.'

'You should charge a shilling to watch. Build a grandstand, Reen. You'd get rich.'

She put her hand on the back of Royce's head and pressed so hard he made a cry. She bunched up the skin about her eyes, and was not holding tears in but rage. And I'm aware now of a quality in Irene I'll call acidic. I must liken her to some substance that burns, something with an ammoniac smell, clean but uric. If that suggests breaking down, she also had a crystalline self; she presented perfect faces, impenetrable.

In hindsight, I'm aware of both, as Irene faces us from her music room; and the mystery – no mystery now – of her holding of the baby's head. She kicked the door and slammed it in our faces.

Phil grinned, cheeky and sore. He rubbed his wrist. 'That got her going. Let's have another biscuit, eh?' We went to the kitchen and ate some more. 'I bet old Lomax sticks it up her too.'

I'd never heard of anything like that. Yet I saw it was possible. I wanted it, desperately, unsaid. I wanted to kill Phil, and rush upstairs and kill Lomax too; and wanted to try Irene myself. A standard set of confusions. It's no wonder we grow old. I grew old. I grew another year or two standing in that kitchen. Phil, though knowing more than I, kept his age.

Outside, I stepped off the scoria path, and heard Irene practising again. It was clean, hard, mathematical, ascending. Pythagorean. It swept my confusions away; and I saw that she was saved, as far as one can be. I mean from being twisted, defiled, not just by her father, by all the many things that work on us. And Kate, I'll tell you this, in case you wonder, Phil was wrong. I hinted the thing to Irene many years later, thinking we were close enough for it, and she screeched and flew in my face like a bat and bloodied my forehead with her nails, and it was more than seven years before she let me speak to her again.

As for Lomax, it comes to me that along with his pointy-faced glitter he had an air of more than defeat, of doom. He was not the shaper but the shaped. When he died in 1922 he left more than a quarter of a million pounds to set up an institute for agricultural research. That, I think, was his cry of rage at himself from beyond the grave.

9

I'm exhausted by all that. He said. She said. It's like tying tabs on specimens and that's not what I set out to do. I want to split things open and see what they're like inside and memory is not the instrument. I'll find out more by saying what should have been.

She should have grown with music all about her. She should have eaten it, bathed in it. (I know, young Noel, you can't eat music.) There should have been singing uncles, fiddling aunts, and trios and quartets in drawing-rooms, and a town full of symphony concerts; then study overseas, London, Vienna; famous teachers; and excellence, perfection, triumph, fame. Instead: a mother who wouldn't have a Bechstein in the house and a father saying tiddily-pomp. There should have been Europe not New Zealand. And no ties on her instead of Royce. Then – but was she strong enough? Wasn't she too fine? And isn't that fineness laughable, isn't it pathetic, keeping one on the sidelines while coarser folk play the muddy game: in her case, keeping her all her life in a house in Jessop, with a wimpish brother, keeping her a tinkler all her life? (I too am saying tiddily-pomp.)

What do I mean by fineness? I mean a kind of fine mesh in her feelings that trapped all painful things as they passed through, and she was sick with them all her life, and grew a slanting face like her dad's.

Yet she was saved. I'll go on saying that. She had no fame or triumph, but in her music room were excellence, perfection. Irene, sick, had only to reach out her hands and pain had no dominion, pain was put in its proper place, and knowledge and beauty became hers.

I loved her, of course. I love her still.

10

I've been sick. I must take care. I want to go on living for a while.

The date is February the first. Kate promised my notebooks back on the first, and stuck to her word, although she doesn't think I'm ready yet. I sit here like a small boy with the mumps. Next week she says I can go on the sundeck and reckons she'll carry me there if I can't walk.

Sitting high, I see mountains and bay but not the town. Helicopters are going back and forth on sight-seeing trips. Their flight path is over my house. They make the spoon rattle in my plate. Motor bikes are kicking up their racket and children are yelling in the river and a crazy dog barking. That's Fonzie from the Tucker house. I watched him all last summer. The kids dive under him and he can't work out where they've gone.

There's a cricket match on in the park. I hear bursts of cheering and shouts as someone asks for leg before. That's all the sounds. Except for a wasp on the window pane.

I called Kate to let him out but she took my notebook and whacked him with it, then picked him up by the wing and carried him out. I had to wipe wasp innards off my book.

Town's a madhouse, Kate says. The tourists won't go home. I'm glad I'm up here. The place is full of Yanks and Scandies with flags sewn on their back-packs. She likes the Scandies, doesn't like the Yanks. They're too well fed, they look as if they've all had second helpings. 'But,' I said, 'the Danes live on pig-meat and pastry, they're well fed.'

'Maybe. But it's not a question of food.'

I had never thought it was. It's a question of politics. She drew breath and began – went on and on. I stopped listening after a while. Looked at her instead. That's the sort of thing that interests me. *One* you can see. *One* you can almost understand.

She came on that Friday and found me shivering in bed, and she's been here ever since. Through Christmas and New Year. I don't remember those days. I remember Archie Penfold standing over me and remember a dispute about homoeopathy – he and Kate making mouths at each other; but their words rustled like paper and I don't know who won.

'I'm sending you to hospital, Noel.' I remember that.

'No,' I said; and 'No,' Kate said, 'I'll look after him. Besides, I need a place to stay.'

'It's all right, Archie, she won't let me die. She wants to write my life.'

I remember bottles rattling one night. Voices. Music. She must have had a party. That's the first time I've thought of it. I hope they brought their own drink and didn't steal mine. I remember something else now. Girls in the door. Frizzy hair, with light in it. They had no faces; glint of tooth as though they meant to bite me. 'So that's what a Sir looks like.' 'Sir Loin.' One of them came in and pinched my cheek. 'Out of there,' Kate said, and closed the door. She had a face.

'Kate,' I yelled, 'I want you.' It came out as a whisper. There's not much more than rags of me left. Rags of flesh. Voice like a bit of used-over bandage. I forgot why I wanted her. She sat on the bed, stitching the sleeve of a blouse, and it's so long since I saw a woman sewing I felt tears in my eyes. My mother sewed, Rhona sewed, and darned my socks, Ruth sewed, and knitted too in the continental fashion, with her fingers going so fast I couldn't work out the sequence of movements. They came about my bed, frowning, soft-footed. I felt a stinging in my eyes and a sense of loss so intense I must have whimpered, for Kate looked at me and said, 'What's up?'

'I didn't think women sewed any more.'

'I can't say I like it. I'm fixing this sleeve so you won't go sticking your tongue in.' That sounds ugly. She spoke with humour and kindness.

'Did I say that?' I remembered that once I'd wanted to. Then I realized I'd written it down. 'You've been reading my notebooks.'

'There wasn't much else to do round here.'

'Except have parties. And drink my liquor. And show me off to your friends through the door.'

'We didn't touch your drink,' she said. 'Not much, anyway. I'll buy you some more. And they looked in before I could stop them.' I was pleased to see her colouring up. Her cheeks go mottled when she's embarrassed. But Kate doesn't spend any time defending. She likes to be swinging, scoring hits.

'They were written to me, weren't they? Kate this, Kate that. Anyhow, I've got a right to see what people say about me. Especially when they want to start licking me.' That had an ugliness I did not admire. But her wildness pleased me, and I said, 'Read away. I don't mind.'

'I will. And you're wrong about me wanting to write your life. I wouldn't waste my time. So you can forget about saying no.'

She took something from me with that. It was as though she whisked away a meal I'd been about to enjoy. I'd changed my mind. I was going to let her. I was eager for her to; eager, rather, for the collaboration. Now I'll have to carry on myself. And yes, if I can manage it, that's best. The girl is really very ignorant.

'What,' I said, 'was this project, then? Or were you only looking for a cheap place to stay?'

'I earn my keep. Looking after you.'

'I'm not complaining, Kate. I want to know.'

She pricked her finger. 'Shit!' And looked at me. 'Shite. If that's OK.' She stuck it in her mouth, and mumbled round it, blood smearing her lip, 'I'm writing grandma's life.'

'I'm not sure she'd want you doing that.' There's a measured response. There's a comment screwed down like a lid on jealousy and rage. I closed my eyes. The bed lifted me as Kate stood up. How much did she guess of it? How much, Kate? My burst of rage that you should choose Kitty ahead of me?

I've tried to be cerebral. I've tried to work always with my brain, be rational. Understand *why* before I act, and if I can't know ends at least know means. Not just in my work but in that part of my life supposed to be private. But the visceral leaps up like a baboon, screams with rage. I chatter, gnash my teeth, roll back my lips, and sometimes weep. I display my scarlet arse at the bars and beat my chest. I piss on all the faces looking at me.

Is this the finish of it? Am I done for? Is cerebration over, my mind's journey, and liver and intestines rule my life?

If I don't get out I'll piss the bed.

'Yes, go on, write it down,' she says. 'It's good therapy.'

I don't do it for that. I do it to keep my mind alive; and in the end I'll achieve some measure. I'll be clear and simple, tell the truth, I'll hold it like a pebble in my hand.

Kate is good for me. We've reached an understanding. I fell out of bed and the thump brought her running and she found me there on hands and knees, leaking like a tap with a split washer. She cleaned me up and put me back and even washed my face. Then she took out the mat and hosed it down.

'You should be ashamed of yourself,' (and I am); but then she sat on the bed and talked to me and wanted to know if I'm upset about her writing Kitty's life.

'I don't think you'll get it finished,' I said.

43

'Maybe not. I'll give it a good try, though. I've got a lot of her old papers, you know. National Archives wanted them but I said they'd have to wait, she gave them to me.'

That seemed a strange thing for Kitty to do; but when I said as much Kate explained that Kitty was trying to help her with her thesis on the New Zealand Labour Party. That's abandoned and now the life takes its place. If I know Kit she wouldn't want anyone poking round in there. Her private life. The public part is another matter, but I told Kate it's well enough known already.

'I'm doing it all,' she said. 'What she was in public and in private. And I'll need your help. You're the only one left who knew her when she was a girl.'

I nearly said Phil Dockery was alive. But I've had Phil eighty years, and had enough of him and don't want him sitting by my bed. I think he never saw a woman whole, with any thickness, and what could he say about Kitty, dimensions without number? So I shut my mouth and agreed with Kate there was only me. But told her I didn't want to go raking over the past.

'You don't mind raking up Irene Lomax. All that garbage. She was a small-town failure, don't you see? I've got letters from her to grandma.'

I kept my cool, as she'd probably say. I've stepped on to a plateau and Kate can't touch me there. I only wondered that she was so aggressive. Has she known too many failures, and what sort? She'd be furious if I told her I think she needs a man.

In the end I agreed to tell her what I know. And I said she could stay here rent-free, but didn't have to look after me. I'd get a nurse.

'No,' she said, 'no bloody nurses.' Does she hate women? 'It's better if I pay my way. But don't get the idea I do it because I like it. Or you either. It's a bargain, OK?'

'Don't you like me, Kate?'

'I'll tell you when it's all over.'

As I said, she's good for me. She keeps me sparking. When it's over I'll tell her if I like her.

I mentioned that her typewriter disturbed me. 'Well that's too bad, I've got to use it.' She brought me some cotton-wool for my ears.

11

Phil Dockery has been. Kate telephoned and told him I was sick and asked him round. It was her scheme to get the two of us remembering Kitty.

I wondered why she brought me fresh pyjamas and combed my hair. Fresh pyjamas for Flea-bag Phil! When I heard his voice in the kitchen I mussed my hair. It's like gravel running through a hopper, but has a kind of boom in it too, a hollowness at the sentence end, a whump like a sack of wheat dropped from a dray. 'Whoit' is gone, exists only in my memory. I'm willing to bet he can't remember it. Somewhere along the line he noticed how people spoke where he wanted to be; so put that roundness in his voice and covered its makeshift nature with a whump! That's quite a feat. I admire him for it. I speak with the standard flatness myself – except on stage, when I can be anyone you like.

In he came, following his chest. I'm one of two or three who know he's got a pacemaker inserted there. 'Gidday, Noel.' He can still do that. 'How are you mate? Off colour, eh? Got the bot?' He came and shook my hand, but the frailness of it startled him and he dropped it fast and ruffled my already spiky hair.

Kate brought in a kitchen chair and he sat. 'You didn't tell me about your nursey, boy. I'd hop in bed myself if I had one like her.'

Kate gave a snaky grin. She went back to the kitchen to make tea. Phil lifted one knee over the other. He was not as spry as he pretended. I asked him how the cogs and wheels were behaving and he gave his chest a thump, but held it back a little at the end. 'My Woolworth's ticker? Have to keep it oiled, Noel.' He winked. 'Needs a shot of Scotch now and then. No, seriously, it's a great piece of engineering.'

'So you're keeping well?'

'Good as gold. I walk down to the club every night. Play a couple of frames of snooker. Indoor bowls, maybe. Have a snifter. Walk back home. See this.' He pointed at a white mark on his forehead. I put on my reading glasses and saw it was a scar, with stitch marks at the sides. It was like a zip-fastener and I felt if you unzipped Phil and looked inside you'd find only two or three circuits open, but hear the crackle, see the flash, of his dozen thoughts, all quick and heavy with himself. He told me he'd got a skinful at the club – beat the city treasurer at snooker – and couldn't remember walking home. The first thing he remembered was standing inside at the top of the stairs and reaching back to switch off the staircase light. Then somehow his feet got tangled up (Kate, at the door, snorted at that) and he fell down the stairs. 'Complete bloody somersault, Noel.' He crashed through the plate glass window on the landing and fell another six feet into the porch and ended up in the cactuses, out cold, pumping blood. The woman in the downstairs flat thought he was dead. But she called an ambulance, and they carted him off and sewed him up, and kept him a day for observation, and the following night . . .

'Don't tell me, I know. You were back at the club playing snooker.'

He grinned at me but was a little anxious. If he's vulnerable to judgement it's been mine. Not that he'll admit it. Never. No. He doesn't give a damn for anyone, that's the principle that rules his life. I could disprove it – what about his voice, for a start? – but I don't want to cause Phil any pain. In fact, as he grinned at me, all I wanted was to make him happy.

'You'll never learn, Phil.'

'Fell from the middle of the bloody house right outside, Noel. Ended up with the potted plants, potted myself. And I didn't have any pretty nurse to pick me up.' He turned to Kate, but she went back to her kettle in the kitchen.

'Does she ever smile?'

'Only at feminist jokes.'

'One of those, eh?' He lowered his voice. 'You know the cure for that, Noel? A length.' He jabbed with his forefinger. Phil's good at dirt. Sometimes he's close to poetic. I told him I didn't have one left and he said he'd be happy to stand in. We sniggered like two schoolboys in the bikeshed. But he confessed that with his pacemaker sex was out. He'd done a deal with his doctor, keep one vice and give up one and he'd kept his Scotch. 'In moderation.' He winked.

As we talked I thought how we'd beaten the averages. I read them in the paper yesterday and we've both had a bonus of thirteen years. So we're doing our bit, Phil and I, to confound statistics. (Although all they'll do is move up a step.) Irene did her bit as well, dying seven years short. Kitty was the only conformist, rebel Kitty, seventy-five. The men are left, the women dead. There's confusion, there's a turnaround.

In spite of his slowed-down legs, Phil looks good for plenty more years. His scar stands bone-white on his ruddy forehead. He tells me he's out fishing in his boat when he goes to Long Tom's, and in town he swims by the yachtclub when the tide is right. Never goes to the beach. 'Hell, Noel, I made an agreement with my doc. I'd be jumping on those topless sheilas out there.' Yes, he'll make ninety, ninety-five. As long as he watches himself with Kate. She heard that last bit, coming in with tea, and looked set to deal with him like the wasps she murders on my window pane.

We talked about Kitty for her. Phil Dockery's world is different from mine and he knows how every last thing in it works. He knows how men talk to each other in every situation touching money, he knows how deals are made and how they're broken and when to move and when to sit still and take a loss, and turn a loss to his advantage. He knows about laughter and how to put a face on and how to speak straight, and crooked too, I guess; and all about goodfellowship and toughness. He knows this, he knows that, male stuff, money stuff. I can't be bothered with that world of narrow boundaries. I won't list the things he doesn't know.

He knows nothing about Kitty but pretends to know the lot. It made me amused and angry by turns. All he remembers are things she said and did. He remembers other things she didn't do. I suppose I should give him the licence I give myself. Kate has accused me of inventing most of the stuff in my notebooks. You can't remember that, exactly what you said, and they, and she, you're making it up. I defend myself by saying it all seems right to me, and quote Tup Ogier at her – 'When we don't know the facts we're entitled to invent' – but it *does* seem right, I believe it; and I've no doubt Phil believes the things he remembers. Like, 'Kitty was the first girl I ever kissed.' He never kissed her.

I know that because Melva Dyer and June Truelove put it round the school – Flea-bag Phil under the bridge with Kitty Papps – and Kitty told me it was a lie. I said to Phil, 'When was that? Where?' 'Under the footbridge.' He remembers the story and the years make it true. It would come out true under a lie-detector. He jerked his thumb at me and said to Kate, 'He thinks his sister was too good for me.' I didn't deny it. He enjoys being Phil Dockery from the Port.

We reminisced, if that's the word, and let Kate plug in her tape-recorder. But she's going to be confused. There were plenty of facts we both agreed on – that Kitty jumped a class, for instance, and caught up with us in standard six, that she asked questions endlessly in class, that her great friend was Irene Lomax and the pair of them saved Mrs Le Grice in Girlies Hole. But even when we agreed our memories – how shall I put it? – reflected different lights. Have you ever seen a rock crystal, Kate? That's limpid quartz, quartz in its purest and most transparent form. Let it stand for Kitty. Now take Phil and me as the two planes of the dihedral summit. We're like that in all things, at right angles, even in our shared memories; and Kitty can be crystal clear to me, and to him, yet we'll face out from her differently. So when he says, 'She used to poke her fingers in Miss Montez's eyes,' he means she was doing what other girls would not dare, but I know she was feeling the hollowness inside. Just like me.

I think, Kate, that you'll agree with Phil. A lady Cabinet Minister who kissed boys under the bridge and poked her fingers for a dare into a skeleton's eyes, that's most appealing. I'd choose her.

12

All the same, you want my Kitty Papps, Kitty Hughes. In good time. First I'll give you my Phil Dockery.

His mother died of TB when he was nine and his father, a shipping clerk, sank into alcoholism and became a rag and bottle man, pushing a cart that made a glassy chatter in the streets. A sister in Hokitika took the four youngest children, but Phil stayed with his father and I remember him – and maybe it's true and maybe not, but at least it's as good as kissing under bridges – a boy with bare feet and scabby knees and snotty nose running from our house with an armful of rags, and Les Dockery, the father, standing by the cart drinking from a bottle, and banging the cork in with his fist, and wiping his mouth with his sleeve. The scene doesn't go on from there, but a part of it – the words under the picture, shall we say? – is that my knees weren't scabby and I had a handkerchief for my nose, and a father who didn't drink, so maybe some adult, invisible now, was giving lessons. Not my mother. She was censorious of those who were up not down.

Phil and his father lived in a street of derelict houses by the port and shifted from one to the other as the Harbour Board pulled them down. Like all town boys I went fishing at the wharves and I had a short-cut through Phil's street. There were picket fences rotting in the weeds. There were porches with the planking stripped off and doors with their panels knocked out and broken roof-slates sliding in the gutters. I saw a rat almost as big as a cat, grinning in the doorway of a house as though he'd just paid off his mortgage.

Phil earned money running errands, delivering parcels. I spotted him now and then darting among the drays and lorries or pinching a ride on the back of a horse tram. I saw him on Saturday afternoons when I went down to the Saltwater baths, my togs neatly rolled up in a towel. He didn't have a penny for the baths. He swam in his baggy pants round the piles of the coal wharf – where the yacht club is, where he swims now, still breaking the rules.

Then Tup Ogier found him, thought he had a worthwhile brain up there. You know all that. Les Dockery pulled himself together, enough to get away to the war, and Phil boarded with us for two months, then went to live with Tup and his new wife, Lotte Reinbold.

We were friends, Phil and I. Had to be. Hadn't we caught Edgar Le Grice, the Jessop fire-raiser? Our names were in the paper – mine first, that was fitting – and in the big-city papers as well. Having Phil in our house though was more than I was ready for. His manners weren't bad. He learned quickly. A word from Mum was enough. Just as he had held himself still at the bakehouse he held himself still in our family. I'd sooner have had him licking his plate or wiping his nose on the tea towels. I felt that Phil, with eyes quick, arms held in, with voice polite, was stealing from me.

My father thought he wasn't a bad chap, but Dad thought that about everybody . He said one day that if Tom Ogier changed his mind it wouldn't be a bad thing to have the boy live here. Now I *was* robbed. I'd had a vital organ ripped out and bled all down my legs and stood in a sticky puddle on the floor; and was cured by the turning-down of Mum's mouth. She didn't want him. Her true centre was on me, which she proved by saying, 'I don't think that would be fair to Noel.'

'I thought he was Noel's mate?' Dad looked at me.

'Yes,' I said, with heart pumping hard and all my blood back inside again, 'but when I go to College I think I'll need a desk where his bed is.' I put an earnest light in my eyes. Remember, Kate, I was an actor; and many's the time I've had to act my pants off.

'Ah,' Dad said, 'ah yes. Well, I suppose it'll be nice not to wipe the lavatory seat all the time. Now don't you say I said that, Noel. I wouldn't want to hurt him for the world.'

How I laughed inside. How roosters crowed in me – doodle-doo! I stood on tip-toes and beat my wings. That night I listened to him sleeping in the bed where my desk would be. Something in his nose made a sticky sound, flaps of tissue coming together and pulling apart. I aimed along my finger and shot him dead. I felt almost fond of Phil Dockery.

Kitty – here's something for you – liked to hear him swearing. She seemed to feel that being tough was his proper function. And now comes a hard part, I'll have to think.

I've said already Phil was a man. Kitty knew it. She was a being full of interests. It was as if things presented themselves and asked to be known and Kitty's task was to hold them still and turn them round; but the larger part of her study was intelligent not simply curious. Does that make her seem cold? She was never cold. How shall I put it? She did not keep the things she collected on a shelf. The increase was not only mental but sympathetic. Coldness came much later in her life.

Now Phil, fresh in his manhood, was of great interest to her. He was of some interest to me too. He showed me his penis erect and it confirmed my poor opinion of myself. I would not show him mine, even though, under my bedclothes, it was doing its best. He measured with his ruler: seven inches. I refused to measure and became moral in defence and threatened to tell Tup Ogier, which frightened him. Now and then we talked a bit of dirt about girls. He was careful never to mention Kitty; but we both agreed we'd like to do it to Irene Lomax.

Kitty though was the one he wanted. You've seen photographs of Kitty? Lomax was right, a pretty girl. And before you get on your high-horse, Kate, let me say good looks mattered to her. She spent hours in Mum and Dad's bedroom, sitting in front of the dressing-table, trying out hair styles. She loved trying on Mum's dresses too. A big girl Kitty, even at twelve – yes, frontally. Phil was someone she could experiment on. One night we sat in the living-room after dinner. Mum was knitting socks, though she hated knitting, and Dad was reading the paper and going tsk, tsk; but in a way that expressed helplessness more than disapproval. 'And Sir John French said it was all going to be over in three months.' (That's the war, Kate. Do you know any history? French was supreme commander. He was talking about the whole thing. A chap called Hamilton was in charge in the Dardanelles. Sir Ian. Believed a nation reached maturity by shedding the blood of its young men. And very fond of poetry, I believe. Our men were in the poppy field about that time. Look it up.)

Kitty came in wearing one of Mum's dresses and not only her clothing was different but her air was ladyish; that is, proper, for us, and seductive, aimed at Phil. How did she know that second part; and how could I pick it up, for it was on a wavelength not for me? But Phil and I, remember, were in a state, and I could not be separated from him.

I thought at first she was a visitor, and half got up from my chair, then flopped back, and watched the little drama concealed in her display. Mum and Dad didn't see it. 'Kit, is that you?' Dad was pleased and put his paper down. She smiled and curtseyed at him, then placed her hands on her hips and turned a circle. 'Does it fit?' she asked Mum.

'Not in the waist. Come here.' She took material in thumb and fingers and pulled it in. 'There, that's better. It's not your colour, Kitty. You want something to tone you down.'

'The pale blue!' She flashed a smile at us and was gone.

I looked at Phil. His nose and mouth had thickened; in fact the fellow was all swollen up with desire. It's a condition that makes one look very stupid. A little fire was burning in the grate for our first cold snap and he stared into it, with hanging mouth and brutish mien and I heard the lumpy coursing of his blood.

Kitty came in skipping, in the blue. She had done something to her hair, made it, somehow, virginal, but in spite of it, because of it, proclaimed her readiness – she stood not on that side of knowledge but on this. I make us sound like depraved children. We weren't that. We were all fast caught in innocence – Phil in his male condition, Kitty learning him, and I aware – we preceded any state

51

of sin. I don't, in any case, believe in sin; but recognize corruption, that's something else. No one was corrupt, or corrupting, beyond what was natural and proper, on that night.

Mum put a stop to it. Perhaps she caught a whiff. She let Kitty pirouette once, and said she looked nice, then said, 'No more. Bed-time, Miss.' And we went to bed.

No sin, you sin-sniffers, in what comes next. We lay in our narrow room with three feet between our beds. The curtains, half open at the window, stirred in a breeze. A little watery light from a quarter moon washed over us. He pushed his blankets down and aimed it at me – huge, dumb, pathetic; not all of them words I'd have chosen then.

'You be a sheila in bed eh, and I'll come in the window.'

'No,' I said; and hissed at him, 'There's someone out there.' He got himself covered quick. He lay with eyes closed and mouth open, terrified, and made no move. As for me – what was there, at the window? I still don't know. Wind in the curtain? Moth, cat, cloud shadow? Or Kitty, my sister, open-eyed? If so, she saw enough for her needs.

We heard movements in the house. Mum opened the door and put her head in. 'Enough talking, you boys. Go to sleep.' We heard her open Kitty's door and say something to her. Apart from whispering, 'Jesus!' Phil did nothing more that night.

And I've got nothing more to say. A couple of days later he was gone to the Ogiers'. He learned a lot, he profited from us. He held himself in and watched and mimicked. Tup Ogier was right, he had a good brain. As for what he gave us, I don't know. He put a little charge in the air for Kitty and me. We weren't the same when he had gone. I won't speak for Kitty, but I, Noel Papps, looked on my body differently; had moved some way to knowing the instrument it was for pain and pleasure. The pain I'm speaking of is mental pain. I'd seen the close connection, body with mind, and glimpsed dark places to avoid. Is this too much to say one randy boy learned from another? I know it's not.

Do you think you'll be able to use this, Kate?

13

Tup Ogier did not make a happy marriage. His confusion makes me sad, even though he learned to take pleasure from his mistake. 'We have to live with our decisions, Noel. No getting away.' In the beginning he was the boy in the cake shop who finds all the goodies made of plastic. (Aren't plastic meals an industry now, with the Japanese?) The promise of Lotte Reinbold must have been immense. I don't mean he simply wanted pleasure, even comfort, although he was a pleasure-loving, comfort-loving man; but that in a sense he sought completion. He sought, through her, a kind of masculation, through her he meant to find his elusive powers. It was, of course, unfair and stupid of him and Lotte Ogier suffered, no doubt, but there's nobility in Tup's mistake. Is nobility a word you'll let me have?

She grew very fat. She scolded him, she nagged him, she would not let him read but came and closed his book and took it away, using his bad eyes as an excuse. She gave up her pupils – except Irene, who gave up her after a while – and fought poor Tup with her piano. Boom! it went, and Bong! with short-arm jabs and round-house swings, then tinkled away out of his reach. He had loved her for her music. Now it gave him headaches and left him out.

Their marriage bed was an unhappy place. Lotte had ample flesh but cold. I have it from Phil; and when I heard it first it made in me the sort of hole it must have made in Tup, for she had been Venus rising in my fantasies. Phil listened in on their unhappiness. He brought me bulletins. What he did not say – I saw it for myself – was that they contended for him. They had no children, though Lotte was not quite forty when they married, but had Phil. She did not welcome him, and it's plain what a lump he must have made in a path she had wanted smooth. But when she saw how Tup began to love him, then she took him for herself. Phil watched it all with a hard, quick eye. He wasn't sure of his place at first. But when he had it sorted out he allowed Lotte to be his ma; and, like her, he left Tup out.

What started thin and bitter soon was abundant, soon was pure. She loved him with a vast maternal love. She trained his hair with oil on her palm, and would have licked it like a cow. She buttoned his coat and polished his shoes and tied his laces. She wrapped him in her arms and sent him off to school sweet with her powder, Port-rat Phil. He began to like comfort very much, and kept himself for himself by sneering at her. I don't blame him. He had to stay clear of suffocation.

Phil brought out in Lotte behaviour I hadn't come across before and took for German. 'Philip,' she cried as he walked in after school. 'Phili-will, my dumpling, my darling.' She fed him on cake, she fed him on cream, and I, as his best friend, got my share; although I preferred my father's cakes, and liked his savouries even better. So did Phil. He sold his torts at school and spent the money on sausage rolls from our shop. 'Sit, sit,' she cried. 'Eat, eat. But a kiss for Mama.' He kissed her. He said, 'Can Noel come in, Mrs Ogier?' For that is what he called her. Pottie Lottie at school; Mrs Ogier at home. She did not complain because she did not hear. She caught her own love as it bounced back and took it for his.

To all this Tup was spectator. Wonky-eyed, he stood and watched, and then he sighed and walked away. There are situations where an imperative rules. Tup walked away. And where did he walk to? Why, to me. He could not love me. The temptation, I'm sure, was never there. But he could experience feelings more in his control – approval, admiration, even delight – as I went my way, and through me claim back things he must have thought were forfeited.

They lived in the cottage that had been Frau Reinbold's – where Edgar Le Grice had kicked the doors out – so Tup became our neighbour, and I could let myself out the gate in our back fence and run along by the park and shin up a cabbage tree and squat on the wall, then pad four-footed down like a spider monkey, and enter the garden shed unseen, where Tup had made a science workshop for me. Unseen by Lotte Ogier in the house, unseen by Phil. Tup was at the door, face all a-grin with crooked teeth and his happy 'Tup-tup' beckoning me. Climbing over fences, what a plus that gives relationships! I've been the one who climbs and the one who waits and I don't know which is more exciting. Well, yes I do. A woman came to me that way once, waiting has the edge. But behind Tup in the shed was the oxidizing flame and the microcosmic salt, and iron, copper, barium, manganese, and girls could not have had more delightful names.

Tup must have spent hundreds of pounds on me. There was no gas laid on in the shed so he had to buy a field burner. He bought beakers, flasks, burettes, pipettes, a Steelyard, a Jolly's Spring Balance, and mineral specimens, crystal specimens, common and rare, and acids and refractors and prisms. He bought a microscope.

I went on fast. It was not all fun. He made me learn the valency tables and the atomic weights. I could rattle through them like 'The Lady of Shalott', I still can, Aluminium, Antimony, Argon, Arsenic, down to Yttrium, Zinc, Zirconium, and pick out any one you want. Try me. Gallium, Ga, 69.72. Tungsten, W, 183.92. Easy. I can draw the periodic table like a two-storied house, with basement for the coal and attic for old furniture on top. I had all that before I went to College so it's no wonder I was dux.

And Tup narrated to me the history of science, and gave me heroes, Lavoissier and Boyle and Priestley and Scheele – my favourite, a boy like me, mixing chemicals in a little room – and I conversed with them and told them I was setting out to join their company. I no longer dreamed of scoring the try that wins the match, I gave a little sniff at that and put on my genius look. I dreamed of – I practised – inventing a piece of apparatus like the alembic, like Boyle's pump, that would leap chemistry ahead; and formulated laws and discovered principles and tried the name Papps against Avogadro and found it lost little in dignity.

I put myself in danger: side by side with Davy inhaled 'nitrous air', and chased fluorine with the pioneers and had that 'wild spirit' flash from its container into my face. I loved the danger (but of course Tup let me have nothing dangerous) and the drama and the poetry – 'wild spirit'. The poetry in shapes – carbon skeleton. There was humour too. Priestley, isolating oxygen: 'This pure air may become a fashionable article of Luxury. Hitherto only two mice and myself have had the privilege of breathing it.' And I tried naming things, undiscovered yet or discovered only in my mind. I had no Greek and so could not make *atom, hydrogen* – but named my new elements Pappsium, Irenium and, feeling pure and stern, Stargon. I held a bit of pretty stuff in solution in the light and saw the sun strike through it and make a colour only I could see. 'Stargon,' I breathed. It was chemical and elixir and vehicle to the stars. There was not a single property I refused it.

What brought me back from this, brought me up short, was the tale of men who sat and thought. They unnerved me, they made me cold and small, I saw my tiny size and knew the shortness of my step. I worshipped them but did not really like them: Dalton *thinking* his way to atomic theory, Mendelyeev sitting in a room, working out the periodic law *in his head*. For Tup it meant that thought was creative, imagination precedes discovery. I sensed that would be too hard for me, I would never travel there, and I got very busy practising skills, learning tables. I became very good at it. Don't run off with the idea that I'm not happy with what I achieved.

But Tup wouldn't let me stop at chemistry. 'The whole keyboard's there in front of you. Why only play middle C?' – although, when he thought about it, middle C was geometry. So we collected bugs and leaves and lichens and shells. We germinated peas, we crossed pollens. For a while we kept two mice in separate cages and fed one on grain and one on meat, but when we put them in one cage to breed they turned out to be males and killed each other.

And so I should not be a philistine Tup gave me 'great books' to read. My father did the same and between them they got me through Thackeray, hard work; and through Dickens. I acted him – Bill Sikes and Quilp and Mr Turveydrop – and liked him better. (That's too tame, I was captivated: that magnified inner life, those monstrous obsessions. My small deceits and guilty fantasies stopped hurting me.)

And I learned the history of medicine, astronomy, philosophy, physics – Archimedes and Aristarchus, Pythagoras and Plato, Galen, Ptolemy, Harvey, Kepler, Newton, Darwin, so on; not all at once, over the years, things outside my school curriculum. Tup had me speak of science as natural philosophy, which I kept up for a while; but people laughed at me and I gave it up. He spoke of dark times when human reason slept and I pictured a great swamp full of black mud and cold vapours, with people sliding round it on their bellies, and priests squatting there, mumbling Latin – he hated priests – and then the sun rising after centuries of night, and dark things sliding down into holes and people turning up their faces to the light and standing upright. I drew it and showed Tup, and he was pleased, but said with a caution that puzzled me, 'Of course, Noel, it wasn't quite as simple as all that.'

Suns rising, suns rolling in the sky, were very much a part of my thinking then. The sun became my symbol for the scientific mind, and that was original at least. I did not care for the moon, I tried to keep her without attributes. But she was the one I was able to look at. I mapped her as an exercise, up in the observatory on Settlers Hill. I don't think Phil ever went there again but I was there on clear nights, mostly with Tup but now and then by myself. I saw the moons of Jupiter and they made a hollow in my chest, as though they'd drawn some of my substance off. I saw Mars and Venus. They looked back and saw me too, hardy at my post. I countered their menace with a litany of facts – fourth in order, period six hundred and eighty seven days, diameter four thousand two hundred miles, distance from Earth one hundred and forty one million miles. That kept Mars in his place, though he loomed large. And so for Venus. And I was even tougher with the moon. If I'd let her have any life at all she would have had me squatting in a corner hiding my face.

The observatory belonged to the Jessop Philosophical Institute and Tup was honorary curator. The building was a Berthon-type with an equatorially mounted clockwork-driven five-inch refracting telescope. I know all this not just because I went there as a boy but because the Lomax Institute took over the observatory in 1937. Tup was dead by then.

He put his hand on the telescope, which now and then he called, 'My optic nerve.' 'I watched Halley's comet through this. I watched it come, and watched it while it was here, and then I saw it go away. You remember Halley's comet, Noel?'

I remembered that whisk broom in the sky. At nine I had thought too much fuss was made of it.

'I'd like to find something up there. Halley's comet. Tycho's star. Ha, Ogier's folly. But I wish . . .'

That was the damage in Tup. He had never been wishful before. Uncertain sometimes, regretful now and then. But he had never said, I wish.

Phil Dockery, that's who I was telling you about. The day before Germany's capitulation the schools were closed because of the Spanish flu epidemic. But the bigwigs got us together, flu or not, and marched us through the streets waving flags, then made us run races at the sports ground. Phil and I went round to Cathedral Square that night and watched a mob burn the Kaiser. We reckoned

Edgar Le Grice would have done a better job. But it gave me a funny feeling to see the Hun up there, with epaulettes and buttons and high boots and moustache. He even wore the helmet I'd worn in the pageant. His moustache flared like straw and armies of sparks crept on his face and turned it black. The helmet fell off and people cheered and a man ran forward and kicked it into the fire. He howled and held his toe. The Jessop City Brass Band played 'Land of Hope and Glory'.

The Ogiers did not show their faces. Les Dockery, the Gasman, was there. Gas caught him in the battle at Ypres, mustard gas (dichloroethyl sulphide ($CH_2Cl.CH_2)_2S$ – I got that out of my head, Kate, didn't have to hunt in any book). It burned his lungs out, ruined them; and I'd say his life ended there, except that something kept on in his mind. He gave the impression of a dead man walking. But something was alive, he talked to someone. He walked ten yards and stopped to breathe, or try to, and walked another ten, grey-faced, in khaki army greatcoat summer and winter, and underneath the wheeze turning in his chest like a rusty wheel, a murmured conversation never stopped.

'Who does he talk to?'

Phil shrugged. He did not want to be an expert on his father. He passed him in the street with just a nod. Even when the Gasman clutched rails in the park and seemed to stop himself from falling over, Phil went by. 'He goes around and tidies up his room,' Tup said. 'He does his shopping for him and makes a cup of tea.' And Tup looked out of his window one day and saw the Gasman in the garden, where he sometimes sat on summer afternoons, and Phil was sitting with the poor ruined fellow and had his arm round his shoulders and was pointing out the sparrows in the dust. But I never trusted Tup when he praised Phil and I'm not sure it was true.

There were plenty of reminders of the war in our town, a blind man, a wooden-legged man, and men funny in the head, and soon we had a monument in the park, a soldier making a bayonet thrust, with more than a hundred names engraved on the plinth; but for most of us Les Dockery was the one who kept it alive. Children named him some time in the twenties – the gay decade, one writer called it, he wouldn't now. Les Dockery, the Gasman. He died on a seat in the park in 1935, and sat there several hours with his head on his chest before a lady tapped him on the shoulder and he fell over. Tup Ogier died in Jessop Public Hospital, of cancer of the bowel. Phil lost both his fathers in the same year.

14

Kate has been going through my photographs. She brought them to my bed in three shoeboxes and tipped them out on the blanket. Then it was, 'Who's this? Who's that?' I set myself to see how many faces I knew and did very well. Occasions defeated me though. That fellow holding Kitty by the hand was Billy Simpson, who went on to be a Presbyterian minister. An earnest fellow, worried about his soul even then, and Kitty's too, which amused her. The girl laughing at Phil was Jessie Mills. She was a nurse. Me and my girl (wasn't that a song?), my girl and I, were laughing too. Nancy Rosser, another nurse. She went out with me for a while but wanted Phil, and that's why she laughed with her mouth so wide. He stood behind Billy Simpson, pretending to be a devil, with forefingers sprouting from his head. His widow's peak and pale mad eyes and grin are devilish. Nancy is pointing at his behind and no doubt saying he should have a tail. Billy frowned. He guessed what was behind him.

I know them all. And know that Nancy Rosser married Billy Simpson and became the moderator's wife. And Jessie Mills never married but ran a nursing home which was closed because the lavatories were dirty. I know that. She was quite rich and went to live in Queensland. But I can't remember where the photograph was taken. There's a banner in the trees but you can't read the name, and two men on a greasy pole are whacking each other with sugar bags full of straw. Perhaps it was a Presbyterian picnic, although we look too smart for that, in boaters and blazers and white trousers. Kate doesn't care. She's interested in Billy Simpson. I told her not to waste her time. Kitty only went out with him because he borrowed his father's car. She told me he was a total sap.

Here's a photo I know more about. We're on a beach, standing in a group, with two dinghies pulled up on the sand. The sea sparkles behind us and an island shaped like a scone sits off the shore. The Papps family and Irene and Royce Lomax came in one dinghy. The

Ogiers and Phil and Les Dockery in the other. The beach is Long Tom's. It's quite a row from Stallards but Phil and I were fit young fellows. We've got our boaters pushed back on our foreheads and we're grinning with achievement. There's his widow's peak again. It's like a pick-axe.

My father took the snap with his box Brownie. I'm standing next to Irene, with whom, by then, I was in love, head over heels; or, as Phil said (interested in violence more than sentiment), arse over kite. Royce, aged four, holds on to her skirt from the other side. I hated Royce. I remember thinking, as I rowed, how marvellous it would be if he fell in and didn't come up. I dived for him, thirty, forty feet, but little Royce was nowhere to be found. Irene wept on my sodden breast. But I'll tell you now, in real life I never even managed to hold her hand.

Phil and I and the girls walked along the beach to the place where the creek flowed out. Phil carried Royce on his shoulders. Small boys are supposed to enjoy that but I saw the way he looked at Irene, and the anxious way she looked at him, and felt their longing for each other. I took up a handful of sand and lectured on it – believing I had arts, and betraying one love for the other.

'Oh, shut up, Noel. We've left school,' Kitty said.

'What a beach,' Phil said. 'I'd like to own this place, eh. And keep everyone off.'

'Why?' Kitty said – or is that simply what she would have said after meeting her husband? Beaches, like the moon, belong to everyone. But she and Phil were out of tune already. He'd seen a place that moved him with its loneliness and beauty, and perhaps as a way of affirming, perhaps in defence, he wanted to own it. Kitty simply wanted to enjoy. Nature's child was one of her personae, genuine – as they all were genuine – and I believe she wanted to strip her clothes off and run naked. Instead she tucked her skirt up and waded across the creek and climbed halfway up the cliff on the other side. Irene, who had Royce back by now, called at her to be careful. What beautiful pitch and tone, what bell-notes in her voice. I was not the least bit worried about Kitty.

We left her and walked back to the dinghies and Phil and I and Tup and my father went for a swim. Irene changed into her togs but Royce screamed whenever she waded out so she stayed in the shallows with him.

'Let's drown the little bugger,' Phil said.

'Let's use him for fish-bait.'

'Now now, boys.'

Irene got dressed and she and Royce went to look for Kitty on the swamp flats by the creek. I have better photos in my mind than this smudgy one. Irene with loose hair and yellow dress, shining elbows, shining ankles, walks on the beach, away from me. (A small boy in a sailor suit trots at her side but I snip him off.) She spins round once – movie, not a snap – to see if Kitty's gone up to the other end of the beach; then climbs among dune grass, pulling with her hands. I've got a slippery eel in my togs and have to wait until it becomes a sprat before I can get out and follow her. Lotte Ogier, sitting on a rug, wags her head. My mother gives a sympathetic smile. Les Dockery, on a driftwood log stripped of its bark, converses with the inside of his head as I walk by.

'Attaboy,' Phil yells from the sea.

Do I catch her? No, I don't. Is violation in my thought? Never! Never! Possession, a spilling of desire, yes, that much, but she's an actor in it too; we adhere, we enter each other by osmosis. How did she reach this willing state? By processes of logic reversed by chemistry. I mean reason was about-faced in my mind by bodily and emotional needs.

It was a painful event and that's why I'm coming at it sideways. I'll try now to look squarely at it. Irene had not found Kitty but had discovered a little tumble-down house at the edge of the swamp. Wild bees had made a hive in the ceiling and homed in from the valley, pellets of light zipping across the face of the trees. I followed her footprints in the mud, saw where she had picked up Royce, and crept on to the porch and looked in a window. What did I see? The termination of my desires? Death of hope. Say it plainly. I saw Irene in an empty room with Royce in her arms, and the child dozing on her shoulder. She walked slowly, meditatively – yet I know part of her slowness, a part of her thoughtful air, came from the pressure that lumpish child made on her arms and hips – and she hummed a tune, something I did not know, a lullaby. Watching, I knew she was never mine. It's as simple as that. Knowledge can come from odd conjunctions that uncover in one things not yet arrived at by the mind, or things suppressed. It's like the discovery of some natural law. One does not argue. A small girl – she never grew more than five feet tall – with high narrow forehead and slanting jaw, walking in a room in a ruined house, with a child too big for her in her arms, and one hand cupping the back plate of his skull: my exclusion, now, forever, was demonstrated. Did Royce's glazing eyes take note of me, and a fat smile show before he slept? Maybe, maybe. Did Irene, turning, spot me in the window and purse her mouth into a silent sshh? Yes, that happened. She closed her eyes as she paced one length of the room, on creaking boards, in dusty light. I backed off and slunk away. The dangerous bees skimmed over my head with their loads of honey.

Kitty was waiting in the sandhills. 'You'd better give up that idea,' she said.

'What idea?'

'Irene.'

'I don't know what you mean.'

She smiled at my feebleness and patted my arm. 'It's not only you she doesn't like. She doesn't like boys.'

'Why not?'

Kitty shrugged. 'She's going to have a different sort of life.'

I sneered at that and made coarse jokes and Kitty laughed – at me, at the jokes. She liked being coarse herself and said what she'd enjoy most would be to pickle Roycie in a jar and put him on the top shelf in a cupboard. But she wouldn't make jokes about Irene.

We went back to the dinghies, where Lotte Ogier and Mum had lunch spread on a cloth, and we ate Ogier cakes and Papps savouries. Irene arrived with Royce asleep on her shoulder, and saved a pie and a cream bun for him.

Later I climbed a cliff and went too high and scared myself. Five feet off the ground is high enough for me. Phil and Kitty crossed the swamp to explore the ruined house – Long Tom's house. Safe again, sitting on a ledge, I saw them walk around it and stop to watch the bees. Then they went inside. If he claims he kissed her there he's a liar. Irene was the girl I couldn't have. Kitty was the girl Phil couldn't have. Natural law.

The day ended – the day ends for me – with the only conversation I ever had with Les Dockery. He was still sitting on the log, had even had his cup of tea and cake there. We made the dinghies ready and I walked along to fetch him. 'Mr Dockery,' I said, 'we're going now.'

'Ah,' he said, and put his hands on his knees and levered himself on to his feet. I went two steps ahead of him. It seemed bad manners to run away. His chest was turning over like a counter-weighted wheel. Halfway to the dinghies he said, 'Noel.' I was surprised he knew my name. 'Wait on, son.' It was not only the first time I'd spoken with him but the first time I'd looked in his face. He was younger than I'd thought. The greyness of his skin made him seem old; the razor scrapes, his Adam's apple like an empty box, and hands, all dry knob and softened callous. His overcoat was like a part of him, half-shed skin. Now I saw what I can only call the young man lost. I saw, startled, what I hadn't known: he was alive.

'What's the name of this beach?'

'Long Tom's.'

His eyelids closed down slowly and the orbs seemed to roll back and look into his head. He gave a little nod and spoke two words that made no sound. Then raised his lids, easy, unfussed, like those garage doors that lift with a finger. I saw something gleam there, in the dark. 'Thank you, son.' With a movement of his hand, he sent me on.

Those are the things I know about this photograph.

15

Today I walked as far as the letter-box and found that Kate has an anti-nuclear sticker on the gate. What's the idea? I wanted to know when I got back to the house. We argued, and I agreed I didn't disagree. I wouldn't back down though, she should have asked me. OK, OK, she said, I should have asked; then accused me of being scared. There's truth in that. I've never been one for declarations. It's more my style to stand in a corner, smiling privately at my better knowledge.

She's being very aggressive. Last week she sent my *Watchtower* lady away with a flea in her ear. I like talking with religious loons, I like their certainty, being a dealer in certainties myself; and I enjoy my better knowledge. The *Watchtower* lady has been coming here for years and we've covered her ground in more ways than I can count, and enjoyed ourselves immensely. Now Kate's spoiled it.

And she told the man who came round with the petition against homosexual law reform to get his grubby bit of paper off her property. Her property! She didn't ask me if I wanted to sign. 'If you'd signed it,' she said, 'I'd have walked out that door and not come back.' She read me a letter she's written to the paper. Something like this: In the matter of homosexual law reform, there's a lot of hatred around, and all of it seems to be coming from Christians. I'm not a Christian myself or I'd quote some texts at them. 'Punchy,' she said.

'Are you sure you should lay yourself open like that?'

She asked if I was afraid they'd come and fire-bomb the house, and that, just for a moment, frightened me. I believe these fundamentalists can be dangerous. If they get in a majority people like Kate will find themselves burned at the stake. Me too – but I'll be safely dead and they'll have to deal with me in effigy. I won't mind that. I mind though the new dark age they'll bring. I don't know what we're here for but it isn't that.

She's been reading my notebooks again. That's what makes her cross. She's decided that Irene wasn't a small-town failure after all but a feminist martyr.

Now she's even crosser. She borrowed some Jessop Girls College magazines from the Public Library and discovered that Kitty was a leading light in the Young Helpers League and was found at the box-opening to have £1.1s.1½d, a record.

'Kitty liked being first,' I said.

'They collected clothes for Sir John Kirk's Ragged School. Jesus!'

'Your life seems full of pitfalls, Kate.'

'The Christian Union. She wasn't in that?'

'Oh yes she was. She went through a very devout phase. Most girls do. Or they did in my day.'

I told her we had been Lutheran, but back-sliding had been our direction, and our church visits far between. These had been to St Bede's, there being large areas of agreement in Anglican and Lutheran doctrine. Irene took Kitty to the Cathedral to sing in the choir, and Kitty was hooked. (Kate approves of that word.) For six months she was a pain in the neck, scolding me when I blasphemed, and crying silently in her bedroom at Mum and Dad's lack of faith. Then she came out. It was as if she'd taken a walk through the fun-house. I mean, things were extravagant inside, with haunted rooms and distorting mirrors, and she found a preference for natural shapes. That was her way, always to come back to her base, with pockets full of interesting things. And through her life she found religion fascinating – not doctrine but belief, and the things it made people do. Billy Simpson might have been a sap but his concern for his soul and for hers, while it amused her, gave him some weight in her eyes.

'She didn't stay in the Christian Union long. Look in 1920.'

I wish I'd been more careful. Kitty wrote the editorial. There's no mistake, it was signed K.P. and no other senior girl and no member of the staff had those initials. Kate read it, breathing through her nose. Poor Kate. She's as reliable as litmus paper. The dislike I announced so firmly is gone; and with it my senescent desire, but curiosity moves me to another sort of possession. Let me begin by treating her as a specimen. I'll name her parts, I'll map her, north to south. And come back to Kitty in good time.

She has hair that my mother would have called summer hair but I'll call blonde. It's rather streaky, inclined to oiliness, and needs more care than she gives it. Her skin is pinkish, not much melanin, and should not be exposed to the sun. I've told her that but she takes no notice. Forehead square, squarer than I like, with a sharp angle at the temple. There's a handsome rounding of the parietal and occipital bones, the sort that leads one, falsely, to think of good brain power. (I don't mean, Kate, you don't have a good brain, that question's open.) She has blue eyes that squint in bright light, but she won't wear sun glasses because they're 'phoney'. They're smallish eyes, lively when not dulled by her resentments. Nose, generous. I'm being less scientific than I intended. What's generous? For that matter, what is handsome? I mean her nose is plumply winged, with broad passages, not the narrow sort poor Irene had. Mouth a little down-turning, lips very red, always unpainted, sharply outlined. She protects them from the sun with a cream that makes them shine, and sometimes makes her look as if she's eaten greasy food. Her front teeth overlap, left to right. Big teeth, saved from goofiness by those spiky canines. She's not too old for orthodontic treatment, but I know better than to suggest it. Small ears, mouse-thin ears. Chin, squarish again, almost mannish, with an overdevelopment of the masseter muscles. She should try not to be so determined.

Those are the parts. How can I make them cohere? How can I demonstrate that, all together, Kate Adams has a lovely face? I can't say where it comes from, this loveliness, though it needs me to see it, and therefore a part of it's from me. There's a tension between what was there to start with and what she puts in, and tension is a well-known provider of balance. There's a tension between perfection and imperfection, using those terms in a structural sense, and between rest and dynamism, and between ageing and youth. Temperament and character also play their part, the tension between them sometimes seems to hum in the air surrounding her.

You don't think you're much to look at, Kate. And you don't care – or, as you put it, don't give a stuff. Why must you prefer ugliness? I think there's a tension in you between what's hard and soft, but hard will win and turn you into stone. You still have time to do something about it.

Her body? Generous. Yes, that will do. But lighter in the upper than the lower part. She seems to have a lot of bones round the shoulder, too many bones – but I'll keep seeming out of it. She's small-bodied to the waist and several sizes larger from there down. Big in the bum. (You don't mind a bit of crudeness, Kate? I'll stop if you will, there's a bargain.) But she has the apple bum, not the pear, chunky not sloping. That's an observation, not a statement of preference. I simply note that one will lose its shape quicker than the other. Her thighs are large and her calves muscular; sprinter's calves. And skinny feet: a corrugation of metatarsals, and elongated toes, monkey toes. She could pick fruit with them. Long fingers too, stretched-out middle phalanges, and short nails like little dabs of glue.

When I think of her body I can dislike her. This is the product of my sour regrets and so worth nothing. There's a tension between wanting and not wanting, and no sort of balance is achieved. But her body's not Kate, and I'll maintain this wanting and not wanting isn't me.

Her mind is Kate. And that's more difficult. Rage and disappointment make a large part of her mental life. There's probably too

66

much idealism there. Idealism always brings ruin in its train: there's nothing like it for denaturing. It deals in simplification, then multi-plication, and in the end there's too much to see, monochrome, gigantically single-celled, and assertion is the only road left open. That's a digression – but it's a fact that Kate simply, endlessly, asserts. That this is so, and this; and both are bad. I wish I could get her out of it. Must I be wishful, like Tup?

She doesn't read much but when she does it's mostly about wrongs done to women – believes in Iphigenia, she does, but won't let Helen have a place – or books about creatures with furry feet and wizards with long beards and magic stones (pebbles I mean, not the other things). Juvenile stuff. She listens to music. She's passionate about homoeopathy and knows a thousand names, and knows all symptoms and complaints and remedies, and has a carry-box, professionally made, that rattles as she totes it about, with tiny bottles filled with tiny pills like snails' eggs. I've asked her to treat my old age, like with like, and she's not amused; gives me bryonia for bilious attacks, nux vomica to keep me calm, and when that fails, cocculus 'to knock my bad temper on the head'. What would she dose me with for fear of death? And herself for lack of curiosity? She knows remedies and symptoms all right, but nothing about the history of homoeopathy. I mentioned Hahnemann and she said, 'Who?' and yawned at him proving quinine on himself. I felt as if I'd discovered some part of her dead.

I asked her once about her degree. She did political science, I knew that much already. And sociology, as I'd expected. She also did philosophy a while; and when I asked her why, replied why not? There seemed to be some promise in that and I settled down to enjoy myself, but found her dreadfully ignorant; as she found me. I did not want her modern stuff, and my ancients she categorized as 'a pack of wankers'. She'd heard of Plato's cave but hadn't bothered to understand it, and when I explained, found it laughable, and, she declared, bloody indecent, people chained in caves, just about what you'd expect from a pack of slave-keepers frightened of looking at 'real issues'. I've no liking for the shadow-shapes myself and was pleased to hear Kate going on, but couldn't agree that what Plato and his pals really needed was a session in the kitchen washing dishes. And there we got to it: feminism. That is where Kate really lives.

I have nothing to say about it. I agree, I agree, injustices abound, cruelties, stupidities, are present everywhere. I agree about the waste, the dreadful waste, and that it's more than time, etcetera. I admit it, we men are ratbags and have centuries of criminal stupidity behind us. And more. And more. But I just don't want to talk about it. And I deny, most strongly, that I'm a rapist. The cheek of that! And how they deny the *single* thing, these idealists.

My God, Kate, I don't like your mind.

She read Kitty's editorial, breathing through her nose.

'There is more to life than success and pleasure,' Kitty wrote. 'As we go out into the world we would do well to remember this, and keep duty always in our sight, and never surrender our ideals. Above all must we remember, we are women, and womanhood means duty. It means service. We must lead good lives. We must make our longings reasonable, and our ambitions modest, and strive not for success, not for pleasure, but for the best and noblest in life; and be the type of "good, heroic womanhood" the poet writes of. The sphere of activity calling most of us is domestic, and goodness and heroism are no less present there than in the world. We must be good heroic wives and mothers.'

Rage and disappointment. There are tears in Kate's eyes now. I tried to explain that Kitty played games, and went through phases, and loved roles and opposing roles and change and variety, and chased approval, and liked to shock; and was a complicated being. On her last day at school, I said, she vaselined the headmistress's door handle. But growth and change seem to be outside Kate's understanding. She can't tolerate inconsistencies; and so she will never write Kitty's life. Or if she does, it won't be Kitty.

16

I never thought I'd visit Long Tom's again. Kate rang Phil and arranged it; or, as she says, jacked it up. He came for us in the silver-grey Austin Princess that used to be the mayor's car; that Kitty looked so stately in, and hated. The man who breeds his horses was the driver. Phil is not supposed to drive any more, but breaks that rule up at Long Tom's.

Kate tucked my mohair rug round my knees, then got in front with the driver; being democratic, or perhaps just getting away from the Old Goat, as she calls Phil. I wonder what my name is.

Town is busy still, with young back-packers coming in at the bus station. I saw a maple leaf on a pack, and the red cross on white, and the yellow cross on blue, and of course the stars and stripes. People will declare their origins and loyalties. In every car window there's a sticker for some radio station or pop group or sporting code; or some brand of beer or for Jesus. And we're becoming passionate, we demand our rights. Gay rights, women's rights, Maori rights, rights to play rugby with whom we want. I'm glad I don't live in this time. I'm just passing through to somewhere else.

We waited outside an accountant's office while Phil went in to do some business. He keeps his stubby finger in the pie. Kate got out of the car and talked with a woman sitting at a little table outside the Trusteebank. She put her name on a sheet of paper and I admired the line of her hip and thigh.

'What was that?' I asked, when she came back.

'A petition against having milk in cartons.'

Just for a moment I felt dizzy. I could not see how milk had got into the world of great events. The driver, Peacock, snorted but held his peace; and Kate explained, but I did not listen. Phil came back, and stopped to sign, and said, 'Pretty girl. I couldn't turn her down.' Then we drove out of town, and through the apple lands that owe so much to me, and round the inlet, through the pine forest, through Stallards, and came to Long Tom's.

When Phil bought the property he found the name changed to something English – I don't remember, Chelmsford or Chugwell, something like that. Now I remember: Worlebury Hill. 'Some bloody name from Pongolia.' He had it off the gate in no time and Long Tom's in its place in wrought-iron cursive script. But he shows no interest in Long Tom. The past doesn't interest him at all. He did not buy the property because he'd wanted it once: he wanted it now.

The road goes down the hill through scrub and crosses a wooden bridge and runs on a causeway over the small piece of swamp that's left. Then you go through paddocks cleared from the bush. His mares and yearlings, lovely things, amble and frisk on the green grass. Breeding is just a hobby with him, but of course he makes it

pay. His English stallion Thundercloud (no prejudice against Pongolian horses) earns him four thousand dollars every time he serves
a mare.

The house is low-slung, Californian style. That's what he says.
It's just a house to me, with too much money spent on it; and far
too big for an old divorcee, bachelor – neither word is right for Phil.
He only spends a few months there in the summer anyway, and
odd weekends. All the same, I was impressed, I was seduced.
Deep-pile carpets, leather armchairs, have that effect on me. They
made Kate disapproving, made her grim, and she drew herself in as
though somehow she might pick up germs. Her nose was up a little
for bad smells. And there was a smell, the smell of money.

We had cold duck and cold white wine for lunch. Delicious. As
my passions cool I seem to be getting my senses back – taste and
smell. They removed themselves for a good many years. My
hearing was dulled too, eyesight dulled. Everything was thinned
and lost its edge and was set further off from me. My senses
somehow failed to find an object, and bad temper, choler, filled
their place. Now, a little bit, they're coming back. Is it Kate doing
this for me?

I drank a glass of wine too much and told Phil I'd earned it, the
wine industry owed me plenty. Tried to tell the story, but he was
bored: wanted to flirt with Kate and possibly sit her on his knee. He
simply had no notion of how impossible that was; and, with too
much drink in me, I found him a little sad. I wanted to tell her to be
nice to him. She wanted to give him a piece of her mind. As for
Phil, I suppose what he wanted was to make everyone happy;
especially himself.

I dozed in a chair after lunch, half listening to them talk about
Kitty. That was Kate's reason for coming. She wanted to know
about their disagreement over the subdivision of Le Grice's farm.
Kitty was mayor of Jessop then and wanted it for a park, but Phil
cut it up for building sections. He won. But they had, as he said, 'a
bar-room brawl'. I stopped listening, this was old stuff, and Kitty as
mayor and Phil as developer were people I'd never had much time
for. Too much ego, too much greed, in both of them. I had a
cat-nap, and woke to see Kate and Phil standing at the window,
where it seems he'd taken her by the plump of her arm to show her
some people across the valley. She freed herself and he gave a

70

shrug of annoyance; and I thought, Be careful Kate or you'll walk home. That was how he treated unwilling girls.

'Jesus freaks,' he said, his face brick-red, and the bit of surgical sewing white on his brow. His anger was not all at Kate. I saw people working in a triangular garden chopped out of the bush on the side of the hill. 'I've offered Stewie Biggers double what it's worth for that bit of land. But his son's one of them, married some God-bothering female from up north. And now old Stewie gets out there himself. Hoeing spuds. Singing hymns. I used to go over there and we'd knock back a quart of Scotch in a night. Now he says the Lord doesn't want him to. "What bloody lord is that?" I said to him. "We're the lords round here mate, you and me." But all he can do is say tut-tut. And he prays for me. So he reckons. The bloody cheek.'

Kate laughed. And I gave a snigger, which he heard. 'Not funny, Noel. I've put a lot of money into this land. And now I've got this bunch of loonies next door.'

The people in the garden were too far away to see properly. Phil brought his binoculars but I didn't bother with them. What was there to see – a dozen men and women working like coolies in the sun? They were too high up the ridge for horticulture. I told Phil not to worry, if they were trying to make a living from the garden they'd go broke, but he said that was only part of it, they had acres under cultivation in the valley next door, Stewie Biggers' place, and were putting in kiwi fruit. 'They don't mind hard work, I'll say that for them.' What annoyed him was the shacks they lived in – did they remind him of the row of houses at the port? – and their bit of garden in his view, and especially their presence on 'my beach'.

'You don't own it,' Kate said.

'I was here first. Do you know what else they wanted? Came over here and asked. They wanted my creek for baptizing.'

Kate laughed. She doesn't laugh much. She showed the whole pink cavern of her mouth. Now and then modern times delight her, she gets quite drunk on craziness. And nothing would do but meeting these people. We watched her walk away up the green fields.

'What's the matter with her?' Phil grumbled.

I told him Kate didn't like being pawed; and that Kitty had told me once Phil had more arms than an octopus. That put him back in

71

his good humour. He offered me a ride in his boat.

We drove down to the shed in a four-wheel-drive contraption – Jeep we used to call them but they're all Japanese now – that rattled my bones. Long Tom's house was gone, no trace of it, just a tangle of lupins over the ground, and a giant collapsing fig tree, covered with purple figs, at the edge of the swamp. I did not remember it. The fruit and huge green leaves and passages to its interior delighted me and I would have been happy to stop there, but Phil was all for fast boats and the sea. We rattled on. The shed is on the inlet at the back of the dunes, with a jetty giving ten feet of water at high tide. It was three-quarter then, with water creeping into the middle reaches of the swamp – in fact, it's salt marsh. A pair of white-faced herons, a pair of pied stilts, an army of pied oyster-catchers, were feeding.

And again I would have liked to stay. To see an oyster-catcher snipping the hinge of a pipi is a lesson in the use of tools. They're neater than lab technicians. And a heron, stepping high and holding still; absolute attention; then spearing in the shallows with her beak, a perfect line, not straight I swear but following the curve of the Earth. She works in millimetres, micro-seconds. I feel a kinship with those birds; will be one if I'm offered a choice. Or albatross. Or shag on a sandbar, in a river mouth.

Phil called me back from the jetty end. 'Get your arse in gear.' He keeps up with the lingo very well. We decided I'd better not try to climb into the boat from the jetty so I mounted in the shed and Phil opened the doors and winched me down the rails into the sea. I felt I was being unveiled rather than launched, sitting up like Jacky, but the feeling of buoyancy under my feet made me want to sing. Phil, of course, has an expensive boat: red and yellow fibreglass, a speedster, a real fizz-boat, with a floral plastic awning over the cabin and stainless-steel fittings everywhere. He jumped in from the jetty – yes, he jumped, how does he do it? – and peeled off his shirt, showing me the scars on his chest, and put on a captain's hat, and prodded a button and we were off. Our speed pressed me back in my seat as though I were a spaceman heading for the moon. The oyster-catchers shot off like a flight of missiles but we overtook them and I could have caught one in my hand. 'Ha!' Phil yelled, and skimmed us along the back of the dune and through the creek-mouth where Kitty had waded and out into the sparkling open sea.

The island stood up high, covered with bush; and nothing like a scone, I thought now. It was just an island in the sea, beautiful. Our speed though, wild approach, hairy approach – Phil did arabesques – spoiled my enjoyment. Round the back, he was content to putter. We went in close to the rocks and saw how they plunged down into the sea. Strange things happen to me where land and water meet in this way. There's a cold sudden rinsing out in my skull, the water touches me *inside* my head; goes bouncing down the white bones of my spine. I want to sink, I want to be lost, I want to breathe that element, be washed empty, be washed clean, and discover ultimate mysteries. It all comes and goes in a breath, and leaves me frightened.

'Feeling OK? Seasick?' Phil said.

I asked him to keep on going slow. We puttered round the island in a circle. The Poms, he said, had tried to give it a name, Steep Holme. He wasn't having any of that. There was some Maori name too, wai or wiri or paku some bloody thing, he'd forgotten. But the guys on the fishing trawlers called it Bucket Island, and that was good enough for him. A tourist launch went by, full of Americans, judging from the voices over the sea. They were pleased to find two old natives in a young man's boat, one of them in a captain's hat and not much else, and with a foot-long cigar in his teeth. They got busy with their cameras and zoom lenses. Phil stood up and held his cigar in front of his shorts like a penis. 'Cut it out, Phil,' I said. But I admired him.

'Bloody Yanks,' he said. 'They think they own the bloody world.' (Phil owns it.)

We made another circuit of the island and then took off for the open sea. We scratched our mark on its sheet of tin, and five miles out Phil let the boat sink forward on her nose, and clipped his rod together and started fishing. The bait stank like nothing on earth but all he said was that it was ripe. He hummed a tune as he fished. He tapped cigar ash into the sea. But the heat in the boat, and the stink, made me queasy. I took my jacket off and unbuttoned my shirt down to the waist.

'There's a shot of Scotch in the locker there.' I did not want any but handed him the flask and he lobbed his butt away and took a swig: playing Blackbeard. My admiration had not survived my queasiness but I did not complain, for Phil, even at eighty, looks for victories over me. Instead I took the photograph from my jacket:

73

Ogiers and Dockerys and Pappses at Long Tom's.

'Ha,' he said, 'when was that taken?'

It didn't interest him. He gave it back and I put it away.

'I reckon old Lotte was the best looker in that bunch. It was all for show though, not for use. Poor old Tup, he was on short rations, poor old bugger.'

'What did she die of? I was away.'

'Diabetes.'

'I didn't know that.'

'She went into a coma. She wouldn't stay off the cakes, the silly old cow. Show me that photo.'

I gave it back to him.

'How did the old man get there? I don't remember him.'

'He came in your dinghy. Who did he talk to all the time, Phil?'

He gave me the photo and reeled in his line to put fresh (?) bait on. The turn of our conversation didn't please him and he lit another cigar before answering. 'Wasn't God, if that's what you're thinking. Or the devil.'

That surprised me. I would have thought concepts of that sort quite beyond Phil. I mean, his concerns were material, and outside things he could touch and own were only things he could taste, enjoy, or put together, break into bits; and transcendental beings were a joke.

He said, 'It was only names. People. Places.' He gave a flick of his wrist and sent the line thirty metres over the sea. The weight made a satisfied plop and Phil seemed to think it marked the end of our conversation. It wasn't enough. Les Dockery had come alive for me. For a moment I almost felt we might pull him up, dark and full of weight and open-eyed and making no struggle, from deep in the sea.

'Do you mean he named his friends? His dead cobbers? From the war?'

Phil sighed. It was strange to hear. It struck me as unnatural – like a dog mewing, a cat barking. 'I've never talked about my old man.'

'What names?'

'People he'd known. Not just in the war. All his life. Places he'd been. Streets he'd lived in. Even pubs. Even horses he'd backed. He was going over his life. So he wouldn't lose it. So he wouldn't die. Do you know the best thing I could ever give him? A new name. One he'd forgotten. I used to lie awake in bed trying to think of one. But I never could. Well, maybe I got one or two. I got Edgar Le Grice. He'd forgotten Le Grice.'

'What happened when he came to the end?'

'He'd start again. Back at the beginning. Remember how he used to stand holding on to something?'

'Yes,' I said.

'That was when he'd ended. He was getting ready to start again. He never went past the war.'

'He asked me what the beach was called.'

Phil turned and looked at me. 'Yeah, that's right. He used to say Long Tom's. The poor old bugger. I suppose that was a real day out for him.' He felt a bite and reeled in his line but the fish was gone. 'The bloody trawlers come in here. They string a net between them and sweep it out like a vacuum cleaner. Nothing left.' He threw the bait overboard and as we left gulls were battling for it.

The inlet was brimming and tufts of rushes stood like islands in the swamp. I stepped out onto the jetty and Phil left the boat for Peacock to winch into the shed. We drove back to the house, past the mares and foals in their post and rail enclosures; and came on Kate with the front of her skirt held up like a sack, bulging with figs. She would not take a ride but walked up when our dust had settled, eating a fig like an apple, skin and all, and her mouth stained with pulp. She was elated. It was as if she'd found treasure. The figs were as fat as peaches, and some almost black, splitting with ripeness, and of course one could not help thinking of a woman's parts, and Phil could not forgo the comparison; but even that did not put Kate out of her good humour. I peeled a fig and ate it, then had to take out my upper plate and wash the seeds out.

Our day did not end with figs though. It ended with a curious act of slaughter; ended with Phil. He had not caught a fish but he could do better than figs, he'd kill me a duck. I thought it would be a matter of wringing one's neck or chopping off its head with a tomahawk. He led me out through the back yard and across a paddock to an enclosure of wire-netting. There a couple of dozen fat Muscovies quacked and waddled about a pond. They seemed to know what Phil's coming meant for they set off in a bum-wobbling scurry for the far fence. They were like a crowd of fat old ladies running from a disaster. And Phil is that, he's a disaster. But he's many other things as well. He's sheriff of Tombstone.

He asked me to choose, but I could not condemn one of those undignified white waddlers; and wondered, with my usual feeling of sickness and apprehension, what bottomless receptacle its spark of life was about to be dropped into. But I knew better than to try stopping Phil. His face had gone deep red, plum-red. He drew his gun from his belt and I saw what an unstoppable thing it was, radiating malignancy. An air pistol, black-handled, long, narrow-nosed. There's no loud bang, no powder smell. The damned thing has a lung and it spits.

He cornered a duck and stood off twenty feet and rested the barrel on his forearm. I saw how he trembled. It was age not excitement. He sighted with his pale eye along that exaggerated snout. He has sniper's eyes – but the shot only kicked a feather from the duck's tail and made it squawk so loudly I thought the sky would fall.

'I got that one we had for lunch with a single shot. Clean through the eye.'

His second pellet smashed the duck's leg and it flapped away, lop-sided, towards its fellows down in another corner. They wanted nothing to do with it. Phil ran stiff-legged, heading it off. He trapped the bird against the wire. It waited there, open-beaked, while he took aim. Of course he would go for the eye, the difficult shot. Phil, in his way, is an idealist.

He carried the duck down the paddock to me. Blood was dripping on his espadrilles. 'I shouldn't have had that whisky in the boat.' Nevertheless, he was pleased with himself. His third shot had knocked the top of the duck's head off. He was pleased with that finality.

17

It's taken me a week to write all that. My hand gets tired and my brain gets tired and shadows waltz in and out of my skull. I've been having dreams. Mostly there's a tree, with leaves as big as door-mats, and figs the colour and shape of female parts, and labyrinths of green leading to a centre where everything's cold and indistinct.

Sometimes I'm a wasp zooming in. It's a sex dream and a death dream and a dream of being alive. I don't know what to make of it, but none of it pleases me much, or frightens me.

Things have changed here in the last week. I'd better fall back on chronology.

I asked Kate how she'd got on with the people over the hill.

'Ha,' she said, 'they'll pray for me.'

She's repelled by their simplicities and by their certainty, which she regards as anti-human, but their happiness attracts her. How can one be happy and a complex being too, that's her problem? Complexity's her right (one she denies Kitty, though) and all possibilities must be open. I tell her the way to happiness can often be a straight and simple thing but she won't agree, and smartly quotes 'the fury and the mire of human veins'. That's nicely put, but I'm sorry to hear her relish it so much.

She'd argued with them; told them there are more stars in the sky than grains of sand on all the beaches of Earth and that makes the Christian God a no-no. I mean, she said, why should he be concerned with us? Or perhaps he's the God of all intelligent species and he's sent his Son in many forms. She challenged them with a crustacean Christ and a chlorine-breathing Christ. And if it's not like that, she said, then he's only one of millions of gods, one for each world – and so on. They just looked at her and laughed. These are not questions.

I find it charming. Kate marching up there to convert them with her silly simple arguments; and they, happy fools, replying with their book. *There's* complexity enough, and happiness in contemplating it.

And what are you? she asked, belligerent. No labels, no labels, I replied. But confessed Tup Ogier made me an evolutionary humanist – by narration, I said, not argument. I was thrilled to my bones by that great drama.

Kate sniffed. 'Evolution's not an issue any more.' Then she giggled – the first time I've heard that girl-sound from her. 'You want to know my name for you?' she said. 'It's The Chimp.'

So there we are, Phil Dockery and Noel Papps, those roaring boys: the Old Goat and The Chimp. I wasn't pleased. I don't mind seeing myself like that, but I've wanted to be something more in Kate's eyes.

It was a fat duck. We ate it for three days and had the last of it for lunch, sitting on the sundeck. I drank a glass of cold white wine and toasted Phil across the glittering bay.

Kate had bought a pot of Cranberry sauce. Soon, to keep the wasps away from our table, she put it on the rail with the lid off. I counted eight wasps on the rim and Kate, looking in, said there was a grand-daddy stuck inside. She lifted it out with a teaspoon and crushed it on the rail.

'There's too many, there must be a nest.'

I think she needed it. She needed a physical act, she needed risk, and it's hardly surprising that in the course of it she found a man. (But you don't have to keep what you find, do you hear me, Kate?) The wasps were there, just below my sun-deck, in the bank. She called me to see; then off she went, lunch unfinished, and I saw her slide through the dry grass and fennel and stop herself on the hurricane wire fence. She climbed over and went with hooked fingers along the wire – Chimp yourself, Kate – until she was opposite the nest. 'A big one,' she called.

'Be careful, Kate.' If she let go she'd tumble into the river.

'There's hundreds. There's a hole as big as my fist.' She held it up.

'Kate!'

'Keep your shirt on.' She studied the nest. I could not see it from my position but saw wasps streaking away and streaking home, and saw her eager face turned up and thought how competent she was. I did not need to squawk like a mother hen.

She came back smelling of fennel, with grass seeds and biddy-bids in her hair. 'Right,' she said, 'they've had it.' She rubbed her hands and would not sit down and finish her lunch but was on her rattle-trap bicycle and off down the hill to the MAF. I watched her cycle across the bridge and along between the plane trees into town. Just like Kitty, single-minded, simple-minded. A dozen paths but one direction.

But she had to wait until dusk before she could do anything. Then she armed herself with a table-spoon and a packet of Carbaryl and a pair of hedge clippers. Grass was growing over the hole and she'd

78

have to clip it away before she could spoon the poison in. She was thoughtful now. She'd had all afternoon to picture that black hole in the ground. It was, she said, like a hole going down into nothing and the wasps just went inside and disappeared, except for sentries sitting on blades of grass. She was a little frightened, by the mystery, I think, as much as the danger; but still she clapped her hands and said, 'Let's go.'

'It's not dark enough.'

'They come back to the nest when the sun goes down. It says so here.' She had a pamphlet from the MAF.

'Get a man to do it, Kate. He'll come with a bottle of petrol and that'll be that.' What a foolish thing to say to a modern woman. I have to take some blame for her stings.

My job was to shine the torch from the sundeck. She slid through the grass again, awkward with her clippers, and crashed into the wire and made it sing.

'Shit!'

'What's the matter?'

'I've lost the spoon.'

'Come back, Kate.'

'Not to worry. I'll chuck it in with my hands.'

This time she went along the inside of the wire. I heard her thrashing in the head-high fennel and saw her face rise like a moon. She'd put on slacks and a jersey but had no veil or gloves.

'Shine that torch.'

She came into the light with the silver cross of the clippers on her breast to ward off demons. I saw no wasps, but saw her stretch her arms and poke at the bank, and heard *snip-snip*. Then I saw them. They swam like tiny goldfish in the light. She did not scream but made a glassy squeak and bitten cries. She beat her arms about her face and fell back down the slope. The fence stopped her. She went on all fours and burrowed into the fennel. The wasps continued their dance and I held the torch on them, thinking I might draw them away from Kate. The clippers and the packet of poison lay by the fence. Then a wasp stung my wrist and I dropped the torch and saw it bounce off the bank and leap the fence and bound away like some creature fleeing, down the hillside into the river. I heard a splash, and for a moment saw a light shining under water before it went out.

I ran outside to rescue Kate. She almost banged me over in the yard and ran into the kitchen with head down and fingers hooked above her scalp.

'There's one in my hair.'

I saw it thrusting with its abdomen and I crushed it between my finger and thumb and pulled it out and threw it in the sink. Then I made Kate sit on a kitchen chair and brought her a cloth to wipe her face. Her hands shook. I hoped she was not going to faint.

'Where did they get you?'

'On my face. On my neck. I need some blue-bag.'

'No, that's alkaline, we need acid.' I fetched vinegar and cotton wool, and because her hands were shaking so much I sponged her stings. She had some in her hair and some on the left side of her face, by the corner of her eye and corner of her mouth and on the hinge of her jaw. I could not help thinking that she'd look determined now.

'On my throat,' she said. There were five there. She dragged in her breath, sniffing vinegar. Then she stood up and peeled off her trousers. They'd stung her through the cloth. There were little blood-red marks on the inside of her thigh. Rage made a thump in my skull. I did not think she'd let me sponge her there, but she sat down and closed her eyes and made no protest as I wiped her skin.

'You'd better go to bed, Kate. I'll make a cup of tea.'

'I'm going back.'

'You are not. I hope you're not allergic. Are you going to pass out?'

'I'm all right.' She opened her eyes. 'That vinegar's no good.' She doesn't believe in antidotes but in like with like, and she ran away and fetched her rattle-box and swallowed ledum; and when she saw me sponging my wrist made me take some too.

Perhaps it worked. I don't know. I've had no swelling and very little itch but that might be because I've got no juices left in me. It certainly didn't work for Kate, as we found next day. But on that night doctoring me put her in a state of reason. She agreed not to go back down the slope. She agreed to get someone who knew about wasps to destroy the nest. We had a cup of tea and went early to bed. I felt that sponging her was a fatherly act. I felt I could safely love her now.

When I woke in the night I walked along the passage to her room and opened the door an inch or two. It was black inside, I saw nothing, but heard her scratching in her sleep, and complaining. I wondered if a bag of ice cubes would help; and knew that if I woke her she'd take my visit for what it was. But in the end I went back to bed. Kitty had told me once, never wake a sleeping child.

18

But she's no child. Oh no. She said to me, 'I'm not a girl. I'm thirty-one.' That was just this morning. But let me keep things in their proper place.

The MAF couldn't recommend anyone so I rang the Lomax and asked for a name, and gave it unsuspecting to Kate. And now we've got a fellow called Shane Worth in the house. Shane! That was a movie. How can you name someone after a movie?

He came on the first of the month, he's our April Fool's Day joke. And when he'd dressed himself in yellow gumboots, two thick jerseys, industrial gloves, and draped a yard of cheese cloth over his cowboy hat and had Kate tuck the ends inside his jersey, he looked as if he should have been blundering on a stage as Caliban. He was armed with a plastic rubbish sack and a spade and a bottle of diesel. Carbaryl, he said, was worse than useless. 'They eat it for pudding.'

He was no better at keeping his feet than Kate. He went down the slope like a wool bale and I heard wires twang and posts creak. 'I think I've bust your fence, mate.'

Kate answered for me, 'Never mind.' It's not her fence! I watched from the sundeck, with the room darkened behind, and she, with brand-new torch, directed him from down 'near the action', holding one of the poles in her arm. Shane – I suppose I'll have to get used to the name – found the hole and rammed the bottle in and left it draining. He collected the clippers from the fence and heaved the packet of Carbaryl into the river.

'Hey,' I cried, 'you'll poison the fish.'

'Sorry, mate. Never thought of that.'

He's sub-normal. He can't think. He simply does the thing under his nose and checks up later that it's all OK. I'm surprised to hear him speaking sentences. And surprised – I'm disbelieving – to hear him say he had three years at secondary school. He says 'yous fellers'; he says 'anythink'; he says 'I rung him up'; but Kate declares he's only putting me on, whatever that means.

They waited under the sundeck for the wasps to die. He told her about himself: how he'd had a PEP job clearing old man's beard from the hills around town and along the river. He dealt with any wasp nests they found, and got the idea of doing it for a living. There was no living in it, he charged thirty dollars a nest and was lucky to get one a week. In his spare time – plenty of that – he helped collect old clothes and furniture for the Unemployed Workers Union.

Kate was stirred by it. A hard luck story, *true* hard luck, with no self pity. I felt her emotion rolling up, and knew how it would be. Clumsiness, simplicity, with social responsibility thrown in. He's made for her. I turned on the lamp by the door and looked over the rail and saw them striped with light, she still hugging one pole and he sitting with thighs wrapped round the other. It rose like a monstrous phallus between his legs. Yes, I knew. But I simplify, and over-state. I'm off balance a little, I'm over-heated. Volatile, that's my state, and crude fancies rise from me like vapour. I'll delete that phallus, it's for show; and declare nothing carnal was in their meeting.

All the same, I knew how it would be.

He dug out the nest and brought the sack into the kitchen for me to see. There was the city, geometrical, amazing, with dead warriors lying in the dirt. Just for a moment I was with them, I was murdered; then looked at Kate and saw what they'd done to her. Her face was huge on one side: mouth swollen as a plum and with a clenched fist in her jaw. One eye peered from a porker-slit and even her nose was lopsided.

'What will you do with them?' I asked.

'Take them home and burn them. I hate the buggers.' He said there'd be strays around the hole for a day or two but the smell of diesel would drive them away. He stripped off his two jerseys, and took his gloves off to pocket my cheque. 'Cash mate, or I'll lose my benefit.' Kate gave a painful laugh. She offered him a cup of tea, but he shook his head and said he wouldn't say no to a beer, he got so bloody hot in those jerseys. So they sat at the table drinking my beer, which Kate found hard with her swollen mouth. She dribbled down her chin and had to wipe her chest with a tea-towel. Laughing hurt her. Her throat was swollen too. Shane Worth was looking hard, trying to see a pretty girl in there.

'That's not all,' she said, and pulled up her skirt and showed her thigh. Not an ounce of modesty in her, but no shame either. It evens out.

'Jesus!' he said. It shocked me too: a great flushed dumpling. When I touched it with my finger – by invitation – I expected to find it hot, but no, it was cold. There's a lardy cumulus under the skin. Shane Worth touched it too. 'Jeez lady, you should see a doctor.'

Kate laughed. She'd had a triumph. She told him she was treating it herself, and dropped the front of her skirt and swallowed more beer. She asked him if he knew about homoeopathic medicine.

'Come again.' (I understand putting on now. He was putting her on.) He took a pair of glasses from his shirt pocket, with black lenses the size of a penny and wire rims. They made him look round-eyed, comical, empty-headed, which he intended; and would have made a different sort of person sinister. He's a big lumping boy – yes, twenty-two – a heavy-built, hairy, gap-toothed fellow, with elf-locks round his head, but thin on top. There's a fuzz of black fur on his scalp. He grins a lot. Yeah, he says, and Jeez, all the time, and Gunna crash, eh mate? That to me, when I went to bed. I took myself out of their way. Kate's eye leaked tears constantly. They ran down the smooth depression between her cheek and nose and she wiped them away with the heel of her palm. She was definitely not at her best. But all the same carnality got in. I saw it in a kind of calculation in their look. I went to bed. I knew how it would be.

But, I thought, with sour prurience, her whopping thigh denied them consummation for a while.

19

She's raising him from the sea. She's finding out his coastline. He's a big one. It's a kind of epeirogenesis she's about and she'll be Asia to his Africa.

When I first saw Kate I thought she swayed, but that was just her youth misleading me. Now I know her better I'm aware she doesn't move from side to side but straight ahead. Her steps, mental, physical, are blunt and short, lacking grace in everything but their quickness. Whether to touch, pick up, put away, she begins all movements of her hands as though she's making slaps or throwing punches; and moves her mind in that sudden way.

But now she's softened, now she's slowed to half-pace. She's not in love, she's in a state of satisfaction. I said, 'Kate, I don't want to see. You keep it in your bedroom.'

'Damn it, Noel,' she answered, 'I don't go in for exhibitions.'

'No parties. No loud music. No pot.'

'I don't use it. Nor does Shane.'

'You keep him out of my liquor cupboard. He can buy his own.'

He pays rent too, and puts in money for the 'kai'. There's an affectation, he's not a Maori. In the mornings he says to me, 'Kia ora, gran'pop.' 'Au revoir,' I reply, waving him out of my way, 'sayonara, auf wiedersehen, ciao.' It makes him laugh – not what I intend – and makes Kate frown. He calls me Sir, salutes me lazily, like a Yank. This morning he called me Lancelot. It's all good-humoured. I don't believe he knows what malice is.

There's malice in *Chimp*.

This is not what I set out to do. I wanted to be exact, and look at me, all over the place. It's time to sit quiet for a while, and then perhaps make a second start.

Things take on their own life, grow too large, grow extra limbs, and what should be purposeful and more in my control rushes ahead or jumps sideways. I mean to stop it. There has to be a centre and a line. There's too much stimulation in the present and so I must make an act of will and face away. I'm interested in structure, but what I've made already's just a mess.

When Tup Ogier started me off in science I knew my first intellectual joy. There was joy even in working on paper. When I balanced an equation, no matter how simple, I felt I'd added a piece to the universe. I must try to do that again.

Here's an equation, a simple one. When Kitty put her fingers in Miss Montez's eyes she did not stop there. She withdrew her hand and felt her own eye socket. She held Miss Montez's jaw in fingers and thumb and worked it up and down, then worked her own. She put her finger in the hole where Miss Montez's nose had been; and pressed the tip of her own nose like a button. What it meant exactly I can't say, but I know she was engaged in giving things their proper magnitude.

Then she gave a nod and turned away.

20

I won a Junior National Scholarship and graduated MSc from Canterbury University, where I was awarded the Travis Martin Scholarship for chemical research. Then came an 1851 Exhibition Science Scholarship and the Orient Shipping Co's Travelling Scholarship, which paid my fare to England. I was at St John's College, Cambridge from 1925 to 1927.

This part of my life, the English part, is not available to memory. It's an object rounded off, put aside. I can admire it and be glad it's mine but soon I want to turn away and look at more interesting things. I was busy, successful, I was happy most of the time, but happiness, it seems, is not a measure. It leaves things aside, waiting another sort of possession, and I have no instruments for that. There are connections I cannot make in streets, in rooms, in gardens not my own. That place is *there*. *Here* predicates. It makes a fizz and ferment, it's rude and beautiful. *There* lies dull and idle, won't be moved. *There*'s inert. I have a hold on myself in Jessop, although I wriggle and slip free. In Cambridge, in London, I'm fashioned, I'm complete – stone fish on a mantelpiece. I'm real fish in my streets; I dart about, there's life hard and slippery in me.

Will that do, Kit? It's you supplying images.

I stayed in Britain until 1933, working at the Fuel Research Station in Greenwich, then came back to Jessop and joined the Lomax Institute as Agricultural Chemist.

Many things were the same and many changed. My mother and father had moved to a smaller house. He still baked the best pies and bread in town and I spent my first night in Jessop down at the bakehouse, feeding the stove, watching this fat little man perform his dance. He told me all the news, giving it a different slant from Mum's, and putting in details she missed out. Les Dockery had died on a seat in the park; but I learned from Dad that he'd sat there dead till the end of the day, when a woman tapped his shoulder and he fell with a sigh along the seat as though trying to find a more comfortable position. Phil had surprised everyone by being upset at his father's death; but from Dad I learned he had cried at the funeral, and made big sniffing sobs like a boy and wiped his nose on his sleeve. Tup Ogier, frail as matchsticks, had to hold the six-footer up and slip a handkerchief into his hand.

Mum was especially dry about Kitty. 'She's all right. They get by. I suppose the children will grow up somehow.' Kitty disappointed us by not going to university. She became a probationer nurse and this seemed a poor choice for such a clever girl. 'I want to start doing something now, not spend years getting ready,' she explained. She was five years at Jessop Public Hospital and married Desmond Hughes shortly after I left for England. 'She broke the rules,' Dad sighed. 'She didn't marry a doctor she married a patient.' It did not bother them that Desmond, or Des as he preferred, was only a working man. Only is a word they'd have rejected. My mother was a saw-mill worker's daughter and her moral cornerstone was that physical labour disposed one to virtue. On this she was unshakeable. In her version of the story, the ruin of the Le Grices began with the father's habit of *strolling*. She had no objection to a bricklayer as son-in-law. She objected to his drawing attention to himself. And anything short of rude physical health in a man was a dereliction. Desmond Hughes chose politics instead of good health.

She was not being completely unreasonable. Des did not look after himself. He was out at meetings on winter nights, he was on street corners in the rain, and on the stage in halls that draughts moved through like rag-ends from a Chatham Islands gale. He smoked, of course, chain-smoked, but we didn't know the dangers then. All the same, his doctor must have warned him that a man with his bad lungs should treat himself better. But Des put all his problems down to the Imperialist war and made use of them as a property. Like Les Dockery he'd been caught in a gas attack. He spent months in hospital in England before coming home. When Kitty met him he had pneumonia and she wondered what kept him alive. It was his passion for a better world, she came to think.

I met Des on my second day home in Jessop. He was sitting on a kitchen chair in his back yard, reading a book. We shook hands, he looked at me and found nothing to alter judgements made on the basis of my type; which was, if I have the terminology, petty bourgeois. He had no curiosity about me or my work. Lack of curiosity horrifies me; and when I found it in Kitty too I felt bereaved, I wanted to weep. And then I wanted to destroy Des Hughes and put things back in their proper shape. I began to hate him and have not conquered it, so you'd better take what I say as lacking balance. Kitty loved him, that much is certain; but I think she loved a Des Hughes she'd made for herself.

He was tall and saucer-chested. A great lump seemed gouged out of him and you felt if you poked where his chest should be you'd find empty space and feel his vertebrae at the back slipping about under a layer of skin. Is that unbalanced? I came to detest the shape of him. I felt his fleshless bones were a figure for the coldness in his mind. He had sunken cheeks and falcate nose and a burning eye – that cold fire that feeds on abstractions – and red hair springing from his brow. *There* was rude health. I imagined papillae feeding on him and all his sap drawn into his hair.

He tried my hand with fingers strong as a builder's clamp. I winced and he moved me further from his centre. That would have suited me, except that he had Kitty there and I did not mean to give her up. Embracing her, I knew that she had lipic qualities and did not have her tissues burned away. The day I left for England in 1925 my father took a photo of us clowning. I've lost it now. No matter, I can see it in my head. Kitty, in her nurse's uniform, kneels on the floor with her arms wrapped about my leg. With raised face she pleads with me to stay. I stride with my other foot at the door. I'm natty in my new suit and gloves, with overcoat on my arm and trilby in my hand. I look into the future manfully. But really I'm a chimpanzee dressed up. She's Mary Pickford.

There was no going back to that sort of thing. Kitty was Mrs Hughes, with sick husband and three barefoot children in hand-me-downs.

'Noel,' she said, stepping back, holding me by the shoulders. She gave me a shake, another hug, and pushed me away. 'You still haven't grown.'

'I'm five foot six.' Her husband's lankiness might be her

87

standard but I wasn't going to have her apply it to me. I was used by now to thinking I was someone.

'A moustache! Oh Noel, you've got to shave that off. Straight away.'

'Don't you like it?'

'You look like a crook. You look like a burglar. Noel, Noel, why aren't you married yet? What happened to that English girl?'

'She married someone else.'

'No wonder, with that mo.'

Although she made me angry, this was Kitty; but it was only the dance of flame before the fire goes out. It surprised her and her eyes grew wide, then she turned to Des and said, 'Well, old boy,' and I knew that meant she was choosing him and was letting him know I was no more than a distraction. All this, you'll say, is as it should be, and I'll agree husband comes before brother. But old affections and shared memories should not just be booted out of the way, and that's what Kitty did. She shoved me into the basement like a piece of furniture she found no use for. Over the next hour I felt as if I'd put my head through a window and some slow wheel, some machine turning counter-clockwise, twisted it off. Extravagant, I know. But that's how it felt – slow, excruciating, against nature. And that lipic quality she had, that weight, that body, was something she drew from Desmond Hughes. I had to alter Kitty in my mind. I had to learn I had no sister now.

'How's Irene?'

For a moment she could not remember Irene. 'Oh, her. Still up there. Living off her fat.' She smiled at Des and he gave a nod.

'Does she do any concerts?'

'How would I know? And where the hell have you been living, Noel? People are starving here. They don't want concerts. They want food and jobs and roofs over their heads. Not music from some tart on some piano.'

To everything I asked she had an answer of that sort. Kitty, I wanted to cry, listen to me, where have you gone? Don't misunderstand me, I didn't object to her politics, never did. They're better than the sort on the other side. I objected to the killing off of Kitty and this clumsy being in her place.

To see how far she'd go, and perhaps twist the screw harder on myself, I asked her if she'd seen Phil Dockery. Kitty hissed. Spit flew from her mouth; and Des, at the kitchen table, reading still, looked up and gave a grin of rage. It was the first visceral response I'd seen from him.

'Dockery? Your mate?' Kitty said. 'If you're being pals with him, Noel, you're not coming in my house.'

'What's he done?'

'Trying to be a rentier,' Des said.

The word was new to me. I looked at Kitty.

'He wants to be the boss of Jessop, Noel. And sit on his bum and rake in the money. But we'll get him.'

'What's he done?'

'Buying houses. Putting up the rent. He goes round collecting it himself. But he doesn't dare stick his nose in my door. No fear.'

'Do you mean he owns this house?' I gave a snort. It struck me as funny: Port-rat Phil growing fat on rents from run-down houses. Then I looked at Kitty's children (the youngest, Pam, would grow up and be Kate Adams' mother) sitting three-in-a-row on the wooden bench that served as sofa, with bare feet dangling and darns in their jersey sleeves, and saw that while a circle might be closed and pleasure felt in it, anger was justified in her.

'Does he charge too much?'

'He put it up last month. Des went to see him.' But now she was confused, and I felt a flash of hatred for Hughes, seeing a kind of deference close to fear in the look she gave him. It seems that Phil had waived the rent increase for Kitty's sake – it was a shilling – and Des refused the favour and the two had a shouting match. Des called Phil a capitalist, a gangster, and Phil – brick-red, plum-red perhaps – replied that Des was a socialist rabble-rouser who'd married a girl too good for him. Des told me that with relish, punishing Kitty; and I was close to saying Phil was right.

'We pay the same as everyone else,' Kitty said. 'We couldn't walk down the street if we took any favours from him.'

Phil returned the shilling by postal note every week, and they tore it in half and posted it back. So the battle went on. I saw the passion spent on it; the energy that went into Kitty's hatred. She was prepared to hate me too, and I saw that she might shrivel up and be a dry shrill woman in a kitchen, wasted thing; or that she might swell, grow huge, and push us all, every one of us, out of her way. I could not retain either picture. Both of those Kittys went away; but just for a moment I understood that Des Hughes would make Kitty into nothing, or that she'd survive and he would be the one who shrivelled up.

21

Now these two, Irene, Phil, who shall I go to? Each visit carries risks. But with Irene I move close to my centre and it's a kind of gravity draws me there.

Night-time of course, starless night. The sky invisible and drizzle in the air. I walk along the empty streets from one fuzz-ball of light to the next. The houses have porticoes and English names and I could be in Dulwich or Esher. But I'm not impressed with English things. I've ambitions to rescue Irene from a life that's second-hand. I've had thoughts of her, thinned-out, beaten flat, while away; persistent nevertheless. The fact I learned standing at Long Tom's window is flattened too. Stood on edge, it's invisible. Many things are like that in the light of my importance. So – coming back to Jessop was one step; coming back to Irene was the next.

The house, in drizzle, swells impressively. The black trees on the lawn are posted in defence. They have the shape of crouching men, but I'm reassured by weeds growing in the path and the absence of red scoria from Auckland. I'm sad for Irene in advance. She has known hard times, that is plain, and I'll rescue her from faded elegance and set her life moving forward again. She welcomes me with music. It comes from a room diffusing light in the warm wet dark, has properties of light as well as sound. It shines into the backs of my eyes and penetrates dark places in my mind, it gleams on water. All music is from Irene, I've not forgotten that, but not, till now, had knowledge of it run like a woman's fingers, her own fingers, on my skin. Do I sound eighteen instead of thirty-one? That is because I stopped off at Irene and could not move, and my experience – by that I mean experience of women, quite extensive – was pre- not post-Irene. Though I spent passion in a prodigal way I was the being who had not loved her yet, so the man-things that I did were boy in fact. Women found me out and married someone else, someone grown up.

I must change this. I'll be deliberate. I didn't choose the present tense, it grabbed me; but I'll shake it off – it wants to stay – and look not only back but down as well. Sharp and cold. Why not impatient? I've little patience with a boy who should have been a man. I'm angry to find him hanging about.

So, back to that wet night, and the music, and the path. I did not want to stop her playing. It seemed the right thing, romantic thing, to listen in the dark and let her finish, and come in on the last chord, so to speak. What's novelettish now struck me on that night as mature. How I seemed to control the event! I stepped off the path and crossed the lawn and stood at the window, to one side, and looked at Irene Lomax at her Bechstein. And strangely enough, though I'm looking hard (and sharp and cold) I can't see her, I can't work my way under the shell I've cased her in. I see myself clearly, I'm in the rain, which is heavier now, and water drips from the brim of my hat. I see my wetness recommending me, as proof of devotion; but Irene, surely, doesn't have her hair up. She doesn't wear a satin gown.

That succubine tense! I'm in it again. Did not! Did not! Let me think. She wore, yes this is it, a cardigan. She wore a brown skirt of some heavy weave, and slippers, and her hair was buster cut. But still the music was the informing agent. I write that after thinking very hard. It's the music that makes me slide about and dresses her up. Music is the thing that sucks at me, music is light and memory, and physical being, and Irene, and Noel Papps; and reason is the thing it defeats.

Let's be still. Let's be calm. Now then.

Irene played. I cannot name the piece. Liquid, slow, connections smooth. Her face is tender. It slopes to one side. It *sloped* to one side. She was in profile to me, but turned her face, floated her face round to semi-full. Her eyes closed down and opened again. I saw the Lomax slant from mid-face to jaw-point. Those are good words. Mid-face. Jaw-point. Two hits to me. The man who came into the frame wants to present himself in a smoking jacket and white silk scarf, but I've got him, I see him, big-bummed boy: big-hipped, fat-thighed, slab-cheeked, with jacket sleeves too short and hands too long, and Charlie Chaplin boots, and slicked-down hair. I did not recognize him. I did not see his age, which was eighteen. I saw what he did. It's cinematic: Papps at the window (it's usually the murderer at the point of view), they inside, contained in themselves, like a moon.

He walked to her and put his hand on her shoulder, and I saw his face, his Lomax face, fatter than Irene's, fatter too than old man Lomax's, but with the same fracture in its line, as though someone with two strong hands had given it a wrench. He listened for a while. (Water trickled inside my collar and made a band of cold about my chest.) Then he stood behind her and put his hands on her throat and began an upward stroking as though working fluids through that column to her brain. I saw Irene shiver. Some little sac of pleasure in her broke. She kept on playing, and Royce maintained the moulding of his palms. Then he touched her ears. He spanned them, finger and thumb; and slipped his fingers into her hair and felt the shape of her, moved across and round her skull, round her cheekbones, over her mouth, and across the hard orbs of her eyes. She closed them to make it easy for him, and kept them closed when he was gone. He moved his fingers back into her hair and laid them full length above her ears; and with them, I knew, had possession of her.

Some bit of their nature was twisted on the skew. I blundered away from it. A wet bush grabbed me in its springy arms. I wrestled my way to the other side, where I squatted and moaned, with fingers hooked in my collar bones. The music stopped. The window opened. Royce said, 'Who's there?' I bit my hand to make myself be silent.

'Reen, there's a hat here on the ground.'

I heard them murmur, heard footsteps on the floor, and then a distant sound of telephoning. Irene cried, 'You'd better go. We're calling the police.' The bell-notes of her voice! They still ring distantly, through dark and rain.

I ran down the wide path of shadow from the bush and tumbled over the picket fence and picked myself up and ran again through the pelting rain along streets whose names I did not know. I'd known them once but they belonged in another life. Yet one of them came up and spoke to me. What it said was, 'Phil Dockery'.

And there, dripping, muddy, I stood at his door. Phil Dockery. I shivered and could not speak, and he, snapping his teeth, pulled me in, and gave me a towel to dry my hair and poured me a tumbler of gin. He said to the pretty girl who blinked at me, 'This is Noel

Papps, Rhona. Least I think so.' And to me, 'Rhona, Noel.' No doubt it's my passion for neatness, for equation, that sees him move us side by side and smile. It's true though, he was getting rid of Rhona that night. But I'm going too fast. Let me go back to my glass of gin. I swallowed it in gulps, and opened my collar and dried my chest, and steam rose off me in the heat of his fire. 'I lost my hat.'

'Lost your marbles, I'd say,' Phil said. 'I like your mo.'

I wiped it with the towel.

'What happened, Noel? Did someone stick you up?'

'I went to Irene's.'

'Ah, so that's it. You should have asked me first, boy. I could have saved you the trouble.'

I took off my shoes and socks and dried my feet. He said, 'See how he clips his toenails, Rhona. A very clean chap, Noel is.'

'What's she doing, Phil. With Royce, I mean.'

'Daddy first, so why not little brother? Why go outside the family?'

I was starting to be warm, and that was enough to make me happy. And the gin. I felt I'd walked a long way heel to toe and now was striding out again. Irene was far away, very small. 'How do they get away with it?'

'No one wants to see. Rhona doesn't know what we're talking about, do you, Rhona?'

'I'd better go,' the girl said.

'Stay a while. It's only nine. Noel will walk you home, won't you Noel?'

'If I can get dry.' I grinned at her; and began to swell up with belief in myself. That's how easily love can be moved over. Conditions were right for transaction, that's the truth. Capital in the feelings could be moved, like shifting it from one account to another; and the only word wrong here is 'love'.

But I'm not leaving it there. Before I go on I'm going back. Irene can't be treated in this way. Nor can I. I want to know what went on before I came into Phil's warm room and met Rhona Clews. Thinned-out thoughts of Irene, did I say? They were fast and shadowy, like bats in the night. English thoughts. Back home in Jessop I approached her with a kind of density in my being, the product of my boyhood, youth, unsatisfied longing; and lust, and guilt and shame, and outrage at the way she had to live. It could not be moved except by chance; this and that, sequentially; which occurred. But what was it? I can't so lightly put it aside.

All I can do is use what I've just thrown out. Take back 'love'. And say that a part of me was Irene, she increased me. And so did Kitty. And, in his way, so did Phil. I may be shallow, shifty, a kind of Aral Sea in my emotions, but if luck hadn't been with me that night – Phil I mean, and Rhona, and circumstance – I'd have found a space in me so great, and had my being thinned to such a degree, I might not have found myself again. I mean that perhaps I would have gone mad.

I do not like this as a meaning of love. I don't much like the person I am. On the other hand I like myself very well. There's something quite appealing, something very human, in shiftiness.

Let's get away from me and look at Phil. He'd thickened up. He'd grown into a man. His chest had that pigeon architecture that made me, through the rest of our lives, think of him, alternately, as hollow or filled with a great coarse-fibred heart pumping gallons of thick blood to his busy parts. His hair had thinned; somehow he was weak in his hair. His widow's peak seemed stuck on with glue. That's all I can remember about him physically – that and his moustache. Yes, he had one, a little brown slug adhering to his upper lip as though with its own slime. I saw why he liked my healthy bush. His nose had fattened up and was thick across the bridge and made him look both greedy and aggressive. I notice noses. I've always felt they show a person's character. He had man-chopping teeth, yellowish, with, like me, mines of black amalgam in his molars when he laughed. Big pink tongue sitting in his mouth like a meal. Blue eyes, sickle-sharp; happy now. That was Phil. A lovely fellow.

He asked about my job at the Institute. He does not want to know things for themselves but for the uses they might have. The Lomax owned some city properties, but Phil soon found I knew nothing about them. Chemistry he looked on as no job for a man. Pouring things from one tube to another, that was girl's work. But I'm putting words in his mouth. He simply shrugged and let the question die. The truth is, I make Phil uneasy. I have a sign on him, and Kitty had it: special knowledge of a part of his life. He could not take it from us and we had power over him. So although he might think

94

my work nothing, because it was *my* work it puzzled him. And although he might want to shuck off poor unwanted Rhona on me, I could say no.

'Kitty's got her knife in you, Phil.'

Here was another thing that puzzled him. 'What've I done? What did she want to marry that twerp for?'

Twerp was the last thing I'd call Des Hughes. In some ways I'd back him against Phil. I'd back him for his rage, and outrage too, and his conviction. And I thought he'd give Phil a good run for ruthlessness.

'Tell them to stop sending that postal note back. It's only a bloody bob, after all.'

'A bob's a lot to them.'

'Well why don't they keep it? It's a gift. Kitty and me were at school together.'

'Kitty and I. You're the enemy, Phil. You're the bloated capitalist.'

'That's what they wrote on the envelope. All I'm doing is trying to make a living. I could pull those houses down, tell 'em that. I will one day.'

He loved wrecking even more than getting possession. When the contractors went in with their bulldozers Phil was there. He loved to see walls come crashing down. In a way I think that was possession for him. He kept a poor-boy fear that someone would come along and grab his pie, and wrecking was gobbling. That got it in his belly and made it safe. All right, a fancy; but most of the properties he bought when he began were buildings marked for knocking down. In the slump, of course, he had to take his losses. The slump grabbed most of his property out of his hand. But he was tough at the end of it. There wasn't much poor-boy in him then, or much looking back. Kitty was the only one he ever sent a shilling.

I did not walk Rhona home. The rain came down more heavily and Phil drove us in his car. She sat in the back. I'd found her attractive in a round-faced pretty way and was disappointed not to see more bone. I like bone in a face, I like a bit of jaw and eye-ridge, cheek-bone. I like a nose that stands in a face. Hollows, angles, do not put me off. Rhona had none of that – and how typical of our relationship that I should start this account of her with negatives.

Sitting in the back, she was in shadow. Light and shade moved on her face and it had all the bone I could wish for then. Who was Rhona? She's a mystery; but that's because I was never curious. The things I don't know about her could have been discovered. I was, with her, desirous, angry, frustrated, pitying, but never tried to find out who she was. I used her, tried to use her, to increase myself. The use she made, or tried to make, of me is one of the things that make me curious now.

'What do you do, Rhona? Do you work?' I was anxious to discover that sort of thing, and I felt a throb of pleasure when she replied that she was a records clerk in a solicitor's office. I began to want her very much.

'She tells me stuff about the clients,' Phil said.

'I do not,' the girl said, shocked. I saw tears start in her eyes. It was enough, I loved her. I was, you must remember, still eighteen, although thirty-one.

Phil stopped at the house where Rhona lived with her widowed mother. 'How about it Noel, walk her up?'

'Phil,' she said, putting her face in light. I saw her pupils shrink. I saw her mouth open and shut like a goldfish mouth.

'I want to keep the motor running. If I stall her she won't start.'

Something in Rhona died when he made that excuse. I put that statement down without firm knowledge; it's more than a guess though. She never spoke to me about Phil, though I made accusations in plenty later on. But something fled from Rhona and I felt it brush me by. It made me cold, it made me still; a pause in time when some particle of life passed from her. Her face, in light, was thick, emotionless. Phil grinned at it. He winked and clicked his tongue. 'Beddybyes, kid.'

I walked her up the path and climbed with her on to a veranda and heard rain rattle on an iron roof. I shook her hand. Her fingers were icy cold. I saw, I think I saw, a smile on her mouth – a tiny thinning of her lips, gone as soon as it appeared. She went inside and turned the key and her footsteps clipped away down the hall, and in a room down there a light went on.

Phil tooted his horn. I ran back to the car and wiped my hair and Phil said, 'Nice girl, that. She's just a bit too serious for me.' He made no boasts and that was hard for him. 'You should try and get a date. She's more your type.'

I replied, 'Maybe I will.' And I said to myself, That's my decision. 'OK, chauffeur, drive me to my door.'
He obeyed.

22

The Lomax Memorial Lecture of 1933 was delivered by Dr Noel Papps. His subject: Developments in Fuel Research in Great Britain. If you look at the list of lecturers over the years you'll see great names. Rutherford spoke on 'Matter and Electricity' in 1925. But in 1933 they were short of money and so chose someone from the staff. I did not let them down. I'm an actor, remember. I can be funny or dignified. My voice can crackle and lash, and fall and reverberate and die. I sometimes think my voice is the best thing about me. It's a voice to open up vistas, and sit you in a puddle on your bum. I'm willing to bet that lecture of '33 was the most entertaining, most 'thrilling', those dignified Jessopians ever heard. And I had a pimple on my nose.

All that confidence, ability. Yet a pimple. It seemed to happen to me all the time. I must be reminded I would never be a man. A creature, Noel Papps, who dreamed of consummations, and peeked in windows, and sat in a wet bush mewling and biting his hand. And ten minutes later leered at a new girl. The toxins in my blood reminded me.

Yet I got up there and performed. I forgot my nose and believed in myself; and they laughed, and they sat breathless, and applauded: the Director, the Bishop, the Mayor, the Chairman of Trustees, and our MP.

My parents were in the audience but Kitty did not come. Irene sat next to the Chairman of Trustees. The lecture was a memorial to her father, after all, and she had dressed for it in the gown I saw her wear that other night, at her piano. Pearl ear-rings gleamed in her hair. The house might need new barge boards and a coat of paint and weeds grow in a gravel path, but there was money still in the Lomaxes.

'Busy men in white lab coats,' I said, 'these are the men of the future. I won't call them a priesthood, there's no room for imprecisions here, but I'll say this: they have a kind of poetry in them. Symbols, equations, valencies, there's a dance equal in importance to any dance of words the poet makes, to any melody from our musicians.'

Irene smiled. She put her head on one side and seemed to concede the argument. It mattered to me, and I knew as I went on that I would never be free of her and that her behaviour – whatever it might be – was her right. Her possession of a part of myself was simply a condition of my life and, partly, no doubt, because of the elation my performance roused in me, I grew elated at my taking from and giving to her, and in my mind struck a bargain: that we should ask nothing, but go on all our lives. I performed for her, with my talk of coal and oil, that ancient treasure buried in the earth. Irene clapped. And when I'd had my thanks, and shaken hands with His Worship Mr Big, and the Hon. Mr Puff, and Bishop Pomp, she took my arm.

'Noel, you've been back two months. Why haven't you called?' There was no dinner with the lecture that night and her gown was out of place, but our town already held Irene eccentric. I felt protective of her and almost put my arm round her waist. Whatever you want to do it's all right with me, I wanted to say. My parents came up, Tup Ogier with them, pleased with me.'Tup, tup,' he said – the last time I was to hear that little measure of his satisfaction. Early November now. Before the end of the month he would be dead. 'Irene, my dear,' he said, and took her hand. She came to his house now and then and played the piano. But science, more than music, was his love. He beamed at me from his wasted face, from his good eye. 'Just a mite flowery, young Noel. Ten out of ten otherwise.' He asked me to call and said he had something to give me. Irene, sly and slanting, said she had something for me too.

I went in the weekend, to Tup first. He still lived in Lotte Reinbold's little house, and his garden, like Irene's, had its share of weeds. Dandelions and stringy thistles sprouted in the brick path where Edgar Le Grice had knocked him down. The rhododendrons, dead at their heart, grew long new bending branches in a fringe, and the sunken garden, concave and spongy with ivy, looked as if it might hide the mouth of an underworld. Tup, in the French doors, withered gnome, called at me to watch my step. His wonky eye rolled without bearing and if I had not known him so straight, if I had been seeing him for the first time, he would have frightened me. His larger nostril seemed to gape more widely and compensate by smell for images lost to his sight. We went into the sitting-room and I saw Lotte Reinbold's collection of busts, her jury Tup called them, on the mantelpiece: Mozart, Brahms, Schubert, Chopin. (Beethoven had been brained by Edgar Le Grice.) Her piano, a wedding gift from Tup, and not as good as the burned one, she claimed, occupied half a wall, and I saw with a start, with a flooding of easy delight, that the music on the stand was *The Harmonious Blacksmith*. Irene had been.

Tea was brewing. Round wine biscuits were on a plate. We sipped and munched and Tup questioned me about my life in science. I told him about the Institute – Fred Gooch's blowflies, Arthur Burroughs' watery core, Billings' work in the cold storage of apples, Dye's on the male genitalia of various insects, and my own suspicions about pakihi – all that solid, all that real old stuff. And about the politics of the place, which didn't interest him. He gave me his magnifying glass, his 'truth teller'; and later we stood in the French doors and looked at Settlers' Hill and the Berthon dome white against the sky. We reminisced about it like old men. Tup advised me not to forget astronomy. The glass, he had told me, banished fear; but a little bit of fear was salutary, and that other glass, on the hill, opened one to it, and showed too how it might be contained. 'There's nothing like astronomy for tension.' He told me how he'd looked out into space and sometimes cried with fear at the spinning suns, and the gulfs between, immeasurable – not, he conceded, by mathematics, instrument, but in the human scale, by the mind. He had watched the comet – Halley's – advance, coming out of deeps beyond comprehension, and had lost, he said, all sense of his being; and regained it, in the end, by an act of will. And when the comet stood at its apogee and filled his lens the margin of understanding over terror was so fine – a crescent as thin as a fingernail clipping – his sanity depended on taking one more breath, just that simple physical *willed* act. And that, he said, is the margin we hold: that's all that keeps us from idiocy.

I won't pretend to go along with this. I told him I did not understand and that depressed him. But we went back into the room and found the tea warm enough for a second cup, and we had more biscuits, and he grinned as though this act, drinking, munching, proved his case. Perhaps it did. Sometimes, these days, I

99

understand it. We hold on by our fingernails, by an act of will. But my grasp of that slips away.

I promised to visit him more often. And he told me not to waste too much time on an old man, but get on with my work, and get a wife.

I laughed, 'Irene?'

He said, 'You leave Irene alone. She's doing very well. I warned Phil off.'

'Does he want her?'

'Phil wants whatever he can't have. But the pair of you are beetles, Noel. Coleoptera. Irene's Chrysopa.' He grinned. 'Go away and look it up.'

I thought about it as I walked to her house. It offended me to be classed with Phil. Our generic difference was plain and Tup, of all people, should recognize it. He was closer to the truth with Irene. 'Chrysopa' got her sparkle and fragility even though it left a good deal out. But what did he mean, she was doing well? I wondered if he knew about her and Royce, then wondered if there was anything to know. It was impossible; but, at once, self-evident; and I lurched on my foundation of sanity and had to take that willed breath Tup had spoken of.

Up the gravel path. Irene standing at the door. No sign of Royce. And more tea offered, although I'm up to my gills in it.

'Would you rather have a glass of beer, Noel? Or some sherry?'

I chose sherry: small glass.

'How was Tup?'

'OK. Good.'

'You know he's dying?'

'Is it close?'

'Oh yes. What did he give you?'

I showed her and she smiled and held it like a lorgnette and looked at me with a huge eye.

'I saw *The Harmonious Blacksmith*,' I said. 'You can't do it without music any more.'

'Oh yes, I can. But he likes turning the pages. Lotte wouldn't let him. He gave me her music stool. And wanted me to take her piano too. But actually, mine's better.'

'What will Phil get?'

'The house. The property. Phil's his "son", after all. And Phil needs property. It's how he measures things.'

'Tup told me he's been chasing you.'

'That's right. I'm property. High-quality goods. But he's given up.'

'Tup,' I said, still bold, 'warned me off. He reckons I'm a beetle. You're a lace-wing.'

Irene laughed. 'Dear old Tup. I don't know what we are, Noel. But I think I'm tougher than that. Anyway, you're not after me. Not any more.'

I thought that last statement ambiguous. It made me cold. I swallowed my sherry and asked for more, and agreed that I wasn't after her; but said, since it was an occasion for honesty, I'd loved her once.

'I know. I loved you too. But never in a way that would have been any good to you.'

We regarded each other with half-amused grins. We were pleased and a little sad, having a past, although I found it shifting in my grasp and not standing still to be seen. She put it well behind us by saying, 'Someone told me you've got a girl.'

'I take one out.'

'Who is she?'

'Rhona Clews. I don't think you know her.'

'Yes, I do. She works in Bowers and Appleton. She's pretty.'

For a moment I could not picture Rhona's face. Then I filled her in, with relief, and agreed she was pretty; and in a kind of fervour to compensate, an eagerness to give Rhona weight, added qualities, until Irene cried, 'All those things? She sounds terrifying.'

All what things? I could not, and can't, remember them. Perhaps I said she was clever and energetic and generous and happy and kind. The truth is, with Irene in my mind, I can't even now give Rhona weight. And while she's weightless, featureless, I slip in and out of that state too. Sometimes when I assemble the actors in my life and run to join them in the photograph, she and I are blanked out: white holes, diagrammatic heads. At other times I see us all too clearly. And then Irene is dark, malevolent. Which is a lie. She never wished me anything but happiness with Rhona. The darkness and the malice come from me. Why I'm so disposed is all too plain, though the object of my feelings won't come clear.

Enough, enough. I'm not satanic. I'm not victim or murderer.

I'm Noel Papps and I won't look beyond the evidence. Or make any statement that's larger than the fact.

Irene said, 'I liked your lecture. I haven't missed one and it's the best I've ever heard.'

'It wasn't helped by this,' I said, tapping my nose.

'Oh, Noel . . .'

'I'll have a pimple on my nose on my wedding day.'

'You will not. I forbid it. No more pimples.' She flicked her fingernail on my sherry glass and made a note that purified my blood. I've not had any more pimples, not on my nose – that's a fact. She said, 'You probably eat too many cakes. It's your father's fault.' But I've kept on eating cakes.

Irene and I chatted for an hour. We were light, amusing. We set a tone; and, over the years, accomplished with it intimacies many married couples never achieve. She played for me and I watched her fingers. That always made a large part of my delight in Irene. Then she said, 'Come and say hello to Royce.' She stood above me and served this on me, a mandamus, and it was my duty to obey. Something, her manner implied, must be got out of the way before we could move on with our present ease.

'Yes,' I said, 'how's Royce? He's grown up now.' I followed her, noticing the slant of her head, and the spikiness of her step. We went past the staircase, past a row of Lomaxes framed, trod lino worn to the boards, and came to the sitting-room on the north side of the house. Bare, a giant box, with Royce in a corner as though all that space frightened him. A bowl of fruit stood on a wooden table. He was shading in, with care, an apple flank and was troubled by its fatness for he rubbed it out as we approached.

Irene said, 'Royce, here's Noel. Noel Papps.'

'Yes,' he said. He stood up, and was no taller than my five foot six. He was, though, better-looking than I'd thought. Although the weight in his body slid to his hips and plumped his behind and made his thighs strain against his trousers, in his face he had the Lomax slant and that gave him a look of suffering.

He had evasive eyes. It didn't surprise me. He had a bitten mouth. What did surprise me was the impression of stillness he made. It was as if he had a hard still core and externals, limbs, behind, were a burden, an embarrassment, no more. That led me to expect some weight and stillness in his work – but I saw, when

Irene opened his folder out, fussy pencil drawings, water colours that looked as if they'd been through the wash. He tried to make trees bend and duck-ponds ripple but achieved only a kind of agitation and emptiness. His work gave me a sense of my own worth. And the boy, the whole of him, put me in a sound position *vis-à-vis* Irene.

'You were just a little chap when I saw you last,' said Doctor Papps.

'I don't remember you,' Royce said. 'Irene says I should, but . . .' He shrugged apologetically and avoided my eye.

I asked if he had left school and he said yes he had, and Irene said he'd left two years ago, he hadn't been happy there, they ran the place like a military barracks, a little Sparta. 'Rugby and cadets and the cane, that's as far as their education goes,' and I guessed that Royce had had a very bad time.

I looked at his work and murmured that I liked it very much. Irene knew I was lying. She frowned, which made her look middle-aged. 'This is just practice. Royce is getting ready. But he mustn't run before he can walk. We go out sketching, don't we Royce? There are some lovely hills in Jessop. Beautiful shapes. And the waterfront is lovely too. Show him your boats.'

'I don't think Mr Papps . . .'

'I'd like to see. Perhaps you'd let me buy one.'

'I don't sell.' He'd gone a girlish pink. 'I'm not good enough yet.'

'Have you thought of an art school?'

'I'm not . . . I'm not . . .' He seemed to have a blockage in his throat.

'He's not interested in that sort of thing. Royce wants to see under the surface, don't you, Royce?'

'Yes,' he whispered. He did not seem to know what she was talking about.

'He wants to lift the skin and see large shapes. That's it, dear?'

'Yes, I suppose.' He blinked. But confused as he was, angry too, angry with her, he still gave me the sense of being unmoved in his core.

Irene stroked his shoulder. 'All right, Royce. I knew you'd want to say hello to Noel. We'll leave the boats for another day.'

I offered my hand and he shifted his pencil from right to left and met my grip with moderate firmness. 'Good luck,' I said, 'keep at it.' An expression of rage crossed his face. I knew I'd trodden on his private ground. But I wasn't about to be alarmed by a boy. 'Perhaps one day you'll let me buy something.' And I went out, pleased with myself; and especially pleased to have found Irene capable of silliness. Royce, with his apples and trees, and his constricting unhappiness, was lifting no skins. Irene was deluded. I saw her as mother to the boy, inventing abilities he did not have. The scene through the window was a dream.

But she restored it to reality. 'Noel, before you go, I've got something for you.' She left me on the front door mat and ran along the hall, where she opened a cupboard, and came back with my hat. 'There,' she said, and put it on my head. 'Now you won't catch cold.'

'Irene,' I stammered. It was a moment of pure transmutation. I spun once over in the air, my body light as a paper-bag, and came down into a world of altered states; and found Irene smiling, glittering at me, both her eyes, all her teeth.

'Not a word, Noel. Not a single word. Now go away. And come and see me soon.'

'Yes,' I said. And went through the sunny spring late afternoon, with my winter hat straight on my head; and a sense of large shapes stirring under a skin.

I saw Royce in a corner of his room. I heard Irene strike up on her piano.

Steady, steady, steady, Dr Papps.

23

Phil did not cry at Tup's funeral. If anything, he was cheerful. 'Not a bad old bugger. He didn't bloody sit there, he had a crack at things. Too bloody right.' It wasn't far from the epitaph I'd have composed. I'd have been more flowery and gone for a bugle note, but the meaning would have been the same: Tup was a battler, a yea-sayer. He was a taker-in not a leaver-out.

Jessop had a new crematorium and Tup was its first customer. We agreed it was appropriate – the scientific end – and I thought of the oxidizing flame and Tup initiating me into mysteries. They had become a part of my everyday life but would never be mundane; and that I owed to my lessons in wonder, to Natural Philosophy, to hypothesis, and the supposition always of the thing beyond the thing. Tup, I thought, ending the occasion with sentiment, knew if there was any Big Thing now.

Phil drove me back to the Institute and I showed him my lab and explained my work. I'd spent most of my first three months on analyses of soil samples sent in by government pedologists doing surveys in North Island districts and on the Coast. The Lomax had contracted for the work and taken me on to carry it out. But I was getting ready for other things. I was staking out a territory for myself, soil analyses were just a beginning. Already I'd set up an experiment to combat bush sickness in sheep, using controlled groups of hoggets and different licks and drenches; and this was soon to show the non-effectiveness of limonite ore and establish the value of soil, in our case Jessop soil, as a supplement in the diet of stock. I meant to look at tobacco soils too and the poor growth of seedlings – and it was my work that showed the harm high pH values cause and determined proper levels for potassic manuring.

But I had only a glimmering yet of my real work over twenty years: the reclamation of pakihi lands, the identification of the deficiencies in the Plowden Hills soil. I can just see a corner of the Hills from my sundeck. You can't tell they're covered with apple orchards. The Coxes and the Galas and the Golden and Red Delicious are harvested now and the pickers are working on the Granny Smiths. Perhaps someone else would have done my work – no perhaps about it, someone would – but it was me, and why shouldn't I claim that they wouldn't be picking anything there if I hadn't come to the Lomax when I did? Kate wouldn't be munching that Gala or having stewed apple with her muesli. They should rename those hills the Noel Papps Hills. I'd sooner have that than be Sir Noel.

I took Phil about and introduced him and the morning ended with me watching him at work. Getting his foot in the door, knowing people, sniffing out possibilities, that was Phil's work. The Lomax was new ground and he explored it with – let me think . . . He was Ramsay filling in a gap in Mendelyeev's list. At the end of it was money, pelf, of course. Phil needed to see that silver shine; but he was not too fond of easy pickings. He was not afraid of hard work, of moving sideways, moving back, of ducking and diving and making a sudden charge to his goal. The Americans have a term: broken field runner. Phil was a broken field runner of genius.

What was he after at the Lomax? He didn't know. He simply saw men working at their jobs, working hard, he sniffed endeavour, and knew it was worth his while to understand. I took him round the chemistry labs and into mycology. (Strange that so many mycologists are women. Is it those curled-in heads, embryonic shapes, and growth in warmth and darkness, that attracts them? Someone should look into this.) Beautiful Pearl Winwood threw him out of his stride, but he recovered, tossed a grin at her, flicked a wink, recovered himself. We went to entomology and found Fred Gooch drawing blowflies. Blowflies were the insects he loved best – 'of infinite variety' he said – and his book on them, illustrated by himself, would make him an international reputation. I have one of Fred's blowflies on my lavatory wall. For my money he's a better painter than Royce Lomax.

I told Fred we'd come from Tup Ogier's funeral, and recalled how Tup and I had watched the mantis eating the blue bottle.

'Ah,' Fred cried, 'Calliphora vicina, one of my beauties. That's a meal fit for a king.' He rolled up his sleeve and plunged his arm into a cage and flies crusted it, with a deafening buzz, and made blue armour-plating on his skin. 'They know me,' Fred said, 'I'm their boss. They come when I call. Did you know,' he turned to Phil, 'a gravid female can bomb you from the air with hungry maggots? Cover your roast beef, my boy, when one of my little Amazons is about.' Fred winked at me. He enjoyed playing mad scientist for a layman. When he withdrew his arm a fly escaped. He opened a window for it. 'Go forth and multiply.'

I refused to put my arm in Fred's cage, though he swore the sensation was more pleasing than a woman's touch, but Phil, grinning, tried it, pushing his arm through the rubber valve and wincing only slightly as the flies bit. Fred washed him with soap and wiped him with an antiseptic cloth. He approved of Phil and told him about the borer house he was setting up on the Lomax research farm at Stallards. Phil got his reward: a tour of that bit of property. After the war, '47, when the Trustees sold the farm and increased the acreage of the experimental orchard, you can guess who set the deal up. You might say Phil made the initial move by putting his arm in Fred Gooch's cage that day.

On we went and looked in to meet the Director, Manifold. He and Phil found interests in common. A pair of shooters: come May, they'd sit together in a mai-mai on the inlet, drinking turn about from Phil's leather flask and blasting away, and you might say . . . Well, Manifold was a nice old fellow, he was a lovely innocent, and burbling on to friends isn't a crime, I've done it myself. When the Institute shifted premises . . . If Kate was taping this I'd say, 'Switch off that machine.' All I'll put down here is that Phil did very nicely. And no one was hurt.

We had a look in the greenhouses and crossed the road to visit the museum, where Phil was bored. Things under glass didn't interest him. He yawned and looked at his watch. I did not want to let him go. I enjoyed too much the sense of my importance; and experienced, for the first time, the Lomax as an extension of myself. In later years, when I moved from practical science to administration, I came to know the risks and injuries – a thinning out, less of the self left to hold on to – but did not suspect them on that day. I told Phil that after lunch I was going up the river to collect some bush litter samples. Would he like to come? We'd look at the arboretum on the way. I hooked him with that. The arboretum was property.

I'm no specialist in indirection. I had no greater ambition than to bind Phil to me for a day and increase myself in my own mind. In stratagems, invention, he left me far behind. When he arrived back at the Lomax Rhona was in the back seat of his car. He had set us spinning on a wheel and gave it another push that day. Whether he took something on the side I never found out, and never will, for Rhona has moved beyond recall. Beyond, I mean, the reach of imagination. I can't move around her, see inside. I can with Phil, but anything I discover could be right. He shifts too quickly for me, Phil Dockery.

Rhona smiled wanly. She was off work that week, nursing her mother. (An alcoholic, I discovered later; a great collapsing ruin of a woman I'd thought part-senile, part-dropsical.) I'll make a guess and say Phil observed how confident I was as Dr Papps and took the chance to show me at my best. The day was full of opportunity. It was a hinge turning on past and future – his and Rhona's, Rhona's and mine.

I put my buckets and spade and trowel in the boot. I sat beside

Rhona on the back seat and, dizzy with anger, fierce in my desire to be free of my ineptitudes, took her hand; which she allowed. Phil scooted his car along the river road, past the old Le Grice farm, where gorse had claimed the hills and thistle the flats, and through the gorge towards the Jessop city water reserve. Dust bloomed behind us like a lily. Rhona answered my questions yes and no. She was passive, inert. Rhona, in fact, was doomed. I had intimations of it that day. There are people doomed from birth – to subjection, to failure in the self, a kind of cognitive failure to find oneself as object. All our healthy stratagems work to this end; but Rhona Clews, Rhona Papps, was born without that skill, or had it stolen, I don't know. I know that my apprehending of her state struck me like a pick-axe in my chest, but lasted only the blinking of an eye, in which time I gripped so hard bones grated in her hand and Rhona cried out. Phil grinned in the mirror. 'Easy, boy.'

I was no boy. I was a man of thirty-two. Phil was the boy. He's been a boy all his life; just as, all her life, Rhona was at others' disposition. Some states there's no escaping from.

We drove past the Lomax arboretum and I pointed out the damage done by fire. Several of the plots were destroyed and others eaten into and I told Phil that the Trustees had almost decided to sell the land and shift the more valuable trees and shrubs to a plot in town. Manifold had told me in confidence, and I passed it on to make myself important. Phil gave me a look I can still see but can't define. Contempt was part of it, pity too; and he was grateful, he was pleased with me. Later on, years later, I accused him of starting the arboretum fire of '34. He shook his head. 'You really think I'm a crook, don't you, Noel?' (He didn't mind being taken for a rogue.) I don't know what to think any more. I know he bought the land and ran grazing stock on it for years and sold it to the Country Club when they shifted into the valley in the fifties. He was on the committee of the Country Club. And I do remember him saying on that day – the day Rhona agreed to marry me – you could make a nine-hole golf course on that land and build a club-house up on the knoll. But this is gossip. No one's going to nail Phil Dockery now.

We drove into the reserve, crossed a ford, parked in a clearing, and I trudged off like an infant at the beach. I collected samples of litter from various trees – the idea being to correlate alkalinity to field observations of the fertility of the soil types – and came back with my buckets and spade and found, as I'd expected, Phil and Rhona gone. I searched. Gum-booted, I burst through scrub, phantasmagoric couplings in my mind; and came on them sitting on a boulder in the river, Phil smoking a cigarette and blowing smoke rings, and Rhona with her arms clasped round her knees and her eyes fixed on the moving water. He flicked his butt away and spoke to her and she shook her head. He reached across and made a little mock punch on her jaw; then pointed at me watching from the bank. Rhona looked up. It's a curious illusion: I seemed to see down tunnels into her head and see a kind of blue immensity, and I believe Rhona surrendered then to nothingness. Phil stood up and yawned. He took Rhona's hand and pulled her to her feet. He helped her across stepping-stones; and, at the bank, made me the present of her hand; and I pulled her across the yard of water and held her for a moment in my arm. I laughed. Rhona laughed.

Phil said, 'I've had enough of this nature stuff. I feel like I'm in a bloody poem. Let's go home.'

He dropped me at the Lomax and drove Rhona home. I was round there that night, and she agreed to marry me. So I took on the job of non-existent Rhona and her monstrous mum, and worked very hard for the next five years.

24

Still reading, Kate? I know you are. You sneak in here at night and find my book dead-centre on the desk. You don't have to go tippy-toes or get the Sundown Kid to put Three-in-one on the door hinge. I leave my notebook out for you to find. I want your opinion. Do you think it will ever see print, my cheating memoir? Do these honest scribblings entertain you?

Give me a line of criticism. Cross out adjectives if you like. You'll upset my judgements but I don't mind; you'll get an inkling, maybe, of things I avoid. If you're patient you may glimpse things that evade me.

But don't interfere with my nouns. My nouns are the truth that I find.

I don't need you to tell me that I'm tired. I know I'm tired. Why shouldn't I be at eighty-two? Tiredness is not a problem to me. In fact

I like it. I can make a meal of tiredness or take it like a mug of Ovaltine. It satisfies me. You're not a problem either, you and Shane, though I wish you wouldn't take me for a fool, with your smirk and snicker. I can work out what a cunning linguist is. And I don't care what you do up there in your room. Just get him to use that Three-in-one on the bed.

Do you mean that my writing is tired? Yes, I agree. There's a stretch I've got to cross and standing here and looking at it brings a weakness in my chest. I feel my stringy heart in there and it doesn't seem to have any blood to pump. It stretches like a nest of rubber bands. I want to write about happy things. I want to tell jokes. My mother-in-law, Doris Clews, hid her port wine under her bed in a chamber-pot. No Kate, not the bottle in the pot, she tipped it in, and fooled us for months. It's an act of cunning that makes me breathless. That old monster, how I admire her. She reached down in the small hours with her tumbler and topped up. And how Rhona screamed when she drew out the pot. Rhona crouched in a corner, screaming.

I started that as a funny story. Things go wrong. I could tell you, Kate, about the time Fred Gooch's flies escaped and we had to evacuate the building. Or about his borer house – how he waited and waited for them to breed and they wouldn't oblige. John Dye went out to give an opinion and told poor Fred the whole of his colony was male. I could spin that out for several pages. Shall I try? Or Manifold drunk day after day on Baxter's Lung Preserver, warbling 'Dressed in your gown of blue brocade' in his office and activating cultures by blasting away with his Boer War revolver. Lomax stories. I've got buckets of them. Unzip your tape recorder, Kate. They're yarns that won't go off in a wrong direction. The trouble is I can't be bothered writing them down.

I finished with the Lomax months ago. And Dockery and Irene Lomax bore me. Tell me some more about Kitty Hughes. Or Rhona if you like, but don't upset yourself.

I don't smirk. I don't snicker.

Kate.

Thank you, Kate. A sign. No, you don't. Your expressions of amusement are frank. I was just giving you a nip with my finger-nails. Shane's a bit of a smirker though.

110

Kitty Hughes? She was frank in everything. Let me think. 'By God, Pam, I'll give you a thick ear.' She said that to your mother when she brought home a bad school report. And she was famous for saying, 'If the Honourable Member for Fendalton doesn't withdraw that remark I'll come across the floor and give him a belt on the lug.' But you'll know that episode. Ersatz earthiness. She prepared the ground for that sort of thing the way Churchill is said to have prepared for his witty sayings. Kitty was an old phoney, did you know? All the same, she was a genuine girl.

I don't go in for paradoxes. Kitty Hughes was a complex being. And there's a mystery in her I've never solved and never will. Kitty was dark and light, still and turbulent, sweet and sour. She was loud and violent, she was quiet. A thick ear for Pam, right enough, and for the boys when they played up; but when they had scarlet fever or the mumps the care they got came from some deep source of love in her. You think I'm being sentimental, don't you? You'll say, maternal feeling, that's nothing to write home about – and probably you'll ask what Des was doing? I'll tell you. He was reading by the stove. He was sitting with his feet in the oven drying his socks and waiting for his slice of bread and jam and cup of tea. No matter what those kids had, mumps or chicken pox or impetigo, Kitty always looked after Des. He got his jam spread thick, and three spoons of sugar in his tea, and a second cup; and she came and took the dishes away and stoked the stove and tied a woollen scarf round his neck. But – there's a mystery. She was rough. And was it the roughness of love, or something else? I thought sometimes she'd like to string him up to a rafter with that scarf.

I never managed to look inside their marriage. Did your mother ever talk about it? Perhaps you can tell me what went on there. I know he hit Kitty now and then. I saw her with a fat lip and black eye. I'm not going to offer the opinion that she liked it, women like it. You'd probably beat me up if I said that. She hated it; and she hated him from time to time. She matched him assault for assault, with her tongue. And now and then she hit back with her fists. I was round there one day and found him nursing his jaw. It was one of the few times I've seen Des happy. 'She got me with a beauty,' he tried to grin. 'Ten Ton Tony would have been proud of it.' After that he called her Tony Galento. (A boxer, Kate, a fat

Italian; and the name wasn't inappropraite. Kitty was growing into a heavyweight.)

But what went on? What really went on? She'd never hear a word against Des Hughes. Assaults on him, and I tried them now and then – have I said I detested him? – she took as assaults upon herself. And I'll say this: that well-matched, mismatched pair, more than any couple I've known, had an identity. He made her, she made him. They generated increase, kept going a creation of themself, continuous. Yet this won't do – for there came a time when she was large and round and Des sucked dry, Des Hughes done for. There was nothing distressing in it (especially for me); it seemed, somehow, part of their bargain.

I'm clutching at shadows. You probably know more than I do, Kate. Here's a day, for what it's worth. It's a Labour Party picnic down on the park at Girlies Hole. The date, March or April, 1938. Jessop has a Labour MP now, lugubrious Bernie Molloy with the bushy hair and honest boots; Bernie from the Back-bench, he came to be called. Des is right-hand man – left-hand, he says, illustrating his role: phrase-maker, ammo supplier. Des isn't a brickie any more, he's a sick man and does some part-time clerical work for the local branch. He's at the picnic to enjoy himself, Kitty says, and she tries to keep him out of Molloy's way.

I'm there too, with Rhona, my wife. Can I change tense? I want to step back and get the racket of kids out of my ears, and the smell of orangeade and donkeys and dung out of my nose. Getting at a distance, that's something I can do for Rhona too. She doesn't – did not want to be at the picnic, and she put herself in another place and passed like a Tibetan through our day.

I wasn't a Labour man, though I voted for Molloy in 1935, and Kitty for as long as she stood. I was at the picnic to be among people. That, for myself. For Rhona, to give her Kitty's company. Kitty was good with Rhona. She found ways through to her. And Rhona softened Kitty. A kind of edulcoration took place and Kitty forgot to sting and bite. On the day of the picnic though, I could not bring them together. Kitty had her children and Des to occupy her, and was loud and frolicsome, athletic – she tucked up her dress and won the women's dash in a rhinocerean gallop – and Rhona, as if puffed on by a breeze, shifted into one of her private worlds. I knew it by a softness on her mouth, and tiny smile, and by a widening of her eyes. She was blind, seeing other things. So I fixed her arm in mine and we strolled about – I strolled, she floated – and I was able to watch the picnic even though I could not join in.

The children were swimming in the river. Your mother, Kate, was like a trout in the water, she was lovely, she was quick, she made a flash of white and pink and brown in the green deeps, and came up open-eyed, bursting up into the sunny day. Shifting a little, smiling myself, I mistook her for the child, Kitty. Your uncles, the boys, a rowdy pair, might have been Phil Dockery and me. They came up begging to me, slippery as fish, and I gave them a florin for fizzy drinks. Pam looked at Rhona, inquisitive, and touched her arm as though trying something out. Then she ran off with the boys to the drink stall; and I glanced at Rhona sideways and saw a little frown on her face. She touched the drops of water Pam had left and gave a shiver, and dabbed them off her skin with a handkerchief. Then, dry, untouched, resumed her dreaming. I took her up from the river, past the coconut shies and the donkey rides, and watched – I watched – the lolly scramble, and admired my ruthless nephews and niece. I thought it inappropriate though that training in capitalism, gaining and getting, should take place at a socialist picnic, and wished that I could make the observation to my wife. I'd keep it for Des Hughes when I found him. I enjoyed setting traps for Des. I'd acquired a taste for his contempt of me. A bit like Kitty, I was increased by Des.

We watched the tug-of-war, sixty people on a piece of mooring rope from the wharves. Town and Port strained against each other and no side won until Kitty changed her allegiance and ran to join her husband on the Port team. I watched her with bewilderment, distaste – her skirt tucked up, teeth bared, fore-arms bulging. Kitty! Kitty! She looked Neanderthal. She had black sweat patches in her armpits. One heave from her and the townies went skidding on the grass. They dug in their heels but it did no good. Kitty dragged them, grunting, sweating, past honest Bernie Molloy, who brought down his arm, 'Port the winner'; and the Port team fell in a tangle on the ground. Kitty waved her fat legs in the air. Des lay panting off to one side, spread out like a star-fish on the grass. His hair was a splash of fire, his face was white. After a while she came and hauled him up by his shirt and brushed him down.

That was our day at the Labour Party picnic. But before I stop, one more thing. Enough was never enough with Kitty Hughes; though it's not her fault. Blame me if you like, always looking for significance. All the same, it happened, though not quite as neatly as I'll describe. We went past the greasy pole, Rhona and I, arm in arm; and there they were again, Kitty and Des. She was everywhere. Do you know what a greasy pole is? I don't know whether you have them any more but they were very popular in my day. You sit on a log mounted high on trestles and try to knock each other off with sugar bags filled with straw. Young fellows used it mostly, but it was more fun with husbands and wives.

If it were an art form you might say it reached perfection with Des and Kitty that day. Skinny Des, made of trellis slats, with paper face and fiery hair; and Kitty in her red dress, black in her armpits, hair unpinned – she lost some votes that day, some of those Labour wives never forgave her – they straddled the pole and whacked each other with swollen sacks. His arm was going round like a propeller, dust puffed from her shoulders with every hit, and bits of straw swarmed like yellow bees about her head. She held on, clamped the pole in her white thighs and locked her ankles. She worked her arm in weighty scything sweeps and knocked him inch by inch to one side. Des bent in the middle. She seemed to fracture him. Her teeth were fierce. She looked as if she'd stretch her neck and bite him on the throat; and his mouth made a woeful O. Down he fell and lay with limbs askew on the mattressed hay beneath the pole. Kitty, not yet done, threw her sack and hit him in the face. She unlocked her legs and put her hands on her hips, and sat there grinning, white-toothed, at the world. Kitty Victrix. There, Kate. Significance. I told you.

But this is not, for me, a Kitty story. This is a story about my wife. While Kitty slugged, and Des tipped slowly over, Rhona must have let go my arm and walked with backward steps away from me, until stopped in her retreat by a fence. There she stood, watching Kitty on the greasy pole, and making little whimpers and moans. I looked for her and found her, with lips drawn tight and the palms of her hands flattened on the fence. I went to her and helped her away, and no one saw.

That's not much, I hear you say. It was a great deal. It was an end for Rhona. She saw a kind of murder. She had confirmation of what she couldn't any longer know.

In a little while she went back inside, to one of her worlds – don't ask me, don't ask me, I don't know – and never came outside again.

25

Thanks, that's useful about Kitty Hughes and Des. You're being selective though, and not very fair. I thought you liked your sister.

Rhinoceros makes rhinocerotic not rhinocerean. As far as I know they don't gallop either.

What was wrong with Rhona? You don't say.

Kate.

26

I do say. I've told you. Stupid bitch! Do you think you can work life out like a sum? This and this and this gives that and that? All right, I know, I said that's what I meant to do, but I'm not a fool, it can't be done. I was skiting. I've told you what I know, and that's enough.

We had no children. You'll want to know whose fault that was. Mine, through no moral or conjugal dereliction. None of the half dozen women I've had affairs with was ever troubled by a pregnancy, although they – and I – were careless enough to make a tribe of babies. And Rhona could conceive, I know that, for her mother told me once about her miscarrying and waking in her bed – being lucky to wake (perhaps unlucky) – with her buttocks in a pool of blood. You asked for it, Kate, and you're going to get it. She wouldn't tell me who the father was but I know, and you can guess. I was, and am, the sterile one, and if you want to make something of it go ahead. But you're probably more interested in sex than procreation.

That's too bad, because I'm going to tell you nothing. I'll tell you it stopped after a while, when she was sick – our euphemism for mentally disturbed. (That's not to say mad, mad came later.) She never liked me kissing her and said once moustaches must have germs, but when I shaved mine off she still didn't like it.

Do you want me to confess I failed her? All right, all right. She looked at me sometimes – what times were those? the dinner table, the fireside chair, the beach, any time – and I saw a pleading in her eyes: Make me forget him. I was not man enough. I could only be gentle or furious, could only say, Be still, it's going to be all right, you wait and see, I love you, Rhona, I'm here love; and touch her with my hands that felt like dead leaves I suppose – or slap her in the face with accusations. Later on her plea was not make me forget, but don't let it come close, don't let it get me. Those are the words I find for the look she gave. I couldn't save her.

And of course I'm guilty, and wear guilt like a mole or wart. It's irrational. I'm *not* guilty of anything, I just won't buy it. But there's this thing I wear. It doesn't trouble me, there's no sting or itch, but now and then I see it and it makes a huge invasion, takes the whole of me, and I stop in my tracks and utter – howl, obscenity – and it's social embarrassment brings me back, or if I'm alone it's the stretching of my face, I start it on its travels, I send it round the villains that I know – Dracula, Kaiser Bill. I call that rubbering, and though it makes me loony it gets me back on balance. You've seen me doing it, Kate, you caught me once, and if you stay long enough you'll hear me howl, 'Baarstid!'

So she went. She took little steps and was thinned in her being as she withdrew. It's my guess she learned techniques of shifting her consciousness. A kind of tinkering went on, she altered things; but when she came back it was alarming. She woke not *from* but *into* bad dreams, and gathered strength and did not stop but flung herself back to her safe place. At last she simply peeped at the real world through some crack or rent in her own. She had glimpses. And one of those, on her last day, set her seeking me. I knew she'd seen, seen *me*. Yes, I knew. Perhaps she'd spent sufficient time in there and was getting ready to come out.

I won't talk about it. It's not your business. Nobody's business but my own.

Rhona, when I knew her first, could laugh. It was a small sound, enclosed by her mouth, and she seemed surprised and swallowed it, and seemed to like the taste for she smiled to herself. She could be passionate. I don't mean in bed. How you people trim language back. Passionate about ending small injustices. Her movements became definite and her sentences stood in parcels above her head

– speech balloons, are they called? Large injustices she never saw. But she marched out into the frozen night and told our milkman that if he didn't get boots and mittens for his delivery boy she'd report him to the police. She prised the boy's fingers from the handle of the urn and ordered the man to take off his gloves and feel; which he did, and said he was sorry. She hacked at a frozen puddle with her heel, as though making a mark to kick a goal. 'That's ice, Mr Boyd. And look at his feet.' She shone her torch on them. 'Yes, all right,' said Mr Boyd. I suspect he watered our milk after that.

Stupidities, sickness, accident – she was good. But cruelties and betrayals she could not handle.

I'm surprised more people don't go mad. We must have minds made of leather.

I married Rhona because I was back home and thought Dr Papps should have a wife. I worried at first that she wouldn't live up to me, but I took her through the Lomax, showed her my lab, talked about my work, and she understood, she saw how important I would be, and gave my arm a squeeze of encouragement. I married her because of my need; and from pity, from my perception of her state; and notions of my strength and maturity. With all that mixed in a brew anyone might believe himself in love. She fitted so neatly into the hole left by Irene. She freed me from the need to discover where it was I had arrived. I can't leave Phil out either. So many phases in our contest, so many battles; and you see how each of us supposed himself victor – though it needed more self-deception on my part. Anyway, there we were, Noel and Rhona Papps, in a villa on Bishops Drive, and Doris Clews in the back bedroom, with a chamber-pot of port wine under her bed.

I grew up. I went into it a boy but in four years was as much a man as I'll ever be. Whole geographies changed. Sandy coasts sank beneath the sea – by that I mean my self-esteem took a proper shape, my notion of myself began to accord with reality. What came up out of the sea was habitable, only just, but, by God, it was real. The soil might be thin and sour, and rocks break out all over the place: but it was mine and would not vanish in a dream . . . It's time I let this figure go. It's leading me to self-praise and I'd sooner keep my cold eye, an instrument of measure.

I'll bring back Kitty as it's Kitty you want. She knocked at our door one night, just after tea. We'd managed to get Doris to eat a mouthful of pumpkin and the eye of a chop, and had her at the sitting-room fire with her port wine watered down; and we were warm and fed and moderately pleased with ourselves. Rhona was darning a hole in my socks, a needless activity but it pleased her.

Rat-tat-tat on the front door, and, 'Who's that?' I said, thinking, as I always did, of Irene, then of Phil. But when I'd padded down the hall in my slippers and opened the door, it was Kitty, shaking rain out of her hair. She stepped inside and closed the door with a bang. 'I've left that bastard. And his bloody kids.'

She had no bag. I saw no marks on her, though I looked. 'Did he hit you?'

'I hit him. And kicked their arses. Bloody parasites.' She grinned fiercely. 'They're howling like the Sally Army band. Let him sort it out.'

'Where are you going, Kitty?'

'To Mum's. I just stopped off to get shickered with Doris.'

'No, Kitty. Rhona . . .'

At once Kitty changed. It was as if I'd spoken the magic word and changed her from a scullery maid into a princess. (She'd hate that simile; would choose to stay scullery maid and start a revolution in the kitchen.) That softness I've spoken of came on her and rounded her face and smoothed the angles of her body.

'How is she? She all right?'

'She's fine. She's good tonight.'

'Want me to go?'

'No, come in. Don't talk about Des, eh? Don't say the kids are howling.'

'They're all right, little buggers. A kick on the bum does them good. Where's Rhona?'

We went down the hall to the sitting room and Kitty touched Rhona on the head and put her hand under Rhona's chin and looked in her face; then kissed her brow. She sat down and grinned at Doris.

'That stuff will give you constipation, Doris.'

'You remember my sister?' It was several weeks since Kitty had been round and Doris's memories did not last so long. All the same, throned in her chair, heavy as a basilisk (though shedding her flesh at this time), and basilisk-eyed, she looked full of ancient knowledge, evil knowledge. Her massive head – I've known no other head give such an impression of being compacted – turned on her neck and her eyes closed and opened in a crocodile, a holy crocodile, way. How misleading it all was. But not deliberately. Doris was not capable of deliberation. Or thought, coherence, memory; and barely of speech. Her life was jumbled in her head like the pieces of a puzzle in a box. Only in the hunt for her next drink could she arrange one thing to follow another. Then she could be clever and move in directions Rhona and I could not foresee.

Her breath was like a basilisk's, poisonous.

I made a pot of tea and brought it in and gave Doris a new glass of watered wine. 'Last one, Doris.' She took no notice.

'Is it still raining out there?' Rhona said; and she and Kitty talked about the drizzle, and then about Kitty's children, and Rhona said she'd knit Pam a pullover – and all the while Kitty made a globe of warmth about them. We put Doris to bed and closed her door and Kitty and I entertained Rhona with stories about our childhood. Kitty discovered memories, and rediscovered a way of looking at things; of shedding toughness, shedding calloused skin. She returned to what I shall call her poetical manner, although it was a good deal more than *manner*. She saw through an eye that took in surfaces and penetrated deeps; and she spoke old words as though they were spoken for the first time and held in them the magic of new-naming. You probably haven't heard of phlogiston, Kate. When I try to put myself at a distance from the Kitty of that night I think of her as being in her phlogisticating mood. That's not altogether accurate. Phlogiston, in the Old Chemistry, was an element supposed to be present in all combustible matter. Flame was the escape of phlogiston. I see Kitty's memories, issuing in language and spirit both, as a dance of flame. Perhaps I'd be more accurate if I said she worked through to her base element that night. She found a kind of carbon skeleton. I don't know. Perhaps I shouldn't look for metaphors in chemistry.

You see, I'm at a distance. It works. Then I creep back and look between my fingers and see as much as I care to see. Whether I should or shouldn't behave in this way isn't the question. It's a question of keeping calm.

We talked about the bakehouse and our father beating dough,

hopping and humming and pretending his white hands were not his own: ghost hands, skeleton hands; then, when we were frightened, turtle doves. Kitty made their cooing perfectly. We talked about Tup Ogier, Mrs Beattie, the patriotic pageant, Miss Montez. And swimming in the river, diving down and seeing the sand puff into cumulus clouds at the touch of your hand, and seeing brown trout resting under the bank. Kitty spoke of rescuing Mrs Le Grice. I told of Edgar Le Grice leaping through the warehouse in his raven coat and the fire running at his side – I left Phil out – and how we faced each other in the yard and how he rose in my dreams to that day; and it was Kitty, I remember now, who gave me the term basalt moon.

We told funny stories and made Rhona laugh. Then we drank more tea and ate wine biscuits and Kitty sighed. 'I suppose I'd better get home and pick up the pieces.'

'Ha!' I said.

'Ha what? We have our fights, Noel. Des is a funny blighter. But I wouldn't swap him for one of your fancy friends. Before I met Des I was nothing.'

'Now you're something?'

'I'm getting there. I'll be branch delegate next time round. Nothing surer.'

'And Des will stay home and mind the kids?'

'Why not? Des is pretty sick, Noel.'

'So you'll do his work?'

'Who says it's his? It's mine.'

'You should stand for parliament, Kitty.'

I was way behind her. She'd thought of it and knew just when it would be. The war made little difference to her plan.

Rhona said, 'I'll come round and measure Pam. And show her some patterns.'

'Better show me. Pam's got no sense. And make it brown or grey so it won't show the dirt.'

'I'd like to make something pretty,' Rhona complained. But Kitty was up putting on her coat and her softness was gone, and her brightness gone. She was swathed and dumpy, and back home in her family, and somewhere forward too, in her future, which could not help being practical and square on its feet. She gave Rhona a peck on the forehead and grunted goodnight to me at the front door. She dug her hands in her pockets and put down her head. Off she went into the swarming drizzle. She hooked with her foot and closed the gate, and didn't look back to see it spring open. Her dark coat – brown or grey, I don't remember – sank in the night and her white calves gleamed.

I closed the door and went back to my wife and we sat a while by the fire, holding hands. I believe, though I'm not sure, Rhona and I made love that night. If so, it was the last time.

27

Five degrees of frost this morning. Snow on the mountains over the bay and the old man wraps himself in scarves and pulls on bed socks over his socks before coming out to sit on his sundeck. Not a cloud in the sky. Autumn reds and yellows, English colours, deck the hills. I'm trying to write the way Kitty would speak when phlogisticating, but Kitty would never say 'deck'. What a word! I considered this: the colours lay spread on the hills like jam and butter, but that's going too far, even though some of those yellows are buttery and one tree – liquid amber – has the colour of strawberry jam. Too much straining for effect. Kitty was not after effects.

Ducks quack and squabble on the river. Thirty-seven ducks sitting out the shooting season on the edge of town. They boat down the rapids and enjoy themselves. Others waddle in the street and cars make a detour round them. I hope they don't decide to fly away because they won't last half an hour out on the inlet.

Kate is being gentle. I don't know why. Does she think I won't make it through the winter? I'll make it. Or not. I won't put in a special effort but I won't give up. Death may be just a step away, nevertheless it doesn't show itself on my horizon. Here I sit enjoying this Pongolian autumn display and it's not an 'issue' with me that it could be my last.

She said, broaching it with hesitation: 'Don't you see, Noel, if there was so much blood she must have tried something. It couldn't be spontaneous. Or else . . .' She means a back-street abortion; arranged by Phil Dockery, of course. She wants me to judge and sentence him. I'm no more interested in that than I am in my death. Leave Phil alone. Leave Rhona alone.

*

Kate is planting ivy round the base of the piles. In a year or two, she says, I'll have it climbing over the sundeck rail to shake hands. She can't be expecting me to die. Shane has built a scaffold along the front wall and is painting the house. That's good of him. The paint and brushes etc. cost me a devil of a lot. But it's good of him. It keeps him busy. If he falls off the scaffold he'll kill himself. It's more than a hundred feet down to the river and nothing to catch hold of before he hits the rocks. He's wearing one of those radios, a Walkman, and God knows where he is while he's on that plank. I wonder if Kate has thought her boyfriend mightn't last as long as me.

She chose the colour, dull green. I don't like it but women say I've got no colour sense – Kitty, Irene, Ruth, all said that. When I told Kate I wanted white she laughed and said all my taste was in my mouth. Green, she said, would make the house merge into the hillside and make it belong there with the trees. Is that what a house should do? She patted me and asked me to trust her, which I've done, because, as a matter of fact, I don't care. White, green, strawberry? Who cares? 'Kate,' I yelled a moment ago, 'tell him to put a pink stripe down the middle. Diagonal. Tell him to paint a mural if he likes.' She squinted up at me and showed her eye teeth. Sometimes I make her uneasy.

'I do like her,' I said. 'In fact,' I said, experiencing one of those surges like water coming back in a plughole, 'in fact I loved her. More than anyone. Anyone in my life. Except Rhona, and Irene, and Ruth. And my mother. But as much.'

Kate laughed. 'Anyone else?'

'You're the one making me confused.'

'For someone you claim to love you say some nasty things about her.'

'Kitty had enough people trying to butter her up. I thought you wanted her warts and all.'

'Yeah.' Kate patted my hand. 'She had more warts than you think.'

I wanted to know what that meant but Kate wouldn't say. I think she's as confused about Kitty as I am and can't decide what to put in and what to leave out. Her book is going not too well, she says. It's got the wobbles. She's even thinking of giving it up. 'Let me read it.' No, she says. She'll keep on, or maybe not, maybe put it away for a bit and see how it looks in three month's time.

'You won't finish.' I was angry. Kitty deserves a book. When wankers like Nash get a book Kitty deserves two or three. Shane's to blame. I told her so. If she put half the energy into Kitty she puts into him she'd have it finished.

'Mind your business,' she said.

All right, I will. But I hope that cowboy falls off his horse.

Phil called to see me yesterday. Kate was out shopping or he wouldn't have got past the door. Is that right, Captain Kate? It's my door, remember, and I'll have what guests I like. In fact, you're a guest here yourself, remember that!

He kept honking into his handkerchief. I had a shot of Redoxon before sitting down with him. With winter coming on the last thing I want is a cold. Phil looked his age yesterday. When he was a boy he looked a man. When he was a man he looked a boy. Always in disguise, always playing roles – that's just Phil Dockery being himself. As tycoon he was chomper of cigars, or malevolent gnome, or number eight putting in the boot. As womanizer he was smoothie, bottom-slapper, winking lecher – dozens of roles. Unbuttoned his wad of notes like his male member. But yesterday the old man of eighty-three with a cold was out of costume – an old man with a cold, sick of things.

I poured him a Scotch and had one myself, hoping it would help kill his germs. We sat on the sundeck in the hot hour of the day and watched a tribe of waxeyes feeding in the fennel. I'm fond of them, their spryness, each a little cupful of life. The ducks quacked on the river and Phil said, 'So that's where the buggers are hiding. Bloody doc wouldn't let me go this year. I reckon I could've frozen this cold out.'

'You'd have killed yourself.'

'Maybe. It's a better way to go than sitting in a chair. In bloody slippers and a bloody scarf.'

He was describing me and I said sharply, 'I'm not going, Phil. Not for a while. As a matter of fact I reckon I'll see you out.'

'Want to bet?'

'All right. You're on. Ten dollars.'

'You always were a piker, Noel. Make it worth my while.'

So we bet five hundred dollars and gave ourselves something to live for. I wrote an agreement on a page of my notebook and tore it out and gave it to Phil to sign.

'We need a witness. Hey, you,' he yelled at Shane, 'come and stick your monicker on this.'

'He's got his music on, he can't hear.'

Phil went to the rail and wobbled Shane's plank. He hooked with his thumb and Shane climbed the rail and took his earphones off.

'We need a witness, sonny.'

Shane read the page. 'Yous jokers know what you're doing?'

'Just sign it,' Phil said, 'and get back to work.'

'I reckon I'll run a book on this.'

'Come on, Shane,' I said. 'Put your name.'

'What's in it for me?'

'If I win you can have the five hundred dollars.'

'Fair enough. Put that down.' He went into the kitchen for a glass.

'Cheeky sod. Who is he?' Phil said.

'Kate's boyfriend.'

'Lives here?'

Shane came back and poured himself a drink. He witnessed the agreement; and I signed and Phil witnessed the second part.

'Long life,' Shane grinned at me, and swallowed his drink. He put on his earphones and went back to work.

'Cheeky bugger.'

'He's all right.'

'A stickman, eh?' Phil was taken with Shane. 'He's bloody big. Dong like a draught horse, I'll bet.'

If you read this, Kate, don't come at me. Go and throw your wobbly somewhere else. I didn't talk about it. You or Shane. I draw the line. But I was pleased to see Phil perking up. Old men sorry for themselves are unlovely creatures.

What else did we say? He made some comment about the trees – how ours were better than the pommie ones, they didn't drop their leaves everywhere; and I asked him what he had against the English. 'You name it,' he said. But it comes down to this: his father didn't say much, couldn't say much, too hard to speak; but he told Phil, 'Those English bastards murdered us.'

'The pommie generals,' Phil said, 'with their riding boots all polished up and their little conductor's batons under their arms. Conducting the war. Ten thousand here, eh? Ten thousand there. Poor buggers getting chopped up with machine guns or lying down and drowning in the mud. For some bloody hill with a shithouse on top. Swagger sticks, that's what they called those things. They bloody swaggered while my old man was getting gassed.' Tears stood in his eyes. He wiped them with his handkerchief. 'I hate bloody colds.'

'Another drink, Phil?'

We both had another. And because we were in the past I asked my question. I don't think you meant to be cruel, Kate. Perhaps you meant to be kind. But it's been there, hurting in my chest, since you planted it. I asked him about Rhona's abortion.

'Who?' he said.

'I know she was just a diversion. One among, how many?'

'Who told you she had an abortion?'

'I was married to her.'

'Did she tell you?'

'Doris did. Her mother.'

Phil frowned, then blew his nose. 'This thing's bloody sopping. Got a spare one?'

I had a handkerchief, almost clean, in my pocket. He blew again and put both away. I don't think he was fixing up a lie. It's just that the past isn't easy for him. He has to grunt and strain at it and shift memories like concrete blocks.

'Maybe she had one. I don't know. Something must have happened.'

I asked him what he meant and he said she'd told him once – he thought they were at the beach but wasn't sure, they might have been out in his boat – Rhona had told him she was pregnant. 'It's fifty years. Leave it alone, eh?'

'What did you do?'

'Can't remember . . . Nothing. Yeah, nothing.'

What did nothing mean?

'I kept on swimming. Or sailing the boat. Then I drove her home. Jesus, Noel, I don't remember. I mean, fifty years. It might have been another girl – you're not going to take a swing at me?'

I wasn't. I should have been disgusted, furious, but I felt only a grim affection for him; and then, piercing it, love for Rhona.

125

'I guess she tried to do it by herself.'

'I would've paid. I'd have arranged it. If she'd asked.'

'Forget it, Phil. Have another drink.' He had kept on sailing his boat and Rhona had waited for a word, and then given up and started to die. I tried to discover what she had felt but could get nowhere. She stood at the end of a tunnel. No way through.

'Nice girl, Rhona,' Phil said.

'Shut up, Phil.'

'OK, OK.'

'Can you tell me the names of your wives?'

'What's your game, Noel?'

'Quizz time. For another glass of Scotch, the names of your three wives, in any order.'

'I dunno why I waste my time with you.'

They were, for your information, Kate, Barbara, Sylvia, Isobel – or Barbie, Silly, Izz. All three divorced him and had their married lives, and children too, with other men. At parties he approached them with a kind of waltzing step and gave them that mock punch on the jaw. 'Are you havin' any fun?' Selective memories. Fiction maybe. That song could be from a more recent time. All I know is he sang it once. And had three wives, pretty girls. And hundreds of others, Rhona amongst them.

We saw you coming, Kate. You rode Shane's motorbike over the bridge, with the sidecar full of groceries. I went inside and put the kettle on.

You weren't pleased – she wasn't pleased to find us drinking whisky and scowled in answer to Phil's flashy grin. Shane, the cowboy, vaulting the rail, got the sharp edge of her tongue. She wouldn't drink her tea with us but sat alone in the kitchen. We three snickered at each other. There's nothing like female disapproval to make a man feel good.

Phil offered Shane work out at Long Tom's. He wanted a paint job done on the out-buildings. His manager had some bloke lined up, but was getting a back-hander, Phil said. He was wake-up to that sort of trick. If Shane could get out there next week he could have the job.

'I'm not a painter,' Shane said. 'I just slap it on.'

'You're doing not a bad job here,' Phil said. 'I'll pay you hourly rate. Twelve bucks.'

'Fifteen,' Shane said, 'and travelling time.' He put his dark glasses on and tried to look like a Mafia boss.

Phil laughed. There's no doubt he approves of Shane. He likes his cheek.

'Cash,' Shane went on. 'I don't want to lose my benefit.'

'Jesus, you young blokes,' Phil said. 'That's my bloody taxes keeping you.'

'Thanks,' Shane said.

'How old are you?'

'Twenty-three.'

'When I was your age – OK, laugh – when I was twenty-three I owned my house, my car, and my own business. How much money you got in the bank?'

'Bank?' Shane looked at me. 'You tell him Noel, I don't know what all these big words mean.'

'If I told you what I'm worth,' Phil said, 'you wouldn't act so smart.' He was getting angry. But ah Kate, I agree with you, young Shane's no fool. He's got Phil Dockery sorted out.

'Do you want to know what I'm worth?' he said.

'Ninety bucks a week. Of my money.'

Shane stood up. He seemed to be four feet through his chest and his legs as thick as my sundeck poles and – doesn't he wear any underpants? – that thing in there was the size of a Dutch salami, I'll swear. He put his head back, swelled his throat. He thumped his chest and sent a spray of sweat out of the hair. I haven't heard a better Tarzan yell. Kitty's boys used to do them, they were good at them; but Shane's yell skewered me from ear to ear, it rattled the top of my head like the lid of a pot and almost knocked me out of my chair. People in houses by the river ran into their back yards and looked at the sky. Kate came running from the kitchen.

Phil flung his hand over his ear and turned away. The colour drained from his face and the pouch of fat under his chin seemed emptied out. I'd never seen it loose, collapsed, before. I won't say that was Shane's doing, he made me notice witherings in Phil, that is all.

He dropped the full rich sack of himself in his chair, making it bend, making it squeak. 'That's what I'm worth, eh. Shane Worth.' Alongside that Phil had nothing. (I had nothing either.)

But Phil's resilient, he comes back. He raised his glass. 'Touché, young feller.' I'd never thought to hear him use that word. He winked at Kate. 'Lucky girl.'

'You bloody men. Playing bloody games. I'm taking that.' She snatched the whisky bottle from the table and flounced away. We all laughed.

'You want that job or not?' Phil said.

'I've got to get finished here. Week after next.'

'Righto. When you want it. Phone me a taxi will you, Noel.'

'I'll take you in my sidecar if you like,' Shane said.

'OK, you're on.'

I watched them ride over the bridge, Phil with Kate's blue helmet on his head. Shane was riding fast. The bike was airborne going off the bridge. Phil enjoyed that. He had his fists clenched over his head.

That's not the end of it. Oh no. I was feeling left out. Shane, whether he'd meant to or not, had challenged me and I hadn't made my answer yet. There's no answer, of course, except in detachment, and I see the way to victory there; but did not see it then and was betrayed by my stupidity.

I wonder if I seized the challenge to escape the hurting in my chest. I don't remember it stopping but it certainly wasn't there as I made my stiff-legged climb over the rail and set myself down carefully on Shane's painting scaffold. The plank is no more than a foot wide. Perhaps I was drunk. It looked as wide as a footpath and with the wall on one side and the safety rail Shane had carpentered on the other it made a corridor along the outside of the house. I didn't look down but shuffled along, humming to myself a song of Phil's, 'Gentleman Jack, the ladies man, he can make love like no man can.' I passed my bedroom windows and glimpsed my ghostly self and saw the white emptiness beyond, with a coloured hill low down; and that made me pause. The plank ended and I had to step sideways to another. It curled up at the end and made a sickening two-inch drop when I put my weight on. A chattering came from the other end, a monkey sound; and I was like a monkey as I shuffled by the living-room windows. I grinned at myself without conviction. But still, I was getting there, the end only six feet away. Shane's can of paint and green-haired brush stood in my way. I decided to do some painting. That would show him. He had nearly finished the wall and I imagined his surprise when he came back and found it done.

'Gentleman Jack,' I hummed, and stepped over the can, nimbly stepped, and squatted on the plank and seized the brush and dipped it in, admiring, almost tasting, the paint: its creaminess, its thickness, its liquid/solid fall. I played a while, lost in sensation, then lightened the brush of its rich load, and went three paces on the plank – and you might say the mirror cracked across and the curse was on me.

I shiver still. After two days it hollows out my chest, hollows my skull. That emptiness. That fall to the river. The wall reeled away. The sky tipped one way and the other and Jessop rocked back and forth like a swing. I dropped the brush and it bounded like a hare down the slope, three jumps, hit the river, and bled its green blood on the pool. Ducks went speed-boating away. I get all this by unconscious recall. I don't remember seeing it. I remember two hands locked on the rail – my hands. They came and went, still there, always there, as, I suppose, I opened and closed my eyes. They were a principle, a law. If I say they were my fundament you mustn't think I'm making a joke.

Heights don't frighten me, they terrify. I climbed a tree in our garden once and made the mistake of looking down, and there I was, not ten feet from the ground, with my arms and legs wrapped round the trunk and my head buried in my shoulder, and I was *never* letting go. My father stood on a ladder and talked to me. He talked for half an hour, gently coaxing, and prised me loose and carried me, locked on him, to the ground. I was eight.

Now eighty-three. Shane spoke to me, prised my fingers loose. He'd delivered Phil to his club and riding back had looked up from the bridge and seen me on the scaffold. I did not know he was at my side until he bent his head in front of me.

'Come on, Sir Lancelot. Let go.'

Kate had the living-room window open and called at him to lift me in. He freed my hands and held me by the elbows. My fingers dug into his forearms. 'Jesus,' he said. He wore Band-aids on the cuts all weekend. (One of them's going septic and Kate says I don't clean my fingernails. I resent that. I'm very clean.)

'Close the window. Help me at the rail.'

But when we got there – shuffle, whimper, sob – he didn't need help. Without letting me go he stepped over backwards. Then he lifted me by the elbows. I felt myself rise into the air and seemed to hear my shoulders creak. They must have come close to dislocating. Sore today, some sort of bruising in the joint. He put me down and Kate held me up.

'Silly old fool.'

'Nice one, Sir Noel. Bloody good try.'

'Your brush,' was all I could manage. 'In the river.'

Kate put me to bed. On my bed. She offered no homoeopathic pills but threw my mohair rug on me and did not bother to uncover my face. I must have looked like a corpse lying there.

I don't blame you, Kate. You've got a lot to put up with here.

Yes, I have. Men who think they're boys. And old men with dirty little minds. Leave Shane alone. He's got a chance. And leave me alone if you don't mind. I'm tired of all your sniping.

You need me, I need you. For a while. Let's leave it at that. Now why don't you write some more about Kitty? And don't try to steal my language, Noel. Words like 'wanker' just don't suit you.

K.

28

At least they show I'm alive. I can still accept new things. Isn't that so, Kate? Or K. You know who he was, don't you? Of course, you're an educated girl. Sorry, *woman*. I hope you never find yourself in his condition.

I was in Prague once, just poking in my nose, a bit of aimless curiosity about alien ways. I left sooner than I had intended. There's nothing political in that, nothing altruistic. I began to feel strange forces work on me, a kind of thumb pressure on my brain, and twinges of alarm made me look up or step ahead or stand stock still. I kept on stopping at the hotel desk to see my passport. *New Zealand Citizen*. It began to seem a fragile description. The ink grew more watery by the hour and my face began to lose weight and not belong to me. So I followed my instincts of alarm and got out of Prague, went to Munich; where I found that Dachau was close by. How had I been ignorant of that? I *couldn't* go. I stayed in town and looked at the Glockenspiel instead. I can't face up to Man, that's why I play monkey.

Does this sort of digression interest you? It stops me from sniping.

I'd rather stay in the present than visit the past. New things, Kate. As long as they come skating over the surface I enjoy them. Let me say what happened on Sunday night.

She's joined a club called the World Record Club and records keep arriving in the post. She carries them down the path like dinner plates; greedy face, ready for a meal. I enjoy them too although the diet's rich and strange. We've had Sibelius. More than once. She's got a taste for big noise, for thunder and crashing seas. We've had Beethoven. And Telemann. And Vivaldi. And Bach. Likes a bit of orderliness too. We've had some flute virtuoso whose name I forget. And various quartets, wind and string. We've had Mozart of course, but Kate's put him away. She went to see a film about his life the other week and he didn't come up to her mark 'as a person'. We've had the Kings Singers. And the Cambridge Buskers. And Stravinsky, who caused some damage in my head. All this makes me think of Irene. Irene and I listen together. Does that annoy you, Kate? What I want to know is, how do you afford these records on your benefit?

That night she put on something strange: Carmina Burana by Carl Orff. I think I've got it right. Choral stuff – I mean 'stuff' in no critical way. I enjoyed it. Lots there to keep me awake, or wake me up. Irene liked some of it too. But Shane could only take a couple of turns of the record. 'Jesus,' he said. He's free with the name. He fetched his Walkman radio from the bedroom and sat on the sofa and switched it on, translated himself out of our world. I gave a look at Kate. 'Dire Straits,' she sneered. 'For ten-year-olds.' We went back to our adult sounds.

We were on side two – tavern songs – when Shane rejoined us. Something in the music caught his attention. He picked the sleeve from Kate's knee and looked at the illustration. Then he snorted. 'Fuck Orff, more like it.' That was no sharp hit, but Kate was hit.

I won't record the insults they exchanged. Well, one each, their beginners: 'Dumb sod!' 'Snotty bitch!' After that it got very wild, and how their faces swelled and throats grew corded. Kate went blotchy, Shane turned purple. Most of my rage these days is infantile, and so was theirs, but it had an adult component: love/ sex/possession. I mean by that, hunger to possess. Things marvellous and terrible have been happening here while all the while I monkey through my days.

So much for skating on the surface. So much for the fun I meant to have. It wasn't any small thing, Kate, I know. Don't be angry with me, I've been engaged in manoeuvres and sometimes I can't tell where they'll lead.

He grabbed a fistful of her hair and forced her against the wall. Her throat was bared as if for the knife. He raised his fist to strike her in the face. Age and horror had me nailed in my chair. I thought I was about to see a murder.

It's difficult to put things in their sequence. In fact, two things happened at once. Kate had no intention of being murdered, even struck. She kneed him in the crotch in the manner she's been taught on TV; and he became aware – beat her by the fraction of a second – of what he was doing. Ask him, Kate. I know you think he cried out because your knee crushed his tender parts. It wasn't that; or wasn't that to start with. Shane saw himself about to murder you – and he stopped. He managed it. Don't think that's easy, Kate. My God, how easy to go on. I'll borrow a terminology I disapprove of: Shane is close to being damned, and yet is struggling to save himself. He'll need our help.

You got him, though. I don't blame you. Right on target. And as he went doubled up to the door and opened it, you followed – she followed him, raining punches on his back; and when he was halfway out she put her foot on his backside, gave a heave, shot him out, and slammed the door. She came back for me.

'No, Kate,' I said. The singers had changed their mood to something softer. That didn't save me, although she seemed to lose heart as she stood me up. She didn't punch. She marched me down the hall by my arm – I'm lucky, I suppose, it wasn't my ear – and pushed me into my room and closed the door. My heart was going thump-thump, whack-whack. The rhythm was wrong, the speed was wrong. I thought I would die. I thought *I* was the casualty, Kate. You too need to control yourself.

I went to bed. Like a child I didn't clean my teeth. I lay in the dark listening for the world outside my door, but no sound came, and when I woke – when my wretched bladder woke me up – the house was dark. I crept up the hall to their bedroom door. No sound in there. Anything might be happening in that silence. Someone might be dead. They both might be lying with throats cut. I opened the door an inch or two and listened for the sound of creeping blood. Kate turned heavily. Water slurped. Have I mentioned that they've bought a waterbed on time payment? She mumbled words in her sleep – not nice words. She was all right.

I hoped Shane was all right too, wherever he was.

He was sleeping in the garage, in my car. Whenever he got cold he ran the heater and he's lucky he didn't kill himself with fumes.

Kate was washing the breakfast dishes when he came in. She did not turn round and after looking at her for a moment he stepped close and put his arms around her. I thought she'd turn and hit him again. It could have gone that way. She was hard and straight. It must have been like hugging a tanalized post. Then she relaxed, she leaned back and let him kiss her on the jaw.

'Get some breakfast. Put on some toast,' she said.

When he'd eaten they lay on the bed – not for sex. After her knee-jab he was probably out of order down there. I heard their voices through the rest of the morning. My guess is they were planning their future.

Shane climbed down to the river after lunch and retrieved his brush from a willow nest. He finished the front wall and now he's busy round the back.

29

They've made a new start. The other night was the rocky climb to a new plateau. There's less absorption now in themselves and a good deal more awareness of each other. That's an improvement. It improves our comfort as well.

Kate has stopped reading my notebooks. I feel the neglect; but think it's just as well. The world I find back there is hardly plenum – it's atom and void, a multitude of bodies rolling about and damaging each other when they come close. I'd like to encourage in her a sense of life's fullness and help her continue in her belief that the solitary isn't our natural state. If only for my own sake.

She's rough and cruel when she suspects the truth.

It's clear to me Kate and Shane won't stay together long.

30

You fly into Jessop over the hills. The city begins without the usual suburbs. You cross the river, following the line of the railway, and almost at once you're over the port, where apple boats and wood-chip boats are loading and the dredge is busy in the channel. Our main street runs south from the reclamation, past the rugby ground, over several bridges, and through the commercial heart – stomach is a better word – and ends at the concrete monster on the hill, our cathedral. In the beginning we were a city because we had a cathedral, but forty thousand people live here now, so we have the numbers. Jessop City. Sun-city, our PR men like to call it. The suburbs spread south along the plain. You see them, and our satellite town, Stallards, as your Friendship turns over the sea and approaches the runway. You come in across the shallows of the inlet, over the sand- and mud-flats, and pass at five hundred feet over Soddy's Point.

I could have mentioned the Plowden Hills, lying south and east, and the apple orchards, and the sixty thousand hectares of pine forest, and the golden sand beaches out beyond Long Tom's, and the maritime park, and the fishing fleet, and the kiwi fruit orchards, and deer farms, and berry farms, and pig farms; and the car assembly plant and the packhouse; and our two schools on the English model, one for girls, one for boys (Kitty a famous old pupil of one, I of the other); and the golf course and Town Beach; all those things. But I started this not for decoration or for civics but to bring myself to Soddy's Point – so back I come.

Seen from the Port Hills or Town Beach, or from Stallards on the other side, it's a lovely place. It curves like a sickle. In spring you can see the red and yellow rhododendron forest behind the main buildings. A clump of native trees grows at the base of the penin-sula and reaches into the mainland. In summer I watch native pigeons take off from the wild plum trees by the river and head over town and I know they're going to feast on karaka berries at Soddy's Point. (It's named after a settler, not the chemist, Soddy,

134

who discovered isotopes.) The buildings are painted white and have red iron roofs. They look like a hotel or resort and visitors mistake them for that. But Soddy's Point is Jessop's mental hospital.

A lot of people say the Point is wasted. It's ideal for a tourist hotel, businessmen say. Phil Dockery wanted to build a casino there. 'With Bunny girls, Phil? And massage parlours?' 'That's a damn sight better than wasting it on loonies.' Then he remembered Rhona. It's one of the few times I've seen him blush.

Rhona went there in 1938 and stayed for the rest of her life. That wasn't long. I visited her on Saturday afternoons and put her arm in mine and we walked on the gravel paths in the rhododendrons and in the gardens on the seaward side. We sat on benches under the Phoenix palms and listened to the dry leaves talking in the wind. They were quarrelling with each other, she said, and she could endure it in trees. And in birds. Black-backed gulls squabbling over a fish head made her laugh. We stood on the low cliffs at the end of the Point and looked at Jessop. The sun shone on the faces of pink and white Mediterranean houses on the Drive, on wharf sheds and warehouses and ships and cranes, and yachts in the bay, the lighthouse on Needle Rock, and the railway bridge and cathedral and Settlers Hill, and the two-storeyed houses where our well-heeled citizens lived. Across the glittering sea Jessop was ethereal. It looks that way still, woven in lace, even with the cement silo and seven-storied DB hotel added. When the tide was out the mudflats gleamed like polished stone. In sunsets they turned pink. I've seen Rhona reach out to stroke them with her hand. Jessop, beyond, now and then in an afterglow, was not the place her previous life was lived in. I'm not sure she had a previous life. I'm not sure what Jessop was. But she faced it and smiled at it across those two sun-coloured miles.

My job was to talk to her. Her doctor thought there was a chance I'd reach her in that way. I told her about my work. I boasted to Rhona. I tried out jokes and anecdotes on her. I told her what was happening in Jessop and the world, confining it to good news of course. I described how Clive Meadows, also working on the apple problem, spied on me from behind the trees. He flitted there like a murderer or the ghost of someone shot, someone *I'd* shot. (Did I say that to Rhona? No, I did not, that wasn't for her.) I told her about the Lomax Lecture, how the Dutch entomologist had put everyone to sleep and how his uppity wife had offended us by describing Jessop as a puddle. *Poddle*, she said. I told her how Irene's German Shepherd had treed me – but not why. I gave her news of Kitty. I told her about movie stars and the two little princesses. But did not mention Hitler, Czechoslovakia, Chamberlain. And, later, did not say a war had started.

Sometimes her grip tightened on my arm. I tried to understand what had provoked it but could not find anything in my words. My silence, though, would make her look at me and sometimes she would shake my arm. I was the being that made the droning sound. When she spoke – perhaps once or twice in an afternoon – it was not to take up anything I'd said. The palms were quarrelling. The mudflats were a floor for dancing on.

I remembered poems to recite, and learned new ones. Lots of Tennyson, she seemed to like the music. The Bab Ballads. Anything with a rumpity-bump in the rhythm. Coles' *Thousand Best Poems* was good for that. Sometimes I brought a book and read to her. I gave myself some pleasure in that way. I read her folk and fairy tales, avoiding Grimm ones. Now and then I sang a song or whistled a tune. And once she surprised me by singing herself:

> Ev'ry morning, ev'ry evening,
> Ain't we got fun,
> Not much money, oh, but honey,
> Ain't we got fun.

She let my arm go and made some lively dance steps on the gravel. Then she sighed and smiled and dreamed again.

When I said goodbye I pointed to Jessop and told her I was going 'over there'. I released her hand and she put it in her cardigan pocket – to keep it warm? preserve my touch? – and turned away. I drove round the inlet to Jessop, where all sorts of things were going on.

One of them was Doris Clews. My mother-in-law was going on. I mean her endless treasure hunt. I did not try to stop her drinking, though it outraged many people to see me taking bottles home for her – and it cost me plenty. Some of them hinted I was trying to kill her – and it cost me plenty. Some of them hinted I was trying to kill her. It crossed my mind. More than once. I'm not going to defend myself. But the fact is, I tried to strike a balance between keeping her contented and keeping her alive. So I watered her port. And I hid it about the house in half pint bottles. I hid it high and low, under and over, behind, in front (the purloined letter trick). I buried it in dirty clothes and buried it in the flour crock and put it in the waste-paper basket and under her mattress and in the cutlery drawer and in the coal scuttle. Think of a place. I put it there. On the curtain pelmet. Hanging from a coathook by a piece of twine, suicide. The idea was to exercise her, make a drinkless time, but let her get her treasure in the end. Treasure is wrong. She didn't hoard it. But she made it last longer because of her great joy in finding it. She swigged half a bottle on the spot but kept the rest about her and cackled over it a good long time.

I kept Doris (reasonably) happy, (just) alive, for more than a year. Then I was tired. I began to listen to arguments that she wasn't my responsibility. The woman I'd hired as daily help quit. And I quit Doris. I gave up and put her in a home. But not before she asked me, told me, this: 'How are we . . . How can we . . . Where . . . What is . . . Why is it? Nothing . . . Nothing can . . . I could never . . . Noel?'

She was marvellously lucid and exact. Among her other questions, she asked me if I knew who I was.

31

At work I had an answer that convinced me: Dr Papps. And looking back, I don't feel too uncertain outside work. I was a man doing his best. Rhona was at the centre of things; and I'll confess I loved her crazy more than I had ever loved her sane. I don't find 'crazy' offensive. Imagine a body with the bones all snapped but its owner happy in his mind. Rhona had a place where she was happy in spite of all the broken things elsewhere, and she spent her time not looking out. She was whole. It doesn't seem outrageous that I enjoyed loving her. I liked being useful too; and liked pity, liked my pain. Does this make me still a boy? It sounds that way. I was just *someone* doing his best, and managing to be useful in spite of his faults. But it's always seemed to me I came to manhood in my marriage.

It's beside the point though, old man's game; a bit of cerebration, nothing more.

*

The Lomax lecture came round again. It brought me two encoun-
ters of some moment in my life – for this stuffiness there's a cause,
I'll come to it. Our lecturer was the Dutch entomologist, Verryt. He
was a most distinguished fellow. Doctor, professor, honorary this,
visiting that. Seven feet of him – well, six – with pointed nose and
pointed jaw and a yellow sunkenness in his face suggesting *deep
thought* and *midnight toil*. All this for insects, I thought, and, jealous
of his fame, considered him an insect himself, tea-tree jack. With
insect wife, a little grub discovered in an apple. Verryt had two
lectures for his tour. One, the better no doubt, was 'The bee in
human history'. I'm told he was severe with Maeterlinck. We got
the dull one – 'Entomological science in the service of mankind'.
How it went on. One thing will eat another, I knew that. Tup had
told me all I needed to know. I yawned and played a tune with my
fingertips on my teeth. I winked at Irene, lovely sharp Miss Lomax,
silken-hatted, down the row.

The little wife, the grub, saw me wink.

She was sitting between Manifold and the Bishop, leaning forward, hands on knees; and, indeed, was forward in her seat so that
her toes might reach the floor. Her head was cocked on one side as
she listened and my leaning forward must have shown in her eye.
My wink ran like a bead on a wire, straight to her. I'm victim of the
instantaneous blush. I had not the wit to turn away, or pick the
gnat out of my eye; or even close my fallen mouth. Her stare was as
bulbous as a frog's, yet had the quality of voraciousness. This
woman was about to gulp me down. No more than two or three
seconds passed, yet it seemed she munched on me. I find, now, the
image of the mantis and the fly. Then *she* winked. There was no
mistake. Behind the inch-thick lenses of her specs one huge eye
was eaten by its lid. Then, because I had trouble understanding,
she poked her tongue out. It appeared like a pink grub dead centre
in her lips – she had a mouth like a blood-red fruit, Satsuma plum –
as though it had wriggled out to see, and then popped back. But
still her magnified eyes kept their stare and I could not mistake the
message. Mrs Verryt was inviting me.

The Bishop saw. He blinked. I found my wits and sat back in my
chair. I pressed myself as deep as I could go. I was horrified and
terrified equally.

Verryt went on – a curious kind of honking and droning that

138

provides the ground for my memories of his wife. Applause, in which, grinning, I joined; which I prolonged, determined to put any sequel off. I willed the Bishop into more and more orotundities – but his thanks were done and there was no safety but in numbers.

'Irene, stay close.'

'What's the matter, Noel? You've gone pale.'

'That woman's after me. Mrs Verryt.'

'What for?' Then she cackled so loudly everyone looked at us. 'Oh, Noel.' I thought she was going to choke. Verryt looked angry. His wife tapped her cheek. And Manifold beckoned me over. I couldn't refuse. 'Stay with me, for God's sake,' I whispered.

'Dr Papps,' Manifold said, 'is our brightest star. He's just about got corky pit whacked. Tell 'em, Noel.'

'It's a matter of deficiency,' I gabbled. 'Composition of the soil not right. God not on the job that day. Sorry, Bishop. But whose fault is it, do you think?'

'Ah, Dr Papps, just your very question is a start. I've hopes for you.'

'But this soil,' Mrs Verryt said, 'surely it is good for something else? Must you grow apples?'

'It's too late to change. The land was promoted as apple land by a company, and the sections were sold, and the orchards planted, and now we've got to make them work.'

'Make good apples from bad?'

'You could say that.'

'You see,' she said to her husband, 'they are not immune.'

'To what?' I asked.

'Greed and foolishness. My husband likes your country. He thought you might be – what is it, Piet, some sort of nature's children, eh? It is not so. This Jessop is a poddle, but nevertheless you are a part of history. That is something, eh? Part of the story of mistake and fixing up – which is further mistake. So it goes on, with little poddle Jessop part of it.'

We did not care to have women talk in this way. But our battery of eyes seemed to stimulate her. 'A little poddle full of croaking frogs. I thought New Zealand would amuse me. But it is boring.'

'I, unlike my wife,' Verryt began.

'You have buildings made of wriggly tin and when it rains you cannot hear yourself. And a cathedral I would not go to black mass in. Do you not know your buildings speak for you?'

'Unlike my wife – '

'And where can I buy some cheese I can eat? Pixie cheese, you have. It is soap. And pixie men. How frightened they all are, unless they golp all this beer down. Then they reach for you with their fingers in the street. Pixilated.'

'On these matters we do not agree – '

'And why do you not open your mouths when you speak? Why do you make the air go up here, into your nose? Such ugly sounds it makes. I speak your English better than you and I am Dutch. I find your country like a little toy shop full of toys.'

'But I – '

'He, on the other hand, is bowled over. Is that how you say it? He finds it a corner of paradise.' She made a face at the Bishop. 'You do not look like angels to me.'

'I'm interested,' the Bishop said, 'in your view of history. Surely your husband's talk tonight gives more hope than that.'

'My husband amuses himself. He plays his games.'

'Now that's not fair, madam.'

'He finds an insect parasite to eat a vegetable one. And then must find a parasite to eat his parasite. He will find perhaps something to eat Herr Hitler and his Nazis?'

'England and France will deal with Mr Hitler. We must trust our statesmen, Mrs Verryt. They have the problem well in hand.'

Mrs Verryt gave an ugly laugh. 'And if they fail God will help, perhaps?'

'Much of our trust must be in God. Yes.'

'Ah, you fools, you do not know. Here in your warm poddle you do not know.'

'We read our newspapers like anyone else,' I cried.

She looked at me with her huge unhuman eyes. 'Give up reading papers, Dr Papps. You must try to make your apples grow. That is sufficient work for a pixie.'

How could I have thought she wanted me? She winked, she poked her tongue out, I insisted, driving Irene home. But it must have been from malice. My God, what a woman! Poor Verryt. What a ghastly woman. And still I use that word, finding a residual need to put distance between us. But –

'I like her,' Irene said. 'She's marvellous. I wish we could have had a proper talk.'

'You're joking.'

'I'm not. She had the whole lot of you going backwards. You know she's a writer? She's almost as well known as Doctor Verryt.'

'What sort of writer?'

'Historian.'

'I'm glad I don't have to read her books.'

I walked Irene to her door. She asked me in for a drink.

'What about Queenie?' – her German Shepherd bitch, who sniffed my fear, and wanted to tear my throat out. Heights and dogs, my two phobias: and when my aching joints make me dream, it's a Dobermann grinding knee or elbow; and sometimes I'm hanging on a cliff-face, holding on with fingernails that tear, and Queenie comes stepping on a ledge, with her tongue dripping like a tap, and sinks her teeth into my ribs. I had a bladder infection once and Queenie chewed my private parts.

'I'll put her in the kitchen.' Which she did, and called me down the hall. I heard Queenie, homicidal, behind the door.

'I don't think you should keep a dog like that.'

'She's useful, Noel. We have prowlers.' Irene smiled. I blushed. But in the living room we fell into our roles and laughed at the Bishop and admired Mrs Verryt – I admired her as a monster – and Irene fetched her dictionary and looked up pixilated.

'It's pixie-led. Wait, it's slang for drunk. Isn't she clever?'

'Too damn clever.'

'If you were pixie-led do you think you'd like her?'

She gave me whisky and poured sherry for herself. Then she sat and watched me, head on one side. She asked about the Lomax and I told the stories I'd tried out on Rhona. With my second glass I talked about Rhona too and Irene asked what would happen to her. I said she'd probably live a good long life, then deleted 'good'. 'Long life,' I said. 'She's well. She's fit. She's even getting fat. They say she eats everything she's served. I take out chocolates for her and she eats them, like this, until they're gone. And she's got no worries.'

'Will you stay married to her, Noel?'

'Yes, I will.' I looked at Irene straight. 'Anyway,' I said, and looked away, 'who else would have me?' I was a wriggly grub myself.

'Lots of women.' Irene mimicked Manifold: 'Dr Papps is our brightest star.'

'Silly old fool.'

'Mrs Verryt wants you.'

'Enough of that. Play for me, Irene.'

She went to the piano. 'Anything special?'

'I've had enough excitement. Something soft.'

I don't know what it was. Nocturne? Lullaby? It moved me to a sadness so deep tears began to leak from my eyes. I squashed them with my fingers and that palping touch followed Irene's touch on the keys. I believed she had reached out to me. I stood up and walked close behind her, walking into a frame as Royce had done. I stood a half inch from her back and watched her fingers move; and knew that in a moment my hands would stroke her throat, touch her mouth, and she would close her eyes, and my fingers in her hair would feel her shape . . .

She stopped playing. The silence rang; it hurt my head. 'Stand where I can see you.' Her needle-sharpness almost made me yelp. I stepped off to one side and looked at her, and was probably cross-eyed, for she was amused as well as cross.

'We got that sorted out years ago.'

'Irene – '

'Go and finish your whisky. I've had enough playing anyway.' She stood up.

'Would it . . .?' I said.

'This is the way it is, or no way at all.'

'Would it have been different – if it hadn't been for your father?'

Now it was her eyes out of line. 'My father?'

'If he hadn't done things, Irene? If he'd left you alone?'

Irene knew what I meant. She made a long ragged indrawn breath; her face seemed to wrinkle and shrink. Light and sharp, and black and grey, withered, dry, she lifted herself and flew at me and fixed her fingernails in my head. They burned like acid. The cry she made was a burning cry; chemical. I stumbled back but could not get away. She was fastened on me. Her face bobbed and slipped and turned on its side and upside down and her eyes bounced like marbles, black and mad. She had no words to say, but cries and screeches ran like knives on me and cut my flesh. I am overdoing it, you think? I don't think so. I bled down my cheeks and over my jaw.

But I got away. I tore her off and flung her down, to save my life. And I ran. Down the hall I went, with Irene after me. I heard her scamper, patter, on the lino like dry leaves. Behind the kitchen door Queenie was berserk. Her claws raked the panels and she made a she-wolf howl. I knew exactly what Irene would do; and to Royce, in pyjamas, at the head of the stairs, I yelled, 'Don't – ' Stop her, don't let her, I meant. Then I was outside, running on the path, with gravel chips leaping from my feet. The gate and picket fence were a mile away and the lawn stretched out. My running was lead-limbed, a nightmare running. Behind me the dog was out of her cage, yelping insanely, making claw shrieks on the floor; then had me in sight and made no sound.

My car, under the street-lamp, was a haven I'd never reach. I might hurdle the fence but Queenie would take it like a gazelle and have me as I opened the door. The distances computed in my brain in a micro-second. I'm pleased now at my clarity. The tree at the gate was my only chance. It was a buddleia, rank and brittle, with branches that might sink me back to ground – but my only chance. One foot on the letterbox, a step and a heave, but the rotten thing collapsed and parts of it hung on my foot as I tried again. I used the bracing strut on the fence; stepped up, made a leap, caught a branch – while in time with me the dog leaped too. I saw her rolled-back lip, teeth sharking up, and screamed and kicked. But she had me. She had me in the crotch. God, how it alarms me to write that. She didn't have me, had my trousers. In the crotch. Then she danced. Only her back feet touched the ground. She hung there, forked in me, a huge new member, while I dangled on the creaking limb and howled.

Royce came lumbering down the lawn with a chain. Unconscious recall. I see him looming ghostly in the dark, in white pyjamas. At that point the bark turned to dust under my hands and I fell off. Queenie thought she had me. She tugged as though to get me to a lair; believed she had me by a juicy part. I grabbed the fence in one hand and tried to pull away. Royce clipped on the chain and joined the tug-of-war. My trousers tore. A ragged piece the size of a doily came out of the crotch. Queenie murdered it as Royce held her. 'Go on,' he yelled.

I needed no telling. I scrambled over the fence in my wooden shoe and head down, hands out, lurched at my car; and was inside.

But wasn't safe. The maniac bitch had broken free. She leaped the gate, and gave a shriek of fury or pain as the chain caught in the palings and spun her like a wheel in the air. She slammed down on the footpath on her back, but was up and squealing, slavering. I fought in my trousers for the key, and found it at length warm on my thigh. Royce, amazing boy, stepped over the fence and came to my window. I saw blood dripping from his palms. But he was measured, he was calm. 'I think you'd better not come back, Dr Papps.'

'Yes, yes,' I cried, and drove away. Was Irene on the lawn? Was that a tree, with white mad flower-face and arms like sickles?

I left another hat there that night, and that one she never gave me back.

32

Three mad females in one night. How I longed to be with my wife.

I put iodine on my scratches and whimpered at the pain but found it restored me to myself. I listened at Doris' door and heard blubbery snores, and turned the key and locked her in. Four mad females. I'd had enough. Then I lay in my bed and cursed all women – and wanted one badly, right then. Not Rhona. I no longer loved Rhona in that way. Mrs Verryt. I wanted couplings brutal, orgiastic; and I groaned the night away in rage and desire.

Next day, with crescent cuts in my brow, I stayed home. I had a bath, then poured buckets of cold water on my head, and once again I was restored. I threw my ruined trousers in the rubbish and considered sending Irene a bill. I thought I might complain to the police and ask to have Queenie destroyed; and I raided the bin and pulled the trousers out as evidence. But one look was enough. That gaping hole made me feel bitten away and I threw them back and went, stomach sick, into the house. What I would do was scratch the silly bitch (Irene, not Queenie) out of my life.

It wasn't till halfway through the morning that I considered what I'd said to her, and saw her behaviour as denial, and its extravagance as justified. Almost. I had not deserved that mad she-wolf and I shivered as I saw her wet teeth rising and felt her hanging in my crotch. I hadn't deserved it. Irene was insane and should be with Rhona at Soddy's Point.

Manifold rang. I told him I'd walked into a tree and scratched my face and was a wee bit shaken still and not fit for work. Happy with Baxter's Lung Preserver, he had just the job for an invalid, he said. Verryt wanted to see my apple plots. Would I show him round? Fred Gooch was going too, and later we could look at the research farm.

'Exactly what I need. An afternoon with a boring Dutchman.'

'Hee hee, now now,' Manifold said, and hung up.

So there we were, two o'clock on a fine Jessop day, walking in the trees, Cox's Orange, Jonathan, Delicious, and I was explaining how these had been sprayed with borax, and these with borax and lime, only last week, and another application would go on in a few days. And these had been top-dressed, half a pound per tree, and what we had to determine was the rate of penetration to the root zone. Over here, now, were injected trees, but we seemed to be getting leaf-scald, and injection wasn't a method orchardists favoured anyway. Now it was Verryt's turn to yawn. His wife yawned too. Have I mentioned she was there? She did not cover her mouth but showed white teeth and curled-back tongue. She stretched her little body and worked her fingers like a pianist. Her hands were roly-poly and her feet plump in her shoes, and I imagined breasts white as dumplings, doughy to touch. That was an unexcited thought. I'd had my way with her in the night. I did not need or want her any more.

'Of course,' I said, 'we've got the same experiments in other orchards too, different soil types. But we know the cause – lack of boron. It's just the methods, penetration, application, we're still sorting out.'

'And these over here?' Verryt asked.

'Oh, that's a nitrogen experiment. There's a dressing of amm. sulphate and dried blood. But you see, we get heavy foliage with too much nitrogen. And then we get woolly aphis infestation. Fred's department.'

Verryt perked up with insects in the game. He used his height to peer down on leaves. He stooped under branches and uncoiled into tree-tops. I began to think he wasn't a bad chap. And Fred was taken with him. They strolled, hands behind backs, and talked of parasites and Fred described the release of the Cinnabar moth for ragwort control, and the Chilian saw-fly for bidi-bidi.

'How do you know these saw-flies won't grow as big as eagles and carry off the babies from their cradles?' Mrs Verryt.

'Ha! My wife makes a joke.'

'Ha, ha,' Fred said.

'I'm not making jokes. This economic entymology – is that how you call it? – everything is guesswork. You assume knowledge of all the forms and factors of Nature. You are aping God.'

'I do not know why she speaks like this. She does not believe in God.'

'He's useful as a concept. He's an interesting model. You, as scientists, should understand that. Doctor Papps spoke of him last night.'

'I was joking.' Dr Papps.

'Your joke had a point. It made your bishop squeak.'

'My wife – '

'Is tired of insects. Dr Gooch will show you where they breed. And you can watch. I will sit in the sun with Dr Papps.'

Verryt said, 'Ah.' He looked at her with a beaky smile and then gave a shrug and said to me, 'Perhaps you will be kind enough, Dr Papps. And Dr Gooch and I . . .' He gestured into the distance with his hand.

What could I say? Verryt and Fred Gooch walked off through the trees and left me with her. 'You were bored with him and he's bored with you. Tat for tit.'

'Tit for tat, actually. You don't seem to approve of your husband's work?'

'I do. He is very useful. But I was born to argue. It is necessary.'

We came out of the shade and stood on a slope dropping to the inlet. A high tide was drowning the marsh. We heard a fizz and crackle as it advanced and smelled salt and iodine and decay.

'Let us sit.' We made places in the grass, three feet apart. Mrs Verryt kicked off her shoes and lit a cigarette.

'You have a wife but she is unwell. Dr Manifold tells me.'

'Yes,' I said, and pointed across the inlet at Soddy's Point. 'She's in there.'

'Unwell in her mind?'

'Yes. No cure.' I told her about Rhona without emotion, watching the white building over the sea.

'That is sad. Also happy. She is happy?'

146

'Yes.'

'But not a part of this any more.' She touched head and breast and I saw she meant struggle and pain, and meant they were necessary. 'And so you have a wife no good to you. And I a husband. The scratches on your head. That is Miss Lomax?'

'I said something stupid to her.'

'It must have been very stupid. You need a new lady to put between you and your wife. So that you can carry on. But not Miss Lomax. Not her, I think.'

'I've got my work.'

'And I have mine. That is good.' She lay on her elbow and looked at the orchard. 'It is the wrong season. I would like to tempt you with an apple.'

'Come back in the summer.' It's a mystery how she made me desire her, this dumpy little woman with her fat hands and feet and froggy eyes. I stalled a bit, asked about her books. She told me she had only written one but would start another when she got home. She was, she said, a medievalist.

'Great days,' I said. 'I'd like to have been alive. A knight in armour.'

'Ha! The terrible worm in the iron cocoon. That is your knight. And murder and pillage and looting were his trade. Chivalry was a game he played with his own kind. Murdering peasants was another game. Atrocious times. All times are atrocious.'

'Surely not –'

'I am not a good historian. I have too many resentments and too much anger. Which increases when I look around me at the world.'

'That's too pessimistic –'

'Another war is coming and it will be worse than the last. Today I will not think of it. Say nothing, Dr Papps. No stupidities or I will scratch. We have warm sun and grass. We will make love.'

I made a show of unwillingness but she laughed. 'I shall call you Plotinus. Plotinus blushed with shame because he had a body.'

'It's not shame. I'm not ashamed.'

'Then what? Do you think I am too ugly? You would like pretty pink cheeks and blue eyes and legs so long?' She cupped her hand on her vulva (the right name but wrong word, in the circumstances. What shall I use? Mount of Venus? Is that better?) 'Ugly face,' she said, 'so you think I must be ugly all through. Ugly down here.'

147

'No, no, of course not. I'm sure it's . . . I'll bet it's . . .'

'You do not like me to be so bold? You think I should sigh and wait for you?'

'No, your husband – '

'He knows. That is why I sent him away. He is a kind man.'

So we made love, there in the grass, in the sun. But first she had to cure me of a cramp in my leg. I used to get them frequently when nervous. I got them in bumpy landings in aeroplanes, and with women, and once had one . . . but I'll come to that. Mrs Verryt pushed back my toes and stretched my leg. She kneaded my thigh, then unbuttoned me, and, as I've said, we made love.

Irene is music. Mrs Verryt is sexual joy. I mean we reached a kind of pleasure plateau and crossed it together and climbed the little peak at the end, and all this with none of the voraciousness I'd feared, but give and take on a very high level. And a marvellous attentiveness. It's possible to be solo in these things, but Mrs Verryt made herself remarkably present and kept me remarkably aware – not just of her person but her self. She, we, did nothing out of the ordinary. I have no tale to tell of positions and gymnastics. You'll get no close-up of busy parts. I have just my tale of the plain Dutch wife who taught me joy.

Later in my life I knew her again. And there's another tale, but I'll tell it in its place. We rose from the grass and became Dr Papps and Mrs Verryt. 'That was fun.'

'It was risky.' The road ran by fifty yards away and the orchard manager's house was round the knoll. I heard his child's squeaky bike in the yard; and imagined I heard Rhona singing to herself, across the stretch of warm brown shallow sea. We had made a star shape in the grass, magnified. But I did not think Rhona would feel betrayed. Her eyes kept their bright incurious stare.

'Love is more fun out of doors. In Holland it is hard to find a place.'

'Holland,' I said, 'is a little poddle.'

She laughed.

'Full of tulips and windmills and smelly cheese.'

She laughed again. I seemed to please her.

We climbed down to the water and paddled in the brine. That hour stands to one side of my life and has no part in its forward rush, or forward creep. It seems like yesterday afternoon. It seems like tomorrow. And sometimes it's a dusty picture hanging in a room in an old old house. Those are occasions when my body affronts me, when my bones creak and belly snores. But I carry that picture to the window, hold it in the sun, dust it off; and feel I can run a hand through my hair and spring up and find her again.

By the way, Mrs Verryt kept her spectacles on.

33

There's a marvellous fellow down south calling for the death penalty for adulterers. A statute of limitations won't apply. He wants homosexuals executed too, and rebellious children. I'm sure he'd make a longer list if invited to. Sabbath-breakers, thieves, pornographers, atheists, abortionists, militant feminists, sex educators, blasphemers, communists, divorce lawyers, prison reformers. I could fill this page up if I tried. Disobedient wives, radical teachers, poets, punk-rockers, over-stayers. Novel-readers, librarians. Quakers, Catholics, Hari Krishnas. Cat-lovers, humanists. He's got a fat face and a burning eye and looks so closely shaven, so squeaky clean, I imagine him drinking Lysol with his meals. Armageddon is coming, he proclaims, and let us rejoice and welcome it. The executioner, evidently, is God.

I approve of this fellow. He makes me pleased with my sins. 'You and Shane will be on his list,' I said to Kate. 'He's on mine,' Kate replied. Every ideology has its hit list.

But Kate is less angry than she was. I notice it in all sorts of ways. When she sets the table she makes sure the knives and forks are straight. She doesn't drop bombs of mashed potato but makes smooth eggs with a tablespoon and lays them in clutches on the plate. She chews her food more slowly and compliments herself on the taste. Let me see. Instead of crumpling waste paper and firing it at the basket she walks across and drops it in. We no longer have balled-up envelopes on the kitchen floor. She used to lean on the sundeck rail and spit at the ducks in the river. (Phil, as a boy, could spit twenty feet but Kate can do better than that.) Now she takes out slices of bread and flies them down like frisbees, and claps her hands when they drop in gardens on the other side. She doesn't butt my ankles with the vacuum cleaner but lifts my feet and cleans under them.

It's unnatural. There's no solid under-pinning for her happiness. It's as if she's practising levitation. Sooner or later she'll tumble down.

Shane is painting the outbuildings on Phil Dockery's stud farm. He's off at seven o'clock in the morning and not back till half past six at night. Kate cuts him a lunch of brown bread sandwiches. Now and then she bakes him a bacon and egg pie. His thermos flask holds four cups of coffee. That much coffee acts as a poison, she believes, but it keeps him warm out there at Long Tom's so she doesn't argue. It's only for a little while, she says.

Shane is bringing home more than five hundred dollars a week. He's as pleased with himself as a stone-age hunter bringing meat. He slapped fifty dollars on the table in front of me. 'That's for all that booze of yours I'm drinking.' 'Come on,' I said, 'you've paid for that by painting my house.' He wouldn't listen. Two or three nights a week he brings home a cauliflower or cabbage from the commune over the hill, or a side-car full of pine cones gathered in the forest. We have fires that roar in the chimney and we sit three in a row on the sofa drinking hot toddies and watching TV. Shane prefers American shows and Kate British, but they're considerate, they have little competitions in self-sacrifice; and Kate will watch *The A-Team*, giving from time to time an ambiguous snort, and Shane will watch *Minder*, and be disappointed in the number of fights. Everything is too noisy for me and I go to bed.

We listen to Kate's records in the day. And he takes his Walkman off to work and listens there.

She's not in love. She's not alone. If I were religious I'd pray for her. As it is, I cross my fingers now and then.

He's not her first man, not by a long chalk. She won't say how many, I'd think badly of her. I don't believe that means she was promiscuous but that her standards have been high. None of her men have measured up so she's tried the next. What is it then she's finding in Shane? Does she sense, along with me, that he's waiting for something? Is it what he will become she's going to love? I don't think she realizes he's scared.

'What would your mother think of him, Kate?'

'She'd like him. Dad's the one who's a snob.'

Pam married out of the Labour party into the National. That's a way of putting it. Kate, probably because of her dad, has come back to base. At university she was in a mixed flat and 'got serious' with one of the boys. 'He was so damn good-looking he should have been framed.' But she quickly found there was nothing to him. 'You could poke a hole in him with your finger and look at the view out the other side.' Now he's 'a poncing little lawyer'. Then she 'got in pretty deep' with a journalist. Her language is a mixture of violence and cliché. I'm sorry I started her off on her men because they make her 'lose her cool'. This journalist was 'a wanker'. She took him to visit Kitty in the nursing home and he started 'greasing up to her'. Wanted to be in politics himself and thought Kitty might be worth having on his side. She saw through him, 'chewed him up and spat him out'.

'I seemed to fall for lightweights,' Kate said; and went on to describe a couple more.

I can see Shane's attraction. Whatever his shortcomings, he's no lightweight. No one will poke a hole in him.

He comes to sit beside me on the sofa and I bob like a dinghy on a wave.

'How much do you weigh, Shane?'

'Ninety-two.'

I convert that to imperial. 'Fifteen stone.' That's more than two of me. He could sit me on his shoulder like a parrot and I could squawk his thoughts for him. That would make no demand on my vocabulary; but there's more than squawk in what he says. Words connect with experience, no gap between. So when he says, 'I'm buggered', there's sweat, there's aching muscle, in the word.

I ask about his life before he came to Jessop. He's had ten jobs in the seven years since he left school. The worst of them: scalder and plucker in a poultry abattoir. Then he thinks a bit. No, he decides, that wasn't the worst. He started in a clothing factory humping bolts of cloth – dogsbody, everybody's boy. It wasn't the hard work he minded. He liked running round, having plenty to do. The bad thing was the women and the game they played with him.

'Oh, Shane,' said Miss Callendar in the office, 'run down to the cutting room and ask Mrs Bracey for the Fallopian tubes.' (Kate snorts and Shane says heavily. 'You think it's funny, eh?') He asks for them and Mrs Bracey hunts and shakes her head. She sends him to the machine shop and the forewoman sends him down to stores. From there he traipses back to the office. 'Nobody knows where they are, Miss Callendar,' he says. 'Oh Shane, they've got to be somewhere. Ask again.' They ran him round all afternoon, couldn't have had more fun sticking pins in him. The next day he had a new name. 'Tubes, clear this stuff out. Pronto, Tubes.'

Shane went down to the library that night and looked up Fallopian tubes in a dictionary. 'Yeah,' he says, 'I should have known. We did biology at school.' He didn't go to the factory next morning but went to a by-products plant where they made fertilizer and pig food. A mate of his worked there. Shane came away with a sack of 'specials'. See him grin now, what a grin of delight. He spills them out for me on the sofa: sheep's feet, fish heads, chicken entrails, feathers, bits of hide, dead kittens from the SPCA. My stomach makes a heave at the naming. He empties the sack on Miss Callendar's desk. She screams as though she's stabbed with a Bowie knife. 'I found the Fallopian tubes, Miss Callendar.'

Kate has gone pale. 'Just like you,' she says. 'Overkill.'

'I was getting even. It's no worse than what they did to me.'

I agree with Shane. But I'm not surprised to hear they ran him in. It was his first conviction. He has two more for disorderly conduct – fighting in pubs.

'Do you like fighting?'

'No, I lose my temper. My mind goes kind of red. I nearly tore one joker's head right off. Lucky they stopped me. I've got it sorted out now.' He does not believe it and the deception makes him blink. 'It's bloody ancient history. Give us a tinnie, Kate.'

'What was your best job?' I help him away from the subject of his rage; for I see rage as a primal condition, and see he's afflicted with connections to a state most of us have managed the step away from – though it chases us, it follows after – and he's afraid. (And I'm disturbed. Let's have optimistic talk.)

'Ah,' he says, 'my last one. Before I came up here. That was a good one. Wish I still had it.'

He worked in a scrap-battery yard, picking up batteries in a truck, maybe five hundred a day. He brought them back and unloaded and stacked them, then pulled on rubber gear so the acid wouldn't get to his skin, and smashed them one by one with a cleaver for the lead. He liked that part, the smashing. Eleven cents a battery, 'And,' Shane boasts, 'I could do a truck in an afternoon. The pitch ones, not the plastic, that's hard yakker.'

'Why did you leave?'

'Had to. My lead level got too high. Up to nine. The Health Department pressured the boss.'

'Well,' I said, 'you know how lead can affect you –'

'It softens your brain,' Kate says, cross still about the sack of entrails. Shane makes a Quasimodo face and lunges at her. He knows he's scored a victory over women that will last. They have a bit of a scuffle and a kiss and sit hand on thigh, hand on thigh, looking smug; and I discourse on lead (IV) oxide, PbO_2, and describe the symptoms of plumbism – wrist drop, lead colic – and Shane lets me look for a lead line on his gums (good gums, good teeth, the boy has); and I go on from there to the match girls and phossy jaw; then my chemists in their little rooms, the Curies with radiation sores on their hands, Davy sniffing 'nitrous air', and so on. It's nice to know an interesting subject. People listen.

'He's a clever little geezer,' Shane tells Kate.

34

She's planning Kitty's life again. This time she's being systematic, making a chart in many colours – green for childhood, blue for married life, red for politics. Little tributaries flow in, other lives run parallel – orange, purple, yellow, black. I'm yellow. I can hardly see myself. 'Sorry,' she says, 'it was the only colour left.' Here and there an arrow comes darting in from the margins. They are named for non-political friends. And enemies. I don't know most of them but Phil is there. And Irene Lomax. Irene has a coloured line during Kitty's girlhood but it stops in 1925. She comes back as an arrow in '41, the year Des died, and her colour runs from there until her death. I'm glad she's purple. I'm glad she comes back and comes as friend.

'She wrote to Grandma when Grandpa died.' Kate fetched the letter – the papers are filed in shoeboxes now – and let me read:

Dear Kitty,

I'm so sorry. Please believe me. I know you think I'm a waste

153

of time but we were *friends*. If I can help, if you want to talk, please come and see me.

Love,

Irene.

She did not write to me when Rhona died. That death should have softened her. She didn't write. She wrote to Kitty when her husband died. Their friendship started up again, and Kate wants to know how important it was. She's anxious to find non-political Kitty.

I told Kate the story of Des Hughes' death. I happened in the winter of 1941. Des wasn't well – but of course he was never well. He spent his days by the kitchen stove, in a cane chair with a flattened cushion, with a hotwater bottle in his lap. He fed in lumps of tea-tree and made the fire roar. When it died down he'd put his feet on the oven door. In spite of this he could not stay warm. The last time I saw him, several days before he died, Kitty had him wrapped in an eiderdown and had draped her overcoat on his head. The stove door was open and firelight played on his face, making it look painted on the wall at the end of a cave. I said hello and asked how he was – foolish question. He did not bother to look at me but read his newspaper, and once he cut a news item out with a pair of scissors. He was still, Kitty said, collecting ammunition for Bernie Molloy.

Kitty asked me to go after ten minutes. Their lavatory was at the back of the section behind a hedge and she would not let him go there but made him use a pot in the bathroom. He would not do that while I was about. I left without saying goodbye. He wouldn't have answered. I was curious to know – I'm curious still – whether, under that coat, his hair was flame-red and springing up.

I don't know what his final rage was about. Kitty never told me. The wind was dropping chimneys that night. I lost a sheet of iron from my garage roof. Hail had fallen in the afternoon and lay unmelted on my window-sills.

Des flung off his eiderdown. The scissors went clattering on the floor. He threw a lump of tea-tree at his wife and struck at her back-handed when she came at him. Brown slippers. Striped pyjamas, blue and white. His red hair was flaming like a torch. (She

154

didn't tell me this but it must be so.) Rage gave him the strength to run. By the time she'd pulled her oilskin on he was gone.

Kitty searched the streets down by the port. She went past the gasworks and along the tidal creek to the reclamation. Then she turned back and went up the hill. The wind was dying down and rain fell straight and thick and icy. She found Des in the park on top of the hill. There's a band rotunda there but he hadn't sheltered. He sat in the open, on a bench. Like Les Dockery, he was on a bench. He could not move, or speak, or see who it was lifting him. By then, of course, though he was alive he'd killed himself.

Kitty half-carried, half-dragged him home. She peeled him naked and put him in a bath that stung her hands, but when she lifted him out his skin was as cold as a stone from a creek. She wrapped him in blankets and put him in bed. Although his eyes were open and he made sounds with his mouth she did not believe he saw or spoke.

The doctor came, and the ambulance, but there was no bringing Des Hughes back. He died in hospital the next day, and Kitty kept herself dry-eyed at the funeral and nodded sharp and hard at Bernie Molloy's praise of him.

'And that's all she told you?'

Not as much as that, I used my imagination. Kitty didn't tell me much at all. Kate's suspicious. She thinks I'm keeping something back, but what I'm doing is not allowing myself to invent too much. Invent is wrong, imagine it should be. I think I could have said how Kitty felt; but she didn't tell me, so I won't.

'Well,' Kate said – there's calculation in her, what does she know? – 'it's going to be a hard chapter to write.'

It's going to be a hard book to write. I'm starting to believe Kate can do it. She's like Kitty in so many ways.

35

Now I'm there. I can't put it off, even though it makes the shape all wrong. Two deaths in a row. That puts an ugly bulge in my story. It weakens the structure all round. One's enough. Save the other for later.

Story? Structure? I'm not playing that sort of game. All I'm doing is remembering and putting down. What does it matter how it's shaped. Let's have *three* deaths. Let me put down that my father died. 1942. Without any fuss. And Kitty cried at his funeral; and I did not keep dry eyes myself.

It was my second trip from Wellington that month. First came Rhona's funeral. I'd sailed out from Jessop on the ferry and had just sat down in my new office, my important job, when the message came. Back I sailed. And two weeks later did the same for Dad.

Kitty cried for Rhona too. Did you ever see her drop a tear, Kate? I'll bet you didn't. A tough old biddy, that's the opinion. Iron pants. Battle axe. One reporter forgot her sex and called her the Labour party's rogue elephant. And it has to be said that she rolled along like an elephant. Elephantine? Elephanterotic? Certainly not. Kitty, in her prime, was genderless.

You see what this is? Evasive action. I should have a stance I can take – but I don't. No position. It gets me differently every time. Rhona's death.

Wasn't there something Kate wanted to know? Irene and Kitty. They were friends again *before* Rhona died.

36

She was on the phone the moment I mentioned him. I thought she'd ask to visit him at his house but she invited him here, the last thing I want. It seems he does his work in the morning and goes out walking in the afternoon. He would be happy to come round.

I'd seen him several times on the river bank, throwing sticks for a huge Alsatian, and I called to Kate, 'Tell him not to bring his dog.' Thinking about it made my scrotum shrink. I was too late, she was hanging up, and half an hour later there he was, crossing the bridge in the drizzle, with the beast at his side. Its shoulders almost came up to his waist.

'It's not coming in the house, Kate. You tell him.'

It seems I have no rights here. It's the size of a timberwolf and it lay by his feet with its jaws on the mat, frowning like a judge and keeping its eyes on every move I made. It's a male, Prince – no imagination – the third dog he's had since Irene died.

'A nice old fellow,' Kate said, patting its head.

Royce grinned at me – yes, grinned, the boy with the furtive smile. 'He's not related to Queenie, Noel.' Noel, at last. And a joke. Confident as he moves into old age.

'He's the same breed. I don't trust that breed. You saw that case last week?' A man in Porirua with lumps torn out of his arms and one of his legs bitten to the bone. Dreadful phrase, bitten to the bone. I shivered as I looked at Prince.

Royce put his foot on the animal's back. 'There. How's that?'

Not much better. He has the body of an elderly dachshund and a pointy terrier face. Did he really think he could control the beast? Yet I remembered him hauling Queenie off and putting his bleeding hands on my car door. He's not a person to be categorized. His dimensions shift as you watch.

Kate made tea and fed the dog a chocolate biscuit, which took its attention away from me. She made some chat about NZ art, sounding both easy and ignorant, and Royce, greedy at his biscuits and sugared tea – 'have some tea with your sugar,' my mother would have said – made polite affirmatives, and seemed to me equally ignorant. Finally he said, 'I don't look much at other people's work. I haven't heard of some of these people.'

'Oh well,' Kate said, and laughed. She was pleased to have that out of the way. 'What I wanted to ask about was Kitty Hughes. She was best friends with your sister, wasn't she?'

'Twice,' Royce said.

Kate grinned, but her teeth looked sharp. She was, I think, offended on Kitty's behalf. 'I was wondering if there were any letters. From Kitty I mean. To Irene. Irene wrote to Kitty, I know.'

Royce took another biscuit.'Heaps,' he said. 'Kitty wrote all the time. Almost once a week. From Wellington, you know, when she was over there in parliament. Big fat letters. Irene used to read bits out to me. She used to let her hair down with Irene.'

'Yes?' Kate cried.

'Some of the people I'd heard of. Nash, I'd heard of. And Sid Holland. Some of it was ripe. Girls together, you know. Irene used to like a bit of smut.'

'So did Kitty,' I said.

'Can I read them? For my book? I'm writing Kitty Hughes' life.'

'Read them?' Crumbs dropped from his lips and he cupped a hand to catch them in his lap.

'If you like I won't say who they were to.'

'But I haven't got them any more. I burned them all. When Irene died.' He saw from Kate's expression that he'd done something terrible. Kate, indeed, looked as if she was punched in the stomach. Her mouth dropped open, her cheeks went white, then started to mottle. 'Shit!' she whispered.

'Have I done something wrong? I read some of them and I never thought –'

'You fucking twerp.'

'Kate,' I said, 'watch your language.'

Prince rose to his feet, with spiky neck, and rumbled at her.

'He's burned Kitty's letters.'

'They belonged to him.'

'They did not. They belonged to . . .'

'You?'

'No. But. . .' Too down-to-earth a girl to say mankind, posterity.

Royce put his hand on Prince's back and forced him down. He'd recovered himself and made some happy munches on his biscuit. 'Well, it's done. *Fait accompli.* Lie still, Prince. I burned lots of stuff. Christmas cards. Invitations. I thought I was doing Kitty a favour. As a matter of fact, I remember her telling Irene to make sure they were burned. And Irene said she'd use them for blackmail. They trusted each other. I had to do what Irene would have done.'

'You did not.'

Royce, for the first time, looked sharp. His nose became a pecking instrument. 'Oh yes I did. Quiet Prince, she's not going to hurt me.'

Kate clenched and unclenched her fists. She controlled herself. 'Fire, rats and female relations.'

'What?'

'The enemies of . . .' Still no acceptable term. 'All right. They're burned. The lot, I suppose? There's nothing left?'

'Oh, the lot.'

'You said you read some. Do you remember what they said?'

'Not much. I didn't read much. The tone was, well, malicious.

Irene was malicious too. I've got no illusions about her.'

'If there's anything you remember, it'll help.' She had become heavy, dull.

'I remember about Nash. He was Prime Minister, wasn't he? The cough drops man.'

'What did she say?'

'It was rather clever. She said he had a widdler – she bet he had one curled up like a little caterpillar.'

I laughed, but Kate, frowning – she'd got a scratch pad out – wrote it down. 'Are you sure it was widdler?'

'Well, it wasn't. Here.' He held out his hand for Kate's pad and wrote a word. Blushing, he gave it back, and Kate grunted.

'They egged each other on a bit, with language,' Royce said.

'What about the others? Fraser? Semple?'

'No.'

'Holland?'

'Oh yes. She said he had a mouth like a baboon's posterior. I remember that. It wasn't original, I thought.'

'It wasn't posterior either,' Kate said.

He blushed again; and Kate wrote 'bum'.

'What else?'

'I can't remember. Honestly, I didn't take much notice. I thought it was all a bit – I don't know – juvenile.'

'She had to relax. She was human too.'

'Oh, of course. I remember – there were other women, weren't there? In parliament? A Labour one?'

'Mabel Howard?'

'Yes. And a National.'

'Hilda Ross.'

'That's right. She said some dreadful things about them. And a woman on the radio, who gabbled . . .'

'Aunt Daisy.'

'Kitty did a marvellous Aunt Daisy imitation,' I said. And I tried to do it, and managed well, having some talent in that way. 'Good morning, everybody. Good moo-orning. And it's glorious weather here in Wellington. The birds are singing, the sky's a lovely blue, and when I got up this morning the sun was shining right up my back passage.'

Kate laughed, and said, 'An old joke. The voice is OK though.'

'She called milk cow-juice. And eggs cackle-berries. Little girl stuff. With Irene, I mean. Not in letters. They were always giggling.'

'And in the letters,' Royce said, 'she was always slinging off. And skiting. And whining.'

'Hardly.'

'Oh yes. People weren't fair. They did things behind her back. That sort of thing.'

'That doesn't sound like Kitty.'

'What you've got to remember,' I said, 'is that Irene was the only person she had. Outside family. Outside politics. Somewhere she could go and be herself. Without being judged.'

'What about you?'

'I judged her.'

'God,' Royce said, and blushed again, 'God was the Pieman.'

'The Pieman in the Sky.'

'Yes. She said, let me see – he was served a mouldy pie by the Pieman in the Sky. *She* was served . . .' He shot a look at me and trailed away.

'Who?' I said.

He shook his head. But I'm in a state of preternatural receptivity to things rising out of that time. Rhona, that was who. I said her name, and although Royce claimed not to remember, I was right. I seemed to feel muddy water lapping at my mouth, and ignorance and squalor all about me. Calculating niece, blushing dauber, unsavoury dog – I won't say where he fell to licking – locked me in. And Irene and Kitty locked me in. Malice, squalor, ignorance. I wanted Rhona's long clear open gaze. Empty. Blue.

I'll be fair to Royce Lomax, he's impressive. He's unpindownable, with his clownish body, comic and soft, but that hard privateness in his mind. He's squashable, he's inviolable. Remember those clowns with huge stiff pants open like a barrel at the waist, and all sorts of things stored down there. Sausages, sledgehammers, boots, balloons. Am I right in thinking they wore just singlets on top, and were thin, pale, bony up there? Breakable. And sad in face, but unbreakable. It's no accurate description of Royce, but it comes a little way at the fracture in his being.

Kate kept jabbing him with questions. She got her tape recorder and made a new start; and wanted my imitation of Kitty's Aunt Daisy. I said I'd do it later. Royce was obliging. Up to a point. He said 'bum' (for posterity) but wouldn't say the other word. Kate said it for him. Then he had another cup of tea. He's a great tea-drinker. That's probably what has dragged all his weight down to his middle and shortened him.

Clouds with grey torn bellies came at eye level from the sea, dropping rain as fat as bantam eggs. It thickened up and thundered on my roof. When I put the new living-room on I made the roof iron (wriggly tin) so I could bring storms inside my house. It's like living at the back of a waterfall sometimes.

Royce likes it. He stood at the window and sucked the weather in through his nose. Lightning cracked like a whip down the hill. 'Nice,' he said. Another Royce. I'll have to start counting. The dog whined and he flattened it on the mat with a finger dab. Thunder came, a hard shallow crack, then a long deep rumble. 'Indigestion,' Kate said, but he made that same finger dab at her. 'Will the river come up?'

'Depends what the weather's been like up in the catchment. It looks like it though.' And I became eloquent. I have a little love affair with the river. 'More moods than a woman,' I said – offensive and trite, it made Kate hiss – and showed how it had changed colour and got a new liveliness on its surface, which meant it was up an inch already.

'When it touches the sewer pipe we've got a flood.'

'Breaks the pipe?'

'Every two or three years. Here come the ducks.'

They boated down, buoyant as corks. The river turned yellow, then brown, and covered the pediment of the bridge. Islands of dead leaves and twigs floated by. 'The logs will start in a moment,' I said, showing off my river.

'She's quick. She's sudden.'

I was jealous of that 'she'. How had he become so intimate with her? I never questioned that it was genuine.

We watched for half an hour and saw a rise of three feet or so. A fresh not a flood, but full of little coils and whips and tongues. Two or three black logs, a piece of foam plastic. A van went up the valley with canoes lashed on top and shortly afterwards the fleet came down, with two metres of headroom under the pipe.

'Sometimes we get jet boats going up.'

Now I suffered that finger dab. He wanted nothing but what he could see and I felt myself anxious that he should have it. Kate had gone to her room. The dog was sleeping. The rain made the roar of tipping shingle on my roof. Houses, cold houses. Gleaming cars. Misty hill with red and yellow, leached and cold. On the bridge, two women. White coat, red coat, slick as satin ball gowns. The quarry face, flayed muscle, slippery. I felt I should offer him that, I felt I was seeing, but he kept me quiet and kept me still; and in the end I stopped collecting things and saw just the moving river and the hill.

At last, when he'd turned away and had his dog at his hip, I fell to grinning and spilled some chatter. I was feeling good. My river, my storm. I'd had him round for a kind of meal and felt the thing had gone off very well. I called Kate and gave her my car keys and told her to run Royce home. 'No, no,' he said; but I gave a lordly wave. My turn now. Last words in my house were my right.

Kate was grumpy, but saw he couldn't walk in the rain. Off they went, and drove over the bridge with the dog sitting up like royalty on the back seat. When Kate came back she parodied him. 'He had a widdler like a caterpillar.' She sat in his chair and put her clasped hands between her thighs in just his way, and made me laugh. She has names for him now – the Caterpillar, the Widdler, the Female Relation. And because she's still sore about those letters the last will win in spite of her feminism.

I didn't want his visit but I'm glad he came. A bit of pain, a bit of pleasure, a dash of mystery. It's perked me up.

I've known Royce all his life and though I snicker at him, and sneer, I find now certain things to admire, and things to like.

37

I'll do a soirée. Sam Weller called them *swarry*. My father did a good Sam Weller act. That's by the way. A swarry at the Lomax house, 1948.

Who was there? Irene and Royce Lomax. Kitty Hughes. Pam Hughes. Noel Papps and Ruth Verryt. Phil and Sylvia Dockery. A lawyer, Bagley. A music teacher, Pauli. The principal of the School of Music. The Dean of the cathedral. Several others, nondescript (important to themselves of course).

I had been two or three years reinstated as Irene's friend. I'd come back to the Lomax at the end of the war. Fred Gooch was gone. Most of the old-timers were gone. John Dye was the new Director and I was Assistant-Director. That was only partly administrative. I was in the field and in my lab most of the time.

I wrote to Irene. I suppose that letter went up in smoke along with Kitty's. I said – and I believed – a new age had started. Wars were over, human foolishness too (I wrote that the year after the atom bomb was dropped), and I hoped Irene would let me call.

She allowed it but did not make me welcome. She found it necessary to make me suffer – so Kitty put it – and playing the grand lady was her way. She always had somebody else there: little Pauli (a big fat fellow), Bagley in his hair-piece that made him look as if he'd had a new top fitted on his head. Bagley sang lieder in bad German and sounded as if his teeth were hurting him. Pauli turned the pages. I stood in a corner and smiled. It didn't punish me, it simply made me fonder of silly Irene. My cheerfulness made her curious, and we talked; and she stopped being silly and we found that we were forty and our minds had taken weight. I don't mean we'd grown intelligent (see above), we just had expectations (some of them) that could be met. We soon arrived back on a good footing. And Irene turned to me as Bagley sang, and gave a wink. Poor Bagley had false expectations. 'He is quite good though,' Irene said. 'He's Jessop good.'

So, I was back, and Kitty was back, both modified; and Phil came once, on the night of the swarry. He came in looking cocky as a defence. 'This ain't my sort of shebang.' Sylvia had dragged him. She sang duets with Baldy Bagley, the Jessop Cuckoo. 'Try not to rock the boat,' I said.

'You playing butler? Buttle me up a drink.' And when I'd brought it – 'So that's your little wop sheila, eh? Sooner you than me, mate.'

I nearly hit him. It was the closest I ever came. Phil's requirements are inhuman – that women at parties be ravishing and submit to him on the spot. I'm calm about it now, yes, I'm calm. I've never told him that my times in bed with Ruth Verryt brought me pleasures he could only dream of. If sex is what we must talk about –

No, why should I? He always manages to lower the tone. Ruth
was more than bed-mate. I'll come to it, and how she showed up in
my life again. I'll even let Phil have a last word here. The Dutch
pronunciation of Ruth was a gift, he smirked and cackled at it,
gleamed his teeth, and all year long asked how she was getting on.
I answered straight and easy, 'Good as gold.' Phil made no mark on
us, did not come near, and when we noticed him felt him deprived.
Last word to me.

Now, this swarry. Which had me in a state of edginess. One of
the reasons I was there was to prove to Ruth that Jessop could
produce something worthwhile. At some point in the evening the
silliness would stop, Irene would play. 'You expect me to believe
that? She is good? That silly lady in the silly dress?' Sometimes I
was close to hitting *Ruth*. But she was there, enjoying it. She drank
up people when they puffed themselves, she savoured their pre-
tentions like wine; they made her very quiet, and gay inside.

I guided her across the room and said, 'Ruth, this is my sister
Kitty. And this is my niece Pam. Kitty shouldn't be here. She
should be in disguise.'

'Ah,' Ruth said, 'because you are a socialist. Then I should not be
here. I am socialist too.'

Kitty was forty-five and in her prime. She had a majestic full-
chinned beauty. Double-barrelled words describe her best: deep-
eyed, straight-nosed, heavy-bosomed, lively-minded. This was the
time of Kitty at her most open. She had not come to roll and lumber
yet, like a water beast, and her mind was free of the ponderous
forward thrust, lightened only by anger, that made her so formid-
able in the years most people think of as her prime. They are
wrong. Kitty's prime was now, two or three years in which she
marked time and was happy.

Irene had tried to improve her dress, tried to teach her make-up,
and had failed. Kitty was neat, Kitty was clean, and that, she
claimed, was enough. Her dresses and skirts were simple and she
usually wore a hand-knitted cardigan. And a brooch. And her
wedding ring. That was all. She hated hats, which made her feel as
if something was sitting on her brain, some silly rule she had to
obey. (Irene loved hats.) On state occasions people used to watch,
and nudge each other: there, off it came, as soon as Kitty could get
away with it. Another thing they watched for was her smokes. She

rolled her own, fine-cut Greys from a Desert Gold tin, and it showed, they said, how genuine she was. But I'm getting ahead. She took out her Desert Gold tin that night at the swarry. Her papers – tishies, she called them – were inside with the tobacco. And Ruth watched with delight the paper held on the lower lip, the stretching of tobacco on the palm; then finger flick, and roll, and lick, all in the space of a breath or two. She asked if she could try it.

Phil came across and joined in but it was Pam who attracted him. A robust girl, big-bodied like her Ma but with a golden colouring, and with that lovely freshness of the young. You want to touch and taste them. They're like apples. To Phil though Pam was a peach. 'That's a peach of a daughter, Kitty.' Kitty said flatly, 'Hands off, Phil.' The girl was out of earshot, rolling cigarettes with Ruth. 'Hey, hey,' Phil said, holding up his hands to show he had no bad intentions.

'My daughter's no bit of property. Look after your wife.' That was Kitty's blunt way. Phil enjoyed it. Her antagonism complimented him. He did not go his ox-blood red but a kind of lolly pleasure-pink. He grinned at Kitty and patted her rump.

'You'll cop one, Phil. I'm warning you.'

He stepped out of range. 'OK, comrade. Don't shoot.' Halfway through the night he started calling her Olga; and this remained his name for her for the rest of her life. (Olga, Comrade Olga, Olga Pappski, and, in his ox-blood state, Comrade Crappski.)

Ruth and Pam had made cigarettes and were giggling in a corner. They looked both delightful and depraved with those white droopers on their lips. Irene sent a frown at them. She was, as Kitty said, dressed up to the nines. The full-length dress, crimson and, I thought, a bit like a nightie, hid her feet and made her seem to slide about the room on castors. Irene up to Kitty and Phil in a sweet curve that glanced off several people on the way: 'I hope you two aren't going to stage a wrestling match.'

'If it'll help to get your party cracking.'

'It's not a party Phil, it's a musical evening.'

'You're not going to let Baldy Bagley sing? Gimme another drink, Noel. And some cotton wool for me ears.'

I can't think of another time the four of us were together. That's why the swarry suggests itself. But what am I to say about us, Irene, Kitty, Phil, Noel Papps? The brainy ones from Standard six,

Tup Ogier's 1915 quartet. Thirty years, thirty-three years later, would Tup have been proud of us? Would he have been even satisfied? Let me think of some words. Adulterer. That's me. Poseur, schemer, profiteer, dissembler; OK, lecher, liar, cheat, let's get tough. Adjectives: violent – no, murderous – indifferent (callous, uncaring, that's to say), pretentious, hypocritical, envious, and secretive, and greedy, and proud: cruel (in many ways), and afraid. I could go on, but that's enough. Share those round. And I could balance things with another list. Generous, loyal. Take it as read. But when they're both complete what have we learned? I can't see anything there except that we were an ordinary bunch. Each one special to himself, herself. That's it, eh? One gets back to being alone. I can say nothing true about the others: well, name and age and outward circumstances. But of course I'm going to try more than that. The whole truth about us is not that we made a set, but the whole truth is impossible and I don't need it anyway. I'll only get the part I need by letting the occasion run along, letting the geometry take shape.

Tup? He wouldn't have been proud or satisfied. Happy. Unhappy. I think he'd have been interested.

Now and then Phil approached his wife. He sidled up, or glided, waltzing step, and squeezed her arm or tapped her jaw, then winked at Bagley and clicked his tongue. She spent her time with Bagley and sang a gluey duet with him late in the night; and several months later, when Phil had kicked her out or she'd left him, she took the ferry with Bagley and started life anew. (That was in the song.) I saw them once, old and bravely smiling, in a television talent quest. They sang about strangers meeting in a crowded room, and they didn't win. They were far from being strangers to each other at Irene's, but the plan they were following was Phil's. He sent them sharky grins across the room.

'Your wife is looking very lovely, Phil,' Irene said.

'Yup,' he replied.

'She and Alan,' that was Bagley, 'sing so well together.' Irene knew something. Phil knew she knew.

'They've both got pretty hair.' A strange thing about that womanizer, he knows how to make a certain type of woman feel safe. He sends a message of neutrality, part matiness, part complicity, and they know it's not them he's after. Some even elbow him or punch him in relief and they screech at his jokes. Irene used her elbow. She didn't screech but whispered catty things about poor Bagley. Phil was my equal with Irene. No other man was. (Royce is a special case.) Bagley, Pauli, later on a violinist fellow, then a flautist, all had music in common with her, but none knew Irene Lomax, little Reen. I thought until the swarry Phil had forgotten her. But he had simply put her on one side and that night he picked her up again. The ease between them made me sulky at first, then began to please me. It worked to increase Irene and there seemed more of her for me to know.

I knew without being told that she had dressed her brother up. Grey flannel slacks, a blue blazer, and round his neck the first postwar cravat I'd seen. He spent most of his night at the window, looking out, and Irene went to him and they stood there privately; and it made me blush, the memories. She turned from him and caught my eye and smiled, and through the back of my head I felt Phil and Kitty watching too. The four of us. We were the orb within the orb, turning counter-clockwise. Even Ruth was part of an outer shell. I heard the muted purr and click of our machinery and felt us brush those others as we went by. Well, metaphor. How beautifully it works, like catalyst, or like an equals sign. It came to me as knowledge, for my need.

'When will she play?' Ruth asked.

'Soon.' Pauli had played and Bagley sung.

'Pack of phonies,' Kitty said.

'Someone should play boogie,' Phil agreed.

I wandered from the room and through the house. A dog smell in one passage turned me back. Nonogenarian Queenie snoozed her life out there, blunt in tooth, blind in eye; but she would know me. Sweat sprang in my armpits at the thought. I climbed stairs. Narrow bedroom, khaki blanket, bed unmade. Royce's cell. It instructed me, it was dogma: Royce and Irene had no further carnal need of each other. Then followed – no step in logic – their connection was a summer, coming on them in its natural time. I could have no quarrel with that; and I've never questioned it since.

Someone started playing Handel – no mean pianist – but I kept on with my exploring for I knew Irene's touch. Her room was a corner room with moulded ceiling and glass chandelier. Bay windows looked across Jessop to the cathedral. Moonlight showed a bed with a blue counterpane. Her slippers peeped out, inclining me to sadness for a moment. Women's footwear often makes me sad. Very strange. Why should it suggest mortality?

I turned on a standard lamp by the bed and made a yellow pool as deep as my chest. Not enough to show the pictures well, but I saw they were Royce's, hills and beaches, creeks and trees, and I didn't feel I was missing much. As far as I could see he'd made no progress. He'd made changes. Here and there a large object lay, or seemed to float, in the foreground: a shell, a stone, a bone. They made the balance wrong and interfered with the perspective, but it did not surprise me to find him awkward still. I thought it kind of Irene to hang so many.

One I took to be by someone else. Then I saw its likeness to the rest. The medium was different, that was all. Oil had increased his clumsiness. Hills like bits of green glass. Clouds like puff-balls, white. A yellow beach, a yellow smile, with reefs, or was it teeth? Oh dear, I thought. Blue sea, of course. But was that a shadow in the sea? Big fish, deep down? And this thing here, this shape, or no-shape, floating in the foreground, was it a cloud, pitch black? Or a head? Was it – whose was the question? – was it Irene?

Just for a moment I was afraid. Then I restored myself by criticism. He did not need the head and fish-shape both. Or teeth-like reef and glass-sharp hills with either. It was cluttered up, too full of stuff, and too much threat meant no threat at all. But in the end I came to think the whole thing accidental. I turned out the lamp and left the room and followed Irene's music down the stairs. She was on, had used Leon Pauli, or perhaps the Dean, as curtain-raiser. Kitty and Phil stood together in not-quite amity. I saw a pointed elbow in them both, but they relaxed and Kitty put her hand on his arm. Irene, I thought, created innocence. Ruth was at the window with Royce. He had a silly grin, as though perhaps she'd poked her tongue at him, and she a lumpy hardness on her face, aimed at Irene. She was surprised and unaccepting. I saw when the slump of defeat came on her and she softened to enjoy.

Sacrarium. I'm silly, sentimental. I want to use that word for the space Irene made about herself at the end of the room. It comes to me, but I hesitate. Piano as an altar. Music-making as an act of worship. That's all nonsense – and I reject it not because I might be thought to blaspheme (I'm no believer) but out of respect for Irene's toughness. When she sat at her piano there was not an ounce of silliness in her. Yet in me, that night, many nights, a feeling I claim validity for. There is, of course, no such thing as ideal beauty. It's all subjective. Yet I'm real. And in my hard centre I'm a fact. And that's where Irene penetrates, and strikes me with her fingers and makes me sound. I'll not try to name the note. I have, as I've said, a passion for naming, and so for bringing things in my control. But this thing, and several others, I cannot name.

When she was finished silliness came back. We clapped, we exclaimed, Leon Pauli led her out by the hand and she made a curtsey. And not long afterwards Bagley and Sylvia Dockery sang, sticky song. How they warbled, how they intertwined. Irene watched them with delight (I'm not sure she listened), and Ruth, at my side, gave a whimper of glee. Kitty caught my eye and questioned me with a little downturn of her mouth, dabbing at Phil. What mischief was he up to? I couldn't guess, but I watched him, apprehensive, as he moved along the side of the room, making two or three steps each time the singers paused. He came to Bagley's side as they finished, and seemed to beam on them with pride. His teeth flashed yellow-white and his friendly arm embraced Bagley's shoulders. Sylvia made her little ducking bow, and Bagley his stiff-hipped dive at the floor. He left his hair-piece in Phil's hand. He shone his white bald head at the audience, while Phil held the thing two-fingered, like a dead rat, for us to see. I laughed behind clamped teeth. I could not help it. Irene laughed. She screeched.

Sylvia ('Who is Sylvia, what is she?' Bagley sang on some other occasion) went white and streamed instant tears down her cheeks. It was not funny. She ran from the room, and Royce, good Royce, followed her, while Bagley, snarling, grabbed his hair and fitted it on. Then he marched out. And Phil, alone, began to look stupid. He sat in a chair and grinned at the floor and sipped his drink and no one approached to talk with him. I did not. Kitty and Irene did not. The sides of our figure flew apart and though we met in pairs and trios many times after we never made a four again; enclosed that space. There are all sorts of spaces though, all sorts of shapes, in my head.

What did Ruth say? Many things. She was excited. She'd had fun. Irene was not superb as I claimed, but very very good.

Excellent. Kitty too was excellent, full of strength. But Phil, he was a monster, rudimentary. 'It is the brother,' Ruth said, 'who is remarkable.'

'Royce?'

'What do you say when you want to talk but cannot talk?'

'Dumb?'

She was impatient. 'Sprakeloos. Having no words.'

'Inarticulate?'

'Yes. He has things in him. Things he must say.'

'Paint. That's what he does.'

'Paint them then. He will do it. Wait and see. Now, no more talking. After all that music, into bed. Time for love.'

Ruth, it seems to me, was remarkable.

38

She did not live with me. The times were not right. I was very careful and she made a game of keeping people just short of certainty about us. Prune-faced looks I got but no one accused us.

She did not live with me. She did not want to. I would become husband, she said, and one was enough. I would imprison her and give her looks of *do this*, *do that*, and *quickly now*, and make a baby-face and small-boy face instead of man. Was she right? Probably. I did not think so at the time; but thought us correct for other reasons. I loved it when she climbed the fence to me. Having a wife in the kitchen would not have made up for loss of that.

There was a day, summer of '48, when I sat in my sea-grass chair in the dappled shade, a glass of beer on the table beside me, a fantail doing aerobatics under the grapevine, my antique gramophone at my feet, with Mimi and Rodolfo in love, and it seemed no bad thing to be alone, a widower. Feet and torso bare, shorts turned up, legs in the sun. Comfortable, released from all that. Good for you, I told the lovers, and: Make the most of it. I knew how their story ended.

My backyard, with lemon trees, with lawn half cut, and tea-tree for my winter fire stacked in a watertank on its side, and underpants and tea-towels on the line, and butterflies and bees and mint and parsley, wooden fence on three sides, tangy with creosote – my backyard was an island outside connections, entanglements, with Mimi and Rodolfo five-minute guests, and fantail, (insect legs like whiskers in its beak) a killer I was not at all disturbed by. Beer delicious. Ham and lettuce salad digesting. No woman in my skull. Peace in my skull. My blood as slow as treacle, cool as wine.

Then she rose. Sun or moon, she rose above my fence. Sun, I think. Yes, she was warm and she beamed on me. But I'll not play sun/moon gender games – or games with her. She beamed on me but I'll keep cool and offer the precision she admired even when she was passionate. So – she had climbed a peach tree on her side of the fence until she could see into my yard, and she cried, 'Dr Papps? Noel?' I heard it as Mimi and Rodolfo drew breath, and I lifted the arm and silenced them. 'Mrs Verryt? Ruth?' I said. I stood up, beer in hand, and walked, paused, walked, and came to the fence. 'It is you, isn't it? Mrs Verryt?'

'Oh yes, it's me. I'm stuck. Help me, Noel. I want to come over.' Her rosy frog-face beamed and her eyes were huge behind her glasses. Eight white fingers with pink nails gripped the top of the fence. She was like that thing children drew at the time, or later:

What's its name?

'Wait,' I said, 'I'll get my step-ladder.' I turned and she gave a cry. 'Noel. Your back.'

'Ah. Marks. From my chair.' She told me later they were like the scars from a whipping. I set the ladder up. I sent a nervous glance at the house next door but my grapevine hid us. Balancing on top, one foot on the fence, I helped her climb; and she, with a hand on my thigh, with a rubber-ball bounciness, hopped across to join me, north to south; oceans and continents disposed of.

I'd given her no more than five minutes of my time since she had gone from Jessop ten years before; and she confessed I'd never crossed her mind. That's very healthy. That made conditions ideal for a second start. I helped her down and led her by the hand across my lawn. It was like bringing home a bride. She sat in my chair, I poured her beer, and, 'Well, well, Ruth. A miracle'; and she, 'Noel, how lovely. How peaceful it is here. How well you look.'

'And you do too. You've lost some weight.' She looked more than ten years older. Have I said she was twenty-eight when she came to Jessop the first time? Now she was thirty-eight and looked forty-five – but had gained in beauty. The petulance, impatience, the greed, were gone from her face, those things that had made little puffy lumps of white muscle in her cheeks, about her mouth; and now she was thinner, she was harder, and somehow all her dross was burned away. A plain woman still, ugly perhaps; but very pleasing to me, beautiful. And I knew – no, I discovered – that she was full of pain, and not dismayed by it, had found herself (that's a cliché) and was inviolable, though all the bad things were not done.

'Ruth, how? Tell me.'

'I heard the music. I thought there was no music in this country. So I climbed the tree to look. And it was you.'

'But . . .?' I meant the house backing on to mine, how had she come there, why was she not ten thousand miles away in Holland?

'We live there. Piet and I. We have come to Jessop. Piet has come. It was hard. We pulled some strings. Is that how you say it? I have come to help him. Then I will go back. I cannot live in a place so beautiful.'

I put that away to think about later. The husband, Dr Verryt, was over there. I watched nervously, expecting to see his top three feet unfold above the fence and turn towards me like a Martian machine. Ruth laughed. 'He is inside arranging his books. You must walk around and visit him. Do not climb the fence. That is the way I will visit you.' Suddenly she said, 'You are not married?'

'No.'

'Your wife . . .'

'She died.'

'And you? In the war?'

'I didn't go. I worked for the government. Soil research.'

'Ah. Ah. Good. I had forgotten such things. That was good.'

'I wanted to go –'

She stopped me. She put her hand towards my mouth.

'Do not. No things that are stupid. Let me hold your hand, Noel. Let me be in New Zealand. Do you make any cheese yet I can eat?'

I brought another chair and another bottle of beer and ham and pickled onions and cheddar cheese. The sun stayed out for us. The fantail made another visit, bringing its mate, and Mimi and Rodolfo fell in love again. Later we had Mozart and Beethoven, and I promised to take her to Irene's where she would hear piano-playing as good as any in Holland.

'The lady who scratched your face? She cannot play. Does she scratch you still?'

'No, that's all over.'

'And no ladies, Noel? No lady friends?'

'No lady friends. I think it wouldn't matter anyway.'

'You are not so frightened now. How frightened you were that day.'

'I guess you were a bit too much for me.'

'Not now?'

'No, not now.'

'All the same, today, I think I will sit and enjoy the sun. It is enough good luck for now.'

We held hands, and we embraced as we said goodbye, and that was enough. As we crossed the lawn she worked out the field of fire from neighbours' eyes. Very serious. 'I will buy a ladder, Noel, like yours, and put it in the corner by that tree. And you put yours there, see? I will step across.'

'I could take a board out of the fence.'

'No. More fun to climb. And be invisible. And quick. I am good at it.'

I had to say, 'What about Piet?'

'He does not care. He will not see, or want to see – or not see. Piet has his bees. I hear them singing in his head.'

She told – a little of it then, and other bits at other times – how he had suffered. But not about her own sufferings. It was bad for him. He could not understand. She understood. It was a thing she had expected; she recognized the hideous face. But it was not a face he was able to look at. 'And now I think he is not alive. Not properly. He is alive only in the part that thinks of bees.'

And for the rest of his life Piet Verryt wrote his giant book that will never be published. He writes it still, or perhaps just lives with his bees – curled up on a bed in a nursing home, blind now, deaf, ninety-five I think, and with a smile on his mouth. I visited him once and seemed to hear a humming sound. But his story is another story, one I don't know, one I can't tell. I can tell a little about Ruth, and about me.

I helped her up the ladder, though she needed no help, and handed her into the peach tree; and in the night helped her climb back, and Ruth Verryt became my wife. I'll say no four-letter words, though wife is one and love another. I'll use no terms like coition, climax. Orgasm? I thought it once a fine grown-up word. Don't like it now. Orgy, chasm. Words are doing funny things these days. Coition won't do, and fuck won't do, even love-making, for our close joinings and achievings, our plain arithmetic of one plus one.

She rose on my life like a sun yet I try to contain her. I try to put her down in dry small words. I measure Ruth out in micrograms and try to find her weight and her dimensions. She escapes me. She won't stay still, and I hear her laugh.

'Ah Noel, Noel, you are a fonny man.'

'Just tell me. A simple yes or no. Do you love me?'

'I do now. And will tomorrow. And next year when I am gone. But in between I promise nothing.'

'Now though? Now?'

'Oh yes, now. You are nice. I love you now. But in five minutes I will stop. Unless you stop.'

I made that mistake, and was careful not to make it again. And I'm not going to make it now. Does it matter what we felt? I'll do better to say what we did and what we were.

We were lovers. We conjoined in many ways. I see that as I take us to bits, but in that year was one way, body/mind. Reciprocal properties, we presented those, and simultaneity, we had that. In chemistry we'd be a compound radical. But enough of that. Easier to say that we held hands and we agreed. Ruth climbed to me over the fence. I shifted my ladder into the corner where it was hidden

by a loquat tree (evergreen) and set its feet on bricks to keep it
steady. On her side she was hidden by a garden shed and a
pepper tree. She crushed leaves in her hands and held them to my
face. The hot smell became a part of our love-making. Her naked
body seemed to release smells of acid and fresh hay. She seemed
to be entirely in my armpit or my groin, in my chest, my head, my
throat. Ruth specialized in attentiveness, being there, and I came
to like presence as much as ecstasy. I could not get enough of her,
and I mean all of her. But there were times when we got away and
could not keep track of ourselves. She was speaking with my
tongue and I with hers. I could not tell whether it was her I held
or me, and when we lay apart, with two points touching, hand on
hand and ankle over shin, our blood was common blood, through
our connections. Words were common too. Who spoke that? Who
spoke this? 'Happy?' 'Yes.' 'Feel my heart.' 'It's alive. It's trying to
get out.'

Ruth had two bargains with her husband. The first was she would
help him to New Zealand, help him settle down, start his work, if
he would let her go after a year. The second, made after she and I
had met again, was that she would give him her days but he must
let her have her nights, and Saturday or Sunday now and then.
He agreed. He did not need her in the nights. Ruth cooked and
cleaned for him. She typed his notes and filed his research – and
found it hard but would not give him one day less than 365. I
stood in the loquat tree and watched her work, a Dutch wife in
her kitchen, scouring pots, while Piet Verryt sat dreaming in the
sun. She said to me that night, 'If you spy on me we're finished,
Noel.'

'I just want to know what you do.'

'Here I am me. Over there I am someone else. Do not spy.'

Now and then she went to look at him; walked to the garden
wall, mounted the ladder. She let me stand beside her several
times. We watched Piet sitting in a deckchair on the veranda. He
drew a five-sided figure in the air, and smiled and considered it,
and drew it again, all afternoon. I had the sense of spying over the
Garden wall, of Piet Verryt as pre-lapsarian, and had to remind
myself that he was mad. Dependent too on his sinful wife.

She said, 'They are ideal creatures, his bees. They reach

perfection. And far beyond his science to discover. Now is mysticism and poetry.'

I thought that a coming down, and said so. She patted me, ambiguous act, and held my belt to keep her balance. 'The life of bees is a magic spring, someone says. The more one lets it run the more abundantly it flows. My poor Piet is swimmer in it now.'

'Drowning,' I said. 'What's he doing with his hands?'

'He meditates on the cell. He makes the cell, one after one. Zeshoekig. How do you say?'

'Hexagonal?'

'He draws it, you see, in the air. Perhaps it is new science, Noel, who knows?'

I made a grunt, ambiguous too, and we watched a little longer, then came down and went inside; but I'll say, from my standpoint, Jessop, 1985, that we're all obsessed, and all alone, and live with the creature in our heads. I was lucky to find Ruth, and she find me. We were freed from our prowling at the window, in the dark. That figure (my obsession) recedes and we are two people holding hands; and that, if we're lucky, we can have, for a while. Do I generalize from insufficient data? Perhaps. But it comes back, that image of the scratcher on the glass; and it won't leave, it will never leave me for long, so I take it as truth, and I'm glad if it's not absolute. As I've said, we held hands, Ruth and I.

Sometimes she knitted by my fire. Sometimes we played chess. She never cooked for me, not once. She never even made a cup of tea. I did that, and took her out for meals, and took her for picnics on Saturday afternoons. But more and more, as the year went on, she wrote down ideas for a book. I did not understand how she could work without a library. I thought history needed research and watched with scepticism as she filled page after page, sitting with her tongue stuck out at my kitchen table. 'I know it all. I have it in my head. When I get home I will put in dates. If you insist. And – ' she wrenched with her fists – 'make it have shape. And this, anyway, is just ideas.'

She was writing a history of 'the Spanish occupation'. 'What's that?' I thought for a moment she had lost her mind. She gave me small lessons in Netherlands history – as much as I could take in, who did not have my own country's history clear in my mind. By some accident of succession the thrones of Spain and the Low

Countries were united. She told me in detail and I objected, 'It's outside your period, isn't it?'

'I've got no period now. Just a subject.' It was man's inhumanity and the feast of unreason. Spanish occupation, German occupation, they were one. Philip II, Cardinal Granvelle, Hitler, Himmler, Nicholas of Egmond ('the madman with a sword') – they all came from one time, Ruth said.

She had heroes, though she was not uncritical. Erasmus seemed to be the chief. And villains whose villainies were accidental: Aristotle, Augustine, those 'splitters of our nature', those 'creators of halfmen'. I could follow, although it was hard for me, and now and then I caught her passion. I saw how the inquisition and the *auto-da-fé* and the tearing out of tongues and the burning on hooks over slow fires, and Titelmann, mad strangler, joking killer (see Motley, I read Motley), followed Aristotle, Augustine, and saw the line Ruth followed through to Auschwitz, Belsen. But there I did not want to go with her. I could not face the things that happened there.

Ruth could. She terrified me. And she exhausted herself, and burned with hatreds, and she was cold and wrung out with our failure. I believe I helped keep her sane, and other times, and other where, she kept herself sane with scholarship. That's my guess. She did not go, as so many do, looking for God to trust in or revile. She tried simply, harder and harder, to know. She's written half a dozen big big books – the one on the Spanish occupation, and one on the Reformation in Holland, and one on Dutch Humanism, and a life of Erasmus. That's the best known. That's the one I've read (not all her books are translated). It's as much elegy as biography. She says, in her preface, mankind took a wrong turning, she can't say where, and is doomed and soon will end. It's getting dark now and soon no lights will go on. She concedes to Erasmus all that part of his life and mind animated by religious faith – could scarcely do less – yet presents him as 'living in his own illumination'. He is 'a figure for our longings'. I'm not sure I know what she means. I seemed to know once. It's more important to me that she doesn't deny him imperfections.

The book has a dedication: *To Noel, over the fence*. It's the only message she's sent me since she left.

39

She stole an hour on a Saturday afternoon. We were sitting in the sunshine in my yard when Kitty came round the corner, wearing a red rosette on her jacket. She was canvassing in my street and she was hot. 'Rustle me up a cuppa, Noel. I'll never make it through to six o'clock.'

I wasn't pleased to see her. I was conscious of Ruth's shrinking time. Her passage was booked, she would sail away. We had seventeen days. And she and Kitty always talked politics and became a couple of quacking ducks. I made tea and watched them from the window: two plain women, two honest girls, being silly. Both were smarter than me, and both knew there was no answer in politics. When I came out with tea and made that complaint Ruth agreed, but said there was no answer anywhere so Kitty might as well keep busy there. 'You vote for her or you'll answer to me.'

'I wish it was always as easy as that,' Kitty said. She took off her jacket and fanned herself with the front of her blouse. *Slurp* she went at her tea. She had that technique, learned from Des, of sucking and cooling the scalding stuff; and when I objected, as I always did, lectured me on the need of working men to get their tea down quickly in the few minutes they were allowed. Drinking tea, or the style of it, was a class thing and Kitty knew where she belonged. Ruth clapped her hands. She enjoyed Kitty. She practised drinking tea the working man's way; and the pair of them rolled in their chairs, laughing at my face. Then Kitty was up and off again, jacket on, rosette straight. Her hard heels clattered on the path, the gate went bang, and soon her knock sounded next door and her laugh, her great *har har*, made sparrows fly. They were National next door, I'd told her that, but she wasn't going to let them get away.

Kitty had to shoulder her way to the candidature. Bernie Molloy didn't want her for a start, didn't want a woman. She bounced him aside. Who was he? Last year's man. Last year in politics was nowhere. And what, she asked, though not publicly, had Bernie done in his thirteen years? There was no reason to let him do something now. Didn't want a woman? She bounced him aside like a prop forward with a nine stone half-back. They carted Bernie off on a stretcher. Then there were those who wanted another

Catholic. They were a cloak-and-dagger group and Kitty countered them by being hearty, being dumb. In private she called them the Irish gang or the Bog boys and when she caught one of them off his ground she trampled him. A Cassidy or Brady who challenged her on some union matter would end up with sprig marks on his face.

She had a lot of union support. For three years she had been secretary of the Carpenters' Union. Perhaps she had taken note of Mabel Howard's career. She had the women on her side too (except those who thought her too bold, too loud, too sweaty, too coarse), but most importantly, three or four cabinet ministers wanted her. They'd had enough of Back-bench Bernie and did not want another one like him. They knew Kitty could talk, they knew she could work, they knew she was smart, and they saw how much support she had among locals – those people who remembered Kitty in the depression riding her bike out to the freezing works and coming back with soup-bones and cheap meat, or a sack of swedes from a farm on the handle-bars, and sharing them round the worst off in the street. Besides, they owed no one a seat or a favour. And Jessop was hardly a safe seat. Bernie held it by eight hundred votes. They wanted someone who could rally voters round. That was Kitty.

'Someone's got to wash the socks, eh? Someone's got to scrub the kitchen floor.' That was the way she promised to work in parliament. 'I'll go into that House as though it was my kitchen. And I'll put plain porridge on the table, I promise you.' Her speeches were full of kitchen imagery. 'You can't thicken the stew without any flour.' It was almost too late for that sort of thing. Kitty just made it to parliament in time. Her style was never right for the fifties. But by then she was a character. Kitty, in her own fifties, became a relic of other times. She realized it and it made her sour, but she was trapped in her role. She talked of peeling spuds and elbowgrease, she rolled her own, and in the end she dredged up language no one had heard in years. Dinky-di. Corker. Biff him on the nose. Poor Kit.

But I mustn't forget, she did huge amounts of work. She held her seat for sixteen years.

Kate knows all this. She has it written down. Why should I bother?

Kitty took Jessop but Labour lost the election. 'Well,' I said, 'you can't have everything.' I had misjudged her. She wasn't crying because Labour had lost but because her majority was down on Bernie Molloy's.

Ruth and I looked in at the party in the Choral Hall. We did not stay, we did not belong, and after our moment at her side, a kiss, a pat, no hug like that she got from other men, we stood by the door and admired her from a distance. Her cheeks were smeared, her lipstick crooked, and she was overlarge, with meaty biceps, meaty calves, and sweat rings in her armpits again. I remembered her in the blue dress, pirouetting to rouse Phil, and remembered her, with skirt hitched up, wading the river mouth at Long Tom's. This was no deliberate memory, and I felt it did more than register a loss; it marked a recognition of her growth and signalled to me that Kitty was free, was separate. Kitty from *there* had come *here*, had come to this – and as much as it's possible *she* had done it. I felt – how sad I felt – I felt like cheering.

Ruth and I walked home along the river. Now and then, from houses we passed, we heard the sound of parties, and car horns beeped more frequently than usual. King Log, King Stork, King Log, King Stork again. The frogs were keeping their spirits up. Ruth scolded me for my cynicism. But she took no optimistic view herself. She simply thought New Zealanders were lucky – look at all the things they were exempt from by an accident of geography. She was sad to be leaving and not so clear-headed that night as usual. Gardeners of Arcady, she called us. 'You sit down here and make your apples grow.' I knew she was remembering friends shot and friends tortured, and would have kept quiet; but it seemed I had to claim humanity for us, and our share of evil and pain. I told her we had thousands dead in the war, and the one before it; and told her we had our torturers too, waiting their time. They would come out when they were called. We were not exempt, we had just been lucky up to now. I seemed to be pleading that we too were atrocious. As for suffering – look at Les Dockery and Kitty's husband, Des.

'Yes,' she said, 'yes. Everywhere.'

I asked her if she'd ever believed in God. 'Once,' she said. 'Not now. There's no dispensation. Good and evil, they belong to us.'

We strolled along, being wise, being silly – take your pick – moving towards the end of our close touching. On the wooden foot-bridge at the end of her street we leaned on the rail and watched the water. It slithered like a creature with a scaly back, but I pushed myself beyond susceptibilities and it became water in the light. And Ruth was Ruth, here, now, and not my wife whom I was losing. Down-river, over trees, the roof of Lomax's warehouse made a black rectangle on the sky. I told her about Edgar Le Grice. I told her how I had dirtied my pants.

'He's come back. Edgar Le Grice.'

I could see the nursing home a quarter mile away on the bend of the river. Jessie Mills owned the place but Phil Dockery had money in it. He'd called on me that week, dragged me out of my lab, and driven me round to Jessie's – Golden West as it was called. 'There's someone I want you to see.' We went through the building to the lawns at the back and he pointed out an old man on a bench. 'Recognize him?'

'No,' I said.

'Take a good look.'

I didn't care for the game, even though the man seemed to be deaf. He sat with his hands tight on his knees, gripping stone, anchoring himself against a trembling in his torso. He was wearing a ravelled cardigan and a green tartan shirt, and slippers and striped pyjama pants. The flies gaped and I saw a grey-haired patch of his belly. Face – nothing to get hold of, stock old man. It had been a big face but gave the impression of being reduced, as though a string enclosing his features was pulled tight.

Phil saw I wasn't going to recognize him. 'Put a balaclava on his head.'

My bowels went loose, but I was grown up and controlled myself. The hammer-blow, the missed beat of the heart, I gave them no more than their beat in time; and I said, 'It's him all right. Where's he been?'

'Living with some sheila out in the country. She brought him in. He's paid for. Jessie'll boot him out when he gets behind.'

'Does he know you?'

'Doesn't know anyone. He's still a bit loopy. Harmless though. Likes his grub, Jessie says.' He bent at the waist, put his face level with Le Grice's. 'Hey, Le Grice.' The old man took no notice, but kept up the fight against his palsy. Phil tapped him under the chin with bent forefinger. 'Lit any fires lately, Le Grice?'

'Leave him, Phil.'

'I should pay the bugger back.' He jerked the cord of Le Grice's pyjama pants, undoing the bow. 'He's going to lose his pants when he stands up.'

I pulled Phil away. It astonished me that he should feel malice. Perhaps it was that which gave Le Grice his power again, over me – Phil seeing him as someone who still had to be got even with. I saw Le Grice. I focused on him, just as he had narrowed himself on to me in the warehouse yard. He sat there, on the bench, hands on knees, power of one. Free from susceptibilities did I say? He narrowed down again to his obsession, that thing before which everything gives way. As Ruth, at times, narrowed down in her obsessive search for glimmers of light. That's why he's here, mixed in with her. I want to allow one no space and let the other have it all. But it doesn't work that way. Those two are equal, those two mix.

Ruth said, 'Come through my house. Climb the fence with me.' We went along by the bedroom, where Piet Verryt hummed like a hive of bees, and down the back path, and I climbed first, Ruth followed, ladder to ladder, pepper to loquat tree. No, no, it's not symbolical. They are just the trees that were there. And our climbing marked nothing significant. It was a bit of foreplay, she was inventive. But I don't intend to make my reader intimate with her. (Who is my reader, anyway?) Or give you ammunition, Kate. The smell of pepper stayed on our palms. And loquats, spring-fruiters, spread their sour-sweetness on our tongues as we paused to try if they were ripe. We whispered and we laughed, I helped her down, and over the lawn we scampered to my bed.

Damn it, words breed words, and the fancier they are the faster they breed. I've just killed fifty. You'll never know what they are.

I won't spread words over Ruth like jam.

She put her glasses on, transformed herself from blind mole into lemur.

'Well, you're not Plotinus any more.'

'Is that all it's been? Just a lesson?'

'Ah no, love. I'm sorry. I'm being clever. That time perhaps. Not any more. I love you, Noel. I don't want to go away.'

'But you're going?'

'Yes. I'm going. I have to go. Don't argue. I don't want to cry.'

I put her on the ferry two days later. It sailed out of Jessop through the cut and its plume of smoke leaned backwards as it gathered speed. I drove home and the years went by. I lived my life in my earthly fashion, and had my share of happiness and satisfaction. But I haven't loved anyone again.

40

There is always, isn't there, that Greek, I forget his name, who led the Persian army through the mountain track at Thermopylae and took the Spartans in the rear? There always is a fellow of that sort.

Kate is reading my notebooks again. Things must be going wrong for her. Is that right, Kate? Have you and Shane reached the bottom of the honey pot? Do you fall upon the thorns of life and bleed? You don't mind my being literary? I'm in good company. Kitty was always spouting Shelley.

> Wherefore feed, and clothe, and save,
> From the cradle to the grave,
> Those ungrateful drones who would
> Drain your sweat – nay, drink your blood?

She quoted that in the House once, caused a real uproar in what she called the Top-dogs party on the other side.

I'm still bringing you stuff Kate, see? How about this? Kitty had lop-ears. Did you never notice those pink question marks peeping from her hair? My mother knitted her a cap, an open-work thing like a basket fungus, and slipped it on her head every night when she was asleep. Didn't work, those ears just wouldn't lie down. But Kitty had thick hair and managed to hide them. Mum closed her mouth too, made her sleep breathing through her nose.

Free gifts, free gifts.

She says, 'Don't you think the composer deserves some credit too?' But Irene doesn't interest her, Ruth doesn't interest her. She's got a bad case of tunnel vision. Only Kitty. Like some stone figure in a desert, eh Kate, a colossal wreck, all alone? That's Shelley again. 'Ozymandias'. Read it.

Kitty wasn't huge, she says, she was middle-sized. She had a good figure. Why do you try to make out she was a whale? You hate her, don't you? It's because you're all shrivelled up. And all this stuff about her sweating, Kate says. You've put that in three times. Everybody sweats. Why keep on about it? Can't you say some good things about her? What about her eyes? Her voice?

OK, lovely eyes, lovely voice. Do you want me to say it three times?

Kate, I put down the things that strike me. Nothing's unfair. I've said I've got a face like a chimpanzee. And Phil has yellow teeth and purple cheeks. I loved Ruth but I've told you she looked like a frog. Do I have to tell lies? Do I have to put things in the order you want? I loved Kitty too. Can't you see it?

What she's done – what you've done, my Kate – after all my heroic defence, is lead the enemy round to take me in the rear.

'How did Rhona die?' That's your question.

Red-hot pokers stand against the white garden wall. Explosive. Acacias, clouds of yellow, overflow the curve of the riverbank. Our winter colours. Bare European trees are printed on the green hill like the map of a river system. That's not bad, but I had a bit of trouble with number there. And I should have mentioned that they're grey.

What is happening in the world? The Greenpeace boat is sunk in Auckland. The All Blacks are not going to South Africa. (Kate jubilant.) A politician punches five reporters. In America President Reagan has had a benign lump removed. I hope he doesn't turn out to have needed it. Locally, nothing. Nothing at all. Forty thousand people get on with their lives.

Phil rang. We had a chat. He's OK. Shane's a bloody good worker, he says. Archie Penfold's nurse phoned to say they're holding a 'flu shot for me. I'm in the group at risk. I told her to give it to someone else. Kate has dosed me up with snail-egg pills – Bacillinum/influenzinum. I wish I could see Archie's face when he hears that.

Why don't you give me calendula, Kate? That's supposed to open old wounds.

Rhona, eh? You think I should face up to things and not leave any holes in case I fall in one and don't climb out. Do you see me in the bottom, curled up like Piet Verryt on his bed? No chance of that. I need to attend.

Since you insist, I'll fill in the hole. It's no big thing. You're not Ephialtes after all. See, I remember his name. Tup didn't let me get away with being just a scientist.

I visited Rhona on the Sunday that I left. Then I took the ferry, as I've said. She seemed her normal self. Unfortunate choice of words. She seemed herself. It was one of those afternoons with limitless sky – the sky no roof, the eye-beam shooting out past invisible galaxies and going on forever; with the curious effect that one feels comfortable being finite and not in any state of awe. Well, I felt it, I felt happy. I was sure of my limits and my abilities, and I was about to be free. What Rhona felt I do not know. She was no sky-watcher but let her eye travel in a line across the sea – apparently without limit too. Its meeting with the sky was lost in shimmer. Jessop, in the east, in the sunshine, was a town made of coloured paper and glass, with a window here and there shining like a torch and blinding us.

I watched her face as I told her I was going away. I don't know what I would have done if I'd seen grief – told her doctor perhaps, asked the nurses to keep an eye on her. But she showed no concern. I did not think she understood. Just for a moment something moved in her eye.

I can't measure the state of her consciousness. I can't say anything about it.

Notice how this account proceeds in negatives. 'I can't.' 'I did not.' 'I don't know.' I'm evading questions no one has asked. 'Speak up,' the judge says. Am I in the dock?

She ate a bag of chocolate roughs. Chocolates were impossible to get. She ate them, every one, but didn't gobble as mad people are supposed to do; consumed them like a lady. The shadow in her eye was puzzlement. She had the means to identify me and foresee changes in her state. Perhaps she could still wish and wonder and connect herself with my world. It wasn't only *that place* she was in. With her arm in mine, her hand spread like a starfish on my sleeve, we walked on the lawns at Soddy's Point. This was no automatic perambulation. We varied it. We? I felt small pressures from her arm. She preferred this path to that. Rhona was able to prefer. I wonder if in the end she would have come back. *Her* state, I said a moment ago.

Was it *our* state? Is that how she saw it still, *our* lives? I claimed somewhere to love her, but that was solitary. I no longer thought of *our* lives.

We stood on the cliff and looked at Jessop. We sat on a bench and she ate the last chocolate rough. I popped the paper bag and made her laugh. Then we went back to the hospital, I kissed her cheek, I patted her, and said I would try to come at Christmas; and off I went and picked up my bags and caught the ferry.

How did Rhona look that day? Youngish. Clean. Pretty.

Damn you, Kate. This is like climbing a mountain. My lungs hurt and my knees hurt and it feels as if that bloody dog has her teeth in my ribs. I can't keep my mind on things if I can't get enough air.

Now. This is what Rhona did. She followed my car down the road. Several people saw her. That is why the search was made towards the entrance and along the road into town. Instead of going that way she must have turned into the trees and walked back to the end of the peninsula. She sat in the sand at the foot of the cliff. They found a hollow there, with her crumpled handkerchief nearby. My opinion is, she watched the tide go out and the mudflats turn pink in the setting sun. Then she began to walk over that polished dancing-floor to Jessop – the faery city where, perhaps, the bad things were all done. The mud is firmed with sand for a quarter mile. You sink down to your ankles. She went a long way before she reached a place where it was soft. There she sank in. To her knees, to her hips. The more you struggle the deeper you go. When they found her mud was up to her chest.

Perhaps she called out. No one heard. In the night the tide came back and drowned her.

I can't breathe. There are knives in my chest. Jesus that hurts.

41

July 16. He has Bornholm disease. I've never heard of it. Nothing to worry about the doctor says, as long as he has proper medication and decent care. With a look down his nose.

Thanks Noel for what you've given me. I know I'm a bully but I can't help it. I'll be around for a while. We'll get by.

K.

42

Did Archie really say it was nothing to worry about? I think it's time I changed my doctor. It nearly killed me. It hurt me worse than any sickness I've known. I say that in a scientific spirit. No complaints.

Bornholm disease (Devil's grippe, epidemic pleurodynia). An infectious disease of sudden onset, produced by a Coxsackie virus, marked by knifelike pains in the chest or abdomen.

Why Bornholm? I asked Kate. Who was he? She did some research in my books and came up with the answer: Bornholm is an island in the Baltic Sea. The virus was first identified there in 1947. That's fine. I like to know the facts. But Devil's grippe is the name I'll use. By God it gripped and squeezed me, head and chest and bowels. It ran red-hot needles into me. And then six weeks of coughing little coughs, night and day. My muscles burned and ached with it and it wore my flesh away. I'm skin and bone. I'm dry sticks and worn hide, an old canoe. In that frail craft I've sailed through to September.

What have I done? Listened to the radio. You can hear the news fourteen times a day, more if you try. The same news, different names, different places. I've listened to lots of programmes with jokes. People with English voices being witty, bringing it off now and then. I mustn't laugh, it hurts me. Lots of songs I never thought I'd hear again. Oh no John, no John, no John, no. It passes the time. I've heard some serious stuff as well, social problems, but find myself wondering mostly at the language. 'Like' it seems has taken the place of 'as if'. 'Less' tips 'fewer' out. Less pedestrians, less immigrants – and it looks like it's going to be another bad year for the farming sector. 'There's dry rot in the timber,' I tell Kate. She laughs and calls me fusspot. As long as people get the drift, she says. And then sits down and tries to write her book!

*

I know how I want to die: spontaneous combustion. I've got to that part in *Bleak House*. A yellow nauseous liquor, greasy soot. The cinders of a small charred broken log. That's all that's left – all Dickens left. What a pity he didn't describe Krook going up. On the other hand, he left it to us; and I suppose an incandescence in the mind, then oblivion. Most attractive. The log can sputter on as long as it likes.

Is it time for the next number, Kate? Forty-three? I didn't do it, she's the one. Likes everything in little blocks.

43

But it does help one change gear. And she's picked up my gear changes well. Kate, it seems we're in this together. Is there anything you'd like to say at this point. No? All right.

I've been half in half out of consciousness. It hasn't stopped me knowing how things are. Phantom beings, voices – but now and then a signal from the real world. That white ghost is Kate, see the sudden redness in her eyes. And that, that's Shane, that wail; voice in anger what it really is.

Shane packed up and left us. No, I'll try again, he didn't pack, just rode off on his motorbike in the clothes he was wearing. Kate has all his gear in cardboard boxes in the spare room, hundreds of dollars worth of stuff, but she doesn't think he'll come for it. She's even got his veil and cowboy hat. That will be useful if the wasps come back.

She still sleeps in the waterbed. Unsentimental Kate. She cries in there. And curses too. Throws heavy things at the wall. I heard something break a moment ago.

How it happened, as far as I know. Let's go back to the time before the Devil gripped me. Shane was still out there at Long Tom's. The painting job was done but Phil had taken him on as a general hand and put him to fencing. Shane could turn his hand to anything. And Kate, though she was watchful, seemed pleased. There were better places to work than a rich man's stud farm, but she agreed that these days you had to take whatever job was offered. So Shane rode off in the dawn, like a cowboy, and was home again soon after dark and I looked forward to his coming and the glass of whisky I drank with him (sometimes he tipped his into his beer), and his yarns about life at Long Tom's. Phil was out there two or three days a week. Not long now and mares would be arriving to foal and then Thundercloud would be on the job. 'What a job, screwing for money,' Shane said. The horse he was sorry for was a little fellow called the teaser who got the mares primed up before the stallion was brought in. 'The poor little bugger, he never gets it in.' 'Do shut up, Shane,' Kate said.

That's how we were for a while. Hard winds, cold nights, old-fashioned stew, and a hot toddy before bed. Shane and Kate grinning at each other and exchanging good-natured abuse. I enjoyed it but didn't believe in it. Loose edges showed all the time. Shane and Kate did not fit together. You know it, Kate. You've admitted it. All the same, they tried, they behaved carefully and showed consideration for each other. Before long it was unnatural.

In the shrunken days of winter it began. He stayed after work for a 'noggin' with Phil. Once or twice he ran Phil back to Jessop in his sidecar and stayed for a 'snifter' at his flat. He used Phil's language, and that indicates his nervousness. Kate was frosty. Cold nights, those.

'The poor old bugger's lonely,' Shane said.

'When they pick you up for drunken driving don't come snivelling to me,' Kate replied.

Then the Devil had me in his grip. Kate won't tell me all that happened so I've had to guess a thing or two. Shane started spending nights out there. He phoned to say it was too wet to ride home. I must say that seems reasonable to me. It's a long way to come on a motorbike, in wind and sleet, especially when home has stopped being home. Don't be angry, Kate, you know it's true. You made me face up to Rhona's death, I'll make you see this. You and Shane had come to the end of your time.

He and Phil got drunk together and had baked beans at midnight and T-bone steaks for breakfast at midday. Shane did not come home three nights in a row. Kate sat on the end of my bed with her eyes gleaming.

'Kate!'

She felt my brow. 'Your fever's gone.'

'Where's Shane?'

'At Long Tom's. With that old man. Go to sleep.'

And she was here with this old man. Perhaps she thought, If we get out, if we go away . . . No, Kate, the old men aren't to blame. Going away would only have put if off a little longer.

The night Shane walked out things went like this: he came in late from Phil's place, Kate was sitting up, I was asleep, and coughing, coughing, melting my flesh away. I heard shouts but they became part of my nightmare. Shane was under the weather of course and as he walked into the kitchen he put his dark glasses on. Kate knocked them off with a swipe. 'Don't you hide your bloody eyes from me.' A good deal of yelling followed, and for me cries of rage became cries of pain, howls of tortured beings, whispers, moans. It was horrible. My apprehensions, transformations, seem correct to me.

'You think you've got me in some sort of bloody prison here.' The logical thing was to chop it down. He started that: ran out to the shed, seized the axe, attacked one of the piles of my sundeck. There's a huge bite taken out. But four hits were all Kate let him have. She ran down the steps into range of the axe and struck him on the run with stiffened arms, bowled him down the bank through the wet fennel, saved my house. (In my dream I felt it tremble.) The fence bulged like a fishing net and sprang several fasteners from a post. Shane must have had a pattern of wire printed on his back. Roaring like a bear, he ploughed up through the fennel. Kate, meanwhile, had found the axe. She heaved it away over his head. Another bit of my property into the river. I'm not complaining, but it does seem to happen all the time.

She ran back up the steps. He caught her in the porch and knocked her down. Murder? Almost. What stopped him? He reached for her. It was time for strangling, for squeezing her until she was dead. She was not going to let him do it and was climbing up to fight. But she didn't stop him, he stopped himself. Kate admits it. He pushed his breath out with a great explosion. Huh! That helped carry some of his rage away. He looked at his hands and gave a shout. His eyes were mad and terrified. Kate says he was terrified of himself. He punched the wall. A great smear of blood was there in the morning. Then, doubled up and weeping with pain, he ran away. She heard his motorbike start and go down the hill, and saw it enter, vanish from, the light on the bridge. That is the last she saw of Shane.

'Gone,' she said in the morning, 'and good riddance.'

'Out to Phil's?'

'Where else? Eat that, I didn't cook it for nothing.'

I ate three spoonfuls of the stuff (hate porridge). And this morning ask, 'Is Shane coming back?'

'No, he's not.' She meant me to understand she would not have him.

'Does he want to?' A hard question for Kate. But she's not a person who runs away. She took a moment, answered square: 'Shane and I were finished. That was it.' Tears sprang in her eyes. She turned her back so I should not see.

Kate tells me to change gear again. She's in a dry condition, saying nasty things about my guesswork. She doesn't, she says, cry in her room. Nor does she throw things at the wall. The crash I heard was her dropping a plate and that was in the other direction, out in the kitchen. I'm going soft in the head, she reckons. She wants me to leave her alone.

Kate, I am not losing my wits. All right, my ears played a trick on me. If you say it was a plate it was a plate. But I see, I hear, and most of the time I understand. Ways have become different, that's all. Now and then I don't get things right. See how you manage at eighty-four, when loud and violent people come pushing up behind. I'm astonished sometimes that I do so well.

As for changing gear, I don't want to go back where you want me. Why should I grind up that hill? I like it where I am, going fast.

Shane is not at Phil's. He never went there: walked out on his drinking mate, abandoned his tools. Phil is sour about it. These young buggers are all the same. Do them a favour, they kick you in the teeth. I try to add another dimension to it. Cowboys always ride away in the end. Sameness starts to make them die. The new range beckons. Shane was a cowboy, I said.

Like Kate, Phil reckons I'm soft in the head.

'Things always go wrong for me,' she claims. By things she means her affairs with men. She makes a list. It seems she's been involved – not in love – with two married men, two mental defectives (the lawyer and the journalist), and a fellow who turned out to be a poofter. Disposes of each of them with an ugly word or a cheap one-liner. She'd like to deal with herself in the same way – tries it but takes it back. She's got too much good sense; and won't go the way of self-pity either. I find it interesting that she doesn't cheapen Shane. She'll mention him and say, as though choosing the word, 'It was *good*.'

She says, 'I don't regret it. No, I don't.'

My belief is that she was in love and I don't think she'll get over it by being Anglo-Saxon.

Sorry, Kate. I know that will make you cross. I'll put a new number down if you like.

44

In the Old Chemistry a menstruum was a solvent – 'to extract,' I think it goes, 'the virtues of ingredients by infusion or decoction'. The belief was that the moon influenced the preparation of dissolvents. Well, I'm solvent for my past, a menstruum, influenced by moons, and I hope I've extracted a virtue or two. (Active quality or power; energy, strength, potency.) The trouble is I don't want to go on. I don't believe there's much left worth looking at. I'll fall to playing games, dressing up, spreading jam – as in menstruum above. I started that to keep out of Kate's way.

She says she wants to know the rest of it. Is that any more, Kate, than a way of keeping an old man quiet? I don't make too much noise, do I? There's noise in my head, a constant buzzing. There are loud bangs now and then – that's my old tympanum heart persuading itself to keep on the job, stepping up the beat; or it's someone dying. It's some huge word from my past, weighing like lead, hitting the floor. There's a gonging too from that direction, potent with meaning, ripe with extensions, but always failing to *signify*. And flashes of light that spit like sodium. The faces they illumine are important but featureless. Does this make me sound mad? It's all quite normal. Maypole dancing as the body gives up its powers.

Phil came and sat by my bed on the kitchen chair. It's catching up with Phil. His knee joints are not working too well. He totters, though I keep that word to myself. He put his hand on the chair back and eased himself down. He's still strong in the shoulders, and strong in his colour too, strong in his eyes, although the whites are criss-crossed with veins and have a sore look. Phil is sore. He feels hard done by. Shane has let him down – and I wonder if Phil wasn't a bit infatuated. He doesn't trust, he doesn't give himself. But he's been hurt, he's in a flushed condition, and some wasting process is in train.

We didn't do each other much good. In fact, I bored him, he bored me. I would have thought Phil in love – for want of a term – would be fascinating, but I was tired and had a touch of the nausea I get now and then. I wanted him to go away. He had nowhere to go, said as much. So, helped himself to a drink and went over his troubles a second time. He told me if I saw Shane, if he came here, to send him straight out to Long Tom's. 'He's chasing some sheila,' Phil said. That was the sort of thing he would forgive.

Kate is going to fill her life with strangers. Lost back-packers. She knows the sad ones by their eyes, and picks them up and brings them home and feeds them. So far we've had a loud Swiss girl who was off-hand with me, taking me for a charity patient too and a threat to her. She walked naked down my hall in the night and peed like a draught mare in a paddock, with the door open. More liquid in her than in the cistern. When I opened my bedroom door to see what was leaking she shouted at me in her language.

'Get rid of her, Kate,' I said in the morning.

'She thinks you're a dirty old man. Yes, she's going. I don't like her.'

Next came an American from Boulder, Colorado (she'll tolerate a Yank now, in her need), a pasty boy who talked about his Mom. He ate us out of ice cream and went into a foetal trance in the shower, using all the hot water Kate needed for the washing. She had to lift him out and dry and dress him. He's on his way, tears in his eyes. And Kate's gone out fishing again. She says she'll be more careful this time.

It's a huge Dane, shambles like a bear. *The Hiking Viking* his banner says. Cheerful fellow, crushed my hand. Although he isn't sad he looks as if he'll eat a lot.

I've had enough of this, I'm going back.

45

Where to go? that's the question. I can think of a dozen places, but none is necessary. The gonging is still there but all it signifies is, time was.

I'll put down a story that restored peace between Kitty and me. She laughed until her cheeks were sore. It's this: they knighted me in 1966 and I made a fool of myself at the investiture. It was time for a knighthood to science. John Dye had been in line for one in the mid-fifties, but he died – saving himself, Kitty said, from the indignity. Borland from the DSIR got it instead. I became director of the Lomax.

Ten years later I was to be Sir Noel and I practised him in front of the bathroom mirror, and practised saying the honour was for science and the Lomax not for me and I hoped my friends would still call me Noel. The usual thing. I'm still waiting for some honest knight to cry, 'Whoopee!'

Kitty stopped speaking to me when it was announced. (Some years later she refused to be Dame Kitty.) She was out of parliament, beaten in 1963, and was Jessop's mayor – mayor, she insisted, not mayoress. Honours routed through Buckingham Palace were a national disgrace; and, with Empire in their name, an insult to the Commonwealth as well. I wouldn't put it so strongly. I just found it ridiculous. It's a pity I didn't find the strength to say no.

Sans peur et sans reproche. That's not me. What I am is *sans* dignity. The clever monkey knelt, he received the ennobling touch – and couldn't stand up. Tipped over on the floor, lay there arched, with face as anguished as the Kaiser's, and fingers dug in thigh, and little yelps coming from his mouth, and some thought he was having a fit and some a heart attack. But Stan Duckham the All Black coach, there to get his OBE, recognized it for what it was, and grabbed my foot and bent my toes back, cured my cramp in good Athletic Park style. He enjoyed it. So did the Governor-General, I think. Most of the others thought I'd let the side down. Duckham helped me to a chair and I sat there, face mottled red and leg out straight: Sir Noel, with gong on chest. As soon as it was over I knew what to do. I telephoned Jessop and told Kitty and heard her laugh. That cramp is a good old friend of mine. I'm fond of him.

He calls me Noel.

Women. Work. There's nothing I need to say about those years. Amusements. Friends. Failures. Trips abroad. Did I tell you I failed to visit Dachau? I thought it might threaten my will to live. So I watched the Glockenspiel instead – well, I went to the science museum too, and some galleries, but Glockenspiel is how it seems to me now. And I measure the loss of self in that choice by the fact that in Holland, the following week, I saw no point in calling on Ruth. I could not find a Noel Papps to present to her.

Deaths: several. Few entrances. That's not to say there were no new things. One of them called for entrances from me. I filled my nights with prancings on a stage. No tragedies, no problems. My face was more for stretching wide than long. We had full houses at the Theatre Royal in the fifties. I became master of the double take – in *Charley's Aunt*, in *Arsenic and Old Lace*. Bodies in window boxes, how I loved finding them. How I loved hitching up my bloomers. It did not matter that I was too old for most of my roles, I made up in bounce, smart-alecry.

Kitty came when she was able to. I heard her laugh. Heard Irene trill. And once I heard Phil Dockery's guffaw. He loved it when the husband hung his hat on me hiding in the wardrobe.

Pleasant affairs came from it. They started, ran their course, stopped with no complications. I'm sure the women would agree with me. We were not even breathing hard. It never crossed my mind that I might marry.

Where did I go? That's a wrong question. I deny being absent at any time. Why can't I find that Noel Papps? All I can find for him is occasions. I know he was with people a good deal – in meetings, at conferences, at concerts and parties. He slides out of focus all the time. The truth is, he was happy and doesn't need me interfering with him. But haven't I said that happiness is not a measure?

One of my mistakes is plain to see. My work, about which I've said very little, exists as the large fact at the centre of my life. If I were drawing a picture of that thing which is no thing, no distinguishable object of thought – my life – it would have work at the centre, so dominant as to be almost invisible. I should put it in with two strokes, a mountain, inverted V, and then not bother with it again but draw in trees and houses, parks and playgrounds at the foot, as I've done. I don't forget my work, but it was mine. Kitty, Ruth,

Rhona, Irene, Phil, do not stroll in and out. My work was never open to their question.

Then I gave it up. I was scientist no more, I was director. I chose 'importance', and nothing important was left to me. Many things happened but nothing was *done*. I did no work, I made no examination. I filled my life with small difficulties and did no one big difficult thing. They knighted me, oh yes. And in those years I had – there's a fine three-letter word – most of my women. But no wife. I need to write down none of their names.

You'll forgive me dramatizing myself? It indicates that my judgement's gone – hooray for that! I'm dizzy with old age and my years are jumbled up and that makes for strange juxtapositions. Things are heightened as if by their natures, and my metaphors are legitimate.

There's something onanistic about this. See how that phallic 'I' stands in my pages. I write it fat, with a swollen head, and rub it up.

Phil would enjoy this.

I was fit companion for Phil.

His marriages produced no children. I've never asked him why. His wives were pretty women, pleased with their rich husband but wanting an ordinary marriage after a while. Unhappy girls. One by one they turned to other men. Phil believes he got rid of them. He's without fallibility, that's the fact he sees when he looks inside. That's his carbon skeleton.

What does it make other people? Goods, I suppose. Disposable property. Do I need to illustrate him again? I don't think so. I'll tell you about one of his wives, Isobel. She was number three, and a real looker, to use his phrase. He chose her for that and for her youth – and from our town's social register, which is not a thing written down but a system of acceptance based on old money, professional status, early coming, established name. No one speaks of it but everyone hears. Phil plucked her out and set her up at his place and enjoyed her in a variety of ways. He swelled visibly. No, rephrase that. He put on condition, his muscles grew springy, a healthier red was in his face. He married her in Victoria Gardens, close by the Eelpond there, making it fashionable for a year or two. But getting her home to his place, having her – this lawyer's daughter (not just any lawyer, Jessop's oldest), private-school girl, debutante, horse-rider, champion golfer – that was the real ceremony, that was ceremony prolonged, Port-boy Phil's announcement of self. No act of joining took place, but an act, continuing acts, of possession.

Of the public kind, let's have a bit of sunlight, good fresh air, let's go golfing on our links by the white-sand beach, with Soddy's Point over the sparkling sea. When I think of Isobel swinging I think of willow wand. She whacked that little ball, that buffalo pill, several hundred yards, or dropped it parabolic on the green, where it stopped as though a gravitational field lay underneath. She had white socks and golden calves and freckled forearms and wore a sun visor that threw green light on her face, making her ethereal even as she whacked. It sounds as though I loved her, but you're wrong. For three hours on a Saturday she was my vision of beauty – I'll not break it down more than that, although I could, I see well enough the molecules cluster – and I tried to put my will in her, make her win.

It was the final of the Jessop Golf Club Ladies Championship. Isobel was favourite, was going for her third straight title in fact. She played off a two handicap, whatever that means, and had been a provincial representative that year, competing for some rosebowl or pennant; and was expected, that Saturday, to have an easy time with the lady (no names) who was my reason for being there. (We had rather pleasant, dull Monday evenings, while her husband was at Rotary. 'Come and watch me, Noel, but don't let me see you or I'll miss my putts.' Those evenings, I think, weren't dull for her. I mustn't boast.) But Isobel quickly fell behind, one hole, two holes, three holes down; and my lady-friend grew hard-mouthed, glittery-eyed, and punched the ball and made it go straight, and roll and roll. No gravitational field worked for her. She drew no arcs, but grew sweaty patches in her armpits (now Kate I am unfair), hitched up her skirt, snapped her teeth, and finally chewed PKs, a thing she believed no lady should do in public. Isobel, with pale green face, began to play. She picked up one hole, two, but could not get the third, for my partner in adultery, who *must* be admired, found, she told me Monday, found herself contracted to a little iron dwarf, dwarfess, sitting between the lobes of her brain, expressing itself as motion to the green, to the hole; and sixteen, seventeen, eighteen, off went her drives, down went her putts. This isn't her story – although I start to like her – but Isobel's. And Phil's of course. He was there. Natty-dressed. Sporting-hatted. He marked Isobel's score on a card for use later on. I saw her look up from a putt that failed to drop, saw them find each other and Isobel look away, back to her task, with a dragging of her eye, as though it were held on his face by a fascination. It's a kind of muted melodrama. I want to laugh. How can I take this thing, this game of golf, whacking of balls, at their valuation? But I can't laugh. I saw what her function was for him – which she strove to fulfil.

My square-built lady won. Good on her. I took her chocolates Monday and enjoyed her muscly strength more than was usual. Later in the week I called on Isobel. I'll be honest – I knew Phil was likely to be out and she alone. I wanted to have a look at her, wanted to settle, name her in a sense, and so take my own sort of possession. I do not often do this for I don't have the vision frequently. Isobel had not left me from the Saturday to the Thursday (Monday night excepted, but that's in the normal course of living); had been there green and freckled, wristy, delicate, beaten, drugged. She opened the door to me without turning on the porch light, and I thought, Ha! what's wrong? Very alert. Receptive beyond what was natural. She told me Phil was out. 'Oh well,' I said, 'I'm here so I'll come in.' She walked ahead of me to the lounge and turned by the fireplace, with a lifting of her jaw, and showed the damaged face I was ready for. A delicate stain of yellow on her cheek, a pastel blush; and round her eye lavender, on which her silver lashes lay like stitching.

'Ah,' I said, 'you're hurt.'

'I slipped, Noel. I hit my face on the edge of the bath.' And as I stepped towards her she took her putter up from the settee to carry on with the practice I'd interrupted. Several balls lay by her feet and a flattened rubber cup like a model volcano fifteen feet away over the carpet. She took a grip on the club, a slanting of ranked fingers, a folding of pigeon wings, lovely strength, amazing delicacy, and hung her head over the ball with a forward slide of the hair she tied with white ribbon on the course, and tapped the silly thing, and sent it running on the carpet to the cup where it fitted in and sat, and waited there, useless egg. Yes, Kate, I can see it, you needn't come smirking at me tomorrow. She didn't want golf she wanted babies. I'm the one doing it, after all. I don't suppose I'll surprise you with what happened next. Tears happened next, love-making on the settee after that; if 'love-making' can be loosely used.

She looked at the ball in the cup and laid down her club and started

to cry big slippery tears. I put my arms around her, knowing roles –
no, no, damn it, enough of that – because I was overcome by pity,
and instantly in a sexual state. 'He shouldn't,' she said, 'he shouldn't
have hit me.'

'Where is he?'

'Out tomcatting. He's been out every night this week.'

'Just because you didn't win at golf?'

'I didn't do what I'm supposed to do.'

There were natural progressions followed then, and very good for
both of us it was. You don't mind a veil of decency? We were, of
course, strangers to each other, but touched at a point as we passed
by, and there's a kind of jewel glitter I see, of red and gold and green,
in the memory; a flash in a dark velvet night. I don't wish to dress the
thing up, but see it bare, and see it clean, and I'm sorry if I've failed in
that.

Low comedy came after: scrambling on of clothes at the sound of a
car that was not Phil's. And lowness in my thoughts later on: I'd paid
him back for Rhona, cuckolded him, lovely term. I was triumphant,
terrified, and my heart jumped in my chest when we met, for a good
long time. But it settled down, I settled down, and take no pleasure
from my victory now, if victory is what it is; but have a small treasure
that I keep.

Isobel stayed with Phil another year and won the golf title a third
time. Then she left. 'I fitted her up with the riding instructor,' he
said. 'But she don't need instructing after me. That lucky sod's going
on a ride.'

I thought of my own ride for a moment; and was angry at my
cheapening of the occasion. Almost said: You didn't fit her up with
anyone, she left you, mate. But kept my silence, had another drink,
heard him out. He had some fun with Isobel, put her in a mucky
yard, with bandy-legged husband, scabby nags; then forgot her,
having her in place. But Isobel and her husband did very well. They
opened a sports store in Christchurch and owned three or four by the
time they'd done. They had a son and daughter and lived together
happily as far as I know.

When I see people standing alone I have a sense of their reality.
Isobel alone, without husband, without Phil. And Kate, without
Shane, there's a solid object. Shane without Kate. Standing together,

supposedly interacting – substance is gone. They become shadowy, they're movements in a pool and have no existence I can hold.

Kitty alone. Phil alone. Irene, little Reen. That's how they present themselves. Yet I think of our lives as a territory and attempt a kind of quadrature.

Perhaps I've made it up, it's all lies. But if I tried again I'd do no better. Let the whole thing stand, all these pages. Let it stand as an approximation.

I've been thinking about Kitty, and I say: In parliament she learned big talk and discovered how small she was. That covers fourteen years neatly. But what about her triumph? After the first loss anything we manage is a triumph.

46

I remember her distress when she lost her seat. Just for the record, her career: MP for Jessop 1949–63. Minister of Health 1957–60. Shadow Minister 1960–63. When she got her portfolio she answered her critics thus: 'I'm a nurse. I can deal with doctors. You watch me.' Not a very clever thing to say, but Kitty was a character by that time and she got away with it. When Labour lost in 1960 she was bitter. She was just getting into things, she said. But 1963 – oh dear, oh dear.

There had been boundary changes, a suburb of state houses bitten off. 'Jesus,' Kitty said, 'that's my freezing workers gone.' She felt it like the loss of a limb and made yells of pain in parliament. Then she settled down to win. She ran her usual style of campaign: Kitty on the cathedral steps flourishing a stethoscope at the lunch-time crowd – 'They use these things to listen to their money in the bank.' And Kitty banging tomato sauce on her pie in the works canteen, and helping dry the dishes afterwards. She worked hard, loved her work, and people loved her; but she lost.

I drove down to the hall at half past nine and found a dozen people drinking tea and nibbling cakes. An old man with a broom was sweeping round them. 'If you're chasing Mrs Hughes she's took orf.'

I drove to the port, where Kitty still lived in the same old house. Some of her party workers were sitting on the porch waiting for her. They had tried the places she might be.

I drove away to one they didn't know. Her red Ford Prefect stood in the street. The light in Irene's bedroom was on and a shadow I took for Kitty moved back and forth. That was all right, she had someone. I went home and listened to more results and went to bed. I had shifted to my house above the river but hadn't yet propped living-room and sundeck over the bank. I lay in bed and listened to the busy river run and celebratory horns toot in the town. 'Poor old Kit' – that was the only valediction I could manage.

I was asleep when she banged on the door. I thought my house was tumbling into the river, and sprang from my bed and knocked myself silly on the wardrobe door. I was staunching blood with a handkerchief and seeing double and trembling with shock as I let Kitty in.

She switched on lights and strode about my house. 'Put the kettle on, I need some tea.' I managed that with one hand, and poured myself a whisky. Kitty had given up alcohol because of her stomach, but poisoned herself with sludgy tea and heaped spoons of sugar. 'Jesus,' she said, looking at what I brought her. She tipped it down the sink and sloshed the pot and poured a new cup, black as tar. 'You heard the result, I suppose.'

'Yes,' I said, and told her I was sorry. But there were special votes to come so she had a chance.

'Don't be bloody wet,' Kitty said. She hissed. 'They were laughing at me down there. They've been waiting for this.'

'Nonsense,' I said.

'What would you know? They hate me. I saw it in their eyes.'

'They love you, Kit. You're mother and favourite child rolled into one. You're Auntie Kitty. This was against the government. It was boundaries.'

'Someone yelled, "You fat silly cow, you've been asking for it." '

'There's always someone like that. One of the Bog boys.'

She grunted and swallowed tea and shoved out her cup. 'Pour me another. And where were you? I thought at least my brother would turn up.'

I told her I had come and found her gone, and tracked her to Irene's where I felt I'd be in the way.

'Bloody Irene. Useless bitch.'

I asked what the matter was.

'I don't know. Sick, she says. She's playing bloody ladies again.

Hasn't got enough to do, that's what's wrong with her.' She went to the window and looked at the town. I brought her tea across but she didn't take it. Lit windows, dim streets, pale grass verges, car lights moving on the black hill over the port: Kitty ground her teeth at Jessop.

'I'd love a bloody earthquake right now.' Then her body quaked and she was crying. I put her tea on the window sill and led her to the sofa and sat her down. I put my arm around her and let her cry. I've said she never cried, or rarely cried, but this was grief of another order. Kitty wept part of her life away. Her tears made a puddle in my collar bone and ran down my chest into my navel. I felt the warm liquid wriggling in and knew our blood union was intact and no one but I could comfort her. She cried herself out. Then she took my handkerchief and blew her nose and went away to the lavatory. I got a tea-towel and dried my chest.

Kitty came back, looking at the blood on the handkerchief. 'Noel, your head. God, I'm selfish.' She sponged the cut with cotton wool and put a plaster on. Then she had more tea and I had whisky and we talked the night away. She told me wicked things about MPs. She told me tricks she used to get her way. We talked about our parents and she phlogisticated. She told me what a fool I was to buy a birds-nest house on a precipice but said she wished she had a place like it. 'Then I could look at Jessop. Bloody town.'

We had another look at it.

'I'm not finished with it yet, Noel. Not by a long chalk.'

'What will you do? Stand again next time?'

'You bet I will. It's my bloody seat after all. But I've just thought, I might stand for Council. Keep my hand in.'

'Good idea.' Anything that kept her bouncing, kept her making positive noises about herself, was a good idea. I walked up to the gate with her. The sky was lightening over the hills and Jessop looked misty and fragile. 'The fools, they've got to do without me now.'

She drove away, and I pulled the plaster off – hate things sticking to my skin – and went to bed and slept until the afternoon, when Kitty woke me with a phone call.

'Noel, they were still on my porch when I got home. Two or three of them. They want me, Noel. They still want me.'

'I told you that.'

'So, do you know what I'm going to do. Why be a tuppenny councillor? I'll run for mayor.'

47

And she did, and won two elections easily and was unopposed in a third. Jessop's Auntie Kitty – 'Just come and bang on my door, I'm always home.' Now and then she rode in the Austin Princess, but she kept her Ford Prefect and that's how people remember her: a fat lady buzzing about in a little red car, and putting one meaty leg out and projecting her bum, then turning, arms akimbo, heavyweight wrestler: 'What's the problem?' Kate will say I'm doing it again, making Kitty grotesque. No Kate, I'm stylizing her, I'm trying to find the shape she made in people's minds.

She didn't try to win back her parliamentary seat. 'No fear. I get more done in half a day than I managed in fourteen years in that place.' One of the things she did was support me on the Lomax Trust Board. Under the terms of the Act the mayor and the local MP and the bishop and the Chairmen of the County Council and the Harbour Board were ex-officio members. Kitty was on the board for twenty-three years. She knew as much about the Lomax as I did.

I got through the meetings by treating them as a sporting event. Well, I thought, I lost that one but maybe I'll win the next. In fact those men did not want me in their little club. Scientists, one told me, haven't got a clue about money. 'The average test-tube wallah,' he said, 'isn't worth two bob. You mix a bit of this with a bit of that and shake it up and if it changes colour, wowee, science. Keep it in your lab, Dr Papps. What we're here for in this room is to maximize Alfred Lomax's investment.' A government appointee, that fellow. Women weren't worth two bob either, in his book. But Kitty and I won a round or two. She soft-soaped the bishop on to her side, and shifted a couple over by argument, and a couple by terror. They were terrified she would become even less of a lady and 'darn it' and 'what in tarnation' turn into something worse. But sometimes all she had to do was show how things really were.

An example. She was new on the Board, on as MP, and I was not director yet and still doing trials on pakihi land. 'Kitty,' I said, 'those stupid mugs, they want to stop my work. They say I'm getting

203

nowhere. But I'm right on the edge of it. It's sulphur, that's the answer, even though it's molybdenum deficiency.'

'Tell them.'

'I've got no access. I tell John Dye till I'm blue in the face. I put in reports. But he's an entomologist, he can't make them understand.'

Kitty thought about it. 'Have you got something we can show them? Have you got some grass growing where there wasn't any before?'

'I'm getting grass over my ankles,' I said. 'But they won't drive sixty miles to see.'

'Leave that to Kitty.'

Within a week she had them in cars and over the hill and had mince pies and cups of thermos tea spread on my grass; with photos of how the land had been. They sat cross-legged and munched and sipped (and burped politely), and passed the photos round, pulling out handfuls of good green grass.

'Remarkable. I wouldn't have believed it. Sulphur, you say?'

Then they strolled about and scared the fat lambs, and the bishop talked of God and the others of profits, and half a dozen happy men they were. But Kitty and I walked to the top of the hill – she could tramp in those days, her legs had not swollen up – and looked at the swamp on the other side, full of red water and sphagnum moss, and Kitty said, 'I like this better. Unreconstructed.'

'That's a funny word for a politician.'

'Is that all you think I am, Noel?'

She moved into mystery when she forced me to consider her; she brought a jolt of fear, and love too, in my chest. Now and then it was so strong it got my head as well, threatened consciousness. I had to hold on, keep myself in place, and defend observed reality with mundane thoughts. I looked at the swamp, saw what she meant; but thought of reclamation, looked for uses – and it was a suggestion of mine, some years later, that led to the use of dried moss as bedding for orchids. Big business now, big sales to Japan. I've done as much as anyone – mundane thoughts – to turn this South Pacific wilderness into the giant dairy farm and sheep run and slaughter-house of today. First the settlers and soldiers, raw encounter, gaining and getting, then politicians rationalizing theft, then men like me with our improvements. I'm not ashamed, I'm not proud either. That is the way it was. Who comes after? I can't identify them properly. The entrepreneurs and the urban peasants. Kate and Shane come from a different world, I know that much. Big city world, city apprehensions. They don't have much of the loot but they understand it. I never will, and don't want to.

Phil Dockery understands. It's a world he helped to make and lives in happily. That putting up, money and buildings both, 'developing'; and that ripping down, and 'ripping off', as Kate would say. We have gangsters, and Wall Street men, smart-money men, and footpads, hunting packs, and there are fights in the streets, with real knives. And the original owners are acting up. They want back what was theirs and I don't blame them. I really don't blame anyone. Except myself, at times, and not very hard, for not understanding it and being glad to be past it all.

Ah well, Kitty and I exchanged a thought or two and came on down and put our reconstructed board members in their cars and sent them home over the hill to Jessop. We followed slowly in mine, up from the pakihi lands, up from the swamps. At the top of the hill we turned off the highway and drove ten miles on marble chips and dirt, with sink holes and limestone on either side, and walked in a beech forest for two miles, in a dry creek bed, with rhino heads, dragon backs, with frozen waves and licking tongues and blind eyes and talons all about, and ferns, and weed-topped pools like putting greens, and a bush robin too, that kept us company – elf-country Kate would recognize from her books – and came to Harkin's Hole, the biggest hole, that drops from its theatre of cliffs, eight hundred feet straight down to the new stream running in place of the dry. We crept on broken boulders by the mouth, went four-footed, sat holding on, feeling the pull of gravity; of desire. I want that fall and dark and oblivion; terror, peace. Terror, then nothing, which lies beyond peace and cannot be imagined or spoken of. The hole does this to me. Kitty felt it too. I saw her shiver. There's no exaggeration in all this. Do you know Harkin's Hole? You could drop a battleship down.

We read a plaque fixed on the wall beyond the boulders, memorial to a caver killed the year before. I threw in a broken stone, we waited a long time: tiny click, tiny echo.

'Come on, Noel,' Kitty said, 'we'll get out of here.' We crept away.

Now the scientist in me wants it explained, but I'm not metaphysician or psychologist and can't oblige. It simply seems to me that the mind – and here were two – at certain promptings enters the realm of supra-knowledge where rational enquiry does not hold; is out of phase with the realities of the place (if *place* it is), and speculation compromised by impurities we bring with us – so one finds the things one is conditioned for; or can, on the other hand, refuse to find and simply travel there without hoping for knowledge to carry home. Comes out with memories though – but treated as data they become compromised in turn. You see the problem? There are no names we can agree on.

Yet Kitty and I stayed in a kind of agreement as we drove home. We sat in my car on the harbour front and ate fish and chips, watching the sun sink into the sea. She placed her hand on mine as it went down . . . then gave a pat, wiped salty mouth: 'Yup, we've got 'em. Easy meat.'

Who was that? It took a moment. Ah, the board.

I dropped her off, went home; and still that coldness, dread and desire, was on my skin, and I lay cold and stiff on my bed; and in the small hours piled blankets on and made myself warm; put it all aside until this day, when it comes back unaltered by the years. But I'm not, as I said, philosopher or guess-man . . .

On that other matter, she was right. They let me get on with my work.

Head-on clash, reasonable persuasion: Kitty was happy with either. And she loved being underhand. The Lomax started charging for advice in the sixties. Alfred Lomax's money wouldn't stretch. We began a consultancy service and had two or three of the staff share their time between that and research. One young man put up a fight – Tim McMinn. He felt demeaned to be charging a dollar every time he uttered a mouthful of words. When orchardists came in he said to them, 'I can't tell you that without charging you. Go home and ring me up tonight.' It got back to the board. 'Fire him,' they demanded, with red faces and bulging eyes. I was not going to do that. Tim McMinn was a good scientist. 'He's feeling cross, let him work it out.' 'Fire him.' They huffed and puffed about loyalty and making an example and Kitty it was who got the thing deferred for a month. Then, when it came up, she said to Victor Richards, the Harbour Board chairman, 'How's your home brew getting on, Vic?'

'Eh? What?'

'Five point eight per cent, I hear. That's pretty strong.' She smiled at Vic with her blunt square teeth and the fellow went white. His offence was no more than a peccadillo; sufficient for Kitty all the same. Vic, she told us, had brought a bottle of his home brewed beer to the lab and got one of the chemists to test it for alcoholic content. It had happened in working hours and Vic hadn't offered to pay. That didn't seem much different from Tim McMinn's offence. Later, when everyone was exhausted with argument, she smiled and said that as we couldn't agree the public would have to judge. She meant that she would talk to the press.

Tim McMinn kept his job.

I said to her, 'Thanks, Kitty. What a storm in a teacup.'

'No such thing. That boy McMinn's got a wife and children. I wasn't going to see him rail-roaded out by a gang of National Party toughs. You tell him though, tell him to watch his step. I can't do it twice.'

She knew her limits more and more. She was growing old and her body was letting her down. After Irene died she came to me. I began to understand that I was her only friend. And, with me, Kitty rediscovered her gentleness. Did you know, Kate, that we had a kind of summer together? If we had not been brother and sister it would have been an affair. In a way it was an affair for it was full of delights and discoveries, of support and silence and company, and it had beginning and end. I was conscious of it and never oppressed but always easy, even when I saw it coming to its close.

She sold the little house where she'd lived with Des and raised her children and been our MP and no-nonsense mayor, and came to live with me up on the hill, over the river. I had been one year retired and my house had sprouted cheekily, living-room and sundeck on stilts. Kitty and I whiled away weekends in the sun, watching the river roll and children play. 'See,' I would say, pointing at a cat on the sewer pipe, his private crossing, or a white-faced heron spearing silver-bellies; or, looking up, two hang-gliders balancing over the hill. Brakes screeched and a car ended up facing the wrong way on the valley road. 'My God, I'm going to do something about the speed limit there. Make a note of it, Noel.' I bought a pair of binoculars and she watched her town. We saw cricket and hockey matches and pipe band displays and vintage car rallies and cycle races and runaway horses and car smashes and a house burn down and a motorbike gang with police car trailing and scrub fires on the hills and pink vapour trails in the sunset as jumbo jets headed west to Australia; and joggers dawn and dusk and in the lunch hour. And the postman bitten by a dog. We watched the monstrous DB hotel go up and saw its neon sign in the night, winking on and off behind the cathedral.

We had a grandstand view of the flood of '73. Kitty was ill that week but she struggled out of bed and stood at the window, wrapped in scarves and dressing gown, and watched the rain and lightning, and black logs race like battleships down the river. They rammed and sank the sewer pipe. Young willows bent, and struggled up, and bent again, were gone. Kitty lumbered to the phone. 'You'll need sandbags in Dougan Street. It's going over.' Trucks arrived and men in yellow slickers built a wall but water lapped the top and poured over in a street-long fall. It ran into back yards and floated firewood out of sheds. It topped the letter-boxes, it filled porches and garages and cars and spread slicks of oil into bean-rows. On the other side of the river a woman waded lawns up to her chest and saved a terrier drowning on its chain. Sheds were swept away, greenhouses crashed. Below my house the weight of the river beat on the cliff. I became frightened that we'd be undermined. 'Kitty,' I said, 'we'll have to get out.'

'I'm staying here.' She swept the binoculars round. She wheezed and quaked and tears ran on her cheeks. Yes, yes, Kitty cried again. But she was hard and quick, and back and forth to the phone in her lumbering trot, on her swollen feet; and later in the day was dressed and gone and I did not see her until midnight. Then she was ill for a month. One reason I keep Archie Penfold as my doctor is the kindness he showed her then.

'Noel,' he said, 'she'll have to give it up. She'll kill herself if she tries to see out her term.'

'Let me,' Kitty said. 'Just let me get the park. Then I'll stop.'

She sat up in her pillows, wearing a pink bed jacket that didn't suit her, with her grey hair done in a single plait. The bed creaked as she moved and a folder of papers spilled on the floor. I could not stop time from slipping about and did not know which Kitty it was I tried to persuade. My sense of her life was inclusive and would not be stopped at invalid or Madam Mayor or the Honourable Kitty – none of her personae would contain her. Kitty Papps. Or Nurse Papps. Or Mrs Hughes with sick husband and barefoot kids. I had Kitty complete, and understood that she would leave me soon and soon be dead. And yet I could speak only of the matter that concerned her.

'All you want,' I grinned, 'is Kitty Hughes Park. It's an ego trip.'

'No more than Sir Noel,' she retorted. 'I'd never sink to that, believe me.'

We made a bargain. She would finish getting the new park for Jessop and then would resign as mayor and look after herself. 'I'll sit on your sundeck and grow fat.'

'Fatter,' I said, and picked her folder up and put it in her lap. 'Get on with it. I think all three of us could do with a rest.'

The third one was Phil Dockery. This was the battle he's told Kate about. He came to quarrel with Kitty in my livingroom and turned his ox-blood hue and shouted at her: 'Comrade bloody Crappski, that's who you bloody are.'

I ordered him out but he stayed to shout some more, and Kitty answered back with fierce enjoyment. I thought if they swelled much more they'd go crashing up through my roof and tower on the hillside, two cloud giants, cumuli, beating each other with wind and storm. Blood went to my head, I shouted too, accusing them, and had to lie down. They came into my bedroom, quiet at last, and stood like parents looking down at me. Kitty put her hand on my brow. 'He's all right. Sorry, Noel. This greedy bugger always works me up.'

'Talk some sense into her, Noel,' Phil said. 'People need houses to live in, not bloody climbing frames and flying foxes.'

'People! Listen to him. He doesn't know the meaning of the word. What are they Phil, these *people* you're suddenly talking about?'

'Don't start again,' I said. 'Please don't start.'

'Bring him a whisky, Kit. That's what he needs, the skinny sod. And have one yourself. Let's drink to the old days. Tup Ogier, eh?'

'Tup would have been on my side. Tup would have wanted a park.'

'Please,' I said.

We drank whisky – Kitty had lime juice – and had a conversation from which, at first, the bottom fell out. They sent sharp grins at each other, stabbed with a finger, hooked with a thumb. I called them back and easiness prevailed. Kitty remembered well, so did

I, but Phil, who had suggested it, had little practice and we kept on surprising him.

'Hey, I remember that. Old Tup with his tuning fork, eh. Men of Harlech. That was a good song.'

'Remember the pageant, Phil? The whoit cliffs? Mrs Beattie stretching your ear?'

'And Edgar Le Grice?' Kitty said. 'Dad had to hide Frau Reinbold in the bakehouse. She ate one of his pies there.'

'Yeah, she would,' Phil said. 'And Le Grice burning that piano. I dream about that joker, you know.'

I looked at Phil with respect. I had never thought of him as dreaming. He seemed gifted, for a moment, with innocence. 'Irene,' he said, 'she was a looker. Boy, did I have a crush on her.'

'I thought it was me,' Kitty said.

'You too. The pair of you. Have you got any idea how you looked to a kid from the Port? With your Lamingtons and mince pies and fruit squares. Jesus, it makes me hungry now.'

'Irene brought her lunch in a wicker box,' Kitty said.

'Yeah. And your white socks, eh. I don't know whether I was after you or your lunches.'

'Well, Phil, you've turned that upside down. I'm from the Port now, you're from Nob Hill.'

By this route they travelled back to their argument. I did not help by mentioning Bucks Hole. Bucks Hole was part of Kitty's park. There would be paths by the river, an adventure playground with log fort and flying foxes, a fitness course, and playing fields on the flat land. The old Le Grice house would be pulled down and changing sheds and a pavilion go in its place. Kitty had a model on display in the foyer at the Council Chambers.

Comrade Olga's toy, Phil called it. 'You should have stuck with dolls' houses. That way you can't do any harm.'

'What to, Phil? Your bank account? Haven't you got enough yet? Are you frightened of starving in your old age?'

'Enough,' I said. 'Out. Both of you.'

They went to the livingroom and shouted some more, and Phil stumped away up the path. Kitty came back to my room, breathing hard. 'I'll give him a heart attack yet.' She looked near a heart attack herself.

*

210

Phil won, as you know, Kate. He had friends on Council and though Kitty was popular in the town most councillors were tired of her and her ways. She had no patience left and showed her contempt. They would not vote money for her park. Phil bought the land and won planning approval and we have a new suburb now on Le Grice's farm. One of the streets is called Kitty Hughes street.

Kitty resigned for health reasons. She went for a holiday to Pam's, your mother's, Kate, in Wellington, and fell ill there and stayed. Our affair, our summer idyll, came to an end.

48

And, Kate says, I let myself go. I deny that. I took a Pacific cruise one year and even managed to flirt with a lady in her forties. I've been out and about quite a bit. I'm a well known figure in this town – or was until I grew tired of the same old faces.

'Exactly,' Kate says, 'you gave up trying. When I came here you were a dried-up little – ' couldn't find the word but I guess chimp – 'with a nasty tongue. And none too clean. You never got out of your dressing gown. At least I got you wearing clothes again.'

Lies! Distortions! Talk about selected memories! All right, I didn't bath as often as I might have. Do you know how hard it is to bath when you're old? You'll find out. That's one of my (nasty) consolations. Everybody finds out in the end, if they last that long.

I'm glad you think I've improved. Describe me now. Go on. What am I like?

She won't do it. Perhaps she thinks she'll have to allow me a good point or two. I still belong to the Jessop Club, Kate. Haven't let my membership lapse. A gentlemen's establishment, unlike that one for players Phil frequents. I'll surprise you one day by going there for a drink. Won't they raise their well-bred eyebrows when I walk in wearing slippers and scarf. Perhaps I'll even wear my dressing gown.

But yes, I'll confess: I let myself go. And, in another way, I fought back. I'm no weakling Kate, I won't have you think that. In all my years alone I never let myself fall into habits. I felt if they got a hold they'd compress me slowly, squeeze me dry, and I'd be dead. So I've been dirty now, clean another time, even bought a stick of deodorant once – threw it away when it made a rash in my armpits. I've eaten this for a season, that for another; muesli, beans on toast; turned my garden over, let it grow weeds. So on, so on. Kept myself alive.

What was missing was a person to reflect me back at myself. And take reflections in her turn.

A pinch and a punch for the first of the month. She's getting chirpy, which I'm pleased to see, even though she bruised my arm. (Arnica, Kate, your box of tricks.) I'm on my feet, and out on my sundeck, in my chair. It's a blue and silver day in the upper air but green, explosive, on the ground. You can see the growth, hear sappy transportations. Kate has juices humming in her too. She sings in the kitchen, chipping plates, and here she comes to plump my cushions up and tousle my hair. The meaning of all this isn't hard to find: she's out of love. That is one of the great feelings.

No more back-packers. Three cheers for that. The last one, a little German girl, a doctor she was, showed me her scalpel for slicing rapists. I could not stop my hands from leaping to protect my private parts. Nausea stirred in my stomach. 'Put it away. Get out of my room.' A man isn't safe with some of these girls. But they're all gone, hooray, Kate's finished with them. Sibelius goes rampaging through the house and after him a breathy flute has its say. There's no yearning in Kate though, and no storms gathering. Good health of every kind beams out of her. I'm just a little frightened that such wholeness is unnatural.

I should have touched wood. There was too much hubris about. But, all the same, she's undefeated. I haven't any doubt she will come through. She talks to herself. 'Shit,' she says. She grins unhappily and angrily. She is learning. Kate is increasing herself with a new growth ring. Victories are possible Kate, but not easy ones.

'Stop mixing your metaphors,' she replies.

Very well then, simple terms: here's what happened. That day she sang in the kitchen, yesterday, Phil Dockery called. 'I've found your runaway boyfriend,' he said.

Phil interests me as much as Kate. I'm not sure he'll survive this. I'm not sure what Phil will become. It's a busy season at the stud.

Phil is spending most of his time out there. Yesterday morning Shane knocked at his door. Stood there grinning, dressed in shorts and bush shirt, with feet bare.

'So there you are, you young prick. Come back with your tail between your legs, eh?' Words I have to guess, but I know Phil and they're likely to be right. I'm not so sure about his actions. I see him throw his arms wide to give Shane a hug. Phil has taken Shane for his son. He loves someone for the first time in his life (although it's possible he loved his father, I don't know). And Phil is suffering, he's in pain. His eyes were red and furious and perhaps he'd been crying.

He said to Kate: 'Can't you hold your man, eh? All you've got to do is give 'em – ' He made an upward thrust with his middle finger.

'Where is he?' Kate said. In her usual way she began to mottle. Out of love? Not quite. Love had a bit of her pinched in its fingers, and made a lightning grab and had a handful. Love or something.

Phil shook his head as though to work off a punch. 'Out there. With that gang of Christers over the hill.'

'The commune?'

'If that's what you call it.' He looked at me and his eyes filled with tears. 'All he came back for was his tools.'

Kate turned away. She got my car keys from the drawer and went out.

'He told me they pray for me.' Phil ran to the door. 'They pray for you, Kate. He said to tell you.'

The car went off. We watched it cross the bridge and go out of sight.

'She won't get him. He's screwing some sheila over there. It's got to be that.'

'But he goes along with the religious stuff?'

Phil nodded. He was frightened his voice would wobble if he spoke. He sat down and held his knees and seemed to want to twist the kneecaps off. He dug his fingers under and held on. In that way he stopped himself from shaking. I asked how long Shane had been at the commune. He didn't know. Told him to get his tools and get to hell off his property. Shane walked up the hill and over the top with the tool kit slung on his back.

'Bloody fool. Bloody young fool. I was going to leave it to him, Noel. Jesus, he would have been rich. I'm a rich man. I've got no one to leave it to. He would've had the lot. All he had to do . . .'

213

What did Shane have to do? Drink with Phil? Be a son? Love him?

I drank with Phil. We drank the afternoon away. I want nothing from him. I don't love him but have a feeling I can't name, made up of pity and respect, and disapproval, and long familiarity. We are, simply, close to one another. It's as if he's in my family and I must love him willy-nilly in spite of all the things I loathe about him.

That came out stronger than I intended. I wrote 'love' and the word isn't right but I can't find one to replace it with.

Perhaps it's right.

I know that I love Kate. It needn't be a secret. And I'm leaving her my property. You won't be rich, Kate. I won't change my mind if you go away. Leave or stay, it changes nothing. But don't act on whims or fantasies. Think a while. You're almost a grown-up person now. I took a much longer time.

She tells me to keep my money. And get away from this airy-fairy crap about love. Now who's mixing metaphors? But I'll do as I'm told. I'll stick to the facts, I'll unstick the facts from me.

I watered my whisky and drank only three or four to his dozen. But still I reeled as I crossed the room to call his taxi. 'We don't need 'em, eh Noel? Stuff the young pricks. You and me, we're buddies, eh? One for the road.' The wrongness of that 'buddies' troubled him. I don't think it's a term he's used before.

The driver honked his horn and finally came to the door, refused a drink, took him away. I boiled an egg and ate a water cracker spread with marmite. I went to bed and slept a painful half-drunken sleep for several hours. A glass of warm milk then and another cracker; and some sleep of better quality. I woke and worried about Kate and opened my bedroom door and turned on my lamp, inviting her to talk when she came in. The clock went round. The moon travelled twenty degrees in the sky. A siren sounded down by the Port. I thought of car crashes and suicide (facts, Kate, facts). She came at last, with rubber steps, with slamming door. And a muttered faecal expletive. (I wish you'd stop!) Refused my invitation. 'Turn off your light, it's half past three.' I heard water gurgle in her bed. Later on she came down the hall and peed like the Swiss girl. Then we slept. I dreamed of Edgar Le Grice. What were your dreams, Kate? I'd like to include them.

In the morning she was up and rattling dishes, scraping toast. She brought me a cup of tea and laughed at my headache, 'Serves you right. I hope that senile lecher's got a worse one.'

I groaned and took a sip, and felt no better. 'How was Shane?'

'Off his rocker. He's got Christian platitudes dripping out his ears.'

And that is all she's told me up till now. Please tell me, Kate. I was fond of him.

She says, 'Have you ever seen that place?'

'No,' I say.

'Impressive. Did I tell you I lived in a commune once? It wasn't religious. Well, I guess the religion was making things grow. And sharing things. I had to get out. I couldn't stand all that forced togetherness.'

'Is that what they've got at Long Tom's?'

She shakes her head. 'It's Jesus there, holding them. He's, like, cement. That's what Shane says. Poor Shane.' She swings between grief and rage. Shane, in her view, is a casualty. He has suffered a dreadful defeat. He's poor Shane one moment and a bloody coward the next.

'They baptized him. They dunked him in the sea. God, what a laugh!' Tears stand in her eyes. Poor Kate. And poor Shane, I agree, even though it seems he's saved himself.

She drove in after lunch, coming down the zig-zag road in low gear. They've cut their gardens from high gorse and manuka and planted shelter belts and toi-toi hedges. From high on the hill it's beautiful, Kate admits. And down below – well, there's nothing Mickey Mouse about the place, they're in business. The usual commune things happen, of course: make your own butter, make your own bread, milk some goats, spin some wool. But they grow for commercial markets – strawberries and kiwi fruit and all sorts of vegetables. They've got cherry trees and nut trees coming on. They're building a big glass-house for tomatoes. That's why Shane wanted his tools.

He pulled her out of the car and kissed her. 'The big slob.' His elf-locks were shorn off. They're squeaky clean, Kate sneers, and what they can't pray out they snip off. He introduced her and everybody smiled and smiled and smiled – they never stop – and said Bless you.

'I'm not your bloody sister,' Kate replied. They coped with her anger easily. 'They've got that half-wit look, as though they've eaten too many greens. Or had their blood supply cut off to the brain. God, they're zombies. Shane too. He's getting it.'

'Come on, Kate. Stick to the facts. Say what happened.'

'Nothing happened.'

She could make no dent in him. She'd gone out there to save or damage him and could do neither.

I think about it. Happy Christians. Sad Kate. But there's no message in it for me. I see them churning butter, picking berries (the season's wrong, but that's what I see) and hear them laugh and see them touch each other, but in the end the thing I'm most aware of is what they haven't got that Kate has got. I won't propagandize. I won't say what it is. In fact I can't. I don't know. Nor does Kate. She walked among them chockful of her passions. She sneered at Shane and called him nasty names. They went down to the beach and sat on the sand and in that lovely place Kate was ugly with him. Why do I see her then as victor? I must, in fairness, say that no contest has been held. There was Kate, there was Shane, in their state of decreasing gravitational pull. That is all; and that's a huge unknowable amount.

'He told me to stop swearing. And blaspheming.'

'What did he talk about?'

'The blood of the Lamb.'

'The wrath of God?'

'They're not into that so much. It's all lovey-dovey.'

I asked a difficult question. 'Does he have a girlfriend there?'

'Oh,' she said airily, 'there's someone. They don't *do* anything. Hold hands, I guess. I could get him. If I wanted him.'

'You tried, didn't you?'

For a moment I thought she was going to cry. But she controlled it. Her features seemed to contract, became tight and dry, like Edgar Le Grice's in the home, pulled closer, too close, by a drawstring. She nodded once, quickly, a sharp blow like a hammer on a nail.

'What happened?'

'I tried to get him to fuck me.' She swallowed: tasting grief? humiliation? 'Undid his fly. Fished him out.'

'But?' I said. I saw her like a surgeon, slicing open, pulling out; and that made it sad and horrible. 'He didn't want to?'

'He wanted to all right. You should have seen. But he wouldn't. He hated me. He would have killed me.'

I shivered for her. Saw her danger. 'What did he do?'

'Ran into the sea. Gave a yell. Like he was shot. Splashed around. Laughed at me. He was lifting water over his head. Smacking his hands on it. Then he started singing hymns.'

'It sounds pagan.'

'I don't know what it was. He kept on calling, "Let Him into your heart, Kate. Give yourself to Him. Come with me".'

'What did you do?'

'I went away.'

'That was right.'

'I parked somewhere and sat around and had a sleep. Then I came home.'

'You couldn't have stayed there. But if he'd come with you – ' I didn't finish. I meant he would have killed her, or himself in some slow way.

Kate, I'm glad. I'm glad he's there. I'm more than glad you didn't get him. You won't like my saying that, you won't agree, but you need my way of seeing things.

'I'm glad too,' Kate says.

49

There's a curve in my tale, a narrowing. Some things are going and will not come back – some people gone. Others are shrinking in importance – people, events – and multitudes are going to be left out. Yet I see the importance of everything. Each thing has its weight. That is what concerned me in my work. A life though isn't measured in that way. How is it measured, how does it move? That's what I'm busy finding out. That's what I'm *not* busy finding out.

I'm not any longer compelled. I'm easy in my choices and casual in picking up this or that. I sit here and think about things and choose not to write them down; or I forget. A morning on my sundeck passes like the turning of a wheel. Time present and time past, now and then, bring their motions into agreement and I know the joys of congruency.

217

Well, that's a mood. I must not be too pleased with myself or some quantity unknown will come along and flatten me.

Here comes Kate with a cup of tea. Now, half an hour later, she's gone. What a pleasant time. We looked at the river and looked at the mountains and took notice of the town in between. Nothing came up to unsettle us. Nothing came creeping out of our heads and there were no great flashes of light. Kate dunked her gingernut too long and half of it fell in her lap as she tried to rush it to her mouth. That was the worst thing that happened. She said nothing about Shane. The Shane in her no longer wants to make his presence felt. She has him fitted in place. That was quick, but she achieved it by symbolic action: packed his things in a tea-chest, nailed down the lid, painted his name on it and the commune's name, called a carrier – retained only the bit of him she can use, the bit she can't get rid of anyway. Well done, Kate. Now she's at her typewriter, busy with Kitty Hughes.

'You can't leave Irene out,' she says. I was not aware of it, but she claims that Irene isn't properly done. It pleases me, amuses me, the bakehouse image. I see my father lifting out loaves on his paddle and dropping them one by one in a wicker basket. I won't accept it though, people as loaves. I mean to leave Irene at her piano. That is my way of seeing her: Irene in mid-life, at her music. That is the measure of little Reen.

But I've been too sure of myself, too complacent, and things have gone out of kilter again. The quantity unknown was Royce Lomax. He's a person easy to overlook but now and then you notice him standing by, wagging his tail. That was a kick aimed at Royce. Why do I want to kick him when the friendly thing, the thing he most longs for, is a pat?

He telephoned half an hour ago. Royce is getting ready for an exhibition of his work. He knows I won't go to the opening so invites me to his house to see the paintings before he takes them to the gallery. 'Some of them will interest you, I think.' I can't imagine what he means by that. Has he painted me spying at the window? Has he painted Irene scratching my face?

I pleaded sickness, feeble thing to do, but he asked for Kate and told her he'd found some photographs of Kitty and a note from her to

Irene, nothing important. She could have them if she called and brought me too. Cheeky devil! Am I goods to be bargained for?

'I won't go, Kate.'

'It'll do you good to get out, Noel. You've been sitting in this house for almost a year.'

'What's wrong with that?'

'Nothing, I guess.' She ruffled my hair. 'Do it for me.'

We're going tomorrow. Kate has promised to make our visit short.

50

First we did some shopping. Kate parked the car in one of those asphalt yards bigger than two football fields together, with little boxes painted up and down. That place is a city square with its heart ripped out. We went into a building called City Centre, past toilets with graffiti spray-painted on their walls. *The Grateful Dead*, says one, very ancient. What does that mean? Is it a message? *No Tour*, says another. That could be a message too.

I bought slippers and pyjamas. All this is of no consequence. Several women stopped to say hello. How they love saying *Sir*. Good God, I thought, after I'd said goodbye, I acted with that one in *Charley's Aunt*. We made love in my car after the party. Damned uncomfortable and I got cramps. She thought my cries of pain were cries of passion and tried to stop my mouth with her own. And today she very nearly bobs a curtsey and addresses me as Sir Noel. But all this is of no consequence.

A hawker was selling copper knick-knacks from a cart. Kate stopped and talked to him and bought a bangle. I started to enjoy my walk in the street. Buskers piped and fiddled outside the bank where the girl with the milk petition had been. I dropped a dollar note in their violin case; and further up the street I bought a raffle ticket for a trip for two to Disneyland. Kate says she'll come with me; and then, I said, we'll go on to New York and London and I'll show you real buskers in Vienna and Copenhagen. But I was more than satisfied with our homegrown pair. The bishop strode by. He's a new chap. I found his purple comic, though he wore it with more style than his predecessor. The young too were in coloured clothes; in coloured hair. I saw girls with yellow lipstick and silver nails and one with a black star on her cheek and one with a gold stud in her nose. Two young men strolled by, holding hands. How things change. But it's not of much consequence. It's fun to look at though. This city, Jessop, floats like a coloured jellyfish in the sea. It grows and it pulses and it throbs. I'm part of it, a cell; that, at least, is how it seems for a moment. And cells don't think, so I won't question it.

Now on we go to see Royce Lomax and his paintings.

I said to Kate, 'You go in first and make sure he's got his dog tied up.'

It's possible I saved my life with that precaution. The animal came leaping from the porch. Kate held out her hand for him to sniff and I felt my own hand full of pains and felt teeth sink in my groin and hip. This is extreme, hysterical, but it's a fact, so I put it down. The barking brought Royce round from the back yard. He led the dog away by its collar and Kate came back to the car for me. She leaned in the window and held my hand. 'I'm sorry, Noel. I should have rung him up. Are you all right? Do you want to go home?'

'No, no,' I said, 'I'm here now. Let's go in. Is it tied up?'

We walked up the path through the weeds. I've seen gardens more neglected and houses in greater disrepair, but this neglect was personal and I had a sense of weeds growing in my skull, of parts of me rusting and rotting and dropping off. Perhaps my recent fear was keeping circuits open for I'm not a person to care about *things* or be sentimental – but I began to stutter with rage and when Royce opened the door I threw words at him like scoria. This, this, this, I cried, this was a disgrace. It was criminal neglect. Royce was a vandal. He didn't deserve it, Irene's house . . . letting it fall into this *leprous* state . . . and so on. He took it well, went pink, grinned like a rabbit. He made no excuses, but said, 'Well, Noel, some things I see and some I don't. I guess I'm blind. It is a bit of a mess, isn't it?' He looked around the porch and said vaguely, 'It could do with a coat of paint.'

'But you won't do it.'

'Noel, Noel,' Kate said, and led me into the house. I blinded myself, I did not want to see, and was in the living-room, enveloped in a chair, before objects made themselves known. Then it was Irene's piano I saw – and I calmed down. I calmed down as though she played me music for that purpose. I – but enough about me. Why should I parade my feelings in this way? They existed, went away, and what profit is there in poking at their corpses? They were yesterday, and located in my head, and where is that, of what significance? What a tiny thing, my head. What a tiny thing, yesterday. And Royce. And Kate. This looms as a discovery. I might as well write the tale of three pebbles on the river bed.

I am sorry about that. Depression sometimes knocks me over like a medicine ball. It was that regiment of 'I's marching on the page. That's an explanation. Lead soldiers in red coats pretending with all their might to be alive.

It was old age. Another explanation. Suddenly your energy, all of your life, runs out. You're as dead as lead. You float away like ashes from a fire.

Making contradictions works as a cure.

Now. Royce gave Kate a wicker box of photographs and went to the kitchen to make tea. She read the letter first and smiled to herself.

'Interesting?'

'Mm. Perhaps.'

'Can I see?'

It was written on paper with a ministerial letter-head.

Dear Reen,

I shouldn't have troubled you with my nonsense. The rain was coming down and maybe there were ghosties that night, and maybe there are ghosties in my head. Who knows what I saw or what I did? Forget it, there's a pet, and that's an order. Eyes front. There's plenty up ahead to keep us busy.

Love,

Kitty.

'Doesn't make sense.' It can't make sense to us, that's what I mean. But Kate just gives a nod and a secret smile. She's playing the expert on Kitty Hughes and I don't mind letting her have the role if it makes her happy. She put the letter in her bag and started going through the photographs. Royce must have taken them. His talents don't extend to photography. They were mostly of Irene and he'd tried to do portraits with a snapshot camera. She was dark and blurred, shadows smudged her. In several her head seemed to bulge and be lopsided. He'd made the dislocation in her face extreme – and now that I say that, I wonder if he meant to? Perhaps his photographs came out just as he intended.

Kate threw those ones in the box and kept out half a dozen of Kitty and Irene.

'Not much good. Except for this.'

It showed them standing by Kitty's little car. Kitty had her hands on her hips and her bosom on attack. Irene, fingers folded at her waist, looked sideways up at her with a sly expression. Though one was large, one small, though one looked out, one in, they were equals in the photograph. I would have liked to keep it for myself.

'Find anything?' Royce came in with a tray.

'I'll keep this one,' Kate said. 'And the letter.'

'Yes, of course. You can take one of Irene, Noel, if you like. Take the lot. They're heading for the incinerator.'

I did not like that. But I need no photographs of her. I have her in my head. Kitty and Irene together I do not have. I told him I'd share the photograph Kate was taking.

She said, 'Did Irene give you any idea what this letter meant?'

'I've never seen it before. It's Dutch to me. Milk in your tea?'

The room was swept and dusted and though the piano was closed it had a glossy cared-for look. I discovered that Royce had a five-roomed house scattered in the mansion – kitchen, living-room, bedroom, bathroom, studio if that's the word – and he kept it neatly. All the rest was dusty, threadbare, peeling, tumbling down. When we'd had our tea he took us to see his paintings. His studio is the big room in the north corner of the house where I'd seen him doing pencil sketches of an apple. Now where has he got to? I don't know. It's a strange place and he's been so alone on the journey that now and then I'm afflicted with an image of this dumpy little man standing like a stone monolith on a moor. It's disturbing, it's bleak and cold, he's bleak and cold – and yet he's such an ineffectual fellow.

'There,' he said, 'these around the wall are the ones for the exhibition.'

I've said I don't like his paintings. I still don't like them. But does the word 'like' have relevance when one is faced with things of this sort? And is the Royce who waits so diffidently, is that Royce? Where does the darkness come from? What are these shapes? What is that light? Who is he?

I said, 'Good God.'

Kate said, 'Crikey,' under her breath. One of Kitty's words.

'These ones here are new. Since I called to see you, Noel.'

They were not hung with the rest but propped against the wall – paintings five or six feet tall and four feet wide. (That's one thing I can be sure about.) They were done on board and the paint was acrylic. (We talked about the chemistry of it later.) They were of my river, my hill. I did not have to be told, although the likeness was poor and the colours taken from outside nature. My green hill was grey or black. My river was black or white. Sometimes it was a black river under a black hill, defined only by strokes of the brush. But black or not, it was a river of light as well as water. There was no sky. How then did I know the black or grey in the top of the picture was the hill? I knew by a shape within the mass. He has always been good at things lying underneath; shapes within; shadows under surfaces. The river never varied in its line. It came in half way up the right hand side, plunged at the hill and was turned aside, perhaps thrown back; flowed out of frame at the bottom edge.

The hill crushed me, the river kept life within my body.

He offered me a painting as a gift. I said they were very nice but I did not want one, they were too big for my walls. Besides, I had real river and real hill.

'There is one painting I'd like if you've still got it. It used to hang in Irene's room.'

He was disappointed. He was crushed. That happens to artists I suppose. They must bounce back because they always seem to keep on going, and keep on going in their own way too. Royce's pain was quickly gone. He's a tough little egg. There's a shape within his shape. We left Kate in the studio and went up to Irene's room.

Terror at closed doors about to open, doors of those we love or seem to love. It ran through me like electricity, making my cheeks jump and eyeballs fizz and my heart bang in triple time – then was gone. I had felt there, for a moment, I was going to know Irene at last and make her mine. It was gone. I put my hand on the wall and stared at the dust in the mouldings. Sanctum? No. It was nothing really, no name fits. Royce opened up and led me in. He tugged the curtains, making golden dust, a swarm of gnats. I thought it was pretty and supplied a tinkly tune, yet had little sense of Irene's presence. Pink roses on the wallpaper, frills on the satin coverlet.

Not Irene. She was tougher, twistier, crueller than this. Her being was too large and complicated for this room.

'That's it,' I said to Royce, pointing at the picture. He took it down and blew dust off and wiped it with his sleeve. We sat on Irene's bed and looked at it. He was puzzled and intrigued.

'I'm not sure I know what it means.'

I touched the black shape over the sea. 'That's Irene. If you turn it round you'll see her face.' I was quite sure. I saw her face looking away from me. 'That's her too.' I touched the shadow in the sea and it seemed to move off slantwise and settle in a new place, deeper down.

Royce said nothing for a while. Then he agreed. 'I suppose you're right. I spent most of my life painting Irene.' He touched the black shape himself. 'I can't remember why she's there. I finished it, then I put her in. It's a rather messy picture though.'

'It's the one I want.'

'That's what she said. She said it was my first real painting.'

He told me that all his paintings, the ones he was famous for, the slitted caves and phallic trees, the hills wrenched askew, the hills that arched their backs like beasts breaking the crust of the land, the clouds like fists, the rivers that tore hills apart, were paintings of Irene, of himself, the inside of his head and of her head; and the shape, the outside, of her head. He used feng-shui, Chinese geomancy, as an aid, a kind of starter, but lately was getting by without intermediate forms. His painting had little to do now with symbols and metaphors. It owed less to the Viennese chappie too, Dr Fraud (Irene's name for him). It still owed quite a lot to phrenology. He and Irene had spent hours feeling the shape of each other's heads.

And I. Not hours. Just once. She was ill. It may have been the last time I saw her. She was in that room where Royce and I sat on the bed.

Irene wore a blue bed-jacket embroidered with lilies. She seemed near shedding her crinkled skin. She was only in her sixties but had no bitterness and no surprise about her death.

We talked about Tup Ogier and I asked if I could feel her bump of harmony. She took my hand and placed the fingers just above and forward of her ear, by the temple. So I touched Irene at last.

'What do you feel, any magnetism?'

'No,' I said. 'A kind of tingling.'

'Harmony is very strong in me. I've got a good bump. Now. Back here.' She shifted my fingers. 'Destructiveness. Very close. That's interesting, isn't it? Feel anything?' A kind of oiliness and inkiness, something cold, malevolent. But I'm suggestible at times – and this was a 'time'. 'Nothing,' I said, and moved my hand along.

Irene toured me round her head. 'Secretiveness, Noel. Very strong. Language. Not so good. Adhesiveness. Oh, I'm adhesive all right. This is Gall's system. Just one of many. Lot of nonsense.'

Suddenly she leaned at me and put her fingers on the base of my skull. I felt her strong key-pressing touch. It was personal and impersonal. 'Yes, I thought so. Amativeness. What a bump. You naughty boy.'

She laughed at me with bell-notes on that, my last visit, the only time we touched in friendliness.

Royce said, 'I know what you think about us, Noel. I know what the whole of Jessop thinks. But it's not true. We should have done it. We talked about it sometimes and we did it in our heads. But we kept on stepping back and putting it off, and in the end putting off was all we ever needed. Not doing it was a kind of act.'

I said I was sorry and he told me not to be. He and Irene lived all those years as man and wife, that's what they were, except in bed. They had a different sex life to take the place of that.

'I hate her,' Royce said. 'That's why – this.' He touched the black shape in the painting. 'But I love her too. She's the only thing I love. I could wring her neck.'

He smiled at me, a smile that made him boyish – nothing haunted. He's not a man to feel sorry for.

'People said my father took her to bed. That's not true either.'

'Yes, I know.'

Royce stood up. 'Well Noel, that's what happened. Or didn't happen. I've always wanted you to know.'

I thanked him. We went back to the studio and talked for a while about oil paints and acrylics and how long they last. Then Kate and I came home. I've hung the painting in the dining-room, which we seldom use.

There are no revelations. There's a filling in of gaps. Nothing surprises.

225

51

I don't mind sharing my house with spiders and silverfish. Or dust mites either. How many dust mites die in a vacuum cleaner attack?

Meanderings, apropos of nothing. Unless it's the fantail that came in this morning and pecked spiders from the rafters in my living room. The trouble is – no trouble – I'm fonder of birds than arachnida. I'd like to share my house with a fantail or two.

I've nothing to put down but that sort of thing. It seems to mean my story's done. A fantail in the house foretells a death (Maori belief?) but I put no credence on that sort of thing. Perhaps it was just telling me I've said all I have to say. But I'm used to my daily scribble and can't give it up. I have a habit.

I sit in the sun. Irene sat in the sun on her side veranda. She sat like Mrs Le Grice, in a rocking chair, wearing a wide-brimmed hat with a silk rose in the band. Now and then she took it off and turned up her face, drinking sunlight in the Swedish fashion. 'I come to think more and more that worship of the sun is the only proper worship.'

'God?' I asked.

'De trop.' That's the sort of thing Ruth might have said.

'Haven't you done some useful work? Haven't we been happy some of the time?' Yes, that's true. Are you telling me lives can be measured in that way? Ah, Ruth. (I spoke aloud – Kate, through the glass, looks up from her desk. A sound of longing, Kate, and love, that's all.)

I am dizzy with you, Ruth Verryt. You recede from me. I try to peer at you and try to touch – and yes, I touch. Are you still alive in your room, out there? I think you are. Statistics are on your side for another year. But statistics are the last thing we need. I'd have felt the drawing down of your blind.

Move away. Yes, you can go. Let Irene back. Irene is easier somehow. Her bright eyes and sick body. How do we come to be housed in this makeshift thing? Low comedy.

I'm a chimp, Sir Chimp, dressed in baggy pants, sitting on top of a boxful of secrets and lifting the lid and letting them out. I turn back-somersaults and scratch my armpits. That's one thing. There are plenty of others. I'm Noel Papps and I forget that my body is old. I spring up and run a hand through my hair – this dream of youth. I dash somewhere.

As well as that, I wait for the comet – the apparition. (Aren't words wonderful, they won't be still.) It's coming and I'll be one who sees it twice. This time I'll observe with knowledge; and, more importantly, interest – (which is the increase on capital).

You might say I'm waiting here dressed in the vestments of my faith, but wearing pink socks and a polka dot bow-tie.

A way to stop this is to give it a name. Put a lid on it. Make it an object. What shall it be? 'Papps.' 'Papps on Papps.' Pappery, Puffery, Lifting the Lid. I could fill a notebook with names.

'Plus Kate.' That's a good one. She came out to see what was bothering me. Nothing, I said. And talked about spiders, fantails, dust mites, tea-tree jacks – that's Piet Verryt! Side-stepped to a 'subject'; entertained her. Maxwell, I said, saw the atom as a world of order and perfection. It was perfect in number and measure and weight. Then along came Rutherford with his joke: 'Some fool in a laboratory might blow up the Universe unawares.' And Oppenheimer said, 'We have known sin.'

One could write the history of science in the language of religious myth.

Kate sniffed at religion but tried a spot of moral philosophy. 'Is and ought.'

'Ah,' said I, 'a lot of good minds have been exercised there. It's a rocky road from is to ought.' And on I went, pleased to find her listening to me. She makes herself absent too frequently. It strikes me she's in a kind of love: possessive and infatuated both. Kitty as a shape to be made, Kitty smoothed and patted and rounded off. Her eyes are glazed and most of the time she doesn't hear a quarter of what I say. 'Mm?' she murmurs at the end of it.

She runs in from the garden and writes things down on little squares of paper and drops them in the tray by her typewriter. When she's gone I sneak across and read. 'Tommyrot!' 'Stonkered.' 'Don't be a sooky-bub.' She's writing down things Kitty used to say. 'Bless my soul.' 'Everything's hunky-dory.' Is this sort of thing worth remembering?

Another afternoon. Lovely day. Listens to me waffle, pats my head, goes away to get on with her work. But doesn't sit down. Rips a sheet of paper across; makes her mind up with a physical act.

Back she comes, purpose in her eye. 'Noel, I've got a problem.'

Now I know what her 'is and ought' was all about.

52

'When I was in the seventh form,' Kate said, 'we had to interview someone old. The school lent us tape-recorders and we recorded them. Then we had to write it up. It was a chapter in oral history. I did grandma. She was on a visit. Kitty Hughes.' She's uncertain who the lady is. 'She said some things – well, I'll let you hear. She asked me to destroy the tape and I said I had. But I've still got it.'

'Told a lie?'

'Yes, told a lie. I used to feel sick about that but I felt if I didn't keep it it would be – wiping out a part of her, sort of. And now it seems she told Irene Lomax. So it's not so bad.'

'The rainy night?'

'The night grandpa died. I've got to know whether to use it.'

I felt that this was going to be a thing I'd rather not know. But I have a compulsion to know – and that sort of thing especially. And Kate had judged me tough enough and Kate wanted to share. *Now* and *then* together I cannot withstand.

She ran the tape halfway and pushed a button. Her young voice said scratchily: 'You told me grandpa – Des – raised you up. What did you mean?'

I have the tape and I'm playing it to write this down.

Kitty said (her voice, when she first spoke, it stopped my breathing, almost stopped my heart), she said, 'He raised me from the middle class to the working class. Now I've slipped back.'

'Is that the sort of thing you used to say in parliament?'

'Worse. I gave them beans.'

'I thought we didn't have any classes in New Zealand.'

'Is that what they're teaching you at school? We've got haves and have-nots. That's our classes. Top dogs and fancy pants and make-believe Englishmen and tax accountants. And the workers on the other side, who do all the hard slog and get nothing.'

'Is this the sort of thing grandpa said?'

'I say it. He raised me up, I've told you that. But I didn't need anyone to tell me what to think and what to say.'

228

'Did you go into politics to carry on his work? When he died?'

'His work?' A slapping sound. Kitty must have slapped the arm of her chair. 'Where did you get that from? It was my work. Des had nothing to do with it. Do you think I'm nothing? Do you think I couldn't do it without a man to show me how? Des could never have got where I got. He just thought about things, moaned about them. I did them. He was in the way, I didn't need him. Not any more. He was stopping me. Everything I said I'd do he laughed at. He sat in front of that bloody stove and sneered. And coughed all that stuff up from his chest, and opened the stove door and spat inside. I can take a lot, but that phlegm sizzling . . .'

'Grandma?' Kate said.

'Don't touch me, girl.'

'Shall I turn it off?'

'Leave it on. Let people hear. There are still people in Jessop who think I went into parliament for him and did it all as a memorial. Des was good once. My God, he was on fire. In that hospital when I met him first he brought me alive. Red hair, it used to burn your hands when you touched it. But after a while he was no good. He was no good for anything but slinging off and spitting phlegm. I didn't need him. He was tied around my neck. I used to dream about pulling a sack out of the river and opening it and inside, instead of kittens, it was Des. And he'd open his eyes . . . That's why I went down the hill when he went up. I knew it would kill him, the wet and the cold, but I didn't care. I'd had enough of Des Hughes. I'd had enough of him. Leave me! Don't touch! He went up. I saw him. I saw his hair flash in the street lamp. So I got my coat and I went down. I searched all the streets at the Port. I took my time. And then I went up the hill past home. He was sitting on a seat in the rain. I knew as soon as I touched him he was going to die. I took him home and put him in bed and I got in and held him and tried to make him warm.'

'Grandma?'

'You needn't think I'm sorry. I'm not. We both knew it might end with him or me. That was part of it all along.'

Silence. I thought she was finished, Kitty done. Then she said: 'I only wish . . . I wish I didn't see him like that. With his hair gone flat and in his eyes. And the water running on his face . . .'

'Grandma?'

'Yes, I'm finished. Switch it off.'

The machine went click.

I knew that if I spoke my voice would give way and I would cry. As I've said, there's just a filling in of gaps. No surprises. What moved me was Kitty's voice, big and old and lost. I waved my hand at Kate for her to take the recorder away. When she came back I was able to speak.

'I would have guessed something like that if I'd thought. When she made you switch it off did she say any more?'

'Not very much. I asked her if it was true.'

'What did she say?'

'She said, "They're ghosts, not people. They're not real." '

Kitty asked Kate to destroy the tape and Kate said she had done it already. She showed Kitty her transcript with Des's death cut out. Now she wants to use it and wants my approval.

'It happened, Noel. They weren't ghosts. And she told Irene Lomax.'

It seems to me Kate is pleased with Kitty. I see a kind of glee in her that grandma killed grandpa. There's something colder too, some bit of ideological approval. I'm damned if I'll tell her to go ahead. She'll have to work it out for herself.

'She put him in a hot bath or got in bed with him. Which is the lie?'

Takes it calmly now that Kitty told lies. Can tolerate inconsistencies.

'Maybe she did both. Or only wished. You work it out.'

I want no part of it. I've got my Kitty. She can make hers.

Everything we did was circumstantial. What if it hadn't been raining that night? What if I'd knocked at the door that other night instead of sneaking round to look in the window? If the inlet had been sandflat all the way Rhona would have managed to get to Jessop. But still I would have been on my way to Wellington. This is futile but it fascinates me.

And now I hate it, now it seems a hard judgement on me that I find myself running this course.

I've had enough. If there's anything to be known Rhona knows, Kitty knows, Irene knows. If not, well . . . That's three black dots too many for good sense.

I'll make a retreat – where to? The Second Law of Thermo-dynamics, a thing to be sure of. I'm ready to surrender my bit of heat and help the Universe run along or down. Down doesn't scare me. Entropy may lead anywhere.

My life has narrowed to a point. I'm no longer a menstruum. Kate, the view from my sundeck, the little bit of springtime that is left, it's enough for me. This strikes me as a healthy state to be in. Imagine such good health at eighty-four.

I'll finish scribbling here but keep on somewhere else. My book is done.

November 28, 1985.

53

I win. Phil is dead.

54

Phil Dockery, 1902–86. Of a heart attack while out fishing in his boat.

The news report didn't say enough. The obituary is a pack of lies. It's full of dates and the names of companies. There's nothing about his belief that what you take from others increases you. In societies where those things were done Phil would have been eater of brain and eye of rival chief. An obituary should mention that sort of thing.

He went out fishing in the afternoon. His manager, George Peacock, winched down the boat and saw him off. When he wasn't back by nightfall Peacock called the police. They found Phil dead in his boat at the back of Bucket Island (I'll give it the name Phil preferred). Cause of death is believed to have been a heart attack.

Kate holds my hand. She thinks I'm upset. I'm not upset, I'm interested. I'm put out to some degree. What was it Phil said about Tup? 'He didn't have a bad life, the old bugger.' So there's nothing in Phil's death to upset me. But he knows too. I'm the only one who doesn't know.

Now we've got the story. Now I can fill in the gap. Yes indeed, Phil Dockery died of a heart attack. Extraordinary that he should finish in that way. I'm pleased to know this thing about you, Phil. You must believe, I don't put it down to increase myself but as a kind of salute to you.

It has been yet another of those Jessop days: the blue that is not colour but light, that green that is not leaf and blade but energy. I sat out in my chair, close to the rail, and was listening to the children and the dog in the river – 'Fonzie, Fonzie,' they cry, and will be too old for it next summer – when Kate showed George Peacock in: someone else with a problem. He's a big man with an insignificant head, chalky face, grey hair like dust mice on his scalp.

I sat him down and heard him confess that he was worried and wanted my advice on what to do. I was, he told me, Mr Dockery's best friend and he had information that perhaps . . . well, I could advise him whether or not he should tell the police.

'Is this about Phil's death?'

'In a way. In a way it is. You might say, yes.'

Here's the story: Phil decided to go fishing on that afternoon and Peacock drove him to the boatshed in the jeep. While he winched the boat down Phil climbed the sandhill to look at the beach.

'He came running back. Jesus, he was fit, Sir Noel. For a man of his age. He yelled at me to give him his gun.'

'The air pistol?'

Peacock said yes.

'Why did he keep that in the boat?'

'When the fish didn't bite he used to take pot shots at the seagulls.'

'They're protected,' Kate said.

'I told him that. And the oyster-catchers. He used to go for oyster-catchers too. And the terns.'

I remembered you, Phil, with your shanghai in your belt, going up the river after ducks; or on the mudflats by the reclamation, shooting at empty bottles hour after hour; all alone.

'Get on with it. The beach.'

'He took the gun and ran back up the dunes. I went after him. I thought there might be shags on the reef. But it was the commune people from next door. They were baptizing someone in the sea.'

Phil ran down the sandhill to the beach and ran towards the reef, where men and women in white shirts were standing waist-deep in the sea. He yelled at them to get off his beach. 'It was Shane he was yelling at,' Peacock said. 'That big feller who used to work for us.'

They took no notice. When he was close enough, some thirty yards, Phil started shooting. Peacock saw the slugs hit the sea. Shane came out and walked along the sand.

My God, I thought, it's a Western shoot-out. Kate, she told me later, thought that too. Phil yelled at him, 'You get those people off my beach.'

'It's not your beach, Mr Dockery,' Shane replied.

'You cheeky bugger. You young prick.' Peacock could not describe Phil's face, but I saw it blood-suffused, with madness and pain in the eyes. 'Take another step and I'll shoot your balls off.'

'Give it to me, Mr Dockery,' Shane said.

He came closer, and Phil, aiming over his forearm, shot at him.

'Where was he aiming?'

'Where he said. But he only hit him in the leg.' Peacock touched his thigh.

'Was he hurt?' Kate mottled up.

'It went in all right. Kind of ran along under the skin. I saw the lump where the pellet was.'

'He'll need a doctor.'

'They've got someone there who does first aid. Just a nick with a razor blade, she'd pop out.'

'What about Phil?' I asked.

'He was shaking too much to shoot again.'

Shane walked up to him – limped up, surely – and plucked the gun away by the barrel and threw it back-handed into the sea. It went fifty yards Peacock claimed. Then he turned Phil round and marched him back towards the creek.

Frog-marched? I wanted to know. But it wasn't that. Shane helped him along, half lifting him with an arm round his waist. 'You'd better look after him, Mr Peacock,' he said. Then he went back and joined the others in the sea.

Peacock tried to help Phil over the sandhill but Phil wouldn't take any help. 'I didn't like the look of him,' Peacock said. 'I told him he should go home. But he wouldn't. Told me to clear out. Got in the boat. Drove away, top speed. There was nothing I could do.'

'When they found him had he caught any fish?'

'There was no rod. He must've dropped it when he had the heart attack. The boat was in the back of the island there. The police reckon he must've been dead quite a while.'

Peacock's problem was whether to tell his story to the police. He thought he might be in trouble for not telling it sooner. I advised him not to bother. Nobody was hurt unless it was Shane and if I knew him he wouldn't complain. Let it lie, I said, why make trouble? That was what Peacock wanted to hear. He shook hands with me, half bowed to Kate, and went away.

That's how Phil Dockery died of a heart attack. The thing you couldn't have, Phil, it got you in the end. For all the tricks and stratagems and ways of attack you knew, you were as ignorant of love as a sandfly, a barracuda. You wanted to take him into yourself. Can't do that, Phil, it doesn't work that way. But don't you see you had him there a moment, when he helped you back with his arm around you? That was enough if you'd recognized it. That would have lasted you for the rest of your days. You did not need to go out there and die.

I wanted Peacock to say you'd caught a fish.

Phil, you're filled in. Dockery, you're docked.

I know the place, the back of Bucket Island, where boulders go down into the sea. I've an urge to come and join you, Phil.

Do you remember your bit of third form Latin? You were always bottom – 'Waste of bloody time!' – so I'll translate. Hail and farewell!

So, the sky and the mountains and the sea. The sun, the river. Kate at her typewriter, making Kitty spiky or smooth.

I've come round to Kitty's view of things: you can take out your eyes and wash them in a basin of cold water.

The comet is there, invisible in our daylight sky. I've been offered a visit to the observatory and turned it down. I don't even want my binoculars. I've spent too much of my life looking through lenses. The naked eye is good enough for me.

I wait, as I've said, in a scientific spirit, but with senses readied and imagination primed. I know it's just a cloud of cold gases in the sky but how marvellous if it should lean to me and burn me in a blue or yellow fire.

Let's burn my notebooks first, shall we, Kate?